VOYAGE
OF THE
DEVILFISH

VOYAGE OF THE DEVILFISH

MICHAEL DIMERCURIO

DONALD I. FINE, INC.
NEW YORK

Library of Congress Cataloging-in-Publication Data

DiMercurio, Michael.
Voyage of the Devilfish / by Michael DiMercurio.
p.   cm.
ISBN 1-55611-291-2
I. Title.
PS3554.I4374V68   1992
813′.54—dc20   91-58664
CIP

Manufactured in the United States of America

10   9   8   7   6   5   4   3   2   1

Designed by Irving Perkins Associates

Illustrations by Barbara Field

This one's for you, Dad.

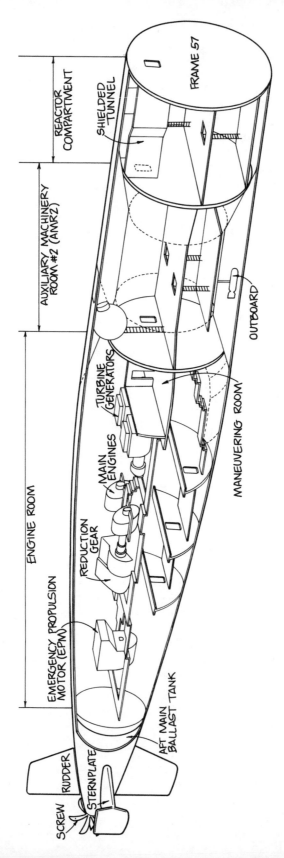

USS *Devilfish* (Piranha Class)
SSN-666 (Aft Section)

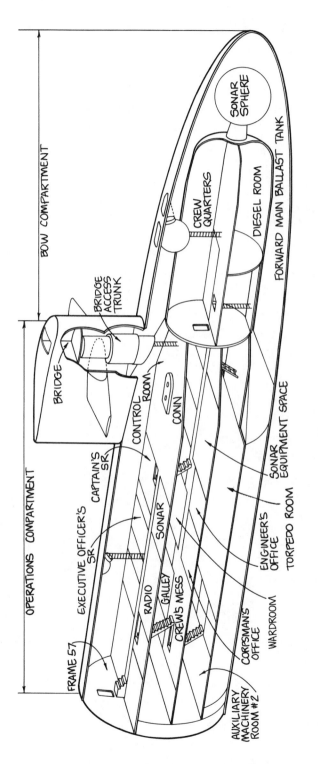

USS *Devilfish* (Piranha Class)
SSN-666 (Forward Section)

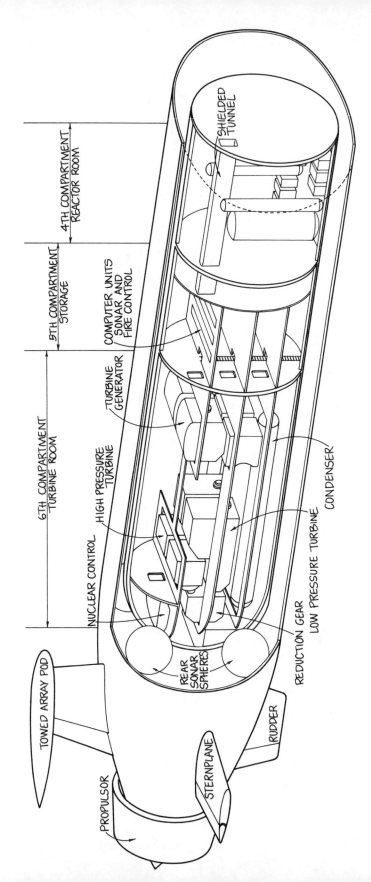

SHIELDED TUNNEL

4TH COMPARTMENT REACTOR ROOM

5TH COMPARTMENT STORAGE

COMPUTER UNITS SONAR AND FIRE CONTROL

TURBINE GENERATOR

6TH COMPARTMENT TURBINE ROOM

HIGH PRESSURE TURBINE

NUCLEAR CONTROL

CONDENSER

LOW PRESSURE TURBINE

REDUCTION GEAR

REAR SONAR SPHERES

TOWED ARRAY POD

PROPULSOR

STERNPLANE

RUDDER

FS *KALININGRAD*
(AFT SECTION)

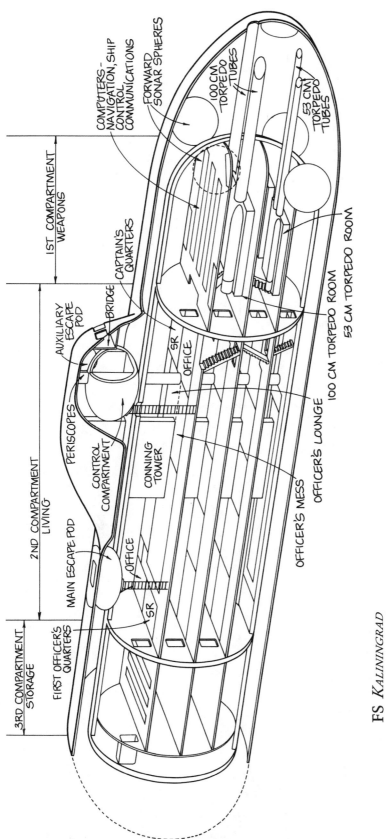

FS *KALININGRAD*
(FORWARD SECTION)

3RD COMPARTMENT STORAGE

2ND COMPARTMENT LIVING

1ST COMPARTMENT WEAPONS

COMPUTERS-NAVIGATION, SHIP CONTROL, COMMUNICATIONS

FORWARD SONAR SPHERES

100 CM TORPEDO TUBES

53 CM TORPEDO TUBES

CAPTAIN'S QUARTERS

BRIDGE

AUXILIARY ESCAPE POD

PERISCOPES

CONTROL COMPARTMENT

MAIN ESCAPE POD

FIRST OFFICER'S QUARTERS

CONNING TOWER

OFFICE

SR

SR

OFFICE

OFFICE

OFFICER'S MESS

OFFICER'S LOUNGE

100 CM TORPEDO ROOM

53 CM TORPEDO ROOM

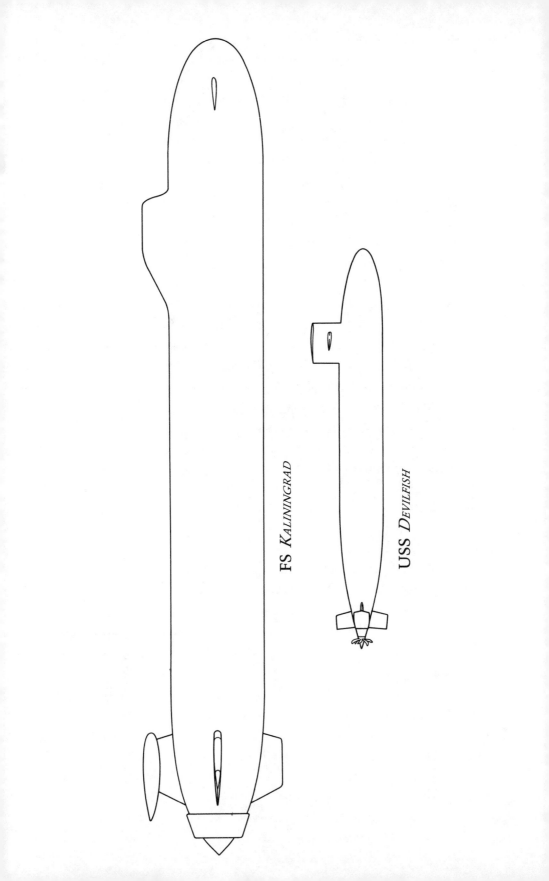

FS *Kaliningrad*

USS *Devilfish*

PROLOGUE

13 DECEMBER, 1973

ARCTIC OCEAN

The USS *Stingray* hovered silently 200 feet below the polar icecap.

The nuclear submarine's control room was absurdly cramped. Filled with consoles, valves, piping and cables it was uncomfortable, but functional. The room was lit by a dim red wash from the overhead fluorescents and the red-masked gages and dials of the ship's control consoles. The only sounds were the whining of the gyros, the low growl of the ventilation fans and murmurs of conversation from the crew in the space.

On an elevated platform surrounded by stainless steel handrails, a tall man with a tightly trimmed beard frowned in concentration at a television screen glowing red. The dim light further revealed a stern-faced man in his early forties, dressed in black overalls with a silver oak leaf on each collar. Over his left pocket was a gold pin resembling a pilot's wings, but each "wing" was a scaly fish facing the middle, with a submarine's conning tower—its sail—forming the center: a submariner's dolphins. Embroidery thread over his right pocket spelled PACINO.

A phone buzzed. Without taking his eyes from the screen, he pulled the handset to his ear. "Captain."

"Captain, radio, sir. The outgoing patrol-report message to COMSUBLANT is ready to transmit."

"Very well, radio." Pacino replaced the headset.

A lieutenant standing at the fire-control console looked up at him on the periscope stand. "Sir, the ship is ready to vertical surface. Ice overhead is one foot thick."

"Very well, vertical surface."

"Diving Officer, vertical surface the ship," the lieutenant called to a chief petty officer sitting behind Pacino at airplane-style controls. At the lieutenant's order another chief at a wrap-around console on the control room's port side pushed the hovering system's joystick up to the BLOW position. The ship started to rise at a steady two feet per second. Every half second the digital–depth gage clicked off another foot.

On the surface above a stiff arctic wind blew the falling snow almost horizontally. The howl of the wind was suddenly punctuated by the sound of the *Stingray*'s three thousand tons crashing through the thin ice. Several ice blocks fell from the top of the black conning tower to the horizontal surfaces below. A tall mast rose out of the sail—the periscope.

A second—the radio antenna—soon followed. It began transmitting a flash priority message to COMSUBLANT, the admiral in command of the Atlantic submarine force. The message reported the position of the newest known Soviet attack submarine, NATO codename VICTOR III.

Four kilometers away, aboard the *Leningrad*, Captain 1st Rank Alexi Novskoyy hunched over a fire-control console showing the position of the American submarine to the south. Long sleepless hours had left dark circles under his eyes, barely showing through the mass of uncombed hair hanging over his face.

He stood and addressed the men in the cramped space. "Attention in the control compartment. As you are all aware, four months ago an American submarine collided with the *Kiev* not far from here. The *Kiev*'s hull was ruptured and she sank with all hands. Our submarine force was disappointed by our official response, little more than a diplomatic protest to Washington. Now we are positioned to deliver the Northern Fleet's *unofficial* response."

All conversation stopped as the four officers stared up at the solid, compact Novskoyy. Only the whining of the fire-control computer and the deep bass of the ventilating ducts could be heard as he lit a cigarette and blew the smoke into the overhead.

Novskoyy looked into his officers' eyes. Each man nodded and turned to his control console. "Weapons Officer, lock the fire-control solution to the target into the torpedoes in tubes one and two and prepare to fire. Deck Officer, open outer doors to tubes one and two. Ship Control Officer, slow to fifteen clicks." Each officer began his assigned task almost before the order was given. He'd trained them well, Novskoyy thought.

The hole in the ice created by the *Stingray* faded as the ship descended to 500 feet and accelerated to five knots. The phone beside Pacino buzzed again.

"Captain."

"Captain, radio, sir. Outgoing patrol report message to COMSUBLANT transmitted to the satellite. The broadcast has been received, it's printing out now. No flash traffic, sir, but we do have the family-grams aboard."

"Very well, radio. Did I get anything?"

"Yessir. Message from your son, sir. Should I read it out to you?"

"No, just send over the printout." Pacino replaced the headset, smiling faintly. Every month or so COMSUBLANT included radio messages from family members—usually less than a hundred words—in their submarine broadcast. For the last three months, it was the only communication from home anyone had had.

"Officer of the Deck," Pacino called. "Time to head home. Come around to the west and clear baffles before you steady on course. I don't want the VICTOR sneaking up from behind and following us home."

"Come around to the west and clear baffles, Officer of the Deck aye, sir," the lieutenant said. "Helm, right five degrees rudder, steady course two seven zero." The lieutenant picked up a microphone and spoke into it. "Sonar, Conn, clearing baffles to the right."

The speaker crackled, sending the voice throughout the control room. "CONN, SONAR, AYE."

Pacino stared at the sonar console, wondering where the

Soviet submarine was. A radioman came to the control room and handed him a metal clipboard with the incoming radio messages. The first page was Pacino's own family-gram, typed by the radioman on the inside of a blank Christmas card.

Pacino grinned as he opened the card. "Nice touch."

DAD —

ANNAPOLIS IS A PAIN. I KNOW, I KNOW—I'M SUPPOSED TO HATE PLEBE YEAR. I'M HANGING ON FOR CHRISTMAS. AND FOR YOU AND STINGRAY TO GET BACK. SEE YOU THEN. GOOD HUNTING AND TAKE CARE, MIKE

Pacino left the center of the control room and wandered back to the navigation alcove; he wished he could have been more of a father during his son's first year at the Naval Academy, but *Stingray* had been at sea so much he'd only been able to make a few calls and send the occasional letter. Still, Pacino thought, nothing would stop Michael from being an officer. He'd hang in there, graduate and maybe fly a jet off an aircraft carrier—or even follow his old man's footsteps and join the Silent Service. Michael would be okay. He had to believe that.

"Tubes report ready, Captain," the Weapons Officer reported to Novskoyy.

"Fire-control ready, Captain," his First Officer called out.

"Shoot tube one," he ordered, and felt the deck lurch beneath him as the heavy 53-centimeter torpedo was ejected from the ship. "Shoot tube two." After the second lurch, Novskoyy leaned over the fire-control console to watch the target disappear . . .

The force of the torpedo explosions threw Pacino into the ship-control console. His head spurted blood over the central panel. Before his eyes the depth gage turned faster and faster, its normal slow clicks accelerating to a mad buzz. The numbers spun by: 1300 feet, 1350, 1400. The ship's crush-depth approached rapidly. Pacino heard the hull creak and pop around him. He heard a scream and water roaring into the room. The lights went out, and soon the deck was so steeply angled downward that the forward bulkhead, the wall, had become the floor. The depth gage continued to buzz off the depth.

Pacino's eyes became unfocused. For a second he thought he saw his son Michael standing in front of him, tall, tanned, handsome and proud in his fourth-class midshipman's uniform.

GOOD HUNTING AND TAKE CARE.

Pacino took his last breath as the compartment around him imploded in slow motion, the wave of water and crushing steel coming at him like a huge thrusting piston.

Blood and icy seawater filled what had been the *Stingray's* control room.

The headquarters building of Commander Submarines U.S. Atlantic Fleet, COMSUBLANT was a massive brick building in an old northwest section of Norfolk, Virginia. The building looked drab and squat, a ghetto gymnasium that seemed half swallowed by the earth. The complex was surrounded by two high chain-link fences with spiral wound razor wire on top. A guard house was perched at the only entrance, manned by two armed Marines.

Inside the building a stainless steel–walled elevator descended to the Flag Plot room sixty feet below the basement level. Inside the elevator was Air Force Brigadier General Herman Xavier Tyler, who wore a blue uniform with an orange tag clipped to his pocket, black block letters proclaiming "VISITOR." Tyler's general stars were brand new from his recent promotion from Offut Air Force Base's Strategic Air Command Headquarters. Tyler's youthful looks tended to rob him of an air of authority, in spite of his steady frown and whitewall haircut, the hair clipped tight to his head. Tyler was enroute to a briefing on the submarine force, a necessary level of knowledge for his future staff duty when he would be shoulder-to-shoulder with Navy officers.

The elevator stopped and the doors opened slowly, revealing a hall with framed photographs on the painted cinderblock walls. Two Marines with M-16's guarded a large steel door at the end of the hall.

The door slowly swung open and the Marines came to attention as a naval officer in khakis stepped out. General Tyler noticed that the steel door was solid and almost a foot thick, with an elaborate spring and counterbalance system to help open it. Several latches showed on the door, each latch over two inches thick. It was a blast door, the general thought. The Flag Plot room must be hardened against all but a direct hit from a nuclear weapon.

The naval officer stepped closer, stretching out his hand. He had the same silver oak leaves that a lieutenant colonel in the Air Force would wear on his collars. For a moment the Air Force general tried to recall what the Navy called that rank. As the officer got closer the general saw pilot's wings over his left pocket. The officer was slim, in his early forties, with most of his head bald. His only hair, once dark but now mostly gray, was tightly trimmed above his ears. The officer walked with a swagger, as if he was carrying a ceremonial officer's sword at a parade. When he reached the general he flashed a wide smile of unnaturally white straight teeth and held out his hand.

"General Tyler? I'm Commander Dick Donchez, COMSUB-LANT Intelligence. Welcome to Flag Plot. The admiral sends his regrets but asked me to show you the operation here."

General Tyler took a moment to look at the gold pilot's wings on Donchez's chest, and noticed they weren't wings at all, but two strange scaly fish facing an old fashioned U-boat–type conning tower. Submarine dolphins, he remembered. Odd to show dolphins as scaly.

The two men started walking down the narrow hall toward the blast door when Donchez stopped short at a framed picture of a submarine running on the surface, the cylindrical cigar-shaped hull plowing through a white wake, a fin-shaped conning tower atop the cigar with horizontal fins sticking out of it.

"Before we go in, sir," Donchez said, "it might help to explain a few things. Have you ever worked with the submarine force before?"

"I was on a staff with a few submarine guys at SAC Headquarters in Omaha, the strategic targeting team, but I really never knew them," Tyler said, looking at the submarine picture.

"Well, let's start with this, then. Newspapers call these boats hunter/killer subs. We call them fast attack submarines. We have about fifty of them, all nuclear, all incredibly quiet and all very fast. None carries nuclear weapons."

The general looked surprised. Every modern submarine he had visualized had a bellyful of intercontinental ballistic missiles. Donchez took him to a photograph further down the hall. This picture also depicted a submarine on the surface, but this one had a long flat back behind the conning tower and looked bigger.

"Sir, this is the kind of sub you're thinking of. It carries ICBM's, SLBM's we call them, stands for Submarine Launched Ballistic Missiles. These boats are officially called FBM's, Fleet Ballistic Missile submarines. We just call them boomers. We only have about thirty of them. They're not under our operational control—they work directly for the President when they're at sea. They just hide, waiting for orders to launch nuke missiles at the enemy strictly on orders from Washington."

Donchez stepped back to the original photo. "But these ships here, the fast attack boats, are our business here at SUBLANT. No missiles, just torpedoes. Their main mission is antisubmarine warfare, since the best way to catch a submarine is with another submarine. But they're useful for missions of covert surveillance too—subs are nearly invisible, and on sonar, and they can hide beneath thermal layers. Surface ships, airplanes and choppers are just no match for a submarine that wants to hide.

"Let me put it this way," Donchez said, "the ballistic missile subs, the boomers, are like one of your monster bombers. Same mission—drop lots of nukes and get in quietly without the enemy knowing you're there."

Tyler nodded.

"Fast attack boats, they're like your fighter planes or interceptors. Attack subs are designed to sink surface ships, like in World War II. Now we have smart torpedoes that can pursue a surface vessel to the ends of the earth, and we're working on some anti-ship missiles that we can launch at a surface target. If we're up against any kind of surface ship we can either let the water in the bottom or let the air out the top." Donchez was on a roll and liking it.

He led the general past the Marines into the blast door and slammed it shut. It took some thirty seconds to lock the latches on the door, and Tyler found himself in a cavernous room with walls twenty feet tall, each wall lined with back-lit charts of the oceans, each chart full of marks and circles and lines.

"This is Flag Plot, sir. Has nothing to do with flags, by the way. Admirals are called flag officers because they fly their flags on ships when they're aboard. Like your staff car has flags on the fenders. This is the admiral's plot room, so it becomes Flag Plot. The admiral in command here is in command of the Atlantic Fleet's submarines but also owns the Mediterranean and the Arctic Ocean beneath the polar icecap."

Donchez saw a momentary flicker of interest from the general at the mention of the polar icecap.

"See that chart there, sir? Arctic Ocean, north pole at the center . . . we've got a boat up there right now trailing a new Russian attack sub under the ice."

Donchez pointed to the chart, which showed a blue X next to a red X, both inside a wobbly circle labelled as the permanent icepack.

"We spend a lot of time trailing their boats. We can get away with that because we're quieter than they are; it's harder for them to hear us. And *every* sub has a blind spot astern of it. We call it the baffles. The screw and engines block out the ocean noises to the rear of the ship, and most sonar gear is located in the nosecone of the sub. So if you're good, you can sneak up on another sub and just follow him in the cone of silence behind the screw. That boat there," Donchez said, pointing to the blue X near the north pole, "is driven by my old Annapolis roommate. He's in trail of a new Russian boat called the VICTOR III. Whenever they launch a new one we try to trail them on their sea trials and see how the new boat does, spy on their exercise torpedo shots, observe their tactics. Since an attack submarine is invisible it can do things no one will ever know about. Anyway, that's the idea."

Enjoying his audience, Donchez went on, "The Atlantic plot here shows a number of blue X's alone. Those are boats on independent operations. Those red X's with the blue X's off the coast are Russian boats being trailed by our attack units. To date no Russian has ever gotten us in trail. How do we know? We check. We'll have one of our attack boats try to sneak up on another of our boats to see if there's a Russian hiding there in the baffles. We call it delousing."

The general stopped Donchez. "What about that big expensive sonar network you people put on the ocean floor for detecting enemy submarines? Doesn't that do all this without having all these big-money attack-boats out there?"

"You're thinking of SOSUS, the underwater sound surveillance system. It is expensive and it's good. But not good enough or accurate enough for us to kill a sub even with a huge nuke weapon. Look here." Donchez returned to the Arctic Ocean polar projection chart. "See the green line?" A green line went from a dot north of Norway's coast to a point near the red and blue X's near the north pole.

"That is the detect on the VICTOR III we were just talking about. He could be anywhere in an area one hundred miles square. Plus he's under ice, and you'd never get him. The only thing that can nail that guy is another submarine, like the *Stingray*, the one who's trailing him now. The SOSUS detection system is picking up the sounds of the Russian VICTOR III but not our own sub—the *Stingray* is just too quiet for us to pick up."

A lieutenant rushed up to Donchez with a notepad. "Commander Donchez . . . there's trouble. SOSUS detected two explosions on the bearing line to the two submarines at the north pole. They reported faint sounds of a hull breaking up and several minutes of bubbles."

Donchez turned to the general, his smile gone.

"General Tyler, I need to ask you to depart Flag Plot. Now. We've got a situation here."

The general was taken off by a waiting petty officer and as he was being pulled to the blast door he heard Donchez talking to the lieutenant.

"Does SOSUS still have a detect on any of the subs up there? He's still got the Russian unit? Goddamn . . . get the admiral on NESTOR secure voice and tell him I'm sending a chopper for him, then get back on NESTOR and notify CINCLANTFLEET, NMCC, the White House—"

The blast door slammed. As Brigadier General Tyler was escorted down the hall, he lingered for a moment at the picture of the attack submarine the commander had been so proud of. So much for the assumed overwhelming superiority of American machines over Soviet ones, he thought.

SIX DAYS LATER, 19 DECEMBER 1973
PIER 7
NORFOLK NAVAL BASE,
NORFOLK, VIRGINIA

A light rain had started about four hours after *Stingray*'s scheduled dock time. The soaked banners read "WELCOME HOME
STINGRAY!" The brass band had long since gone. Families
huddled in groups, their conversations hushed, apprehensive.

The Squadron Seven Public Affairs Officer was nearly
mobbed when he walked onto the pier.

"Ladies and gentlemen, I have an announcement concerning
the *Stingray*." Family and friends of the *Stingray*'s crew
crowded around the podium. "I'm reading now from a statement from the Commander in Chief, U.S. Atlantic Fleet,
CINCLANTFLEET: Unconfirmed reports indicate the USS
Stingray may have been lost at sea in mid-Atlantic while returning from a classified deployment. Search vessels have been
in the vicinity for the last several days. The announcement of
the *Stingray*'s possible loss was delayed in the hope that she
might have suffered a mere loss of communications and surfaced today as scheduled. Now that she is overdue by almost six
hours we must begin to believe the worst. Search efforts will
continue until further notice."

At first, they stayed on the pier, as if thinking the *Stingray*
might still round the turn any minute and put her lines over the
pier. But soon the drizzle turned into a driving rain, and when
the pier floodlights came on hours later, the crowd had finally
dispersed. Only the dark submarines of Squadron Seven remained, tied up on each side of the pier, with a conspicuous gap
left for the mooring of the *Stingray*.

U.S. NAVAL ACADEMY
ANNAPOLIS, MARYLAND

Commander Donchez entered the office and put his cap on the
single desk. He rubbed his hand over his balding head, a habit

when he was uncertain, and looked around at the office. The room was normally occupied by the officer of the watch at the Academy's Bancroft Hall, the enormous, forbidding granite dormitory for the midshipmen. The room hadn't changed since he'd been a midshipman himself, the wall still done in dull brown ceramic tile, like a large bathroom. Donchez looked out the window onto the flood-lit bricks of Tecumseh Court below, remembering the view from his and Anthony "Patch" Pacino's room some twenty years before. As the late Anthony Pacino's best friend and former Annapolis roommate, it had fallen to him to tell Pacino's son about the loss of the *Stingray*. The sinking had not yet leaked to the press; they had not even told the families on the pier.

The door to the room opened and latched with a crash. The officer of the watch delivered a tall, thin, close-cropped midshipman in a black shirt and trousers. The midshipman took three large steps into the room, pivoted in front of the desk and came to stiff attention, eyes frozen at infinity as required of plebes at the Academy.

"Midshipman Fourth Class Pacino, sir!" he sounded off.

Donchez sighed. "It's me, Mikey, Uncle Dick. Carry on."

Donchez nodded to the lieutenant, who left and shut the door behind him.

Pacino looked confused for a moment, then a dark cloud came over his face.

"Commander Donchez," he said, unable to drop the formality in the midst of his regimented plebe year, "it's dad, isn't it?"

Donchez nodded. "Mikey, the *Stingray* sank off the Azores in mid-Atlantic about a week ago. We couldn't confirm it until she was due in. She failed to show up at the pier today. I'm afraid we have to presume your father is dead."

Pacino sank into a chair, a thinly padded steel legged seat. His mouth opened and shut twice before he found his voice.

". . . what happened?"

Donchez inhaled, preparing for the lie. The world would never know that the *Stingray* was intentionally downed—the very fact that U.S. sonars were capable enough to hear the sinking was still highly secret. A protest to Moscow would only alert the Soviets that American ears could hear them from continents away. More to the point, the *Stingray*'s top-secret mission had been to spy on the Russians, and an admission that she was under the polar icecap would be a confession to the Soviets that she'd been ordered north for covert surveillance. The President would not appreciate a media frenzy over a spying American submarine sunk by the Russians. But the multitude of valid national security reasons to cover up the sinking did not make the lie any easier, not when he had to look into Michael Pacino's eyes.

"We think she had a hot-run torpedo that blew up inside her bow compartment," Donchez said. "Probably someone doing maintenance on the weapon screwed up, and it started its engine, armed, and detonated before they could jettison it. Goddamned Mark 37 torpedoes. They hot run all the time." Donchez dropped his eyes. He himself had been the author of the official cover story.

Eighteen-year-old Pacino shut his eyes and put his head in his hands. Donchez looked on, feeling helpless, wishing he could hug the boy, comfort him somehow. When young Pacino started to shake, Donchez could no longer stay still. He pulled Pacino up and put his arms around him.

"Dad . . ." young Pacino said to no one, his voice shaky.

Did he really believe Donchez's story?

Someday they'll pay, Donchez thought. Was his old friend's son possibly thinking the same thing?

CHAPTER

1

MONDAY, 13 DECEMBER 199-

WESTERN ATLANTIC OCEAN

The anniversary of the sinking of the *Stingray* had never been marked or even mentioned in any way by the Navy. Nor had the Soviets mentioned it. Nobody was *that* keen on a nuclear war. But nobody felt easy that somehow it would not repeat itself.

This anniversary, over two decades later, was a rehearsal for a reprise. A U.S. fast-attack submarine was again within weapons range of an enemy submarine. The Piranha-class submarine ran quieter, deeper and faster than the *Stingray*. Her electronics and fire-control and sonar were more accurate, her nuclear reactor and engines more powerful, her layout more efficient and her torpedoes more deadly.

Two conditions about the USS *Devilfish* were very much reminiscent of the old *Stingray*: Her control room was just as cramped, and her captain's nametag read PACINO.

Commander Michael Pacino frowned down on the fire-control solution from the periscope stand. His green-hued eyes and crow's-feet wrinkles around them were hidden by the dim light of the fire-control television monitors. At six feet two inches he was almost too tall to qualify for submarine duty. Pacino was as slim as the day he had graduated from the Naval Academy, mostly from skipping meals and running in place between the broiling hot main engines. He had a mustache and his hair was a thick black mass in need of a regulation Navy cut. But as the son of a legendary submariner lost at sea with his ship the USS *Stingray*, he was not about to be denied his role. Over the years young Pacino had lived with memories of the day Commander Donchez had brought him news of his father's death. Even more, with imaginings of what had happened and how. He had tried to believe the official version, but somehow had never quite bought it.

Since Pacino had ordered *Devilfish* to battle stations ten minutes earlier, the control room had been filled with twenty-one men, most wearing headsets and boom microphones. They called it an "exercise," but it was one in name only. Sooner or later it could be the real thing. As far as Pacino went, it couldn't be soon enough. In front of Pacino, showing the *Devilfish's* position in relation to the enemy submarine—designated Target One—were the computer screens of the fire-control system, displaying the distance to Target One as well as its speed and course. The readings were educated guesses aided by the multimillion-dollar Mark I fire-control computer, though subject to error.

"Attention in the fire-control team," Pacino said. "It looks like Target One still doesn't know we're here. Let's hope he won't until it's too late. I intend to fire two torpedoes in a horizontal salvo. Be ready to evade if Target One fires back and be alert in case he runs from the torpedoes. If Target One zigs we'll do a quick maneuver to get his new solution and turn the weapons . . . Firing-point procedures—tube one Target One, tube two Target One, horizontal salvo, thirty-second firing interval, ten-degree offset."

Officers at the panels checked the target solution and locked it in. The final program was readied for the two Mark 49 Mod Bravo Hullbuster torpedoes twenty feet below on the lower-level deck of the operations compartment. The torpedo tubes of the *Devilfish* were twenty-one inches in diameter and twenty-one feet long. All four were set in the lower level of the operations compartment amidships. Unlike previous submarine classes, the Piranha boats had the main sonar gear in the nosecone and the torpedo tubes amidships, each tube canted eight degrees outward from the ship's centerline. Tubes one and two were the upper tubes; number one on the starboard side, number two on the port. Each tube was flooded and equalized with sea pressure, and the torpedo tube outer doors were open.

At Pacino's order to man battlestations, the Mark 49 Hull-busters had received power to spin up their navigational gyros. Their central processor computers came up after a self-check and reported back to the fire-control computer. With their central processors, each torpedo had roughly the same intelligence as a golden retriever, which for a weapon was near-genius level. As the central processors reported the results of the self-check, the Weapons Officer at the control-room firing panel began to load the run instructions, which sounded like an alien language: "Unit one, you are in tube one. The mother ship is on course 180, depth 546 feet. When you're launched, turn to course 240 at 45 knots and dive to 800 feet depth. Arm the warhead when you are 6000 yards away from mother ship, your run-to-enable. Then start your 25-knot active sonar search at depth 300 feet. The enemy sub, Target One, is currently at bearing 225, and will drive into your search cone at a range of 2000 yards. When you get three confirmed return pings in a row, accelerate to your 50-knot attack speed. When you detect the iron of the enemy hull, detonate your explosives. If you turn more than 180 degrees, you may start homing in on the mother ship. If that happens, shut down your engine, flood and sink. If the target zigs we will turn you toward him with further instructions using your guidance wire."

With each downloaded instruction the Hullbuster torpedoes acknowledged. Two faithful golden retrievers, wagging their tails and panting near the master's hand, waited for the command to go.

In the control room, the furthest forward space in the three-deck-high operations compartment, Captain Mike Pacino watched the fire-control solution and the red television sonar-repeater screen on the port side of the periscope-stand conning-console.

The Officer of the Deck, Lieutenant Scott Brayton, reported, "Ship ready."

The Weapons Officer, Lieutenant Commander Steve Bahnhoff, called out, "Weapons ready."

"Solution ready," said Commander Jon Rapier, the Executive Officer.

Pacino opened his mouth to speak as Lieutenant Stokes, the officer on the central fire-control panel, said, "Possible zig, Target One."

"Zig confirmed," Rapier said. "Time-frequency plot. Possible maneuver to starboard—"

"Check fire, tubes one and two," Pacino told the executive officer, aborting the launch sequence. Target One had turned and would no longer be where Pacino had been about to send the torpedoes. Launching a torpedo was something like throwing a touchdown pass—the torpedo was sent to where the target would be. If the target changed course, zigged, the firing solution was no good and the torpedoes would miss.

"XO, get a curve and get it quick." Into his cordless boom microphone he spoke to the sonar chief in the sonar room aft: "Sonar, Captain, do you confirm a zig on Target One?"

"Conn, Sonar," came the reply in Pacino's single headphone, a custom configuration allowing him one ear for the sonar-phone circuit and one for the control room. "We're investigating . . ." Pacino waited impatiently. "Conn, Sonar, zig confirmed. No change in engine RPM. Target One is at the same speed, turning to his . . . starboard."

"Any sign of a counter-detection by Target One?" Did the son of a bitch hear us? he thought, trying to read the mind of the opposing commander.

"No . . . he's steady on course now, sir."

Pacino spoke to Rapier. "XO, you got a curve yet?"

Rapier, the most senior executive officer on the Squadron Seven pier, was about Pacino's age, thin, with silver hair and the same crow's feet around his eyes that Pacino had from hours of squinting out of the periscope. Rapier was overdue for command of his own boat but his replacement was late. He leaned over Lieutenant Stokes' shoulder.

Stokes sat at the central fire-control console, Position Two, and stared intently at the screen as if willing his dot-stack of sonar data to line up. But the sonar sensor was passive—it only listened and gave the bearing or direction of the enemy sub, not its range, course or speed.

At the base of the screen were knobs that could dial in trial enemy ranges, speeds and courses—the combination of range/ course/speed of the enemy submarine making up the "solution." It was found by driving the *Devilfish* back and forth and seeing the effect on the bearing to the target. With the computer to help, Lieutenant Stokes could dial in any number of guess-solutions, but he started from a reasonable one and refined until the bearing dot-stack was vertical. It all worked fine when the target stayed on course. When he zigged, only an expert like Stokes could reach out with his intuition and capture the target's motion.

Finally the dot-stack was vertical and Stokes announced his arrival at a solution: "XO, I have a solution." From Stokes, a fiery ex-football player from western Kentucky, it came out, *Eh-yecks Zoh, ah've a slooshun.*

"Time-bearing, what's the status?" the XO said.

"XO, gotta curve, bearing-rate right, range . . . ten thousand yards," Ensign Fasteen reported from a manual-plot board.

The XO immediately reported it to Pacino: "Captain, we have a curve and a firing solution."

"Firing-point procedures," Pacino announced again, "horizontal salvo, first fired unit, tube one." He paused a moment, then said, "C'mon, guys, let's get these fish out. Target One may detect us at any moment and zig again. Okay, first fired unit, shoot on generated bearing," Pacino ordered, starting to feel intensely alive, and sweating. This was the point of no return.

"Set," Stokes said, sending the final solution to the firing panel and to the weapon in tube one.

"Stand by." Bahnhoff, on the firing panel, taking his trigger lever all the way to the left, the "Standby" position.

"SHOOT," Pacino commanded.

"Fire," Bahnhoff said, taking the trigger lever all the way to the right, to the "Fire" position.

The whole ship jumped and a booming roar slammed the eardrums of all twenty-one men in the control room. Pacino's white teeth, upper and lower, were all visible. This was a sweet sound, the crash of a torpedo launch.

"Tube one fired electrically, Captain," Bahnhoff reported, resetting his panel to address the weapon in tube two.

"Conn, Sonar," the sonar chief's voice came into Pacino's headpiece. "Own ship's unit, normal launch."

Pacino looked at the digital chronometer. The thirty-second interval was coming up quickly.

"Tube two, shoot on generated bearing."

"Set."

"Stand by."

"SHOOT."

"FIRE."

Again the explosive pressure slammed the crew's eardrums.

"Tube two fired electrically, sir," Bahnhoff reported.

"Conn, Sonar, second fired unit, normal launch."

In the ocean outside the skin of the *Devilfish*, two high-speed Hullbuster torpedoes screamed in the direction not of the enemy submarine but toward a point in the sea where the enemy sub was calculated to be six minutes ahead. The control room crew was quiet, waiting for the torpedoes to go active. From this point on the weapons were "units"—friendly weapons launched by "own ship." A "torpedo" was a threat launched by the enemy.

Pacino watched the third fire-control console, Pos Three, waiting for the torpedo to report its status. Three minutes later Pos Three's status indicator blinked that the first fired unit had gone active, pinging a sonar beam forward as it tried to see the enemy a mile ahead, and if it did it would go after it at maximum speed of 50 knots. No matter what the target did, as long as the unit had fuel the target had had it. No 30-knot or 35 knot submarine could outrun a 50-knot Hullbuster. But if the enemy detected the unit and zigged before the unit went active, he might escape.

"Conn, Sonar, Target One's screw is cavitating . . . he's speeding up . . . definite target zig, Target One. Captain, he's detected the first fired unit and he's running. Max speed."

"Damn," Pacino muttered. "Helm, right fifteen degrees rudder, steady course north, all ahead standard. XO, you've got a one minute lag to get a new curve and steer the weapons. After that it'll be too late."

"Working it, Cap'n," Rapier replied.

At least the target hadn't yet fired a weapon in response. Not yet, anyway.

"My rudder's right fifteen degrees, sir," the helmsman at one of the airplane console–style seats on the forward bulkhead said, turning his wheel. "Maneuvering answers ahead standard. Steady course north, sir."

Pacino frowned at the fire-control console. The first zig had been routine, but a target zig with target acceleration was much more difficult to deal with, particularly when their own ship was turning. Now the sonar data had become a mass of relatively meaningless numbers. Computers were useless at times like these. Only human judgment and intuition, and perhaps some luck, would put the torpedoes on the alerted target.

Michael Pacino shut his eyes, rubbed his temples and imagined a God's-eye-view of the sea. What would he do if he were the "enemy." He opened his eyes, moved off the elevated periscope stand, nudged aside Lieutenant Stokes, grabbed two solution guess-knobs and twisted in a guess-solution. "Keep that in," he told Stokes, whose expression betrayed he thought Pacino's solution flawed.

For the next thirty seconds Pacino really sweated. Two sonar bearings came in and lined up vertically. His solution was dead on. He punched Stokes' massive shoulder and pointed to the computer console. Stokes just shook his head.

"Weps, steer the first fired unit to course one seven five," Pacino said to Weapons Officer Bahnhoff on the firing panel. "Steer the second to one eight zero."

He looked over Bahnhoff's shoulder as he programmed the firing panel with the steer-commands; the firing panel talked digitally to the torpedo-room console, which relayed the instructions to the tubes, which passed on the steer-commands through a neutrally buoyant wire the size of a stereo-speaker cord, snaking out the tube to the ocean beyond through twenty miles of wire to the units. The units heard the order and turned to the south, listening to their pings. One unit got a ping return in its search-cone almost immediately.

"Detect," Bahnhoff announced, smiling at Pacino. "Unit one . . . detect. *Homing, unit one.* Go, baby, go."

The first fired unit had heard three returns in a row, deciding that Target One was a valid target. The torpedo sped up to 50 knots, its attack speed. The faces of the control-room crew lit up in anticipation.

"Unit two, detect," Bahnhoff said happily. "Detect. Lost it
. . . Come on, sweetheart. Detect. *Acquisition*, unit *two*. Captain, we've got him."

"Conn, Sonar," Pacino heard through his headset, the volume
suddenly loud. "Torpedo in the water, bearing two three five!"

Target One had finally returned fire.

"Helm," Pacino ordered, "all ahead flank. Maneuvering cavitate. Diving Officer, depth fifteen hundred feet, 35 degree down
angle."

Four ominous BOOMs shook the ship as its main reactor-
coolant pumps were switched to fast speed. Aside from a torpedo launch, the check valves in the coolant piping made the
loudest noise the *Devilfish* could make. The deck began to vibrate as the ship came up to flank speed, 35 knots, her dual
main engines shrieking far aft in the engine room, her screw
spinning wildly and cavitating—boiling up sheets of angry,
noisy bubbles of steam in the ocean.

Pacino looked to the forward bulkhead at the ship control
panel's gages. The control team was three men seated at controls, two in front on either side of a central console and one in
the middle to supervise the other two. In the port seat was the
sternplanesman, who put his control yoke to full dive. Two
hundred feet aft the huge control surfaces, driven by high-pressure hydraulics, went to the dive position, forcing the submarine to a down angle. Her speed, and the fair-water planes in a
diving position on the sail, nosed her down into a steep 35-
degree dive. Every man at battlestations held on to keep from
falling to the forward bulkhead. The hull of the submarine
groaned and popped as seawater pressure increased with the
depth. No matter how many years a man spent at sea, submerged, the sound would always be eerie, ominous, Pacino
thought.

"Loss of torpedo-control wires, units one and two, Captain,"
Bahnhoff said, not yet registering that the target had counter-
fired. He was so caught up in his two torpedo hits that he didn't
realize it.

"Torpedo room, Conn," Pacino ordered over a hand-held microphone he had grabbed, "cut the wires to tubes one and two,
shut the outer doors and drain tubes."

Suddenly the deck levelled out at 1500 feet, test depth, her deck still vibrating as 30,000-shaft horsepower blasted her through the water at flank speed.

"Conn, Sonar," Pacino's headset crackled, "incoming torpedo now bears two three three. Slight right bearing drift. It's range-gating."

Outside the hull they could hear a high-pitched pinging that got louder, more frequent, more insistent. The torpedo knew exactly where they were. And Pacino knew his only chance was that by going flank speed he might draw out the chase long enough to make the torpedo run out of fuel.

"Maneuvering, Captain," he said into a mike, "unload the turbine generators as much as possible and load the battery. I want every ounce of steam we have going to the main engines. And raise T-AVE to 520 degrees—you'll have to override the cutback."

A speaker in the control room overhead boomed harshly through the previous quiet.

"UNLOAD THE TG'S, LOAD THE BATTERY, MAXIMIZE MAIN ENGINE STEAM, T-AVE TO 520 AND CUTBACK OVERRIDE, CONN, MANEUVERING, AYE."

Pacino strained to check out the speed indicator. Thirty-five knots and steady. He watched to see if he was getting a bit more speed from the reactor but it was no good. The incoming torpedo would be at the hull at any minute.

The torpedo pinged louder.

Pacino looked at the geographic plot, then at Position One on the fire-control screens. Position-One's officer was trying to get a solution on the torpedo, but without maneuvering the ship it was all a guess. The weapon could be five thousand yards away or five hundred.

"Conn, Sonar," Pacino heard in his headset, "torpedo still incoming, range-gate narrowing. Within one thousand yards."

Pacino shook his head. He'd gotten two hits on the enemy, so what? The enemy weapon was zooming in at over 50 knots and *Devilfish* was only doing 35. That put torpedo-impact less than two minutes away.

Pacino looked toward the rear of the control room at the ship's framed Jolly Roger flag with the *Devilfish*'s motto sewn above and below the grinning skull and crossbones of the pirate flag. The motto read:

IF YOU AIN'T CHEATIN'

YOU AIN'T TRYIN'

Every watchstander in the control room of the *Devilfish* had frozen, waiting for torpedo-impact. The sound of the torpedo's screw was now louder, huge fingernails scraping a giant blackboard. While Pacino stared at the flag, and its motto, an idea came to him. He mounted the periscope stand and called to the Chief of the Watch at the portside ballast-control panel: "Emergency blow the forward group."

"Blow forward, aye," the chief said, his tone betraying how odd he thought the order. Nonetheless, he reached for one of two large levers, hit its plunger and pushed it up to the stop.

Immediately a sudden loud roar filled the control room, the sound of ultra-high-pressure air roaring into the ship's ballast tanks and blowing out the water. Dense fog filled the room, condensation from the leakage around the blow valve. Visibility shrank to less than a foot. The chief grabbed a small lever and pulled it to the right, sounding the alarm throughout the ship for an emergency surface. OOH-GAH, OOH-GAH, OOH-GAH. It was not the submarine's klaxon horn of John Wayne movies. The alarm was generated electronically and sounded like it came from a cheap video arcade game amplified to a distorted, earsplitting volume.

The chief pulled a hand-held microphone from the panel: "SURFACE, SURFACE, SURFACE."

Pacino shouted over the violent roar of the emergency blow system: "Chief, emergency blow aft."

"Emergency blow aft, aye sir. Blowing aft."

The noise got worse, the roar louder than a torpedo-launch, and instead of a quick crash it was a sustained kind of scream. The fog in the room grew thicker. The ship-control party pushed their faces close to the panels to read their gages.

In the *Devilfish*'s main ballast tanks, filled a moment before with seawater, high-pressure air forced the seawater out. The tanks went dry fifteen seconds after the aft-system blow, and suddenly *Devilfish* was hundreds of tons lighter. Nothing would keep her submerged for long now.

"Secure the blow," Pacino ordered.

The room went quiet again, only the sound of the pinging and torpedo screw could be heard. The depth gage clicked once, twice, several times. The fog began to disperse. The deck floated upward, becoming steeper a degree at a time.

Pacino's voice reverberated throughout the ship on the circuit-one microphone: "This is the captain. We are emergency blowing to the surface to try to avoid the torpedo. We may get lucky—if it's like ours the weapon will be programmed not to go above a ceiling. If we can get shallow fast enough and above the ceiling we may be able to get away from it."

The deck inclined up and up, 20 degrees, 25, to 45 degrees. The sternplanesman held full dive on the sternplanes. Without the planes on dive the boat would certainly have been vertical. The ship's speed indicator showed 40 knots. Pacino was hanging from a stainless steel rod above the number-two periscope. The depth gage reeled off the depth—750 feet . . . 500 . . . 300. *Devilfish* was rocketing to the surface.

Pacino glanced at the sonar repeater. He might evade the torpedo but he might have made things worse—once they punched through the thermal layer, if there was any kind of shipping above it was about to get 4500 tons of nuclear submarine rammed into it at 40 knots. The force of such a collision would surely sink both vessels.

The USS *Diamond* was an ugly surface ship, a typical salvage vessel. She was the range-safety ship for the day's highly realistic submarine-versus-submarine torpedo-shot exercise. Her sonar showed *Devilfish* had gotten off the first two shots, the USS *Allentown* had been slow to get off a counterfire but had nearly sunk *Devilfish*. Both of *Devilfish*'s torpedoes had hit their mark, but as the *Allentown*'s torpedo zeroed in on the *Devilfish* the sonar officer on the *Diamond* pulled off his headset and shouted, "*Devilfish* is emergency-blowing, bearing north."

The pilothouse, in a near-panic, put the rudder over hard-right to head south and away from the submarine emergency-blowing to the surface. The wake boiled up at *Diamond*'s stern as she tried to run from the area. The off-watch crew gathered at the fantail aft to catch sight of the sub about to come screaming out of the depths.

Suddenly the sea directly astern of the retreating *Diamond* exploded, a tower of foam leaping in a column from the water. Following the foam, a streamlined nose leaped from the ocean. Almost in slow motion, the rest of the cylindrical shape came out of the sea, black on top, dull red on the bottom. In less than a second the massive three-hundred-foot-length of 32-feet-diameter steel shape came roaring out of the water at a 50-degree angle, jumped completely out of the sea, a spray splashing over the salvage ship as the submarine's huge brass screw became momentarily exposed. The behemoth fell crashing back to the water, a tidal wave coming over the transom of the *Diamond*, soaking the men at the rail and nearly washing one overboard. As the *Devilfish* bobbed in the water in a field of white foam and angry bubbles, most of the drenched *Diamond* crew cheered in appreciation . . . it wasn't every day they saw a submarine so blatantly break the rules and win.

One soaked chief petty officer turned to another: "The captain of that sub is going to pay for that stunt with his dolphins."

The other shook his head. "No he ain't. That there's the *Devilfish*—she cheats at *ever'thang*. Gets away with it, too."

Abruptly the angle came off the ship, throwing Pacino into the back of the Diving Officer's seat. Although he and his crew had won, he couldn't shake a sobering thought: Would the tactic have worked against a real Russian torpedo? He relinquished the periscope to Officer of the Deck Lieutenant Brayton and spoke to the crew.

"We seem to have been successful in evading the torpedo. We'll have to wait to see if the *Diamond* confirms a kill for us on Target One. Carry on. Helm to Maneuvering, switch main reactor coolant pumps to slow speed. All ahead one third, right fifteen degrees rudder, steady course two seven zero. XO, secure from battlestations."

Near Pacino on the periscope stand a speaker came to life, static sputtering out of it. Pacino stooped down and turned up the volume. It was a human voice booming through the depths.

"Deep . . . deep . . . deep . . . coming up . . . echo . . ."

It was the underwater telephone, the UWT, an active sonar system that transmitted voices instead of pings or pulses. The coming-up call indicated another submarine was coming up to periscope depth or to surface.

"Put the scope on it," Pacino said.

The Officer of the Deck turned the periscope over to Pacino and waited for the USS *Allentown*—their opponent this afternoon—to surface. Pacino's mission had been to sneak up on the attack submarine and fire a Hullbuster shot without being detected. But even being tipped off beforehand hadn't helped the *Allentown*, Pacino thought. She didn't even know the *Devilfish* was there until the Hullbusters went active.

Commander Henry Duckett of the *Allentown* had been Michael Pacino's old squad leader when he was a plebe at the Naval Academy. Duckett had, in fact, made life miserable for Pacino, to the point of nearly hazing him out of Annapolis. But today Duckett commanded the *Allentown*, a new Los Angeles–class attack submarine. And today, the *Devilfish*, the older Piranha-class attack boat, had snuck up on her, scored two hits and evaded a 50-knot attacking torpedo. Not too shabby, Pacino thought.

The UWT sputtered to life again: "*Devilfish*, this is *ALLENTOWN*. Over . . ."

Pacino recognized the voice. Duckett. He turned the periscope back over to Brayton and picked up the microphone, hit a toggle switch and spoke, his voice that echoed back at him sounding like the voice of a giant bouncing off the ocean floor.

"*Allentown*, this is *Devilfish*. One in, over."

"*Allentown*'s surfacing, Captain," Brayton reported from the periscope.

"*Devilfish*, this is *Allentown* . . . report Uniform Whiskey Mike . . . I say again . . . report Uniform Whiskey Mike . . . over."

"Hell!" Pacino snapped to Rapier.

"Uniform Whiskey Mike" was NATO code for "you missed me."

"It's bullshit, Cap'n. We kicked his ass," Rapier said.

"*Allentown*, this is *Devilfish*," Pacino said into the microphone, "negative Uniform Whiskey Mike, repeat, negative Uniform Whiskey Mike. Duckett, I hit you fair and square. Twice."

"Captain, look at *this*," the Officer of the Deck said from the periscope. Pacino took the scope as the OOD mumbled, "Low power on the horizon, bearing two three zero."

On the television periscope-repeater Pacino's crosshairs were centered on the sail, the conning tower, of the USS *Allentown*. And sticking in one side of *Allentown*'s sail and out the other was one of Pacino's torpedoes that had impaled the rear part of the sail.

"Off'sa'deck, line up the periscope still camera. We need a few pictures of this for posterity," Pacino said.

"Lined up, sir," the OOD replied.

Pacino moved up to the UWT transmitter: "*Allentown*, this is *Devilfish*. I say again, negative Uniform Whiskey Mike . . . advise you to check your sail . . . it's got a Hullbuster sticking clean through it . . ."

Duckett's aggrieved voice was recognizable in spite of the UWT distortion: "*Devilfish*, this is *Allentown*. Cheaters never prosper. Out."

Pacino keyed his mike.

"*Allentown*, this is *Devilfish*. Old budd, don't you know? YOU AIN'T CHEATIN', YOU AIN'T TRYIN'. *Devilfish* out."

The *Allentown* rolled in the gentle swells on the surface. Her Officer of the Deck stood in the cramped bridge cockpit at the top of the sail and scanned the horizon with his binoculars. The ship was stopped, waiting for its opponent the *Devilfish* to head toward the traffic-separation scheme outside of Thimble Shoals Channel. The sun was low on the horizon, the Atlantic air cool and fresh after two weeks submerged.

Lieutenant Ron Graves, the OOD, picked up a microphone at the forward lip of the cockpit. "Control, Bridge, raise the radar mast and bump up the Bigmouth antenna."

The communication box crackled with static and a loud distorted voice said, "BRIDGE, CONTROL, RAISING RADAR AND BIGMOUTH."

The OOD replaced the microphone and again trained his binoculars on the shrinking form of the *Devilfish* as she sailed to Norfolk. He waited for the thunks of hydraulics raising the masts from the sail, but all he heard was a brief grinding noise from aft. He dropped his binoculars and turned to look behind him. Neither mast had risen. He was about to call the control room again when the bridge communication box sputtered to life.

"BRIDGE, CONTROL, CAPTAIN TO THE BRIDGE."

"Captain's coming up, Bridge aye." The OOD wondered how the skipper could know so soon that something was wrong. He stepped to the far starboard side of the cockpit and hinged up the deck grating to the access tunnel, which plunged down thirty feet to the deck.

Captain Henry Duckett hauled his bulky frame up the tunnel with surprising speed. Large and solid, Duckett was large enough to force his men to duck into side rooms whenever he walked down the ship's narrow passageways. Solid enough to make the offensive line of the *Allentown*'s inter-squadron football team the terror of the fleet piers. He was also not known for his sweet temperament. Now he pushed the OOD out of the way, leaned far out over the starboard lip of the bridge and peered aft.

"I'll be god*damned*." He shouldered past Graves and climbed back down the access tunnel. "Damned fiberglass sails." His voice floated upward. "Goddamned Pacino."

"Good afternoon to you too, sir," OOD Graves said, looking down at the retreating form of his captain, then leaned over the starboard side of the cockpit to see the current source of Duckett's foul mood.

Not ten feet behind him, protruding horizontally from the fiberglass flanks of the black sail, was the stern of a Mark 49 Hullbuster torpedo, its propulsor blades still spinning. There would be hell to pay.

CHAPTER 2

MONDAY, 13 DECEMBER

The Severomorsk Naval Complex near Murmansk on the Russian northern coast was the size of a city. Within its barbedwire fence and concrete barriers were two sprawling shipyards, repair yards, submarine and surface-ship operating bases, a weapons depot and the many buildings of Northern Fleet headquarters. It was drab and massive. Shipyard workers crowded the walkways. Sailors and naval officers were almost as numerous. In the submarine building yards a half-dozen gigantic building-ways and drydocks were centers of frantic activity, three shifts a day, seven days a week.

The largest construction drydock, Building Dock 4, was over 500 meters long and 20 meters deep. A six-story building could have been built in Dock 4 without rising above the rim. The dock was pumped dry of the brackish channel water. Nestled in the dock was a submarine, the first ship of the Project 985 class of attack vessels.

Outside the security building for the dock two men met and shook hands. The first was a barrel-chested man in a long greatcoat, the red epaulettes on his shoulders showing four gold stars. His head was covered by a fur cap also displaying four

38

stars. The second was bundled in a long overcoat with a suit and tie showing at the collar of the coat. The shipyard workers avoided him.

"Colonel Dretzski," the man with the stars said.

"Admiral Novskoyy," said Dretzski. Ivan Dretzski was assigned to the KGB's First Chief Directorate, headquartered at Yasenevo. His specialty was nuclear weapon intelligence.

Novskoyy motioned Dretzski into the security building and pointed to a row of white visitor's hardhats. The sentry handed Novskoyy a special gleaming red hard hat. The hat had the emblem of the Northern Fleet on the front and words in block letters above and below the emblem: ADMIRAL A. NOVSKOYY, SUPREME COMMANDER, RED BANNER NORTHERN FLEET.

Novskoyy looked at the hardhat and turned to Dretzski. "This is why we can't build a quality submarine within budget, Colonel. We spend too many rubles making *hardhats*." Novskoyy tossed it back to the sentry. "Hand me one of the visitor's hats," he said, taking off his fur cap and putting on an old scratched hardhat.

Novskoyy then motioned Dretzski out a door in the far wall of the security building to a deck overlooking the drydock. Below the men the vast submarine stretched to the vanishing point in each direction.

Dretzski heard his own whistle.

"*Yolki palki*, admiral. Enormous!"

Novskoyy nodded. "Two hundred meters long. sixty thousand tons of submarine, Colonel. Six times bigger than the Los Angeles–class sub. Its reactors produce over three thousand megawatts of power, enough to light the lights of Moscow. Project 985. My design. Beautiful. Enough weaponry to sink a fleet and enough cruise missiles to wipe out a continent. This ship is the *Kaliningrad*. The Americans call it the *Omega*. The last letter of the Greek alphabet. The end-all, the ultimate."

For a moment the two men watched a huge crane below move a periscope into position for lowering into the teardrop-shaped conning tower. The black hull was oval in cross-section, making it seem fat. The tail section had a teardrop-shaped pod mounted horizontally on the vertical tail fin. The screw was shrouded in a cylindrical cover. Up forward two hatches were open and men and supplies were passing in and out from the gangway to the drydock rim.

"The ship is ready to be floated out of the dock, but first I want to show it to you from below."

Colonel Dretzski followed Novskoyy downstairs to the drydock floor. Novskoyy walked under the keel of the ship. When they were underneath it, a waiting shipyard worker walked up with a ladder. Novskoyy had the ladder erected at an open passage through the skin of the submarine above and climbed the ladder and disappeared into the hole, calling down to Dretzski to follow. Dretzski grimaced and climbed the ladder into the black hole above. He found himself standing inside the hull in a black space. A flashlight clicked on. In its wandering beam he saw Novskoyy a few meters away. He was in some sort of tank. The top surface, the ceiling, was three meters above his head.

"Amazing, isn't it, Ivan Ivanovich?"

"Admiral, what is this?"

"This is a ballast tank. The *Kaliningrad* is a double-hulled submarine, a ship within a ship. Look up there." And Novskoyy shined the light upward. A man could stand on top of another man's shoulders in the tank and still not hit his head on the ceiling. "That is the pressure hull. We are standing inside the steel outer hull. This doughnut-shaped space between the inner and outer hull is filled with water when the ship is submerged. An enemy torpedo would have to penetrate five meters of water to get to the inner hull. The water is a sort of armor. The inner hull is a titanium alloy, the strongest submarine hull in the world. This ship is practically invulnerable to all but a direct hit from a nuclear warhead."

Dretzski was impressed. "Now, Alexi, you did have some reason to bring me here other than to show me a ballast tank."

Novskoyy motioned Dretzski down the ladder. Once they were back on the floor of the drydock, the shipyard worker bolted a louvered grill over the hole in the hull and the two men climbed out of the deep dock back up to the deck by the security hut.

At the end of the drydock an officer motioned for the pump house to open the flood valves. Water jetted out into the dock from eight huge holes in the dock walls. Instantly the floor of the dock was filled with water, which then rose at a meter every minute. For a time they watched the ship in the flooding dock as the water began to lap at the keel. In a few minutes the water began to climb up the hull of the vessel.

Dretzski began: "It's worse than we thought, Admiral, much worse. The Americans' nuclear-tipped land-attack cruise missiles, the Javelins, are still loaded aboard their attack submarines. Peace dividend is rhetoric. We're guessing they have about two-hundred-fifty of them."

Novskoyy's eyes narrowed, staring down at the dock and the mammoth ship. "Yes, exactly. While *our* weapons are waiting to be destroyed in front of a U.N. team. The latest negotiating round featured another reckless offer to eliminate sea-launched cruise missiles, all in storage in the Severomorsk arms depot. The Americans' cruise missiles remain deployed on their nuclear submarines. Submarines that can sneak right up to the northern coast and launch dozens of their missiles at treetop level, ready to detonate on target . . . Did you hear about the latest Javelin test?" Novskoyy asked.

Dretzski nodded. "Yes, a Los Angeles–class attack submarine launched a cruise missile from a point in the Atlantic about 300 kilometers east of Jacksonville, Florida. The missile went completely undetected by civilian *and* military radars. It flew over Florida's panhandle, through Alabama, Mississippi, Louisiana and into Texas. A hundred kilometers over the Texas state line it flew to its target, a village constructed for such tests at the Lone Star Naval Weapons Station. The target was a three-story building behind a five-story office building in the center of a 40-block downtown. The missile not only hit the target building, it hit the target window in the target floor . . ."

As they spoke, the two men watched the dock continue to flood so as to launch the *Kaliningrad*.

"Our leaders are making peace," Dretzski said heavily. "People don't seem to be worrying—"

"In the United States, presidents come and go," Novskoyy said quickly. "Not long ago they elected a tired old actor who joked about dropping bombs on our people. The one after him loved his wars . . . They still put billions into Star Wars. They are building the Seawolf-class submarines as we speak. They still have Stealth bombers and fighters. Phased array radar-defense networks. Don't forget . . . America is the one that dropped two atomic bombs on civilians just fifty years ago. Why must *we* always make the good-faith gesture?"

"Admiral, we agree on all that," Dretzski said, "it is what brought us together in the first place. Do you have some plan to change this situation?"

Novskoyy nodded, seemingly to himself, and stared into the distance of the channel.

"I do. Some may consider it extreme, but I am convinced it is necessary for our survival. We must get rid of the threat of their terrible destabilizing missiles . . ."

Dretzski began to look uneasy, although he was the one who had originally briefed Novskoyy on the American advantage when no one in the Kremlin or Russian Republic would take action. In fact, he had been recently passed over for promotion in the KGB, being labeled an antiquated Cold War holdover.

"I have one-hundred-twenty attack submarines prepared to go to sea. Each has been loaded with one SSN-X-27 nuclear-warhead-carrying cruise missile, which I managed to acquire from the arms depot. They will take station off the eastern coast of the U.S. and target every port with submarines that have the missiles aboard. When we inform *both* our government and theirs, there will be no missiles left. The threat will be gone."

"It sounds very risky."

"No. Under the threat of our missiles, poised to deliver, we will restore the balance we once had. The naïveté of our present leaders that somehow the U.S. has gone pacifist, that its military-industrial complex has actually given up and not made contingency plans to retain destructive weapons secretly is nothing but wishful thinking. What did one of their philosophers say? Those who ignore history are doomed to repeat it. It is to their advantage, my friend, to see us completely disarmed while they, as you yourself have said, maintain capabilities to destroy us."

Novskoyy looked closely at Dretzski to see if his lecture was sinking in—and being believed. More than once he had asked himself if he thought his plan would work without needing to fire a shot, and had tried to convince himself that it would. But if not, well, he would deal with that contingency when and if it happened. He was a man who had already destroyed an American submarine for what he believed in. He remembered, he had never forgotten, the incident over twenty years ago under the icecap when he had commanded the *Leningrad*. If necessary . . .

Dretzski felt it necessary at least to play devil's advocate. "Admiral, remember Contingency 12, the one we got from the spy Walker. If an American submarine commander comes to periscope depth and is convinced that his nation is the victim of a surprise attack—ongoing or potential—he is authorized to use his missiles. What about their forty submarine captains at sea—"

"We monitor their deployments with our trawlers and satellites. And there are not forty at sea at any one time."

The water in the drydock was now three-quarters of the way up the sides of the *Kaliningrad*, and a loudspeaker crackled across the dock:

"LIFTOFF FROM THE BLOCKS. THE UNIT IS WATERBORNE."

Novskoyy gripped the handrail tightly and smiled. "Colonel, I am beginning to worry about you. Let me remind you that nuclear weapons are *your* responsibility. If it ever comes out that I was able to take these weapons without your knowledge, it will not be to your advantage, to say the least. If you decide to do anything so rash as to report prematurely what I have told you, I promise you, you will regret it."

Dretzski knew the admiral was right. He was caught up in this, willingly or not. "But what if word gets out, Admiral, that the submarine fleet has departed?"

"Colonel, you know the answer to that. It is just another deployment exercise."

"But won't the authorities get suspicious if you don't return in a week, at least? And it will take that long, will it not, to get your boats into position . . ."

"Yes, they may get suspicious, Colonel. And that is where you fit into the plan. You may not be the most popular man in the government, but it should not be too difficult for you to convince them that all is normal, routine. They will not suspect you of further endangering yourself. And in any case, once they realize, if they do, what I am doing, it will be too late. We will have the U.S. ports under siege, with the threat of destruction. What can they do in Moscow or anywhere else?"

"Still, sir, suppose Washington learns from Moscow of your deployment? Learns its real purpose. The American submarines could be waiting for you."

"Again your job, Colonel. Your plant in the American military, Fishhook, better known as General Herman Tyler, I believe, will insist that this is an exercise, and that this is no time to show distrust of the Russians, who have been so cooperative . . ."

"Fishhook? But, Admiral, that would put him in danger of blowing his cover. The KGB placed him in the U.S. Air Force nearly thirty-five years ago. It seems he is a brilliant officer but a mediocre agent . . . stubborn and argumentative. At SAC headquarters he never produced the target list he had been put in place to provide. Eventually we even considered removing him, but decided, flawed as he was, to keep him on as a contingency. It had been a mistake, I believe. He became a general, and then incredibly was named as the Chief of Staff of the Air Force and a year later Chairman of the Joint Chiefs. An overwhelming and unexpected intelligence victory, you might say. But not so. If word ever leaked out that the Americans had a Russian penetration agent so high in their government they would clean house like never before, become once again paranoid as they were in the Fifties. We've pretty much left Fishhook alone ever since he became a general officer."

"Nonetheless, Colonel, given his high station, he should easily convince his leaders that this deployment is an exercise. Remember, the Americans themselves conducted an exercise such as this will seem in 1984. And remember that first we thought it was a preemptive strike and then realized it was a drill. They will react the same way now."

Dretzski did not like it but realized there was little more he could say in opposition, except to ask the admiral how he planned to give instructions to his fleet once deployed. The answer, as he suspected, was that the *molniya*, the "go-code," would be issued by the admiral from the *Kaliningrad*.

Below them, the massive caisson door at the seaward end of the drydock was being pulled open by a tugboat now that the level of water in the dock matched the level in the channel. Soon the giant ship would be able to be towed out of the dock to a waiting pier.

"*That* is how we avoid detection," the admiral went on. "I will take this ship north to the polar icecap while my fleet heads to the Atlantic. There I will be invisible, hiding a quiet submarine among the noise of the shifting and creaking ice. I will remain undisturbed and untouchable. The *Kaliningrad* is a fortress flagship. When it is time, I will surface through the ice and transmit my messages to Washington and Moscow. And, if it becomes necessary, I will send the *molniya*."

Tugboats now began to pull the *Kaliningrad* out of the dock.

Novskoyy held out his hand to Dretzski, who ignored it. "I don't like this, Admiral. It is terribly risky—"

Novskoyy dropped his hand and nodded gravely.

"Of course, you are right, Ivan Ivanovich. But it is all that has been left to us. Come, I will walk you to your car."

As Dretzski followed Novskoyy to the security building, he took one last look at the gigantic *Kaliningrad* being towed out of the dock to the deep water channel beyond. At that moment he hated the ship, and the man who would command her. And what of himself, of Colonel Ivan Ivanovitch Dretzski? How did he feel about *him* . . . ?

CHAPTER
3

MONDAY, 13 DECEMBER, 1545 EST

THIMBLE SHOALS CHANNEL, CHESAPEAKE BAY

Directly astern of the port side of the *Devilfish*'s control room, in the centerline passageway of the upper deck of the operations compartment, Pacino sat in his stateroom facing a fold-down desk and a stack of paperwork—shovelling the currency of the Navy's overweight bureaucracy being the price Pacino had to pay for operating their prize possession, the *Devilfish*.

He had been up most of the night chasing the *Allentown*, and now the combination of paperwork and the ship's gentle side-to-side motion was making him drowsy. He had called for coffee and had just taken his first sip when the bridge speaker-box hissed and crackled to life.

"CAPTAIN, OFF'SA'DECK, SIR."

Pacino flipped a toggle switch and spoke into the communication console between his desk and a table at the opposite wall.

"Captain."

"CAPTAIN, OFF'SA'DECK, SIR. RADIO REPORTS RECEIVING AN IMMEDIATE MESSAGE FROM COMSUBLANT, SIR. IT'S MARKED PERSONAL FOR COMMANDING OFFICER."

"Anything else?"

"YESSIR. CONTACT SIERRA FOURTEEN, OUTBOUND

TANKER, IS PAST CLOSEST POINT OF APPROACH AND OPENING AT TEN THOUSAND YARDS. NEW CONTACT, SIERRA FIFTEEN, OUTBOUND MERCHANT VESSEL, HEADING OUT OF THE NORFOLK TRAFFIC SEPARATION SCHEME, RANGE TEN MILES, BEARING DRIFT RIGHT."

"Off'sa'deck, Captain aye. Keep an eye on him, he may not see us. Where's the *Allentown*?" Pacino had given orders to get ahead of her and run flank speed into Norfolk. The victor got the best spot on the pier with no waiting. The loser waited until the pier crew was done mooring the first boat.

"*ALLENTOWN'S* ASTERN, CAPTAIN, OUTSIDE VISUAL. RADAR HAS HER AT BEARING ZERO NINE FIVE, RANGE 25 MILES."

Pacino smiled. "One more thing," he said. "You got the Jolly Roger flying up there?"

"YESSIR. FLYING TALL AND PROUD, SIR."

"Captain aye." Pacino flipped off the toggle switch, leaned back in his chair and yawned.

At ten feet square the captain's stateroom was by far the largest private space on board. Pacino's desk was beside the entrance door, a fold-down stainless steel sink behind it. Against the far wall a table and two chairs folded into a bunk. The aft wall had a display of remote instruments showing ship's course, speed and depth, a TV monitor that could be patched into the periscope or a VCR, and a door to the stainless steel–panelled bathroom Pacino shared with the XO.

The only decoration on the stateroom's imitation wood formica panelling was a large flag in a mahogany frame with a glass cover—a grinning white skull and crossbones, the Jolly Roger.

Whenever the *Devilfish* got under way or returned from a mission, another Jolly Roger flapped in the breeze next to the American flag. The crew enjoyed the flagrant violation of U.S. Navy Regs. Every month Pacino received a memo from Squadron Seven staff not to fly the flag, and he always posted it on the bulletin board outside the crew's mess. He suspected the Squadron Seven Commodore knew it had more than a passing significance for Pacino and let him get away with it.

At fifteen, Pacino had enjoyed a week of fishing at a hideout cabin in Wyoming with his father and then Commander

Richard Donchez. Once, while trading sea stories with Donchez over a fire, Pacino senior had commented wistfully about what a kick it would be to sail into Norfolk after a big mission with a Jolly Roger flying from the sail.

Years later, on a rare day of liberty for plebe midshipmen, Pacino had found the flag in a dusty antique store and bought it to give to his father as a Christmas present when he returned from the deployment of 1973.

For years after the sinking, Pacino had not been able to bring himself to remove the flag from its gift-wrapped package. Once he finally did, seeing the old skull and crossbones seemed to fill just a little of the void his father's watery death had left inside him.

The flag seemed to capture the spirit of what his father had been—a courageous submarine officer, a seafarer, a leader, a warrior. Sometimes Pacino found it draining to stare at it for too long. Usually, it was his source of strength. He still hoped one day to do something to make up for what had happened to his father . . .

A knock sounded at the door. Pacino opened it and the Radioman of the Watch handed him a metal clipboard with a radio message printout.

132045ZDEC

IMMEDIATE   IMMEDIATE   IMMEDIATE

FM   COMSUBLANT NORFOLK VA
TO   USS DEVILFISH SSN-666

SUBJ   SMALL BOAT TRANSFER
COPY   CONSUBRON 7 NORFOLK VA
REF   (A) COMSUBLANT SUBEX 13DEC

CONFIDENTIAL   CONFIDENTIAL   CONFIDENTIAL
PERSONAL FOR C.O.//PERSONAL FOR C.O.//PERSONAL FOR C.O.
//BT//

1. SMALL BOAT TRANSFER WITH USS DEVILFISH WILL BE EXECUTED AT MOUTH OF THIMBLE SHOALS CHANNEL AT COORDINATE 12 OF REF (A) AT 1630 EST.
2. TRANSFER SHALL REMOVE COMMANDING OFFICER CDR. M. PACINO FOR TRANSPORT TO COMSUBLANT HEADQUARTERS FOR MEETING WITH COMSUBLANT.
3. ADMIRAL R. DONCHEZ SENDS.
//BT//

Pacino shook his head as he read the message. What could be so urgent that he'd be pulled off the ship with only a two-hour transit left of her trip? Even if the brass were unhappy enough with his illegal emergency-blow tactic to relieve him of command they'd still let him drive in and see his replacement standing on the pier with the commodore. It made no sense.

"XO," Pacino called over his shoulder through the wall to the XO's stateroom. Rapier tapped on the door and entered through the bathroom between the two rooms.

"XO, better get the small-boat transfer-team ready to go. The boat will meet us at the entrance to the channel."

"Who are we transferring on? Or off?"

"Me. You'll be acting captain of the *Devilfish*. Be careful with her."

Rapier frowned. "What's up, skipper? Is this about your emergency surface? You think the brass are pissed off?"

"I guess we'll see," Pacino said.

The topside crew of the *Devilfish* caught the lines of the 40-foot boat maneuvering alongside. The submarine and the transfer boat cruised at 5 knots, just enough to maintain steering. The boat was winched in tight, touching the *Devilfish*'s steel curvature. Pacino, in a heavy green canvas parka and flaming orange lifejacket, moved close to the edge of the sub's treacherously sloping cylindrical hull and grabbed the outstretched arm of one of the sailors in the small boat. When he had been pulled aboard, the transfer boat took in its lines and slowly pulled away from the submarine. Dimly Pacino heard the P.A. Circuit One announcement booming over the submarine's bridgebox, "*DEVILFISH*, DEPARTING."

The boat's diesel motor throttled up, its wake turning to white foam as it accelerated away. Pacino stood at a rail and looked back at the *Devilfish*, still going dead slow ahead.

The ship was graceful and powerful, her black cylindrical hull so low to the water that she was practically submerged even when rigged for surface. The water climbed smoothly up nearly to the forward hatch as the ship picked up speed and drove by the small boat. The conning tower was placed far forward, near where the hull started its slope down into the water.

The sail was a beautifully crafted 25-foot-tall fin shaped like a long teardrop in cross section, vertical on its leading and trailing edges, curved on top. Two officers with green parkas and binoculars stood on the bridge, the cockpit at the top of the forward part of the sail. Behind them a ten-foot-tall stainless steel flagpole flew the American stars and stripes and the stark black and white of the Jolly Roger. Coming out of the sail were two horizontal fins, "fair-water planes," shaped much like a jet airplane's horizontal tail surfaces. Rising high out of the sail, looking like two telephone poles, were the periscopes. The forward one was a simple and rugged World War II–era device. The one aft was a high-tech radar-invisible mast that was part-periscope, part-video camera, part-electronic countermeasures device, part-radio receiver. Further aft of the periscopes was an even taller, slimmer telephone-pole mast—the BIGMOUTH multifrequency radio antenna.

Behind the sail the hull extended far aft, smooth and cylindrical, until it sloped slowly into the water. The aft slope was much gentler than the forward slope, the hull gradually lowering into the sea. After a long gap of water the rudder jutted out of the water, shaped like an airplane's vertical tail. The only surface characteristics visible were white draft marks on the rudder.

Devilfish displaced 4500 tons, was 292 feet long and 32 feet in diameter. Her screw was submerged and invisible in the water. Pacino remembered the first time he had seen her in a drydock, she had looked huge and fat with no water to hide beneath. The tail section was complicated, with another rudder under the ship, horizontal fins—sternplanes—and the screw aft. The screw was a spiral-bladed shape with ten long curving blades, each looking like a scimitar sword, the hub of the screw extending far aft of the junction of the blades and the hub. A long tube extended from the skin of the ship aft to a horizontal tail fin, the sternplane and further aft beyond the screw. It was a fairing for a towed sonar array the ship could pull several miles behind her.

Pacino could stare for hours at the *Devilfish*. Aboard the transfer boat he imagined the salt breeze of the wind on his face on its bridge, the snapping of the flags behind him, the hum of the rotating radar mast aft of the flags . . . He felt his grip on the rails tighten, hoping he wasn't being relieved of command. It wasn't his career he worried about but the thought of never driving the submarine again, never feeling her deck vibrate beneath him as she plowed through the sea at flank speed.

As he watched, the *Devilfish* shrank into the distance so that all that remained was the vertical fin of the sail and the horizontal fins of the fair-water planes, forming a cruciform shape against the backdrop of the land beyond.

When the small boat landed at a jetty it was almost like being awakened from a dream. Pacino took one last look into the distance and stepped onto the dock. As he did a lieutenant came to attention and saluted, her hair pulled up into a tight bun under her oddly shaped female officer's cap. Pacino saluted back and followed her to a black staff car. He didn't ask what was going on. He would know soon enough.

CHAPTER
4

MONDAY, 13 DECEMBER, 1920 EST

NORFOLK, VIRGINIA
COMSUBLANT HEADQUARTERS

The staff car pulled through the gate of the COMSUBLANT compound and parked at the main entrance to the thirty-year-old main core of the building, a squat brick gymnasium. Beyond and above it the new glass-walled wing minimized the eyesore of the old core.

Pacino got out of the back seat of the car, feeling the chill of the December evening. The sky was black, no stars visible because of the glare of the floodlights. He and the lieutenant walked through the entrance, presenting their identification for entry. While he waited Pacino looked at a row of oil paintings on a far wall, each showing a different submarine class driving on the surface, going back to World War II ships. He lingered for a moment on the painting of the Piranha class. To its right was a painting of the newer Los Angeles class, a submarine the fleet considered a giant step backward in technology from the venerated Piranha's. The Los Angeles boats had suffered from the budget crunches of the 1970s and early eighties, considered too expensive to build right.

The lieutenant led Pacino down a cinderblock corridor into an atrium of steel and glass that arched to the top of the new wing. After an elevator ride to the top floor Pacino found himself in the plushly carpeted outer office of COMSUBLANT, the admiral in command of the Atlantic Fleet's submarines. Immediately he was led in by the receptionist, and both the receptionist and lieutenant quickly left, leaving Pacino alone with the admiral.

Pacino walked up to the massive oak desk made from timbers of a Navy frigate that had fought in 1812, removed his cap, came to attention. "Commander Pacino, USS *Devilfish*, reporting as ordered, SIR."

The bald man at the desk looked up, a slow smile spreading over his thin face, the white-capped teeth near-perfect beneath his graying mustache. He stood up, looking slim in his dress blues with rows of ribbons splashing color over gleaming gold dolphins and endless gold braid on the sleeves. He gripped Pacino's hand in a firm handshake.

"Mikey!" He stepped around the desk and put an arm around Pacino's shoulders, guiding him back to the door. "I'd offer you a drink but we need to get down to the Top Secret Conference Room."

"Hello, Admiral," Pacino said, "Sir. Uncle Dick."

Donchez looked Pacino over, opened the door and led the way back down the corridor to the elevator. "Mikey, you look great. How's Squadron Seven treating you?"

"Fine, sir," Pacino said, somewhat uncomfortable. Donchez had stayed in touch over the years but Pacino had kept a certain distance. Partly to avoid giving the impression of having connections with the brass but also because Donchez reminded him too much of good days gone by, and of the awful day Donchez had broken the news of Anthony Pacino's loss at sea with the *Stingray*. As Donchez had climbed the bureaucratic ladder of the Navy he had become more distant. Finally, as a three-star admiral in command of the fleet, they almost never saw each other.

"I heard about how you kicked ass today," Donchez said in the elevator, pulling out one of his cigars. "Good job. It's good to see a Piranha beat a Los Angeles like that. I liked the balls you showed getting away from that torpedo. Not many left in the force think like that."

"Thank you, sir," Pacino said, relieved.

"How's Hillary and your son?"

Probably sore as hell, Pacino thought, both on the pier waiting for him to disembark from the boat. "Both fine, sir. Tony wants to be a race driver, zooms around the house yelling *vroom*. Drives his mother crazy, I think she wanted a girl . . ."

Donchez said, "Maybe he'll drive a sub when he grows up."

As the elevator doors opened to a sub-basement Donchez led the way down a hall to another security scanner and sentry, through the door and another hall with a blast door at the end. He hit a large panel and the solid steel door slowly swung open with the hum of a powerful motor.

Another hall had four doors set off of it, with one double door under a sign reading FLAG PLOT. They went in one of the doors labelled TS CONF RM 1. The room had a large wood table in the center, big enough to seat over a dozen people with another dozens seats against the wall. Pacino sat at the briefing table, remembering he'd been briefed in this conference room when *Devilfish* deployed to the Mediterranean earlier in the year. Admiral Donchez sat across from him, and finally spoke.

"You want to know what you're doing here," he said, shrugging out of his dress-blue jacket. His white shirt had cloth shoulder epaulettes with three stars and anchors, and Pacino realized he was still in his khakis, the oily smell of the submarine still in the fabric.

"We have an emergency, Mikey. We need the best Piranha-class submarine we've got to go on an urgent OP. Up north, under the polar icecap."

Pacino felt excitement at an emergency operation, mixed with some disappointment at the timing. *Devilfish* had spent the last six months on a deployment and had been scheduled for a month of "stand-down"—R and R for the crew. He glanced at his watch—the date on the Rolex's dial showed the number 13, and abruptly he realized that it was the anniversary of his father's death on the *Stingray*. In the rush of battle with *Allentown* and the flush of victory afterward he hadn't realized. With the realization now came grief, an old friend, and guilt.

"Admiral, *Devilfish* has been submerged over 230 days this year. My men have barely had a chance to say hello to their families. Over 120 days without surfacing, Admiral—"

"Sorry, Mikey. You and yours are it." His tone turned chillier.

Donchez dimmed the room lights and pulled a computer keyboard off a shelf on the wall and set it on the briefing table. He hit a key, starting a computerized slide show on the far wall, a television projection driven by a computer display. The COMSUBLANT emblem dissolved into a projection map of the north pole.

"A chart of the Arctic Ocean," Donchez said. "You've been there a few times. The boundary of the ice zone is shown in green." The chart slowly zoomed in to the Russian northern coast. A city named Severomorsk was highlighted in red. "As you know the Severomorsk Naval Complex is a major shipbuilding facility, ammunition depot and command center for the Russian Northern Fleet, including the biggest and most capable arm of the Navy, the Submarine Force."

The screen changed to a view of the Severomorsk complex. Pacino could tell by the odd slanting lines through the photograph that it was a shot from a spy satellite. On a clear day a satellite could peer over from its path to get side-angle photos like this. The perspective made it much more valuable than the usual God's-eye-views satellites provided. It was like being there.

Clearly visible in the photograph was a giant drydock filled with scaffolding and equipment and the dots of workers. The dock's immensity could be told from the tiny trucks parked along the security barrier. Cranes on rail wheels surrounded the scaffolding in the dock lowering massive pieces of equipment into place.

"The old Cold War is over, but submarine-building *continues* and at a fast pace. We've been watching during the past few years as one particular class of submarine has been built. The lead ship of the class is almost ready to get under way. It happens to be the newest, most advanced attack submarine in the world, at least so far as we know."

"Not much of it to see," Pacino said, thinking the OP probably involved trailing the new Russian submarine under the polar icecap.

The screen changed and Pacino blinked hard. The same perspective but now the clutter had been removed and a behemoth of a submarine was clearly visible in the dock. Her lines were graceful. She would be very fast. The boat had a teardrop-shaped sail forward, not the sheer-sided fin of American boats but a gently sloped bubble leaning forward. Far aft, where the long hull of the boat finally tapered to the screw, a pod shaped like a long teardrop was mounted on top of the rudder fin. Aft of the rudder was a shroud. None of the screw blades was visible. Pacino looked at the ship in frank envy, wondering what it would be like to drive.

"This is the OMEGA-class Russian fast-attack submarine."

The picture changed to a blueprint of the ship, streamlined, her nose and tail sections elongated elliptical curves. Inside the lines of her shape was a second long shape.

"Double hull," Pacino said, and stood up and walked to the screen to look at the drawing up-close. He concentrated on the gap between inner and outer hull. The Piranha and Los Angeles submarines were single-hull ships. A hole in the skin of an American sub punctured the "people tank," flooding the ship. A puncture in the skin of the Russian sub would do no real damage. The only disadvantage of the double-hull ship was weight, the extra metal and water would slow the ship down.

"The inner hull of the OMEGA is titanium," Donchez said. "Strongest submarine-hull material in the world. Outer hull is plate carbon steel. The annulus, the ring, between inner and outer hull is about fifteen feet on the top and bottom, about twenty-five feet on the sides. That's twenty-five feet of water a torpedo would have to blast through to get to the interior."

Pacino looked at the blueprint's end-on drawing. The inner hull was cylindrical while the outer hull was oval shaped. The annulus was filled with tanks and air bottles and batteries and piping, all leaving more room inside the pressure hull.

"Omega's 656 feet long," Donchez went on, "Eighty-two feet wide, longer and fatter than our Trident. A Trident sub—which I consider to be a giant underpowered hog to drive—is eighteen thousand tons submerged. This ship is *sixty thousand* tons submerged."

"She'll be slow," Pacino said.

"A lot faster than a Piranha," Donchez said.

"What?"

"It has twin-reactors, each liquid-metal cooled. We're guessing about three thousand megawatts between the two of them. Pretty big when you think that the Three Mile Island plant is only twelve hundred or thirteen hundred megawatts. That gives her about six hundred thousand horsepower at the screw."

"Six hundred *thousand* shaft horsepower? Jesus." Pacino thought a moment. "There's no way a conventional screw could accelerate a boat like that with that kind of horsepower. The screw would cavitate, just spin in a cloud of steam."

He was thinking of the lectures at the Academy . . . a rotating screw blade in seawater created a low pressure area on one side of the blade, high pressure on the other. The high pressure pushed the ship while the low-pressure side sucked the ship forward. But if the pressure got too low the vacuum effect would form bubbles of steam, which would shriek as they collapsed in the high pressure of the sea away from the screw. The noisy bubble effect was called cavitation, the blades making cavities in the liquid water . . .

"No cavitation," Donchez said. "No screw, for that matter. She's got a ducted propulsor. She'll do forty-five knots easy. Maybe fifty."

Pacino looked at the blueprint. Under the shroud aft of the rudder were what looked like several rows of turbine blades. The submarine had essentially a water-jet propulsor. It would be quiet and efficient and fast.

"If she can do fifty knots," Pacino said, "she could outrun a Mark 49 Hullbuster torpedo. Not that it matters. I doubt even a Hullbuster would do much damage to her hull, not with steel over water over titanium." He shook his head. "Well, even if this thing is fast, it must take an hour for her to get up to speed."

"Look at the bow section," Donchez said.

Pacino saw torpedo tubes going forward to the nose of the ship. And a sphere of equipment at the very tip of the inside of the nosecone.

"No," Pacino said, "not polymer injection . . ."

"Yes, polymer injection. Enough for ten minutes. She'll squirt a layer of polymer out the nosecone, make the skin slippery and she'll just glide through the water like a ghost. She'll accelerate fast enough to leave her paint behind."

"Polymers won't work in arctic-temperature water—"

"I hate to tell you this, Mikey, but it works down to 28 degrees Fahrenheit."

"Why don't we ask Congress to buy us a few of those?"

"Not funny, kid," Donchez said, checking his watch. "Let's finish. This guy can dive to 7500 feet, and with the way titanium flows before it ruptures he can probably go down to 10,000 feet for a few minutes. That's over six times deeper than you can go, Mikey. And yes, our Hullbuster torpedoes would implode from sea pressure at that depth. He's armed with conventional 53-centimeter torpedoes, the new 100-centimeter Magnums and SSN-X-27 nuclear warhead land-attack cruise missiles—that is, if they're cheating on the treaty and still loading cruise missiles . . ."

You ain't cheatin', you ain't tryin', Pacino thought.

"And the 100-centimeter Magnum torpedoes can pursue at sixty knots for sixty nautical miles with a nuclear warhead. And even if you can evade one, it just drives back to the point where it thinks you *should* be and detonates. It doesn't have to get close to kill your delicate little hull with a nuclear explosion. Meanwhile the OMEGA submarine is running like hell using his polymer system and avoids damage.

"And finally, the OMEGA has a thicker anechoic coating than previous classes. The coating does to sonar pulses what a stealth bomber does to radar pulses—absorbs them without reflecting them. In addition to quieting the submarine, any torpedo going active would not hear a return sonar ping from her hull."

"This boat is fucking invincible—"

"Damn near. Mikey, we need to get a recording of this boat's sound-signature. And I want you to get it."

An SPL, Pacino thought. Sound Pressure Level. Obtained by putting an American attack submarine about ten feet away from a Russian submarine and using sophisticated recording equipment to record the different sounds and tonals from each bearing. In effect, a map of the target ship's radiated noise. Each Russian submarine class made different noises. Machinery rotated at a particular speed, created a distinctive note like a tuning fork's pure tonal frequency. Each class had a few tonals that American sonars could detect and classify from miles away.

The only way to get an SPL recording was to drive right up to less than a tenth of a shiplength away and maneuver around the

target without him finding out that he was being recorded—
literally driving circles around the target submarine.

There was always, both Pacino and the admiral knew, the
risk of collision.

Pacino looked up at Donchez, who had been studying him.

"Sir, the Russians are laying down their cruise missile nukes
before the U.N. Someone must have forgotten to tell the shipyard that the Cold War is over. Or maybe they're finishing this
thing to provide jobs." He was just testing.

"We know what we see, Commander."

Donchez stood up, his face stony. "Come on back to my office. I've got something to show you."

Back in the admiral's office Pacino sat in a deep easy chair and
accepted a cigar from Donchez's humidor. The sky outside the
plate glass windows was dark. Pacino's watch said it was almost
eight in the evening. His stomach growled.

Donchez's head was stuck in a safe, looking for something.
Finally he found it. Pacino picked up Donchez's lighter, a worn
Zippo with the emblem of the USS *Piranha*, SSN-637, lead ship
of the class. Donchez had commanded her years before. Pacino
lit the cigar and tasted the smooth smoke on his tongue.

When the admiral sat back in his chair, his expression was
dark. He flipped Pacino a bound report marked "SECRET" in
black letters on the binding.

"What's this?" Pacino asked.

"It's been more than twenty years, Mikey," he said. "It isn't
declassified yet. The report on the loss of the *Stingray*."
Donchez's tone was thick.

"Admiral, why are you showing me this?"

Pacino felt like he did the day he was a plebe and Donchez
had come to the Officer of the Watch's office and told him his
father was gone.

"It's exactly what I told you that day. I wrote that."

"Yes, sir?"

"And it's all bullshit, pure bullshit." Donchez's voice wavered.

"What do you mean?" His old, faint suspicions at the time
reviving.

"Mikey, that report as written would suggest that your dad screwed up. Didn't turn the ship in time to inactivate the hot-run torpedo. Didn't set material condition in time."

Donchez looked down at his desk and continued softly. "Commander Anthony Pacino was the best damned combat submarine officer I ever knew. Except for one." He looked back up at Pacino, who said nothing. "Patch Pacino did not die in the Atlantic Ocean. And he didn't die from his own damned torpedo. Patch Pacino was a hero, which are in short supply, especially these days. The USS *Stingray* was on a top-secret operation under the polar icecap. She was getting an SPL of a VICTOR III."

Donchez walked over to a wood cabinet and opened twin doors, revealing a large television monitor. He took a VCR tape out of the safe and inserted it in the VCR deck below the monitor.

Pacino shivered from the cold of the office, which only a moment before had felt comfortable. He watched as the TV picture went from fuzz to focus on a minisubmarine hanging from several cables. A submersible. The cables lowered the submersible into the sea. Donchez began a commentary, his voice noticeably hoarse.

"This is a submersible that was used by Doctor Robert Powell of Woods Hole. The guy who went down to the *Titanic* and the *Bismarck*. Well, he also took this baby down to the *Thresher*, our sub that sank in '63. The submersible was designed to dive to Russian submarine wrecks and recover data. It has three spherical pressure hulls, its own manipulator arms and thrusters, and a remotely piloted vehicle, an eyeball. It can carry a video camera into tight spots.

"Last year we decided to try to find the *Stingray*'s wreck under the polar icepack. Instead of using a sidescan sonar from a survey ship we had to cut holes in the ice, drop a sonar probe down and listen. For a year we came up with nothing. We drilled, dropped and listened at hundreds of sites. Finally we found it, made an icecamp and sent the submersible down." The TV picture showed an encampment in the arctic, tents and quonset huts gathered around lifting-derricks. It also showed the submersible being dropped through a deep hole in the ice. "We found the *Stingray*'s remains under 11,500 feet of very cold water. The initial shots on this tape were taken from the remote swimmer camera that was sent to the interior of the hull's wreckage. This shot is of the bow compartment."

The inside of the *Stingray* was all wreckage, mangled pipes and pieces of steel. Pacino tried to speak but his voice was gone, his throat thick.

"This is the operations compartment," Donchez continued as the view shifted. It was like staring into an open coffin, Pacino thought, wondering why Donchez would subject him to it.

"We did find something recognizable here."

The light from the remote eyeball's floodlight wavered as it swam by a grotesquely bent frame. An object came into view slowly, then focused. It was a baseball cap, the thread embroidery still plainly legible above and below the submarine dolphins: USS STINGRAY SSN-589.

Pacino felt a sudden exhaustion, like a shock wave.

The TV view shifted to an outside shot. "This was taken with the video on the main cameras of the submersible," Donchez said. The disembodied sail came into view with sand in the background, one fair-water plane buried in the sand. "The sail was ripped away from the main hull by hydrodynamic forces. Part of the hull was flattened like a wing. The hull hit the bottom at nearly a hundred miles an hour. Back aft you can see that the hull, instead of flattening like the forward parts, was accordioned. The conical hull was forced inward, compressing the smaller part of the cone into the larger part. The force required to do this was immense. Here's the bow compartment, which didn't crush like the rest of the hull. It was equalized with sea pressure."

The video shot showed the rounded bow compartment, the torpedo doors rusted at the far point of the hull's nosecone. The shot showed the hull coming around. Soon the flank of the bow was in the picture, a gaping hole in it.

Donchez stopped the tape at the shot of the hole in the hull. "Mikey, you've got a PhD in mechanical engineering. You tell me, was this an explosion inside or outside the hull?"

Pacino slowly rose from his seat and walked to the TV. His back was wet with cold sweat, his khaki shirt stuck to his back. He pointed to the star-shaped fingers of the jagged edge of the ten-foot-diameter hole.

"These points of the hole go *in*, not out. It was an external explosion. *Stingray* was gunned down, wasn't she, Admiral," Pacino said, a statement, not a question. No more guessing or wondering now.

Donchez barely nodded.

"Why was this kept secret? Why was it covered up—"

"Mikey, you've been up north. You know about the game. At the time it seemed the thing to do. Should we have whined to the U.N.? What would we say to Congress when they demanded to know how in hell a Soviet could sneak up on one of our best and put it on the bottom? What would become of our northern surveillance? How could we tell the world that we *knew* what they'd done when the SOSUS network that discovered it was highly secret?"

Pacino said nothing at first, then: "So why have you decided to show this to me? After all these years?"

Donchez turned off the TV and pulled out the VCR tape. In the heavy silence that followed he opened his safe, returned the sinking report and the VCR tape, at the same time removing a purple file folder. He slammed the heavy door of the safe and spun the tumbler, finally turning to face Pacino, whose face was tight with anger at the scene of the *Stingray*'s control room. He slapped the purple folder on the desk in front of Pacino. "Open it."

Pacino did. Inside, staring back at him, was the face of a man in a Russian Navy uniform, four stars on his epaulettes. Thick graying hair hung over a dark face, lined by the years yet still commanding. The eyes seemed to stare off into the distance, slightly narrowed.

"This is Admiral Alexi Viktoryvich Novskoyy, Supreme Commander, Russian Northern Fleet. A reactionary hawk who *still* wants to bring back the old discredited Soviet Union, when he and his ilk were riding high."

Pacino waited.

"He is also the man who murdered Patch Pacino."

Pacino looked at the photograph, stunned, his eyes finally rising to look into Donchez's face. *"You know this for a fact?"*

"Alexi Nosvkoyy, commanding officer, fleet submarine *Leningrad*, a VICTOR III attack submarine, the *only* VICTOR III, I might add, from 1973 to 1976. He was the new construction commanding officer. Awarded Hero of the Soviet Union medal in 1973 for classified action. In the Arctic Ocean. That's him, there's no doubt."

"And now? That was a long time ago—"

"The new Omega submarine got under way three hours ago, Mikey," Donchez pointed to the folder. Pacino put the photo of Novskoyy aside and looked at the satellite photo beneath, a God's-eye-view looking directly downward that showed the huge Omega submarine angled away from her pier and pulling out.

"What do you see?"

"Sub getting under way. One last line on the pier. Topside crew getting ready to pull the line in. Two cranes on the pier. Probably one for shorepower cables and one for the gangway."

"What else?"

"Car on the pier. Limousine. Flags on the fenders. Stars on the flags."

Pacino looked up. "Admiral's limo."

Donchez nodded. "And how many stars?" he said, offering a magnifying glass.

Pacino studied the photo with the glass. "Four stars."

"Correct. And do you see flags flying on the OMEGA?"

"Yes. Northern Fleet Banner. Russian flag. Commissioning pennant."

"And?"

"And a flag with stars on it. Four stars." Pacino looked into Donchez's eyes. *"Admiral Novskoyy's on board!"*

"Bingo. Novskoyy's on board the OMEGA. The mission, as we understand it, is a one-week trip under the icepack. Sea trials. And the admiral is along to see how his baby performs. He designed the OMEGA himself."

Pacino sat back in his chair. Suddenly he understood the urgency of the OP. And for him in particular. The son-of-a-bitch who'd killed his father was aboard—

Pacino jumped as the phone rang. Donchez nodded at it.

"It's for you, Mikey."

Pacino shook his head. How would Donchez know who the phone was for?

"Pacino here."

"Captain, XO here." It was Rapier. "They said you were in a briefing but they put me through anyway."

"Go ahead," Pacino said, looking at Donchez.

"Sir, we're moored at berth 7. I took the liberty of bringing on shorepower and ordering the reactor shutdown . . . Something very strange is going on here. The squadron sent over some guys from the tender with about ten forktrucks full of food. They're loading it aboard right now."

Pacino stared at Donchez, who returned his look. "Yes, XO. What else?"

"Arctic gear, sir, four pallets. Squadron wants to load that on, too, in the ship's office and the fan room. I told them to hold off until we talked. There's also a truck here with five torpedoes. They're painted red instead of green. Tender says they're a new weapon system. Mark 50 torpedoes. They call them Hull-crushers. Squadron Weapons Officer is here and wants permission to load *them* aboard. I said hell no. Sir . . . you got any orders for me?"

Pacino didn't hesitate. "XO, you have permission to load weapons and Arctic supplies. And notify the crew that all liberty and leaves are cancelled. We sail at dawn tomorrow. While you're at it, request a clearance message from COMSUBLANT for transit—"

"Sir, I'm holding the clearance in my hands right now. I suppose you'll be letting me know what's up?"

"It's a secure phone," Donchez broke in.

"XO, *Devilfish* will be getting under way for a classified OP tomorrow morning. You can let the crew know they won't be home for Christmas." He broke off the connection before Rapier could protest.

Donchez pulled his long cold cigar out of the ashtray and lit it, looking out the plate glass window to a plaza across the street where construction vehicles had been parked for the night.

"You know, Mikey," Donchez said, "the polar icecap is a lonely place. Things can happen there that no one on earth will ever know about. Look at *Stingray*. Only a few men know what really happened to her." Donchez swivelled around in his chair and looked directly at Pacino. "Those Mark 50 torpedoes, the Hullcrushers, they're new, experimental. They have shaped charges designed to penetrate and blast through double-hulled submarines with one hundred times the killing power of the old Mark 49's. And as far as your tubes and fire-control systems are concerned, they'll look exactly like Mark 49's. No system modifications necessary. They'll go fifty-five knots. Their sonars have improved doppler filters. And their crush-depth is deeper than 10,000 feet. We figure they're the antidote to the OMEGA."

Pacino's mind raced, wondering whether Donchez really meant what Pacino thought he did.

"In fact, Mikey," Donchez went on, "those torpedoes are so new and so experimental that we've never had a chance to take inventory of the five on the squadron truck. Why, if you came back from up north and those torpedoes were missing, well, no one would ever notice. As far as squadron and SUBLANT are concerned, those torpedoes don't exist."

Pacino stood up, hands balling into fists.

Donchez stood up and held out his hand.

Pacino saluted, turned and walked to the door, putting on his blue baseball cap.

"Merry Christmas, Uncle Dick," he said and closed the door behind him.

Admiral Richard Donchez sat back down and said, "Merry Christmas, Mikey . . . and good hunting."

He looked out again over the grass to the plaza across the street. The construction going on was for a contract he had written personally: to build a marble monument in honor of the officers and men of the USS *Stingray*.

Donchez took a long puff on his Havana cigar. "And Merry Christmas to you, Patch," he said softly, "and rest in peace, old friend."

CHAPTER
5

MONDAY, 13 DECEMBER, 2350 EST

SANDBRIDGE BEACH, VIRGINIA

Sandbridge Beach, a small village of beach houses, fish restaurants, convenience stores and bait shops, was bathed in the moonlight of a cloudless night sky. The large beach houses were quiet in the off-season. A few were decorated with Christmas lights. As midnight approached, the lights of all but a few houses were off.

Michael Pacino's old Corvette rumbled to a halt in the carport under a large three-story redwood house on stilts overlooking the water. He turned off the engine, brought back to the present by the silence, surprised that he had driven the forty miles from the base to the house without conscious thought or motion.

Slowly, feeling like an old man, Pacino emerged from the cramped car, pulling a duffel bag from a cubbyhole behind the seat. He stood, watching the waves break on the beach on the other side of the property, then climbed to the second-floor entrance to the house. Hillary had bought the beach house with her own money. Commander's pay might afford a modest colonial in the suburbs but never a house on the water, not on Sandbridge. It had bothered him some, living here. As he searched his pocket for his key the door opened.

Hillary's face was always a welcome sight after a long run on the boat. She had beautiful tanned skin, dark blue eyes over high cheekbones and perfectly full red lips. With long blonde hair, she was tall and thin. Her own complaint about herself was that her breasts were too small. He had no complaints.

She was also a high-strung, thoughtful, at times brooding woman. On many nights after Tony was in bed she'd spend hours on the deck overlooking the beach, smoking cigarettes and staring out to sea, sometimes writing poetry in a notebook she never could bring herself to let Pacino read. When he was assigned ashore she would tend to come out of herself, laughing and talking more. Frankly, she once told him, she was scared to death of losing him, and that fear was a live thing between them. She had tried to convince him to leave the Navy and come to work for her father, an executive for DynaCorp International, a defense contractor. Pacino couldn't see it. Money meant little to him. He still drove his midshipman car, the beat-up '69 Corvette. To Pacino, resigning from the Navy was just unthinkable. He was a submariner, his reason for living was to poke holes in the ocean, to be where he was needed. Like his father. He understood her feelings, worried about them, but he couldn't quit. And she was no clichéd rich bitch who selfishly wanted it all her way. She had tried hard, as he had, but it hadn't been easy . . .

Tonight would be a repetition of the old conflicts, he suspected. Once through the door he found he was right.

"Michael, we waited on that pier for hours. Neither you nor squadron gave me any idea you wouldn't be on the boat. I had to find out from Jon Rapier that you got called downtown. And now Julie Rapier calls and wants to know why you're taking the boat out to sea for Christmas. My God, Michael, what's going on?"

She trailed him upstairs as he pulled off his uniform, the khakis still smelling like a submarine, shrugged into an old black sweatshirt with the faded legend on the front reading "DEEP, SILENT, FAST, DEADLY—U.S. SUBMARINE FORCE." Once in his jeans he took the stairs down to the lodge room and headed for the bar. Once he found the Jack Daniels he splashed the gold liquid over four ice cubes in a highball glass and drained half of it in one gulp.

How, he wondered, could he tell Hillary what he was about to do? If he *could* tell her, she might understand, but this trip was top secret.

"Hillary, please—" and stopped as he saw the tears. He was about to go to her when he heard Tony calling out from the loft above. He hurried to the stairs, and as he climbed the risers saw Hillary going out on the deck.

At the top of the stairs Pacino took Tony in his arms and carried the boy to his room, turning on the light, taking up the boy's teddy bear and sitting down in the easy chair where they read together on the rare nights when he got home at a decent hour.

"Daddy," Tony said, "mommy said you're going away for Christmas. She said she doesn't know when you're coming back."

"Tony, I *have* to go. I'm sorry but there's something very important we have to do on the boat. I'm really sorry, Ace, but it has to be done now. I'll be back soon, though, and when I'm home we'll have our Christmas then. Okay?" Of course not okay. Tony's tears proved it.

"It's way past your bedtime, and I've got to pack. Let's get you tucked in."

As Pacino repeated the words of Tony's prayer—"if I die before I wake, pray the Lord my soul to take"— his eyes seemed to get heavy. He hoped Tony wouldn't notice. But Tony's eyes were shut, and by the end of the prayer his son's breaths were slow and deep.

Pacino kissed Tony's cheek and moved out of the room, shutting the door gently. Darkness. Hillary already in bed. A single dim light in the kitchen. Pacino went down the stairs, intending to try Hillary's therapy of staring out to sea when the phone rang, making him jump.

"Pacino."

"Duty Officer, sir." Lieutenant Stokes. "You wanted a zero one hundred status report, sir. Are you awake?"

"Go *ahead*, Stokes," Pacino said, forcing himself to concentrate on the needs of the *Devilfish*, to respond to the request to start up the reactor, to hear the package of data needed to plug himself into his ship from forty miles away and guide the actions of young Stokes.

"Station section three watches aft and start up the reactor," Pacino ordered. "Divorce from shore power and get the squadron crane on the pier by six. When you're ready take off the shore-power cables."

"Aye aye, sir," Stokes said, repeating back the order. "Sir, should I call for tugs and a pilot?"

"No tugs, Stokes, and no pilot. *Devilfish* will get under way on her own steam."

"Aye aye, sir. Do you want a call when the reactor's critical?"

"No. I'll see you in a few hours. Make sure the coffee's very damn hot."

"Aye aye, sir. Good night, Captain."

"Good night Stokes."

Pacino put the phone down slowly, moving in a sea of molasses, his eyes roving to the pictures on the wall, the wedding photographs, the crossed swords at the Naval Academy Chapel, Hillary kissing him under the swords of his classmates, Hillary holding newborn Tony, himself saluting on the deck of *Devilfish* at the change-of-command ceremony, his whites starched and shiny in the Virginia sunshine. So long ago. So very damn long ago. Finally his attention went to the one faded photograph of him and his father taken during his plebe summer, his father in dress whites with the three stripes of the rank of commander, looking so damned proud.

For the next two hours Pacino stood on the deck facing the Atlantic. He considered waking Hillary and talking it out but knew it was a dumb idea. Finally he went in to pack, washing his khakis, ironing some shirts, filling the duffel bag with his gear. After an hour he decided to write a note to Hillary and one to Tony. It occurred to him that if he didn't return he wanted Tony to hear the story from him firsthand. He let it spill from his pen—not the specifics of the mission but that he was going especially because of *his* father. He tried to push a lifetime of fatherly advice and love into one twelve-page letter, remembering how he had searched his own father's effects for some sign, some note. How there had been nothing.

He wrote a second letter to Hillary, telling her how he felt, trying to bring her back to the days when they were drunk with their discovery of each other . . . the first time they made love in her car, the windows steamed up on the parking strip of

Halsey Field, and how the Jimmylegs security guard had pounded on the window with a flashlight, how she had giggled at him as he tried to get back into uniform, his shirttail hanging out, his hair a mess, lipstick all over his face from her kisses, how he'd told her about when he'd been placed on report for the infraction, a "Class A" offense for public displays of affection, and had been restricted to his spartan room in Bancroft Hall for six weeks. After he had tried to evoke the good times, and a few of the bad, Pacino sealed the letter and inserted it into the coffee can in the freezer, where she was sure to see it in the morning long after *Devilfish* would have slipped away from the pier. Tony's letter, intended to be read only if Pacino failed to come back from the OP, was placed in the file cabinet in the folder marked WILL, where Pacino knew it would be found if . . .

He checked his watch. The night had evaporated. He hurried into his khakis, put his bag by the door and went up the stairs to Tony's room. For a moment he watched his sleeping son, so quiet and handsome in his sleep. He touched his hair, and left.

Hillary was curled in a ball in the center of the bed, lying on her side, a pillow between her knees. Pacino walked to the head of the bed and kneeled down so his face was even with hers, kissed her lips and she sighed, and for a moment a trace of a smile was on her face.

Pacino's wristwatch alarm beeped—time to go.

He looked at Hillary one last time, then left the room, shutting the door quietly.

CHAPTER
6
TUESDAY, 14 DECEMBER, 0756 EST

Norfolk, Virginia
Norfolk Naval Base
Pier 7

The sun was just rising over the Squadron Seven piers as Pacino pulled his duffel bag out of his car and began walking toward *Devilfish*. The dim orange light gave little warmth. The air was crisp and cool.

Pacino walked up to the end of the pier and returned the salutes of the guards, then reached for his identification. Pier 7 had changed quite a bit in the last two decades, he thought. At the head of the pier concrete crash barriers had been set up, along with a barbedwire double-chain-link fence. The guardhouse was manned by a contingent of U.S. Marines, all armed with M-16s. Every submarine tied up at the pier had a sniper with a high-powered rifle in the sail. The quarterdeck watch sailors no longer carried Colt .45s with the ammo in their belts. They had loaded machine pistols. Such anti-terrorist measures hadn't existed in the fall of 1973 when his father's *Stingray* had sailed for deployment.

That day the families and children and girlfriends had all been on the pier. The squadron staff made a bon-voyage party of it— brass band playing, crepe banners in red, white and blue, a banner reading GOOD LUCK, STINGRAY, tables covered with cookies, pies, sandwiches. The crews of the other boats waving. Michael Pacino in his fourth-class midshipman's uniform, his brass anchor pins on the lapels, saluting the officers who passed by.

This underway would be different. *Devilfish* would leave without fanfare. A crowd on the pier was considered a security problem. It was as if the boat was already gone.

Pacino walked down the pier, the eyes of the bridge snipers on him. The other boats were quiet. By his request, *Devilfish* was always parked at the very end of the pier so he could drive out without tugs. To Pacino it seemed somehow inappropriate for a warship to pull out with two tugs. The sleek destroyers and frigates two piers down would pull out with a Back Emergency–Ahead Flank under way, their wakes boiling up astern, their radars rotating in quick circles, flags fluttering smartly from the masts, smoke pouring out their stacks. Envious submariners would watch the cocky surface officers while two tugs pulled their delicate submarines gently away from the piers, being careful of the fiberglass nosecones covering the sonar spherical arrays. No, no tugs for Pacino.

When he reached the berth of the *Devilfish*, he received a salute from the Duty Officer, Lieutenant Stokes.

"Good morning, Captain. I thought you'd want a report before getting onboard, sir."

"Go ahead, Stokes."

"Sir, reactor's critical. We got a normal full power lineup, reactor main coolant pumps in two slow/two slow, divorced from shorepower, main engines warm, clutch disengaged, section three watches manned aft. I've had the shorepower cables removed from the ship. The XO has gone over the pre-underway checklist with department heads and reports the ship is ready in all respects to get under way. XO briefed the officers, and the Chief of the Boat briefed the men. XO recommends stationing the maneuvering watch in preparation to get under way. Sir, request permission to station the maneuvering watch."

Pacino looked at the river, measuring the wind and current. He turned back to Stokes. "Station the maneuvering watch. Rig out the outboard, raise and lower masts as necessary and when you're ready, rotate and radiate on the radar." Pacino had just saved the Duty Officer three phonecalls for permission. "And send the XO to my stateroom."

Stokes repeated back the captain's orders and walked to the boat. Pacino lingered on the pier for a moment, looking at *Devilfish*'s sleek hull, then crossed the gangway.

"*DEVILFISH* . . . ARRIVING," boomed throughout the ship, announcing the captain's arrival. Pacino saluted the topside watch and crouched over the operations compartment hatch, the same hatch used to load weapons.

"Down ladder," he said, tossing his bag down the hatch, then lowering himself through the small opening. The smell of submarine hit Pacino. A mix of lubrication and diesel oil, stale cigarette smoke, cooking grease, ozone, old sweat and raw sewage. The smell wasn't particularly bad, just strong and characteristic. It lingered on the clothes, in the hair. Hillary hated it, and who could blame her? He heard the sounds of the boat—the high whine of the ship's inertial navigation system, the low roar of the ventilation ducts. He climbed down the ladder, and his feet hit the deck of the operations upper-level passageway across from the XO's stateroom.

The narrow passageway forward opened into the control room. One door to starboard was the sonar room. The door to port was the captain's stateroom. Between the captain's stateroom and the control room was a steep staircase to operations middle level, home of officers' country and the crews' mess.

Pacino opened the door to his stateroom, noting the room clean and tidied, a steaming cup of coffee on the table. The Duty Officer must have had it sent to the stateroom when he was walking down the pier. Pacino tossed his bag onto one of the seats of the table, opened his fold-down desktop and sat down to drink the coffee from the mug with the *Devilfish*'s emblem painted on it.

The *Devilfish* name and emblem had been controversial from the beginning. A circular field framed a leering ram's head. The ram's horns curled up and back in a curving spiral. Between the horns was the shape of a modern nuclear attack submarine seen from the side. Above the ram's head were the words USS DEVILFISH, below the letters SSN-666. The hull number had inspired someone in NAVSHIPS to name the boat *Devilfish*. Protests were lodged with Congress but controversy had never reached the front page. Nixon had resigned that same week. With no media outrage to fan the flames the *Devilfish* name-flap had died out. Pacino liked it. It sounded vicious and fierce.

On his second sip of coffee he heard Stokes' Kentucky twang boom out over the P.A. Circuit One announcing system: "STATION . . . THE MANEUVERING WATCH."

A knock came on the door from the head, Commander Rapier coming to brief him on the ship's readiness.

"Come in," he said. The door opened and Rapier walked in from the head, wearing a canvas green parka over khakis, hands full of papers and the radio message-board. He handed the clip-board to Pacino.

The XO tour was considered by many the hump of a Navy career, defined as making another man, the captain, happy, taking the paperwork burden off him and allowing him to concentrate on tactics instead of plans, weapons employment instead of weapons inventories. The idea was to suffer through the XO tour, doing the hard work while the captain got the credit, so that when it was your turn another officer would do it for you.

Rapier looked down now at Captain Michael Pacino and for a moment he could forget all his gripes. With Pacino on the boat, with the hatches shut and dogged, the boat rigged for dive, life changed. Suddenly the submarine created its own universe, and he and Pacino alone took it on, fought the elements, the cold depths of a sea intent on killing them at their first inattention. Submerged with Michael Pacino, life had purpose. Sometimes he wondered whether the captain had the power to brainwash him, so powerful were the feelings of his own dedication when he was at sea. But just when an OP would be clicking, with the submarine and himself and Pacino operating together like a machine, they would pull into port and the paperwork mountains would be brought in by forktruck . . . messages demanding reports, sailors demanding evaluations, medical reviewers wanting radiation records of the personnel, fiscal auditors wanting to see the ship's operating funds, supply auditors wanting to review the ship's food service, *admirals* coming and going, hours of cleaning the ship, the gear breaking, the parts missing, the men stressed by demands on their time to fix the boat in port while annoyed wives and children wanted them home.

And now the cycle was to start again. A fresh OP. A fresh

attitude. Just them and the boat and the sea. Rapier inhaled slowly.

"Morning, sir."

"Morning, XO." Pacino smiled slightly. "How pissed off is the crew?"

"Very, sir. I think the *Devilfish* Wives' Club is hanging us in effigy."

"Me, you mean. Can't be helped. I'll brief the officers once we're submerged."

"How long'll we be out, sir?"

"Could be as few as three weeks."

"Must be important."

Pacino looked at Rapier over his coffee mug. "It is. What's the status of the underway?"

"Engineering is ready. Propulsion is on both main engines. Lines are being singled up topside. Forward spaces are rigged and ready. All checklists completed last night. All personnel onboard and ready. We're go, with the exception of getting permission from Squadron to get under way."

Pacino drained his cup. His communication console speaker blasted out a call from the bridge.

"CAPTAIN, OFF'SA'DECK, SIR," Stokes' Kentucky accent boomed.

Pacino clicked on the speaker toggle switch.

"Captain."

"OFF'SA'DECK, SIR. COMMODORE IS ON THE PIER WAITING FOR YOU, CAP'N."

"Very well. You ready to get under way up there, Stokes?"

"YESSIR. SOON AS YOU GET BACK ABOARD WE'LL PULL THE GANGWAY OFF WITH THE LAST CRANE AND WE'RE ALL SET. AND THE JOLLY ROGER FLAG IS UP HERE, READY TO RAISE WHEN WE SHIFT COLORS."

"Captain, aye," Pacino said. "I'll be up after I see the Commodore, XO. See you later."

Rapier walked out toward the control room, and Pacino climbed back out the operations upper-level hatch to the curving deck topside, blinking in the cold early morning sun.

*   *   *

In the bridge cockpit, a small space atop the sail, Lieutenant Nathanial Stokes accepted the cup of coffee handed up to him from the bridge-access tunnel by the messenger of the watch. He had been up all night getting the ship ready to go, with last minute pre-underway checks, last minute repairs, the arctic gear and the emergency supplies. It didn't take a rocket scientist to tell that the ship was to go under ice.

Stokes and the Duty Chief had gotten out the Standard Operating Procedure for under-ice operations, which required them to put duct tape on every crack or hole in the top surface of the hull to further quiet the ship. The most minute cracks or holes on the hull could cause a flow-induced resonance, with a noise like a hillbilly blowing over a bottle neck, noises that could give them away.

Stokes, of medium height, dark-haired, a tight beard on his chin and thick neck, was built like a bull, huge shoulders, thighs to match. A southerner and damn proud of it, the first thing Stokes' molasses-thick Kentucky accent would say to someone he met was that he was from Mayfield, Kentucky, and anywhere else on God's green earth was a sorry disappointment by comparison. A star offensive tackle on the varsity football squad at Navy, his twin claims to fame were his interception of a short over-the-line pass at his senior year's Army–Navy game, which he had run in for the go-ahead touchdown in the fourth quarter, and his seduction of the Naval Academy Superintendent's daughter, having been caught in her bed by the admiral himself. The only thing that had saved Stokes from dismissal from the Academy was the daughter's temper tantrum over his pending Conduct Hearing. Stokes had reported to *Devilfish* with his reputation as a ballplayer and ladies' man preceding him.

Stokes drained the last of the coffee and stowed the cup, then heard the communication box boom out, "BRIDGE MANEUVERING, REQUEST TO SPIN THE SHAFT TO KEEP THE MAIN ENGINES WARM."

"Maneuvering, Bridge," Stokes replied laconically into his microphone, "Spin the shaft as necessary."

"SPIN THE SHAFT AS NECESSARY, BRIDGE, MANEUVERING AYE."

What was the holdup for getting under way, Stokes wondered

in his fatigued impatience. The sun was starting to climb in the cold December sky. It was time to get this damned bucket of bolts to sea.

The enlisted phonetalker nudged him. The captain was emerging from the operations compartment hatch, climbing out on deck into the sun.

As Pacino crossed the gangway to the pier below, Stokes clicked the P.A. Circuit One shipwide announcing system microphone and gave the crew a dose of his accent.

"DEVILFISH, DEPARTING!"

Commodore Benjamin Adams was waiting on the pier. Actually he was a Navy captain but was addressed by his station in life as commanding officer of the submarine squadron, just as Pacino was called captain when he was only a commander. Adams was a paunchy balding man in his fifties, with a gravelly voice, a brisk manner and a dry sense of humor. Pacino walked up and saluted. Adams smiled and returned the salute.

"Well, Patch, you all set for this mysterious mission of yours?"

"Yessir," Pacino said, pleased to hear his father's nickname applied to him.

"You want to let me in on what you're doing on this run?" It was not unusual for squadron commodores not to know the mission of one of his squadron's ships. When in port the ships came under Adams' administrative control. Once at sea the submarine commander answered only to COMSUBLANT. Since submarines were under orders to maintain radio silence at sea a submarine captain was essentially on his own when submerged.

Pacino made a zipping motion over his lips. Adams nodded.

"Okay, Patch. Wherever the hell you're going, good luck."

"Thanks, Commodore. Request permission to get under way, sir."

Adams looked over at *Devilfish.* "Your tugboats late?"

"No sir."

"No tugs?" Adams asked, knowing the answer.

"No tugs, sir."

"No pilot?"

"No pilot, sir."

"Get under way, Captain. And I guess this is it till January. Oh, Patch, no pirate flag this time. Right?"

"Right, sir."

There was an awkward silence between the two men, friends separated by the gulf shaped by their respective jobs.

Adams shook Pacino's hand. "Well, good luck again, Patch. And good hunting."

Pacino walked across the gangway, again struck by how different this day's underway was from his father's.

"*DEVILFISH*, ARRIVING."

Pacino walked forward to the leading edge of the sail, climbed up the steel ladder rungs set into the flank of the sail 25 feet up to the bridge. Stokes and the phonetalker were crammed into the small cockpit of the bridge. Aft, poking his head from a trapdoor, a clamshell, was the enlisted lookout. In the crawlspace between the bridge and the lookout cockpit was another enlisted-man phonetalker, shoehorned into a tight black hole with no view and no breeze. His job was to act as back-up in case the bridge communication box failed. Whenever the OOD gave a speed or rudder order, the phonetalkers simultaneously relayed it to phonetalkers in the control room below.

Pacino climbed to the flying bridge at the top of the sail behind the bridge cockpit. Steel handrails, temporarily screwed into the top of the sail, were set up above and behind the bridge cockpit. Standing there, Pacino could see for miles. He checked his watch.

"Off'sa'deck, let's lose the gangway."

A crane on the pier pulled the gangway off *Devilfish*'s hull.

Pacino nodded to Stokes. "Let's go."

Stokes took the bullhorn and shouted down to the lifejacketed men on the deck and on the pier, "Take in line one. Take in line two."

The linehandlers on the pier pulled the heavy lines from the bollards and tossed them to the linehandlers on the boat. The ship's bow started moving away from the pier, the current pushing her away.

"Take in three. Take in four." Stokes leaned over the starboard side of the sail, looking aft at the linehandlers. As the pier sailors tossed the thick lines to the boat's linehandlers, he picked up his microphone.

"Shift colors!" An air horn at the base of the cockpit blasted an earsplitting shriek for eight seconds, announcing that the warship was no longer pierbound. Simultaneously the American flag was struck on deck, a bigger American flag raised on the temporary flagpole behind Pacino, and on the other lanyard next to the American flag, the Jolly Roger was raised to flap proudly in the breeze.

On the pier, Commodore Adams smiled in spite of himself.

Pacino climbed down into the bridge cockpit with the Officer of the Deck and the Junior Officer of the Deck.

"Flying bridge clear, Off'sa'deck," he said to Stokes. "Raise the radar mast, rotate and radiate."

Stokes passed orders to the control room, and above and behind them the radar hummed and squeaked as it rotated, helping the control room crew below navigate out of Norfolk. Both periscopes rotated furiously, taking visual fixes as the navigator, an Irishman named Christman with red hair and temperament to match, directed them out.

"BRIDGE, NAVIGATOR," the bridge communication-box rattled, "100 YARDS TO TURNING POINT. NEW COURSE, ZERO EIGHT ONE."

"Navigator, Bridge aye," Stokes drawled into the microphone.

Pacino looked at the sky and the sea. The wind was stiff and cold, numbing his windward left cheek. The sky was a deep blue with white clouds in layer-thin wisps. The sun was bright but cold and low on the horizon. The southern mouth of the Chesapeake Bay was choppy in the wind. The water looked a dirty green, small whitecaps on every wave. Pacino looked through his binoculars down the channel after the next turn and saw a merchant tanker lumbering down toward them, inbound to Norfolk's international terminal.

"BRIDGE, NAVIGATOR, MARK THE TURN TO COURSE ZERO EIGHT ONE."

"Helm, Bridge, right fifteen degrees rudder, steady course zero eight one," Stokes ordered. Pacino nodded.

"Helm, all ahead standard," Stokes called into his microphone.

"Off'sa'deck, shift pumps," Pacino said, "we're about to haul ass."

The ship began to react to the speed increase of 10 knots, the bow wave rising over the bow until the hull forward of the sail started to get wet and the wake aft to boil white.

Stokes spoke into his microphone: "Maneuvering, Bridge, shift reactor main coolant pumps to fast speed."

"SHIFT REACTOR MAIN COOLANT PUMPS TO FAST SPEED, BRIDGE, MANEUVERING AYE . . . BRIDGE, MANEUVERING, REACTOR MAIN COOLANT PUMPS ARE RUNNING IN FAST SPEED."

Stokes acknowledged. He looked at Pacino, standing beside him on the crowded bridge.

"Flank it, OOD," Pacino said, training his binoculars again on the inbound merchant ship and the Thimble Shoals Channel beyond.

"Helm, all ahead flank," Stokes ordered.

"ALL AHEAD FLANK, HELM AYE . . . BRIDGE, HELM, MANEUVERING ANSWERS ALL AHEAD FLANK."

The bridge box sputtered with Rapier's voice: "BRIDGE, XO. CAPTAIN TO THE IJV PHONE," requesting that Pacino pick up the IJV phone circuit, a more private line than the P.A. speakers.

"Captain," Pacino said into the handset.

"XO, sir," Rapier said. "Recommend we keep the speed down in the channel, sir. Last time we flanked it we got a speeding ticket from the Coasties. Max speed in the channel is 15 knots."

"The Coast Guard has their priorities, we've got ours, XO."

"Your hide, sir."

The bow wave climbed up the hull until it was breaking aft of the sail. The water stream climbed the sail itself, spraying the bridge officers. The hull vibrated beneath them with the power of the ship's main engines, two steam turbines driving a huge reduction gear and the single spiral-bladed screw. The wake boiled up astern. The wind blew in the officers' faces, making communication possible only through screaming.

Devilfish rocked in the waves, five degrees to port, then back to starboard. The periscopes rotated, the radar mast whistled as it spun in circles, the flags crackled in the wind and the bow wave roared.

Usually the sounds of getting under way filled Pacino's soul with a near-pure contentment.

Today, all he could think about was his father, and a Russian admiral that had put him on the bottom.

CHAPTER
7

TUESDAY, 14 DECEMBER, 1100
GREENWICH MEAN TIME

ARCTIC OCEAN
BENEATH THE POLAR ICECAP

In the winter, the polar ice almost reached the northern Russian coast. An icebreaker had to clear the way for the fleet submarine *Kaliningrad* to get under way, and now it proceeded at full speed under the icecap.

Admiral Alexi Novskoyy unpacked his duffel bag into the spacious lockers of the commanding officer's quarters. Captain 1st Rank Yuri Vlasenko had been surprised by Novskoyy's arrival on the pier, saying he had not had time to arrange conveniences for an admiral and his staff. Novskoyy had waved the protests aside. There would be no staff, just himself. Vlasenko had quickly given over his captain's stateroom, where the admiral was now settling in.

A knock came at the door of the outer room of the stateroom suite, which led to the second-compartment passageway. Novskoyy shut the lockers and unlocked the outer room door.

Standing in the passageway was Captain Vlasenko, dressed in his underway uniform of olive green tunic over pants tucked into boots. Novskoyy waved him into the suite, pointed to a seat and locked the door after him.

Vlasenko was a short but powerful man, a champion wrestler at the Marshal Grechko Higher Naval School of Underwater Navigation. His shoulders were so big that his uniforms required special tailoring. Now in his late forties, he was losing a little of his muscle tone. His once blond hair was now grayish silver and wrinkles surrounded his eyes.

Vlasenko stared for a moment at Novskoyy's hip, where the admiral wore a gleaming leather belt, a shining holster and a fleet-issue semiautomatic pistol. Just as on the *Leningrad*, Vlasenko remembered, feeling the bile rise. The man affected airs like the American general he'd read about . . . what was his name? Patton, wore pearl-handled revolvers like a fancy cowboy . . .

"Sir," he began, "I came to invite you on an inspection of the ship."

Novskoyy smiled slightly at Vlasenko. Why would his old subordinate offer to parade him through the ship he had designed himself? All the credit belonged to him. Vlasenko was the captain only as a result of his benevolence.

"No, I have no time for a tour. I have urgent fleet work, Captain. And besides, I know this ship better than any man alive, including you. I will assume—I will demand—that it is combat ready. Your job, Captain. Dismissed."

Vlasenko stared at the admiral, managed to nod and leave. As he stood in the passageway, he heard Novskoyy lock the door from the inside.

Vlasenko tried to fight down his anger. Declining a ship tour with the captain was an insult, a violation of protocol for a visiting admiral. Vlasenko wondered just what this trip meant. *Kaliningrad*'s original agenda of machinery tests for sea trials had been cancelled by Novskoyy the moment he had come onboard. Taking an untested vessel under the icecap for a mission was not only unprecedented, it could be suicidal. And Novskoyy was acting like *he* was in command of the submarine. Vlasenko felt like a First Officer instead of ship's captain.

He concentrated on the ship's inspection. Novskoyy's ride wouldn't last long—in a week or two he would go back to fleet HQ, leaving him in command of the most modern nuclear attack submarine in the Russian Northern Fleet. At least an inspection would get him out of his closet of a stateroom to where he could talk to the men, the kind of walkaround that the arrogant Novskoyy would never bother with.

Vlasenko walked out of the First Officer's stateroom, now that Novskoyy had appropriated his own suite, and moved along a narrow passageway lined by bleached panelling toward the starboard side of the vessel that terminated at the main shaft, the fore-and-aft running upper-level passageway. At the intersection was the ladder to the main escape pod, an enormous 7-meter-diameter titanium ellipsoid.

The *Kaliningrad*, so automated that a relatively few enlisted ratings were required aboard, was manned by 18 officers, 13 warrant officers and 16 enlisted men. In an emergency the main escape pod, accessed from the second compartment upper level, would be able to evacuate about 30 of the ship's 47 men. The rest would use the control-compartment escape pod, which was designed for 18 men. But many of the *Kaliningrad*'s missions were under ice, where an escape pod was useless.

Vlasenko continued forward through the main shaft, past the galley and messroom on the port side to the officers' lounge, a large parlor with video equipment, books and easychairs. Vlasenko remembered how cramped the *Leningrad* had been by comparison. Well, these officers were a different generation, raised on peacetime, however uneasy the peace. He felt more than years separated him from them. He had seen more combat than he'd ever wanted. Witnessing the sinking of the American submarine . . . the *Stingray* . . . under the icecap by the *Leningrad* had been a shock. He had been the Weapons Officer under this same Admiral Novskoyy. He himself had actually pressed the firing key that sent the torpedoes out to the American vessel that day far in the past but never forgotten. He had tried to rationalize it . . . Novskoyy had ordered it, backed up with the threat of his service pistol . . . It never quite worked. He still had nightmares. And now, decades later, Novskoyy once again was a presence looming over him.

As he was about to leave the lounge he was outraged to note that the door to the captain's stateroom suite that opened into the lounge had been stitch-welded shut. A brand new submarine and this man comes onboard and welds a door shut. Why?

Vlasenko reentered the main shaft, turned left to go forward, passing the other door to Novskoyy's stateroom. He couldn't help trying the knob. Locked. What the hell was Novskoyy hiding?

He moved to the forward bulkhead of the second compartment, a watertight boundary between the compartments. One compartment could flood and still allow the ship to survive; if two compartments flooded it was more serious but the ship might still survive. The second compartment was designed to be the most survivable—no weapons that could explode, no seawater pipes that could rupture, no oil lines or tanks that could catch fire, no heavy equipment that could jump out of their foundations. And so it was chosen to contain the huge main escape pod.

Vlasenko ducked to pass through the automatically closing watertight hatch to the first compartment—the weapons spaces. He inhaled, relishing the smell of the ozone from the electrical cabinets in the first compartment's upper level that housed cabinets of electrical and computer gear for the communications and navigation equipment. It was the high-voltage cabinets that spewed ozone, with a smell particular to a submarine since the ventilation system could not quickly disperse it. Vlasenko now doubled back to the hatch to the second compartment, where a narrow, steep stairway led to the middle deck. He climbed down, and the whole environment changed. This was the middle level torpedo-tube space, the home of the three 100 centimeter tubes and the Magnum nuclear-tipped torpedoes.

The immense size of the weapons was a shock. The torpedoes were the size of the minisubmarines used in World War II by the Japanese, and they were the fastest underwater weapons in the world, able to go nearly 110 kilometers per hour. With their huge girth, they also had tremendous endurance; they could go on at attack-velocity for over an hour, covering over 100 kilometers. No submerged adversary on earth could outrun a Magnum.

The Magnum torpedoes were painted glossy black, gleaming and deadly in the bright lights of the compartment. Over the red-taped barricade warning of the nuclear torpedoes' radioactivity, Vlasenko reached out and put his hand on the smooth cool surface of the topmost weapon. Immediately a cold pistol barrel nudged his neck.

"Turn around very slowly and put your hands behind your head."

Vlasenko did, and stared into the face of Warrant Officer Dmitri Danalov, chief of security aboard, his heavy mustache nearly obscuring his upper lip.

"Captain!" he said, lowering his pistol and holstering it in his wide shiny black leather belt. "No offense, sir, but no one touches one of the nuclear weapons without me knowing about it."

Vlasenko waved off Danalov's apology. "No, no, what you did was proper. I commend you for it."

"The admiral wouldn't agree, sir . . ."

"The admiral? Novskoyy was here?"

"He was looking over the Magnum an hour ago."

"Did he say anything? About the Magnum?"

"Yes, in fact, he did. He said he hoped the scientists who designed them knew what they were doing."

Vlasenko stored the comment. "Warrant, I'm going to the lower level. Want to come?"

"I'd better, Captain. I don't want my torpedo officer killing you if you surprise him."

They made their way to the ladder to lower level, the area with the six 53-centimeter tubes. Following Vlasenko down the stairs, Davalov was impressed at how fit Captain Vlasenko looked at forty-eight, then remembered he had been a champion wrestler at Marshal Grechko Higher Naval School of Underwater Navigation.

The men now reached the base of the stairs, where young Senior Lieutenant Vasily Katmonov, the Torpedo Officer, came to attention.

"Is there something I can do for you, Captain?"

"No, just wandering the ship."

Vlasenko looked around at the space. It was clean and fresh looking. The lower-level compartment was the home of the six 53-centimeter conventional tubes and their 53-centimeter torpedoes. The weapons lay on two large racks with hydraulic rams to maneuver them into the tubes. These torpedoes were painted a dull black, as sinister looking as the Magnums above.

Vlasenko complimented Katmonov on the lower two levels of his compartment, adding he was especially pleased with security. "Warrant Officer Danalov here is an asset to this vessel."

Katmonov and Danalov shared a quick look. "That is not what the admiral said," from Danalov.

"What did he say, Lieutenant?"

"He wanted me to demote the Warrant Officer. He said Danalov should be disarmed. It seems Danalov put a pistol to the admiral's head when the admiral was looking at the weapons. I don't like the idea of an officer carrying a loaded pistol, sir. Neither did Danalov. But Admiral Novskoyy refused to hand over his weapon, a serious violation of Fleet Regulations, sir, particularly in the weapons spaces. I don't know what I should do, sir. How do I tell an admiral he's violating Fleet Regs?"

"You don't, Lieutenant. You tell me, I handle it."

He left them and made his way back to the second compartment's main shaft and again stared at Novskoyy's locked door. It occurred to him that he knew where there was an extra key to the door, but dismissed the thought. Don't provoke the man on this trip—the admiral would soon be gone and the boat would again be his.

Vlasenko turned away from the door and went to the ladder to the lower level, where he found Captain 3rd Rank Vladimir Ivanov standing ten meters aft in the passageway outside his stateroom door. Ivanov, normally the Operations Officer, was responsible for Weapons, Communications, Sonar and the ship's tactics, but on this run he also became Acting First Officer when the second in command of the *Kaliningrad* took sick.

Ivanov motioned to him, and Vlasenko walked aft down the passageway.

"Good morning, sir. We have a problem. Two problems."

Ivanov was in his mid-thirties but seemed younger. He could drink vodka all night and was unofficially the ship's number-one bachelor, usually not one to take life too seriously, but ever since he had assumed the duty of Acting First Officer when the ship had pulled out of Severomorsk he had seemed agitated and tense.

"Go on, Ivanov."

"Technical problem first, sir. The multifunction transmitter cabinet is blowing fuses. It's eaten two circuit boards for the signal drivers. We're trouble-shooting it now, but I'm beginning to think the UHF to the satellite may be out of commission for some time."

Vlasenko shrugged. Routine trouble and they would soon be under the arctic ice cover where there would be no need to transmit to the satellite. Emergency systems could handle the communications if they needed a rescue.

"Well, sir, that leads us to the second problem. Admiral Novskoyy . . . he wants the UHF systems of the multifunction antenna ready at all times, commencing now."

Son of a bitch, those were orders that should have originated with him, Vlasenko thought, not with a visiting flag officer.

"I will talk to the admiral, Ivanov. Meantime, keep working on the problem. Are you going forward?"

"Yes, sir. I expect I will be there until the equipment works. The admiral wants the gear to be up by this evening."

"Tonight? Did he say why?"

"No, Captain. Just that I will be sorry if the equipment is not working by then." Ivanov looked ready to deal with Novskoyy personally as he hurried up the ladder to the upper level. Vlasenko understood, but hoped the young headstrong Ivanov could keep his temper under control this run. He knew it wouldn't be easy . . . not for any of them.

Vlasenko, aborting the tour of the second compartment, headed aft to the nuclear control room. Nuclear control was really just a large waist-high computer console that wrapped around a right angle with an elevated platform behind it. The platform had a command chair reserved for the Chief Engineer, who was sitting in it and looking altogether regal. Captain-Lieutenant Mikhail Geroshkov plainly loved his job and little wonder. The propulsion plant of the *Kaliningrad* was far superior to any other in the fleet, for that matter was much more advanced than anything the Americans had, with their low-power density, water-cooled cores. The *Kaliningrad* had two reactors, each cooled by highly conductive liquid sodium. Pumps had no rotating parts and pushed the coolant through the loops using magnetism. It was very quiet.

Vlasenko did not pretend to know much about nuclear power.

The Russian fleet was split into two tracks—the seamanship officers, of which he was one, and the engineering corps that had the responsibility of running and repairing the plants.

"Any problems with the plant?" Vlasenko asked Geroshkov.

"So far, perfect, Captain."

"Computers working out okay?"

"Very well, sir. I was skeptical at first but they make this operation very efficient."

Vlasenko watched the screens for a while, wishing he shared Geroshkov's optimism about the computers. "Did the admiral happen to come back here?"

"No, sir. Why would he?"

"No reason. I'm going forward. The spaces look shipshape."

Vlasenko had intended to confront Admiral Novskoyy over the admiral's giving direct orders to his men, but on reaching the upper level of the second compartment a messman indicated the admiral was in his stateroom sleeping. Well, he'd check out the control compartment and wait to confront Novskoyy after figuring out exactly what he would say. He didn't want to start a war aboard his own ship. Still . . .

CHAPTER
8
TUESDAY, 14 DECEMBER, 1014 EST

Western Atlantic Ocean
40 Nautical Miles Northeast of Norfolk, Virginia

Commander Jon Rapier started his walkthrough of the submarine, ensuring the ship was rigged for sea. This had always been Pacino's duty—the captain insisted on seeing every corner of the boat himself. But today he had asked Rapier to do the walkthrough and had remained in his stateroom. Something was definitely wrong with him, Rapier thought. The last two years had been tough with home life and navy life seemingly at crosspurposes. But even during the stormiest times Pacino had kept a sense of humor.

This run was different. Something had changed the captain and it seemed to be much more than any family squabble.

In his stateroom Rapier had changed into his underway uniform, a one-piece cotton overall with his name sewn above the right pocket. He strapped on his khaki belt and radiation dosimeter, pinned his dolphins on, got into his at-sea boots, left his stateroom and walked forward along the central passageway through operations-compartment upper level and down narrow stairs to the middle level, then turned left to officers country. Each "stateroom" occupied by three officers was six-by-six feet, with two chairs and two fold-down desktops, a few lockers recessed into the fake wood panelling and three "coffins," racks shaped like drawers in a morgue except each had a side-entrance curtain and a reading light. The coffins were stacked three high in the staterooms, four high for the enlisted men. Those high-ranking enough got coffins to themselves; many hot-racked, shared a coffin with someone on a different watch section. That still left about twenty men who had to make a rack on top of the torpedoes in operations lower level.

At the aft end of the officers-country passageway was the wardroom, about twenty-by-fifteen feet with a table in the center. At the aft end was the door to the small pantry, which further aft opened into the main galley. The wardroom was used as a dining room, conference room, briefing room, movie-screening room, tactical-planning room and end-of-watch reconstruction room.

One of the largest open areas aboard, the crew's mess, could seat about thirty men. The starboard bulkhead was painted with a mural of two square-rigged ships sailing on a stormy sea. The central columns were covered with hemp rope spiralling around, with brass lanterns at the top. The forward bulkhead had a mirror framed in more hemp rope. The leather bench seats and tablecovers were done up in blue. The deck was tiled in blue and white. Actually the mess looked more like a cheap fish house than a combat submarine. Never mind, Rapier told himself, at least the crew liked it.

At the aft end of the crew's mess was the Trash Disposal Unit room. The TDU was a vertical torpedo tube used to eject compacted trash through a ball valve at the hull. The garbage was sealed in plastic and weighted with lead bricks so no floating waste would give away their position. By the TDU room was a steel ladder to the lower level that Rapier slid down.

Rapier's inspection now took him through the gyro room below the crew's mess, to the Auxiliary Machinery room, then the torpedo room. In each space he made sure there was no unsecured equipment that could get damaged if the ship took on a severe angle or suddenly went into a roll.

He lingered in the torpedo room, a long wide space built for weapon storage. A central aisle threaded between the waist-high storage table for the upper tubes. The port and starboard tables were packed with Mark 49 torpedoes, each painted green and stencilled with white block letters—MOD B HULLBUSTER. At the centerline were the experimental Mark 50's, painted glossy red and stencilled HULLCRUSHER and looking long and graceful and fast.

Forward of the weapon-storage area was the central-torpedo local-control panel, where the torpedo chief flooded and drained tubes and where the weapons could be moved from the panel with powerful hydraulic rams. On either side of the local control panel were the tubes themselves, canted outward from the centerline because the torpedo room was amidships. Since the torpedoes were so-called smart weapons, it no longer mattered in which direction they were launched . . . they would turn toward the target impact point by themselves. The tubes were embedded in water tanks, which were piped to the ship's high-pressure air-system. Air pressurized the water tank, which was open to the aft end of the torpedo tube. The pressurized water pushed the weapon out of the tube, flushing it out. No air bubbles would escape to allow them to be detected.

On each tube's inner door hung a sign, WARSHOT LOADED. Rapier checked the tubes, found them dry, their interlocks functional. He nodded to Chief Robertson, who sat at the local control panel. He then called control to tell them he was going to look into the battery compartment below the torpedo room. He lifted the hatch and peered down. The space was three feet high, thirty feet long, twenty feet wide. Once inside, a person would be lying on top of the batteries. Entry required removal of all metal objects on the body to avoid shorting the cells, each of which was the size of a household's water heater and full of sulfuric acid. Satisfied, Rapier stood, lowered the hatch and left the torpedo room.

Rapier knew the nuclear spaces aft would be ready. Chief Engineer Matt Delaney's troops, the nukes, always were more squared away than the operations and weapons sailors, at least they thought they were. He crossed the centerline passageway to the captain's stateroom and knocked. No reply. He opened the door and saw Pacino sitting at the table, staring into space.

"Sir?"

Pacino focused and looked at Rapier.

"I've completed my tour. The ship is rigged for sea, sir. No major discrepancies."

"Very well, XO," Pacino said, his voice a monotone.

"Anything else, sir?"

Pacino shook his head, and Rapier got out of there. Clearly the captain had a lot on his mind.

As the door shut gently and Rapier's footsteps faded down the ladder to operations middle level, Pacino shook off memories of his father and the Russian admiral somewhere out there . . . He got up from the table and made his way forward into the control room to the navigation alcove. Even at flank speed they would not be able to dive until mid-afternoon because the continental shelf was some 150 miles east of the Virginia coastline. The *Devilfish*, after all, was designed for submerged speed . . . on the surface she could only do 20 knots because of the need to fight the bow wave. Pacino checked his watch impatiently, and began to calculate the time it would take to get to the marginal ice zone north of Iceland.

Twenty minutes later the wardroom table was crowded with officers around the table, some clasping their hands together on the blue leather cover, some doodling on spiral notebook pages. Executive Officer Rapier took his seat to the right of the chair near the end reserved for the captain.

Navigator Ian Christman stood at the corner of the room at a curtain. Christman had two modes of operation: frantic or sleepy.

Pacino walked into the room, accepted a cup of coffee, sat at the head of the table and waved at Christman.

"Go ahead, Nav."

Christman stepped into the pantry, the small closet between the wardroom and the galley, shut its outer door and threw the bolt. He shut both wardroom doors and locked them, sealing the room. Back in the corner of the room by the captain's chair he drew the curtain aside, revealing an Arctic Ocean chart and a blueprint of the Russian OMEGA submarine, both stamped TOP SECRET. He turned to the men in the room and pointed to the chart.

"Gentlemen, this is the Arctic Ocean, and this is the Russian OMEGA-class attack submarine." Christman loved a dramatic opening. "Our mission this run is to find this son-of-a-bitch, just completed this week and now submerged for sea trials. Once we find it we get an SPL and bring it home to the geniuses at COMSUBLANT for analysis. The plan is a little complicated so listen up. Our sonar search has a problem . . . no boat has ever *heard* the OMEGA before. Our tonal search gates are configured for the AKULA class. We hope the propulsion-plant configuration is at least similar . . ."

"Yo, Nav," Stokes interrupted to Christman's annoyance. The contrast between the hyper Christman and Stokes' southern calm made for constant friction between them. "If we can't hear this bad boy with our tonal gates, how do we 'xpect to snap his ass up? We could sail right by him 'n' never know he's there."

Hick or not, he'd made a crucial point, Pacino thought.

Christman frowned at him. "The truth is that we may never find him during our allotted mission time. But we may get a hint of him from a careless transient noise. We may get lucky and detect a torpedo exercise . . . several other Russian attack submarines in the area, each of which *will* be detectable in our search gates. Or we *could* get a radio message from COMSUB-LANT that he's been detected by SOSUS. Not likely, I admit. SOSUS won't be much use for a quiet contact, and this far north the position uncertainties could put a good detect in a thousand square mile area. Our last card is PHOTOINT. You know, satellite surveillance. Maybe we can pick up a surfacing with an infrared scan from the polar orbit KH-17."

"Odds are," Stokes drawled, "this here boy won't be surfacing at all. Why would he?"

"Might not, but then, if there's one thing we've learned about the Russians, it's that they're unpredictable." Even Stokes had to nod at that. "Our track is marked in black, taking us to our search position here. We're scheduled to transit under the ice in three days. Our search position grid is located at the operation area where COMSUBLANT expects the OMEGA to be doing its sea trials." Christman pointed to an area marked in red far north of the banana-shaped island of Novaya Zemlya. "As you can plainly see, it's a large area and not much help to us in finding the OMEGA. Okay, so much for the search phase. Now, assume for a moment that we have a good detect on the OMEGA. This is where we start the SPL. I hate to break this to you first-tour officers but against the Russians, an SPL is a hell of a lot different than the exercise we did against *Billfish* in the Med. We'll be less than five yards away from the Russian's hull, circling him and recording him. And unlike our exercise with the *Billfish*, the Russian is not under orders to be nice and control his course and speed for us. He could go nuts at any moment, smash right into us and breach the hull. Or worse, shoot at us."

Pacino cut in. "This next is Special Compartmented Information, Top Secret—Tophat. A few years ago one of our boats, a Piranha class, ran into a Russian attack sub during an SPL. The Russian launched two warshot 53-centimeter torpedoes at her. A nasty way to end a northern run . . ."

"What happened, Cap'n?" Brett Fasteen, the Electrical Officer, asked.

"Our boat had gone to flank, and by luck it managed to avoid running into an ice-pressure ridge. One torpedo was a dud, the other ran out of fuel after a twenty-minute pursuit. But let me tell you, twenty minutes is a long time to spend on the business end of a Russian warshot torpedo. The commanding officer hung up his dolphins after that run."

Pacino looked around the room. If there had been any lingering doubts about the importance and the danger of this OP, they had disappeared. And they still didn't know the half of it . . .

Pacino, in his stateroom, looked at the briefing sheets of the OMEGA that Donchez had sent over before *Devilfish* got under way, thought about that other half . . . somehow avenging his father's death by confronting and destroying Novskoyy, the man who had sent him to the bottom, the man who Donchez had told him was on the OMEGA. But how? How . . . ? Fantasy took over . . . *If he could collide with the Russian, maybe the OMEGA would shoot first. If a torpedo was screaming in at them, no one would question the captain's order to fire back, the only problem would be evading the Russian torpedo—*

An insistent buzzing sound broke him out of his farfetched reverie. Farfetched . . . ?

It was the phone from the Conn.

"Captain," Pacino said, sweat pouring off him.

"Off'sa'deck, you asked for a wakeup call, sir."

"Thanks. I'll be out on the Conn in a few minutes."

He stretched, ran hot water on his face and looked in the mirror. He'd let his beard grow on this run. Normally he didn't do that . . . it made his face look too much like his father's. Good, this was the time for it.

Now 160 nautical miles northeast of Norfolk, *Devilfish* was still running on the surface but she was rigged for dive, the watch already transferred from the bridge to the control room. Lieutenant Stokes, the Officer of the Deck, hugged the number-two periscope on the raised stand, slowly rotating it over the horizon.

Pacino walked now into the control room. In the forward end sat the four men who drove the submarine. Two seats were stationed behind a large panel with a console in between. Each seat had a steering wheel in front. One seat was positioned behind and between the two seats. The panel wrapped around to the left side where the Chief of the Watch sat. Actually it looked much like the cockpit of a large airplane.

The left "pilot's" seat was the fair-water planesman, whose job was to control the horizontal fins on the sail. In the right seat was the helmsman, who steered the ship with the rudder and controlled the sternplanes, the horizontal fins in the far rear of the vessel. The seat behind them was the Diving Officer, charged with the ship's angle and depth; he supervised the two planesmen and the Chief of the Watch on the left wraparound panel. The Chief of the Watch's panel controlled the various tanks in the ship, the ballast and weight distribution and the hovering system.

Behind the control station was the Conn, the raised platform, eight-by-four feet, penetrated by the two periscope poles. A console with a remote sonar display, microphones and computer gear was on the port side.

To the right of the periscope stand, the Conn, was a long row of computer consoles—the fire-control system. To port, on the outboard side of the Conn, was the SHARKTOOTH under-ice sonar console. The SHARKTOOTH, which looked up and forward to find the ice, was an active pinging sonar but faint to being nearly undetectable. In the far rear left corner of control was the chart table, and in the rear center of control was the Ship's Inertial Navigation System equipment, the SINS.

"Off'sa'deck, your report," Pacino said.

"Captain, the ship's rig for dive was checked by Lieutenant Commander Bahnhoff, Ensign Fasteen and Lieutenant Brayton. Straight board. Bottom sounding is 670 fathoms. One contact, tanker, bearing two zero five, range twelve thousand yards, angle on the bow starboard one twenty degrees, past closest point of approach and opening. We are on course zero three five, all ahead two thirds. Latest fix by NAVSAT shows us two miles northeast of the dive point. SINS agrees. Request permission to submerge the ship, sir."

Hands in his pockets, Pacino looked at the television monitor showing the view out the periscope. He stepped up to the Conn and took a look at the remote sonar display, then stepped back down and looked at Pos Two, the central of the three TV computer displays for the fire-control system. He disappeared around the other side of the periscope stand, studied the chart for a moment and checked the depth sounder. He returned to a position by the Diving Officer of the Watch seated between the planesmen.

"Off'sa'deck, submerge the ship."

Stokes nodded. "Diving Officer, submerge the ship to six seven feet."

Fasteen repeated the order. "Submerge the ship to six seven feet, dive aye. Chief of the Watch, open the vents on all main ballast tanks. Sound the diving alarm, over the P.A. Circuit One, dive, dive."

The Chief of the Watch Chief Robertson flipped eight solenoid switches to the up-position and saw eight lighted green bars on his panel turn into red circles. "Vents open, sir."

He pulled a lever in the overhead, and throughout the ship the diving alarm sounded.

OOH-GAH. OOH-GAH.

"DIVE, DIVE," Robertson announced on the P.A. Circuit One.

Stokes trained the periscope view down and forward, and a huge cloud of white spray rushed out from below his view. "Venting forward," he called out and rotated the periscope aft.

More clouds of water vapor rushed out of the aft vents as Pacino and the crew watched on the periscope TV monitor.

The rear deck of the sub was now settling into the sea as the white foam washed around it, and Stokes called out, "Decks awash."

Soon the aft end of the ship vanished and the waves were getting closer to the periscope lens.

"Four five feet, sir," Diving Officer Fasteen announced.

"Very well, Dive," Stokes replied.

Steadily, the *Devilfish* settled into the waves. After the deck vanished, the sail was all that was visible. Soon the fair-water planes, the horizontal control surfaces protruding from the side of the sail, splashed the waves, then also vanished underwater. The top of the sail settled until it too was obscured. Only the tall number-two periscope rose above the water, lowering until it only poked above the waves by four feet, a small foamy wake trailing behind it.

"Six seven feet, sir," Fasteen called out.

"Vents shut," said Chief Robertson.

"Get a trim, Dive. Helm, all ahead one-third." Stokes never removed his eye from the periscope as he continued to train his view around in slow circles, switching between low and high power, then looking upward in search of aircraft, the submariner's lethal enemy.

After ten minutes of pumping and balancing, Fasteen had *Devilfish* at neutral buoyancy.

"Captain, we've got a good one-third trim. Request to go deep and head north, sir," Stokes said.

"Off'sa'deck, proceed to five four six feet and continue northeast at flank," Pacino responded.

American submarines cruised at odd depths like 546 feet, the idea being to avoid collisions with Russians, assuming the Russians measured depth at the keel and cruised at even depths measured in meters. Pacino always wondered if they cruised at depths like 334 meters to avoid collisions with Americans . . .

"Helm," Stokes called, "all ahead two thirds. Dive, make your depth five four six feet." Pacino watched the periscope view showing on the remote TV monitor to the right of the control station, where the view of the sea grew more restricted as the vantage point got closer to the waves.

"Six eight feet, sir. Six nine," Fasteen reeled off.

The periscope view hit the waves. Foam boiled up around the periscope lens. The view cleared. Waves again.

"Scope's awash . . . scope's awash . . ." Stokes called out.

"Seven zero feet, sir," from Fasteen.

One final wave came up and splashed the periscope view. Then the view showed the underside of the waves. The field of view trained upward and looked at the waves from the bottom side, watching them get further away. When they were 40 feet overhead Stokes snapped the periscope grips up, reached into the overhead, rotated a large metal ring and said, "Lowering number-two scope." The periscope optic-control section vanished into the periscope well, and the stainless steel pole lowered thirty feet until the top of the scope disappeared into the sail. The periscope television repeater automatically turned itself off, and the deck angled downward as the ship went deep.

"Helm, all ahead flank," Stokes ordered.

The hull creaked and popped as the ship went deeper into the increasing sea pressure.

"Off'sa'deck, maneuvering answers all-ahead flank," the helmsman called.

"Very well, Helm."

"Off'sa'deck, passing four hundred feet," Fasteen reported.

"Very well, Diving Officer."

Stokes looked at the remote sonar display. One lone contact, the supertanker, was fading astern.

"Off'sa'deck, depth five four six feet."

"Very well, Diving Officer."

Stokes picked up the P.A. Circuit One microphone. "RIG SHIP FOR PATROL QUIET."

Pacino looked at Stokes, who leaned on the periscope pole, arms crossed over his chest.

"I'll be in my stateroom," Pacino said, and walked aft.

Five-hundred-forty-six feet beneath the waves, the USS *Devilfish* continued northeast, enroute to the polar icecap.

Enroute to Pacino's fateful confrontation.

CHAPTER
9

TUESDAY, 14 DECEMBER, 1135 EST

NORFOLK, VIRGINIA
COMSUBLANT HEADQUARTERS

Admiral Richard Donchez lit his first Havana of the day, ignoring the pained expression on Captain Fred Rummel's face. Rummel, the SUBLANT Chief Intelligence Officer, had called Donchez to the Top Secret Conference Room for an urgent brief. Donchez had been in the office before the sun to work on plans for a *Stingray* monument. The memorial had been kicking up objections from Naval Intelligence, which wanted the entire affair forgotten.

"Sir," Rummel began, "CIA PHOTOINT sent us this."

The room lights dimmed and a slide projector clicked on to show a view of the Kola Peninsula on the Russian north coast. Most of the countryside was a cool blue, while bright orange dots lit up half a dozen points on the coastline.

"Infrared," Rummel said. "Blue is cold, orange is hot. As you can plainly see, we're getting hot spots at the submarine bases of the Northern Fleet along Russia's northern coast."

Donchez nodded. "Power plants, buildings with poor insulation, floodlights. Lots of thermal sources."

"Right. That's why it took a few hours for us to get around to looking at this."

The slide changed to a closer view of one of the submarine bases.

Donchez stood up slowly. "Oh shit," he said softly, dropping cigar ashes into the carpeting.

"Indeed, sir. As you can see, each of the twenty-five submarines here has an orange spot showing mid-length in her hull. Those thermal traces are reactor cores. They look like that when they're critical, making power, but also when they're shut down. But look aft of each reactor. The steam lines inside the turbine rooms are *also* glowing. These submarines are all hot, the reactors are all critical. They're making steam."

Rummel now clicked the control on the slide projector and the machine ran through a dozen similar shots, each a different Kola Peninsula base, each showing nuclear submarines with reactors and engine rooms hot.

A knock came at the door and a petty officer looked in at Rummel, handed him a sealed envelope lined with a red banner and quickly left.

"How old are those photos?" Donchez asked.

"Three hours, sir."

"We need to see what's happening *now*."

Rummel opened the envelope. "This is hot off the TS fax machine, sir." He pulled out a long strip of paper with the same kinds of coloring as the slides.

Donchez turned up the room lights as Rummel spread the fax out from one end of the long table to the other—every fourteen inches was a photo of a submarine base.

Donchez looked from one photo to the next. "They're *gone*. Every goddamned one of them."

Rummel nodded, face tight.

Each photo showed the same bases as the three-hour-old shots, but in the new photos the piers were empty.

"How many attack subs are in their Northern Fleet?"

"One hundred twenty, sir."

"Any in dock for repair?"

"No, sir. Not one."

"Any activity out of Vladivostok?"

"No, sir. The Pacific Fleet is dead quiet. Almost all their submarines are in port, shut down, getting routine maintenance. This activity is altogether confined to the Northern Fleet."

Donchez sat back down in his seat while Rummel folded up the fax. The cigar's tip had gone cold. "Get SOSUS on NESTOR," he ordered, referring to the secure UHF radio telephone to the Sound Surveillance System Control Room on the eastern shore of Maryland, the receiving and analysis point for the ten thousand miles of U.S. sonar-array cables laid on the Atlantic.

In the two minutes it took to get the SOSUS duty officer on the line, Donchez had summoned his own duty officer to the conference room.

"SOSUS CONTROL ROOM. DUTY OFFICER," the speaker rasped out to the room.

Donchez nodded at Rummel.

"SOSUS, this is SUBLANT. Report any detects in the North Atlantic and Barents Sea that are new within the last three hours. Over."

"SUBLANT, SOSUS. SORRY FOR THE DELAY—THERE SHOULD BE AN IMMEDIATE MESSAGE COMING OVER YOUR UHF SATELLITE NETWORK NOW. WE HAVE MULTIPLE SONAR DETECTS, TOO MANY TO DISTINGUISH. CONTACTS SEEM TO BE WARSHIPS WITH SUBMARINE-TYPE SCREW PATTERNS. BEARINGS GENERALLY CORRELATE TO THE NORTH ATLANTIC AND REGIONS IN VICINITY OF KOLA PENINSULA AND NOVAYA ZEMLYA. OVER."

Rummel acknowledged and broke the connection. Donchez turned to the SUBLANT duty officer.

"Assemble my staff in this conference room, then get on NESTOR to CINCLANTFLEET and tell Admiral McGee I'll be briefing him in a half hour."

The Duty Officer left in a hurry.

"What do you think, Rummel?" Donchez asked, pulling his Piranha lighter from his jacket pocket to relight his dead cigar.

"A deployment exercise . . . what else? Things are pretty cozy between us and them these days . . ."

Donchez pointed to the fax photographs. "Does that look cozy? Get on the horn with Langley and ask about the Russian SSN-X-27 cruise missiles' status. Put the same question to OP Oh Nineteen at the Pentagon. I want to know if these attack subs are loaded with anything that could be tossed at us. Cozy, my ass."

Rummel took off without a word.

Donchez watched the smoke from the Havana rise toward the ceiling, and wondered what in hell Admiral Alexi Novskoyy was up to now.

ARCTIC OCEAN
BENEATH THE POLAR ICECAP

Captain Vlasenko knocked on the door to his commandeered stateroom. It was time to take back the ship.

Novskoyy called out, "Who is it?"

"Captain Vlasenko, sir."

Through the door Vlasenko heard the rustling of papers, the sound of books being shuffled and the safe door being shut. Finally the door mechanism clicked as it was unlocked. The door opened and Vlasenko saw Novskoyy's back as the admiral returned to his seat at his desk. The desk's papers and books had been covered by a chart, laid blank side up, revealing only the TOP SECRET stamps on its blank wide surface.

"What can I do for you, Captain?"

The glance at the stateroom had momentarily thrown Vlasenko off balance.

"Sir, I had wanted to talk to you about, well, about what you are doing aboard. You've practically taken over this ship, aborting my sea-trials agenda without letting me brief the crew on what we're doing, giving direct orders to my officers, threatening my Security Warrant Officer, transmitting messages from my control compartment without my signature, assigning maintenance schedules to the Communications Officer. Sir, I am the captain of this vessel, these orders should come through me . . ."

He had run out of steam, and was furious with himself. It sounded like a plea for Novskoyy to give him back the ship . . . please? sir?

Novskoyy seemed to have barely heard. "Whatever you like, Vlasenko. Now you'll excuse me, I have some matters to attend to. By the way, I've instructed the Deck Officer to use the topsounder and find the nearest polynya. We will be surfacing as soon as there is thin ice overhead."

Vlasenko stared. What was Novskoyy doing? An order to surface along with his demand that the radio sets be fully functional . . . ? Vlasenko started to protest but Novskoyy cut him off.

"*Captain*, shut the door behind you and set the lock, if you please."

He hadn't so much as looked at Vlasenko's face as he said it, his eyes focused on the far bulkhead. Without further word the admiral began to unlock his safe again as Vlasenko moved out, locking the stateroom door behind him.

In his stateroom Vlasenko again thought of the spare key to the captain's—Novskoyy's—stateroom. It was in the First Officer's safe, and the combination was set so that it would be easy to remember—his graduation date from the Marshal Grechko Higher Naval School of Underwater Navigation: right to zero five, left twice to twenty-eight, right again to sixty-eight. The small safe opened, and at the bottom was an envelope with a single key. The key to the captain's stateroom. No question in Vlasenko's mind now—after what he had seen . . . or rather not seen . . . he had to get in and find out what Novskoyy was up to.

Admiral Novskoyy stared at the room's door after Captain Vlasenko left, eventually shrugged and returned to his study of the deployment of his submarines. They would dictate the disarmament of the U.S. Dictate and if necessary force . . . Excitement, exhilaration over the plan now moving to fruition mingled with a wash of exhaustion. It was a heady feeling, one he had not known since twenty years ago when the USS *Stingray* went to the bottom . . .

Vlasenko sat at the polished oak foldout table, hating his situation, being deprived of his ship. He had been with the *Kaliningrad* through its five years of construction, since the first beam of structural titanium had arrived from the west by railcar. He was there when the beam was rolled into a ring, at the first hoop of framing, when the keel had been laid. He had watched the gigantic hull grow, module by module, deck by deck. And every day of those five years he had waited for the moment when she would submerge under the waves, with Vlasenko in command.

He had devoted thirty years of his life to the Navy, almost all of them at sea. He had never married, never made love to a woman, unless you counted the Severomorsk and Vladivostok prostitutes. When he died his name would die with him. He had given it all up for the submarine force. Not to be Novskoyy's errand boy.

Vlasenko shut his eyes, let his mind wander, hoping it would somehow take him away from the pain. Instead, it returned to the epicenter of the hurt. Clear as day he saw himself some twenty-five years earlier, the day he had pulled in on that run under the ice, the run when Novskoyy had shot and destroyed the American attack submarine . . .

It was December of 1973. It had been blowing wet snow the entire ride in. The waves were violent, spraying cold seawater onto the shivering officers and men on the bridge, coating them with its gritty salt. At the time a senior lieutenant, Yuri Vlasenko had been Deck Officer. Normally he would have been proud to drive the new attack submarine into the Polyarnyy piers, but this time he was exhausted and overcome by a deep unease. As the *Leningrad*'s lines were thrown over to the men on the pier, a long black Zil limousine drove up to their berth. Twin red flags fluttered on the fenders, each flag displaying five stars—the limo of Fleet Admiral Konalev, commander of the entire Red Banner Northern Fleet. The car skidded to a halt on the ice-coated pier, and Vlasenko put down the bullhorn, the line handlers having finished securing the ship. He called down to the control room to have nuclear control parallel into shore-power and shutdown the reactor. Captain Novskoyy looked ready to leave the bridge. Vlasenko decided to speak his mind, cautiously.

"Captain . . ." Vlasenko began.

Captain Novskoyy frowned. "What is it, Vlasenko? The admiral is waiting for my report."

"Sir, I was just wondering . . . what are you going to tell the admiral?" His meaning was clear. Would the captain tell the admiral he'd sunk an American submarine without any real provocation, only because the American had been trailing them for a time, actually risking a nuclear conflict with the Americans?

Novskoyy's face seemed to grow as dark as the storm that blew around them.

"Vlasenko, you are impertinent. However, to enlighten you . . . I will tell Admiral Konalev the truth."

"The truth?" The words escaped Vlasenko's lips before he could stop them.

Novskoyy stared clear through him, his expression now blank, controlled. He leaned over until his gray eyes were within centimeters from Vlasenko's. "The truth, Lieutenant, is that the American submarine ambushed us with an offensive salvo of torpedoes. We fired back to save ourselves. After we outran the American weapon our torpedoes sent the enemy to the bottom, which he deserved." Novskoyy continued to stare down at Vlasenko.

A bead of sweat dripped down Vlasenko's chin in spite of the cold. He was, by too long conditioning, literally frozen in place. Novskoyy finally broke off his stare, opened the tunnel hatch to the control room below and went through.

If he had stopped and looked back up at Vlasenko, he would have seen a lieutenant standing stiff at attention. If he had looked into the man's soul, he would have seen profound hatred, smothered below layers of fear. It would take years to peel them away . . .

NORFOLK, VIRGINIA
COMSUBLANT HEADQUARTERS

Admiral Richard Donchez walked into the conference room and shut the door.

"Attention on deck!" someone shouted.

The room's officers came to attention. Donchez waved them to their chairs and sat at the head of the table.

"Good morning, gentlemen. Today at zero nine hundred Greenwich Mean Time our Bigbird II reconnaissance satellite passed over the Kola Peninsula and the Russian northern-coast submarine bases. The Bigbird satellite found all the piers empty. *Empty.* The previous pass, approximately four hours before, showed all 120 nuclear attack submarines in port. SOSUS hydrophones reported a large number of submarines under way in the Barents Sea. They seem to be heading in the direction of the North Atlantic. Toward us . . . ?

"This remarkable deployment, we suspect, may well have to do with the commander of the Northern Fleet, Admiral Alexi Novskoyy. Last night Novskoyy was reported by intelligence assets to be embarked aboard the new OMEGA-class attack submarine *Kaliningrad*, which left Severomorsk for the Arctic yesterday, supposedly for sea trials. And meanwhile his fleet is deploying with speed and precision. Novskoyy is now at an undetermined location under the polar icecap."

Donchez let the news sink in.

"What he is up to is anyone's guess. The DIA, CIA and NSA are on the case. But they don't ever have to face an opponent at sea. We do. Therefore, I am ordering the immediate deployment of the east-coast attack-submarine force. I want repairs accelerated until every vessel is underway submerged. Unfortunately, that is only sixty-seven ships, which means each one of ours will have to trail two of theirs. The classification for this information is TOP SECRET THUNDERBOLT. Any leaks and I guarantee the leaker will spend the rest of his career in Leavenworth Military Prison. That is all. Dismissed."

NORFOLK, VIRGINIA
NORFOLK NAVAL BASE
PIER 7

The mid-afternoon sun gave little warmth as Squadron Seven's leader Commodore Benjamin Adams, shivering in a light khaki jacket, stepped off the long sloping gangway of the *Hercules*, Squadron Seven's tender ship. The diesel engines of Pier Seven's four cranes rumbled as they removed shore-power cables and gangways. Two of the squadron's submarines were in the channel already and one was taking in her lines now.

Adams walked down the pier to the berth of the *Billfish*. From the sub's flying bridge Captain Toth saluted Adams, who returned the salute and gave him a thumbs-up. The tugs pulled *Billfish* away from the pier and towed her to the center of the channel at the pier's end. Tossing off the tug lines, Toth ordered ahead standard, the wake boiled up around *Billfish*'s rudder and she surged forward.

Ben Adams watched the same scene played out for the *Spadefish*, the *Archerfish*, the *Whale*, the *Barracuda*, the *Pargo*, the *Sturgeon* and the *Piranha*. When the sun set, Pier Seven was empty except for the tender ship *Hercules*.

Bill Sweeney, commodore of Squadron Twelve, joined Adams on the pier. "Can you believe this?"

"Did you get everyone under way?" Adams asked, ignoring the question.

"All but the *Charleston*," Sweeney told him. "She was blowing resin in drydock. Word has it they're throwing her engine room and reactor compartment back together, sending her to sea with no resin refill."

"Jesus," Adams breathed. The ion exchange resin of the purification system, he knew, kept the radioactive particles in the nuclear coolant down to a minimum. Without resin the engine room could become a high-radiation area. COMSUBLANT wouldn't order a boat to sea without resin unless the situation was damn serious . . .

Sweeney took a deep breath. "I haven't seen anything like this since '82, and even then, it turned out that COMSUBLANT and COMSUBPAC had a bet on who could scramble their sub forces the quickest."

"I remember," Adams said. He had been XO of the *Whale* at the time, but talk of the deployment exercise had gone on for years.

"You don't send a boat to sea without resin for a bet," Sweeney said.

"What do you hear in the wardroom?" Adams asked. The wardroom was the seat of scuttlebutt.

"My intel officer was reluctant to brief me. Can you believe it? My own damn intel officer worried I'd leak it."

Adams hadn't had time to consult intelligence. The rush to get the pierside boats under way had taken all his concentration and time. "Bill, tell me what the hell's going on. I haven't heard anything."

"Well, it seems the Russians went to sea this morning with 120 attack submarines. Every damn ship in the Northern Fleet. No one knows why. They must have been nursing those boats for months getting ready for this. Their maintenance problems are supposed to be worse than ours."

"Why? They're not crazy. What's it supposed to mean? Why are *we* reacting this way?

Sweeney shrugged. "I'm no intel spook, Ben. I'm gonna head home and watch CNN until my eyeballs fall out. Not much to do here."

When the ships were at sea their skippers reported directly to Admiral Donchez, COMSUBLANT. The commodores had no tactical control.

Adams waved at his counterpart and walked back up the gangway to the *Hercules*, exhausted. He climbed the ladders to his stateroom, gathered his briefcase, waved to his Chief of Staff and walked back down the ramp to the pier and the parking lot. His Mercedes was in the first reserved space at the end of the pier.

As he started to unlock the driver's side door he saw a *Devilfish* sticker the size of a dinnerplate plastered to the window, its grinning ram's head staring out at him.

Patch Pacino's son's way of saying good-bye. Good hunting, he murmured, wishing he were more than a damn pierside jockey.

CHAPTER
10

WEDNESDAY, 15 DECEMBER

ARCTIC OCEAN
BENEATH THE POLAR ICECAP

Admiral Novskoyy stood in the *Kaliningrad*'s control compartment and watched the topsounder display table. The short shriek of the topsounding sonar was audible through both hulls of the ship as it searched for a polynya—the open water that formed when heavy rafts of ice were torn apart. The open water of a polynya might last all of ten minutes, the admiral knew, before skinning over and freezing in the subzero temperature, and within days the two disparate rafts would again be welded together into a solid mass of ice.

Novskoyy peered at the navigation display tied into the high-frequency-contour sonar. The topsounder "sensed" the ice's thickness and mapped out the shape on the navigation display. The plot was two-dimensional but using a hybrid holography technology, it looked three-dimensional, a tight grid deformed into mountains and valleys and plateaus. The mountains corresponded to thick ice, the flat plains to thin ice. In the center of the nav plot was a "bug," a small illuminated circle that symbolized the ship, which now was in the middle of a large elliptical field of flatness, a valley surrounded by large but distant ridges. Clearly the polynya was big enough to allow surfacing four vessels the size of the *Kaliningrad.*

Captain Vlasenko, the Deck Officer for the ascent, stood in the periscope well. "Ship Control Officer, pump centerline amidships variable ballast to sea. Establish one meter per second vertical ascent."

The Ship Control Officer, Lieutenant Katmonov, touched his panel in the fixed-function-key sector. In front of him the screen was selected to display a multicolored graphic of the variable ballast systems, a series of tanks in the belly of the huge ship linked by a piping network, and the heart of the system, a positive displacement pump the size of a truck. A three-way valve on the display, the one to the centerline amidships-tank, changed color from white to green. The valve was open. The graphic of the pump flashed "ON" and "4000 LPS" as the pump pushed thousands of liters per second from the tank. As the tanks emptied, *Kaliningrad* grew lighter and the forces of buoyancy began to move her upward. The depth graphic steadily counted off the meters and sixty million kilograms of attack submarine rocketed toward the thin ice above. As the ship rose through the ocean, the light around the hull became slowly brighter, until at 30 meters, the hull could be distinguished from the black water around her.

The deck trembled gently and the deceleration from the halted ascent made Novskoyy momentarily weightless. The ship had surfaced.

"Captain, depth zero," Katmonov reported. "We are on the surface."

"Very good, Ship Control. Bubble the ballast tanks and rig for surfaced-at-ice."

"Aye, Captain."

"Captain-Lieutenant Ivanov, take the deck," Vlasenko said. "Admiral, the ship is surfaced-at-ice."

Novskoyy nodded and sat down at the communications console, typed in the command to raise the multifunction antenna, concentrating on the communication console screen and a binder full of notes. It was clear there had been a reason for him to order Ivanov to repair the systems. Vlasenko could not wait any longer. He had to find out what the admiral was doing.

"Admiral, permission to go below," Vlasenko said.

Novskoyy waved a dismissal, still typing into the computer.

Vlasenko moved quietly through the main shaft of the second compartment upper level, past the doors to officers' messroom to the first compartment bulkhead.

To his left was the captain's stateroom door. He could not afford to look hesitant. He was the captain. He was unlocking and entering the captain's stateroom, *his* stateroom. Right.

He unlocked the door and pushed his way in, went directly to the inner stateroom's tactical safe and dialed in the combination. He drew a breath and pulled the lever.

The safe opened.

Inside were some musty and dated publications like the Emergency Warsaw Pact War Plan and the Prolonged Naval Warfare War Plan. Also the Nuclear Release Code. On top of such dusty pubs was a chart marked TOP SECRET and a binder, a slim volume of red plastic that looked like the one Novskoyy had thrown across his desk to conceal his papers.

Vlasenko pulled out the chart and unfolded it. It was a chart of the Atlantic Ocean, with dozens of red dots marked in the ocean east of the U.S. coast. A hundred blue circles were drawn around cities on the east coast. Clusters of blue circles were drawn around Washington, New York, Boston, Philadelphia. Other cities such as Portsmouth, New London, Norfolk, Charleston, Jacksonville and Port Canaveral had blue stars. All the blue stars were U.S. Navy bases.

Why? Novskoyy could hardly be thinking of a ballistic missile assault against the U.S. The ballistic missile submarines were nearly all decommissioned. Even when operational they had been under the control of the officers of the Strategic Rocket Forces. Novskoyy couldn't order an attack with them. The blue dots at sea—launching positions?—seemed too close to the targets. And there were at least 100 of the dots . . . the fleet had only two dozen ICBM-equipped submarines. Even a depressed trajectory ballistic missile needed several hundred nautical miles for a standoff range . . . but a city-assault *could* be done by *cruise* missiles if the fleet were armed with them. And if the fleet was in position. But to do that, the dozens of submarines would all have to be at sea, which would mean months of preparation, and Vlasenko knew very few of the Northern Fleet's submarines would be ready to make a run to the mid-Atlantic on short notice. Besides, such a move would make a lot of noise, he would have heard about it from his fellow skippers.

So it *had* to be some kind of wargame, a drill . . .

Except *why* would Novskoyy be so secretive if it was a drill or communication exercise?

Vlasenko turned to the red binder and opened it. The first page was answer enough.

** FLEET BATTLE STUDY 93-1169 **

T.O.T. NLACM U.S. EAST COAST ATTACK

PURPOSE: TO EXAMINE THE EFFECT, IF NECESSARY, OF A TIME-ON-TARGET NUCLEAR LAND ATTACK CRUISE MISSILE (NLACM) ASSAULT ON THE UNITED STATES BY A FORCE OF ATTACK SUBMARINES DEPLOYED TO THE WESTERN ATLANTIC.

ABSTRACT: THE ATTACK WOULD REQUIRE A MINIMUM OF 100 SSN-X-27 NUCLEAR LAND ATTACK CRUISE MISSILES FIRED FROM AS MANY PLATFORMS AS POSSIBLE TO AVOID UNIT LOSSES. THE T.O.T. ASSAULT WOULD INSURE THAT ALL WARHEADS, REGARDLESS OF FLIGHT TIME, WOULD DETONATE AT THE SAME INSTANT.

THE EFFECT OF A TIME-ON-TARGET ASSAULT ON THE EAST COAST OF THE USA COULD ACHIEVE CASTRATION/CAPITATION STRATEGY OBJECTIVE.

Vlasenko slammed the book shut, put back the volume and chart and locked the safe. He looked around the stateroom, to make sure that no trace of his search was visible, moved into the passageway outside and went quickly to the First Officer's stateroom, slamming the door behind him.

He tried to reassure himself with the words "if necessary," "could achieve." Novskoyy wasn't crazy, he just had a contingency plan. Maybe he was planning to target U.S. cities, not actually fire on them—but even that was inevitably dangerous. The admiral, self-convinced of his course as always . . . Vlasenko could not forget the wanton sinking of the U.S. boat years ago. He was frustrated by the dismemberment of the old Soviet Union and with it so much of his power. He had concocted this operation. For Novskoyy, an enemy was an enemy forever. He was an old man from another era who couldn't believe he had ever been wrong. No, he wasn't crazy. It was worse. He was a desperate man, highly skilled, who never doubted his righteousness. Much worse than mere crazy . . .

Novskoyy would have to be stopped.

LOW EARTH ORBIT
ARCTIC CIRCLE

The KH-17 Bigbird II satellite sent up that year had been launched into a polar orbit. Such an orbit facilitated looking at the Chinese activity in the antarctic as well as monitoring the Russian naval force strength up north. The latter was the key to the Naval Disarmament Treaty. As Reagan had said years before, "Trust but verify." The KH-17's were built to verify.

As the twelve-ton spy-platform crossed the Arctic Circle, it trained its high-resolution visual mirror to search to the east of track. The prime-viewing area this orbit was deemed to be to the right side of the Bigbird's path over the icepack.

While the optics trained over, the infrared sensors followed, scanning the same swath, searching for heat attributable only to warm-blooded life or a man-made source in the frigid cold. For the last hundred orbits, only seven arctic heat traces had been scanned. All had been polar bears.

Now the Bigbird's computer found its eighth heat trace, much larger than the others. Twelve meters long, five meters high. The computer searched its memory as its program commanded. Nothing in its flight history to date had been this big. The next program step told the onboard radio to send an alarm message to the Langley CIA Reconnaissance Section control facility.

As the alarm message transmitted, the third program command instructed the optical telescope to train over the heat trace and zoom in. The Bigbird relayed the telemetry back to Langley until the images shrank and were lost in the clouds over the horizon.

Start to finish, the detection episode had lasted less than four minutes.

Four thousand miles away, in the east wing of Langley's CIA Reconnaissance Center, the four-minute-long optical trace slowly printed out on the high-resolution facsimile machine.

The senior duty analyst pulled the image trace from the machine. Probably another polar bear, he thought.

He laid the image out on the table to the side of the fax machine and emitted a low whistle.

It was a submarine's conning tower that had pushed through the ice. A damn *big* conning tower. He reached for a secure phone and dialed in the code for COMSUBLANT Headquarters, Norfolk, Virginia.

CHAPTER

||

THURSDAY, 16 DECEMBER

N orfolk, V irginia
COMSUBLANT H eadquarters

Admiral Richard Donchez stared at the Flag Plot room's North
Atlantic electronic wall chart, at the mass of red X's blinking on
and off, as they cleared Great Britain and headed to the west
Atlantic. Just offshore, Donchez felt certain.

The neighboring chart, the western Atlantic, showed blue X's
moving away from the coastline. His fast-attack submarines
headed out into a zone-defense of the coast. With some luck, his
ships should be able to confront . . . or intercept . . . the
Russian boats as they pulled up at America's east coast. Except
the Rules of Engagement said that no offensive action could be
taken until one of the enemy ships *did* something—no fair hitting unless the other guy hits first.

Donchez shook his head as he crouched over a table with the
CIA photographic intelligence of the OMEGA submarine surfaced at the icecap, the detail fine enough to see the rungs of the
handholds going up the side of the sail to the bridge. It was
more than an implicit revenge sanction now, he thought, in the
context of officially making Pacino's mission one of getting a
probing sonar profile of the guts of the new OMEGA. Before the
Russian deployment, he had let Patch's son believe his mission

was also a belated payback for *Stingray*. But now . . . Novskoyy and the OMEGA had to have something to do with the Russian deployment. And Novskoyy must have anticipated some sort of counter-deployment, he might even be expecting a U.S. attack sub to visit him. This was turning into a potential general skirmish . . .

Donchez handed back the intelligence-update message to the radioman and stepped back to look at the plots. One thousand miles northeast of Norfolk, one blue X was all alone. Black block letters beside the X read USS DEVILFISH SSN-666 SUBMERGED TRANSIT.

Donchez tried to visualize Pacino and the *Devilfish*. Would it be better to tell Pacino the OMEGA was surfaced now and later tell him about the major deployment? No doubt there was enough turmoil in Mikey's mind with the implicit and explicit mandates. It would be best to wait at least until evening for further developments before giving the *Devilfish* a mission update. Soon, though, he would have to tell Pacino that the OMEGA might be expecting him, even gunning for him.

Three hours later Donchez was joined in Flag Plot by Admiral Casper "Bobby" McGee. Donchez pointed his cigar at the advancing blinking red X's on the chart, now approaching the middle of the Atlantic.

"The red X's are the Russian attack submarines," he said. "The blue ones off the U.S. continental shelf are mine."

McGee stared at the wall chart.

As Commander in Chief U.S. Atlantic Fleet, CINCLANTFLEET, he was Donchez's boss. He was slightly shorter than Donchez, heavyset with bushy gray eyebrows and jowls. He looked like a caricature of an authoritarian southern traffic-court judge, and hailing from Waycross, Georgia, even sounded the part. Appearances were deceiving; anyone who mistook his folksiness for ignorance could find themselves up against a ruthless intelligence. Still, he was not a submariner.

"Why them red ones flashin'?" he asked Donchez.

"The flashing means their position is only approximate. We have a position within five hundred square miles from SOSUS, sometimes within one hundred square miles. The position is good enough for you and me to see the progress but not good enough for us to . . . shoot at him. I know those red ones are there, plus or minus an inch or two on that chart, but I can't sink them—"

"Who's talkin' about *sinkin'* 'em? Maybe I missed something but a couple red X's on a chart . . . it's still an exercise."

"Looks kind of threatening for an exercise, Admiral. This isn't like the surface navy. We can't see these guys. Sending them out like this in an instant and sending them south can't exactly be interpreted as a peaceful gesture. Sir, the track projections take them right to our east coast. Their ETA is two days from now—"

"So they come. What are they gonna do, shoot red flares at us? Their guns ain't loaded anymore, they destroyed the cruise missiles this very week. We got confirmation—"

Donchez frowned. "I didn't expect this sort of reaction from you, sir." It wasn't like McGee, who had once been an avid hawk. Sign of the times . . .

"I was also surprised," McGee said, "when the White House called to say they had information that this was happening. Which means the White House knew about it before we did. The Russians, it seems, gave the President a call and told him not to sweat this, that it's just an exercise."

"But, sir, why did it take so long for word of this so-called exercise-notification to get down to my level?" Translation: Why, Admiral, didn't you tell me this before?

"Sorry about that, Dick. After the missiles were destroyed it just didn't seem like such a big deal. Pentagon figures they got bored with the Arctic Ocean and headed for some tropical weather. Who can blame 'em?"

"Sir, we should brief the White House on what's happening. This could still be some kind of . . . trick." Donchez knew it sounded paranoid but what else could he say?

"We can't brief the top brass until you can prove some hostile intent, here, Dick," McGee said quietly. "Besides, the White House staff ain't the only people I got phone calls from. Got one from General Tyler at the Pentagon, too. He even mentioned you by name, Dick. Said he didn't want to hear any damned doomsday talk from you about this here exercise. You know how the ol' boy feels about this kind of thing. He made it sound like the Russians practically asked White House permission to do this submarine deployment. So I'm telling you, Dick, you rattle your sabre about this Russian thing, General Tyler'll break it off in your ass."

"Sir, all due respect, but General Tyler couldn't find *his* ass with both hands."

"Careful, Dick, this is the Air Force Chief of Staff you're talking about. Also, the next Chairman of the Joint Chiefs. Our future boss."

"Until he's my boss he's a horse's ass."

McGee sighed. "It's not all his fault, Dick. He's Air Force. Hell, it's all *I* can do to understand this submarine crap. I'm a pilot, not a sewer-pipe sailor." McGee had been COM-AIRLANT, chief of the aviators, and before that captain of an aircraft carrier, and before that commander of an F-14 fighter squadron. "Look, I've gotta run, Dick. Keep me posted. But remember, I need something more than just goddamned ship movements if we're going to ask for modified Rules of Engagement. You can trail 'em, but don't mess with 'em."

Donchez stood in his office and stared out the plate-glass window at the *Stingray* monument construction site across the street. A cement mixer was pouring a foundation. He pressed his intercom and summoned Captain Rummel to his office.

"Yessir," Rummel said as he entered.

"Those SSN-X-27 missiles, the cruise missiles . . ."

"Yessir?"

"There was a U.N. team that witnessed their destruction?"

"Yessir."

"What are the chances that they saw exercise units destroyed?"

"Zero, sir. First, they broke open the weapons to inspect the warheads. No mistaking plutonium with a Geiger counter. Alpha radiation, the works. Every weapon, sir. Those units were the real thing. And they're history now."

"What's the possibility that the Russians had some cruise missiles that we didn't know about before?"

"Slim. Maybe one or two escaped us. Maybe a dozen on the outside. But if you're thinking that attack sub fleet is armed with 'em, no chance. We'd know if there were a hundred and twenty of them out there."

"What if only ten were on the boats and the rest were exercise units, units that flew like the real thing but had dud warheads. That could cause enough confusion to screw us up, couldn't it?"

"Well—they would all fly in at tree-top level so if exercise units were launched with an attack, they'd be stealthy as the real thing."

Donchez thought a moment. "Any chance that only a few Russian boats have nuke cruise missiles and the others are protecting the boats with the nukes?"

Rummel shook his head. "All the boats are separated. They all have different approach vectors. Different destinations. They aren't in some kind of escort formation."

"They're asking me to just sit here and wait for the worst to happen. I can't do it."

"Sir?"

"Never mind, Captain. Let's go. It's time to tell our boys what's going on."

Back in Flag Plot, the Duty Officer stood at attention.

"Duty Officer, two messages to go out FLASH priority. You ready?" Donchez said.

The Duty Officer's pen was poised over his notebook. "Go, sir."

"First message. Addressee, USS *Devilfish*, currently enroute the polar icepack for rendezvous with Russian OMEGA-class submarine Unit One. Mark the message Personal for Commanding Officer. Message classification: TOP SECRET— THUNDERBOLT. Message subject: Mission redefinition." Donchez read the body of the message. "You got all that? Read it back."

Donchez listened as the Duty Officer read back the message.

"Good. Get it on the wire, then come back for the second."

As Donchez waited for the Duty Officer to hand the message to the Senior Chief Radioman, he and Rummel looked at the Arctic Ocean plot, seeing the flashing X that symbolized the unknown position of the OMEGA Unit One.

When the Duty Officer returned, Donchez started in on the second FLASH message.

"The boat that got damaged the other day, Lieutenant, the 688-class boat, who was that?"

"That would be the *Allentown*, sir."

Donchez glanced at the Atlantic Ocean plot to find the *Allentown*. She was several hundred miles off Norfolk, in line with the other Atlantic Fleet submarines forming the zone defense of the coastline. Donchez frowned. He had never liked zone defenses, much preferring man-to-man or sub-to-sub. But the Russians had him outnumbered two to one.

"Did she get her sail fixed?" Donchez asked.

"No, sir," the Duty Officer said, as if it was his fault the Los Angeles–class submarine had remained damaged. "The shipyard was two-blocked with work, sir, and they didn't get to the *Allentown*."

"What's *Allentown* got as far as Javelin cruise missiles?"

The Duty Officer scanned a computer printout on his clipboard. "Sir, she's one of the VLS equipped Los Angeles boats. Fully loaded out."

"Okay," Donchez said. The Vertical Launch System used on the most recent attack submarines meant that in the forward main ballast tanks twelve vertical torpedo tubes had been installed in a space that would otherwise be wasted. The tubes were loaded with Javelin cruise missiles, freeing up the torpedo room for more torpedoes. *Allentown* would be loud and rattling with her sail damage, too noisy to trail one of the Russian boats heading for the coastline. That made her a perfect candidate for Donchez's next idea.

"Okay, Duty Officer. FLASH priority, addressee USS *Allentown*, currently orbiting in the VACAPES OPAREA. Mark this one Personal for Commanding Officer. Message classification: TOP SECRET—THUNDERBOLT. Message subject: New mission directive. Message body to read: Paragraph one will be the same as for *Devilfish*, telling Duckett the current situation. Paragraph two: *Allentown* to transit north to Barents Sea off Russian northern coastline. Use wartime submarine safety lanes to transit north as set forth in the CINCLANTFLEET SIOP WARPLAN. Use maximum speed of advance consistent with ship safety and take a position off of Severomorsk as dictated by the Warplan's Station Number One—"

Rummel looked up sharply. Station One was a hold position for U.S. nuclear submarines directly off Severomorsk Naval Complex, intentionally inside Russia's territorial waters, a dangerous place for an American sub. "—Paragraph two: *Allentown* to maintain passive radio communication on VLF and ELF frequencies, on maximum wartime cruise-missile alert. Paragraph three: Javelin cruise-missile targeting shall be in accordance with the SIOP WARPLAN, Military and Naval Base Facilities Priority section. Paragraph four: Continuous alert to be maintained as a precaution against Russian aggression. *Allentown* shall be within three minutes of Javelin launch at all times. Paragraph five: Vital *Allentown* remain undetected. Paragraph six: Destroy this message immediately . . ."

It would not do to get captured by the Russians with a message onboard ordering them to violate Russia's territorial waters. The contingency plan for capture included the immediate destruction of sensitive documents and war plans, but the most sensitive document contained orders to sail covertly inside the 12-mile territorial limit of another country.

"Paragraph seven: Our hope is that you will not be needed. Good luck, Hank. Paragraph eight: Admiral R. Donchez sends."

The Duty Officer read it back. Donchez nodded and the Duty Officer hurried to the radio consoles. Rummel looked at Donchez, speechless. Donchez stared back at him for a moment.

"The best defense is a good offense, Captain."

MID-ATLANTIC
USS *DEVILFISH*

Pacino moved through the narrow aisle between the Ship's Inertial Navigation System binnacle and the NAVSAT receiver cabinet to the navigation alcove in the aft-port corner of the control room. The chart was taped to a table below a moveable fluorescent light. Pacino leaned over the table and toyed with a pencil, looking at their track-line heading northeast. Where was the OMEGA? Where exactly was *Devilfish*?

He focused on the last fix, obtained by bottom-contour sonar. The BC sonar set pinged and listened to the return on the ocean bottom. Its computer matched the contour under them to a memory of the ocean bottom taken by survey vessels and other submarines. If the sea floor had rocks and valleys and peaks, the fix quality was excellent, putting the ship's estimated position within a few yards of where it actually was. If the floor was sandy, the ship being tracked could be anywhere.

"We're the Fuggawee Indians," the navigator Ian Christman said behind him. Which was to say, Where the fugg are we?

An old joke. Pacino didn't laugh.

"We need a decent fix, Captain," Christman said. "The bottom's been flat as a pancake for twelve hours." The navigator drew a circle around the dot on the track corresponding to the *Devilfish*'s assumed present position. The circle was three inches in diameter. "That's the fix-error circle. We could be anywhere within that. Right now it's only forty miles across. But it's getting bigger every minute without a fix. And going flank speed makes the circle get bigger that much faster. We need to come to periscope depth and get a GPS fix off the NAV-SAT."

The Global Positioning System satellite network gave any owner of a receiver his position to within tens of feet, but going to periscope depth, Pacino was thinking, required going dead slow to avoid ripping off a delicate periscope mast or radio antenna. But since there were no submerged mountains in the area, the risk of a navigation error was acceptable given the overwhelming need to get north and rendezvous with the OMEGA—and Novskoyy—before it headed back to Sever-omorsk.

"Can't do it, nav," Pacino said, shaking his head. "Going to PD means slowing down, clearing baffles to make sure there're no surface vessels on top, going four knots until the fix is onboard. That's forty minutes lost right there. And radio will want to catch the broadcast at the quarter-hour. And the Supply Officer will want to dump the trash out the TDU. The engineer'll want to blowdown the steam generators. It'll just take too goddamned long. We'd be seventy miles behind track. No way. We're due under the ice in a few days. We'll come up to PD before we transit under the ice. Until then we'll just have to live with an expanded fix-error circle. Any chance we can collapse the error circle with SINS?"

Christman shook his head. "The error curves on SINS are getting irregular. Northern latitude. We need an honest-to-God NAVSAT fix to settle out SINS."

"Do the best you can, nav. This OP is urgent. We have to continue deep at flank. If we cut the hull open on a submerged mountain I'll take the hit. You can put it in the ship's log if it makes you feel better."

As Pacino shouldered by Christman he could *feel* the navigator's look. It wasn't like Pacino to take risks like that on navigation—the navy was unforgiving when it came to navigation errors. But for Pacino, *Devilfish* was late for an appointment, an appointment overdue for more than twenty years.

The phone was buzzing as Pacino opened the door of his stateroom. It would be Stokes on the Conn. Instead of answering he turned around and walked back into the control room and stood next to the periscope stand. When he caught Stokes' eye, Stokes put down the phone he'd been holding to his ear at the console aft of the periscopes.

"Cap'n, radio says we gotta come shallow. They're getting an ELF call sign. Looks like ours. Request to slow and come up to 150 feet in preparation to go to PD."

Pacino shook his head. "No, off'sa'deck. Keep flanking it north. I'll be in radio looking at the ELF message."

Pacino walked out and aft down the centerline passageway past his stateroom and sonar.

The door to radio had a combination lock. Pacino pushed the combination buttons and rotated the latch. The radio room was little more than an aisle between two tall rows of equipment racks. A small bench locker was the only seat. Beyond it a printer on a shelf rolled out from one of the racks, hummed, waiting for input.

The radioman, Petty Officer Gerald, was older than Pacino, overweight, barely able to move in the space. Pacino had always liked him—he hustled and was a pro. He would have been a chief petty officer years before if not for a tendency to get drunk in port and throw the first punch.

Gerald looked up. "Afternoon, sir. We're picking up a call

sign on ELF I've got two letters on board already, BRAVO and DELTA. One more to go."

Extremely-low-frequency radio waves were the only ones that could penetrate deep into the ocean. The cost was speed: It would take several minutes to receive a single letter with ELF. The transmitters out of Annapolis were mainly used to transmit a boat's call sign as a signal for her to go shallow and get a burst communication from a satellite.

"What's our call sign today?"

"BRAVO DELTA WHISKEY," Gerald told him. "Here it comes now."

The printer spat out a row of W's, the WHISKEY of the call sign.

"That's us, sir. Someone sure wants to tell us something."

CHAPTER
12

THURSDAY, 16 DECEMBER

Atlantic Ocean
Virginia Capes Submarine Operation Area
(VACAPES OPAREA)

The control room of the USS *Allentown* would look roomy to any Piranha-class sailor. Its layout was planned, not like Captain Henry Duckett's last Piranha-class boat, the *Spadefish*. The control room had the elevated periscope stand by itself in the center, the navigation chart immediately aft so the OOD could see the ship's position without walking off the Conn. The Chief of the Watch's panel seemed impossibly far away to port, and similarly far off to starboard was the long line of fire-control consoles. To a submariner the roominess of the space was like a breath of topside fresh air. The sonar room, the ESM room and radio all opened directly from the control room, not from an aft passageway like on the Piranha class. And this allowed face-to-face discussions with minimal disruptions to the critical combat centers.

The Radioman of the Watch's voice crackled from the overhead speaker: "CONN, RADIO, WE HAVE AN ELF TRANS-MISSION COMING IN ON THE LOOP ANTENNA . . . WILL ADVISE."

"OOD, you have the Conn," Duckett said, moving into the radio room. He was gone for six minutes.

"What is it, sir?"

"We're ordered to periscope depth. Get us up quick, no baffle clearing."

"Aye aye, sir. Helm, all stop. Dive, make your depth five four feet, ten degree up bubble. Sonar, Conn, ascending to PD. Lookaround number-two scope. Helm, all ahead one-third."

The OOD raised the type-18 periscope and the *Allentown's* deck inclined as she ascended to periscope depth.

The young lieutenant rotated the periscope in circles, his body hugging the deck-to-overhead periscope and optic module, his pelvis pressed up against the optic module, dancing with the fat lady. Duckett leaned against the pole of the attack-periscope, the installed spare.

Finally the radioman brought in the message board with the flash message.

The first paragraph nearly made Duckett's heart come full stop. 120 nuclear-attack subs heading for the coast? Jesus, Joseph and Mary. Duckett read on to the paragraph directing *Allentown* north to Warplan Station Number One, directly offshore from Severomorsk Naval Complex in Russian waters. With cruise missiles armed and ready . . .

"Off'sa'deck," Duckett called, "muster the officers in the wardroom for an urgent brief. And send down the SIOP WARPLAN."

The OOD's eyes widened. "The warplan, sir?"

"That's right, Lieutenant. You got a problem with that?"

"No, sir. SIOP WARPLAN, coming up, sir."

Good for him, Duckett thought. Because he sure as hell had one.

NORTH ATLANTIC

The *Devilfish,* responding to orders, rolled in the long swells at periscope depth. Pacino stood at the number-two periscope, doing slow circles, unable to see much but the mountains of the waves crashing over his view as the storm raged above the ship. Every few minutes he prodded the OOD for the status of the satellite radio transmission. They'd lost it the first time as a wave splashed over the BIGMOUTH radio antenna sticking out through the waves.

The submarines could get a broadcast-burst communication only on the quarter-hour. Since they missed it once, it would mean staying at periscope depth for another fifteen minutes. And even then another wave might drown out that burst transmission.

Pacino called to the OOD without removing his eyes from the periscope, "Off'sa'deck, hit the satellite and get the broadcast onboard."

"But, sir," Stokes said, "if we transmit to the satellite to request our messages we could be detected. It may be a burst comm but the Russians got receivers with direction finders."

Pacino shook his head. "You think we've been stealthy this run yet? We've gone through a thousand miles at flank with the reactor main coolant pumps at fast speed. And now we're sitting here with two telephone poles sticking out of the sea just waiting for someone to eyeball us. Hit the goddamned satellite, get the broadcast onboard and let's get deep where we belong."

"Aye, sir," Stokes said tonelessly. "Radio, Conn, hit the satellite."

Stokes reached for the radar-wave-receiver volume-knob on the phone console in time to squelch the screech of the ship's transmission. The receiver made noises, mostly *boops* and *beeps* when enemy radar beams hit the periscope. It also detected the BIGMOUTH transmitting. Same frequency range.

The speaker in the overhead squawked as hydraulics thumped, indicating the lowering of the BIGMOUTH antenna by the radioman.

"CONN, RADIO, BROADCAST ONBOARD, PRINTING OUT NOW, LOWERING THE BIGMOUTH."

"Take her deep," Pacino immediately ordered.

"Diving Officer," Stokes drawled, "make your depth five four six feet, thirty degree down angle. And step on it."

The next mountainous wave splashed against Pacino's periscope-view, and for a few moments he looked at the underside of the waves, training the periscope-view upward as the waves grew distant overhead. Finally all was dark.

"Scope's under," Pacino called, rotating the hydraulic control ring. "Lowering number-two scope."

The periscope optic module vanished into the well and continued down until it reached the stop 30 feet below.

Pacino watched the depth gage as the hull popped and cracked. By the time it reached 546 feet the speed indicator had climbed to 34 knots and the deck began its vibration. Pacino went back to the navigation plot to see how the NAVSAT fix came in. As he studied the chart, wishing the distance to the ice would melt away, Radioman Gerald handed him the metal message board and the top-secret log.

"Flash traffic, sir. Top secret."

Pacino signed for the messages, opened the clipboard cover and read the message that had been urgent enough to call *Devilfish* up from her deep transit.

* * * * * * * * * * * * * * *

* FLASH *

* * * * * * * * * * * * * * *

150354zDEC

FLASH FLASH FLASH FLASH FLASH FLASH FLASH FLASH FLASH FLASH FLASH

FM   COMSUBLANT NORFOLK VA

TO   USS DEVILFISH SSN-666

SUBJ MISSION REDEFINITION

REF   COMSUBLANT OPORD 54-0964A DATED 13 DEC

SCI/TOP SECRET—THUNDERBOLT

PERSONAL FOR CO//   PERSONAL FOR CO//   PERSONAL FOR CO
//BT//

1. NEW INTELLIGENCE HAS DETECTED DEPLOYMENT OF ALL NORTHERN FLEET ATTACK-SUBMARINE UNITS FROM BASES ON NORTHERN RUSSIA COAST. SORTIE OF OVER ONE HUNDRED ATTACK SUBMARINES OUTCHOPPING THE BARENTS SEA TO THE GI-UK GAP. SPEED OF ADVANCE HIGH. VECTOR ANALYSIS INDICATES PROBABLE DESTINATION U.S. EAST COAST. OMEGA UNIT ONE MAY BE LINKED TO THIS DEPLOYMENT. AS YET ANALYSTS UNABLE TO VERIFY SUCH A LINKAGE.

2. OMEGA UNIT ONE DETECTED. ITS POSITION DEEMED RELIABLE AT COORDINATE ALPHA TWO ONE DECIMAL TWO TACK FIVE THREE DECIMAL SIX, CHART Z-SUB-ONE.

3. UNIT SURFACED AT POLYNYA WITH ONE ANTENNA UP. NO RADIO TRANSMISSIONS DETECTED. POSSIBLY UNIT IS LISTENING AND IS NOT TRANSMITTING YET.

4. DEVILFISH ORDERS REDEFINED. DETERMINE POSSIBLE HOSTILE INTENT OF OMEGA SUBMARINE AND DETERMINE ANY LINKAGE TO ATTACK-SUBMARINE FLEET HEADING TOWARD U.S. COAST. SUBLANT RULES OF ENGAGEMENT NO LONGER APPLY. DEVILFISH ORDERED TO TEST OMEGA UNIT USING ALL METHODS SHORT OF ACTUAL WEAPON RELEASE. DEVILFISH COMMANDER AUTHORIZED TO USE ALL REPEAT ALL INITIATIVE IN THIS ENDEAVOR.

5. FURTHER INTELLIGENCE WILL BE RELAYED AS IT IS RECEIVED HERE.

6. GOOD LUCK AND GOOD HUNTING, MIKEY.

7. ADM. R. DONCHEZ SENDS.

//BT//

For the first time in a long time Pacino allowed a smile. The question of how to get the crew to engage the OMEGA had just been answered. Fleet deployment that intelligence didn't foresee. Perfect sanction for his confrontation with the OMEGA.

"Officer of the Deck," Pacino called, "change course to zero four five. Get the XO and Navigator up here now."

As Pacino waited, doubt crept into his mind. Could the deployment info be for real? Why would Novskoyy be surfaced in the first place? He pushed away the thought and concentrated on his confrontation with Novskoyy. He could approach the OMEGA while it was surfaced at the polynya, hover beneath and do a vertical surfacing . . . but instead of breaking through the ice hit the OMEGA. But if the OMEGA had its engines shut down it might take an hour for it to get under way from the polynya. And the OMEGA, quiet even in open ocean, would be quieter than the ice around her if her engines were not running. So he might never find her at the polynya. And a sub that big could take a helluva wallop without being damaged. To wake her up would take a crash violent enough to damage *Devilfish* herself . . . Was this mission survivable?

Rapier and Christman having arrived at Conn, Pacino let them read the flash message together.

"We've got to find this bastard, Skipper," Rapier said.

"And hammer him," from Christman.

"Don't forget, gentlemen," Pacino said, "we *don't* have a weapons-release authorization here. We can shoot only if he shoots first."

Rapier shook his head. "COMSUBLANT said the Rules of Engagement no longer apply. We don't need to wait—"

"No, XO, he also said use methods short of weapon release. He said to use our initiative. And *that* is what we're going to do . . ."

CHAPTER
13
THURSDAY, 16 DECEMBER

Moscow
The Kremlin, Defense Ministry Subwing
Hearing Room Four

Colonel Ivan Dretzski studied his notes for the final remaining minutes before the hearing on the Northern Fleet's deployment to the Atlantic was called to order. Its purpose was to determine why the fleet had sailed without permission from Moscow, and what to do about it.

The room looked like a Russian version of a Senate hearing room. On the back wall, perhaps four meters tall, the faded outline of the old hammer and sickle showed, its shape indicated by the contrast of the dirty wall with the clean spot where the symbol of the Soviet Union had once hung. He thought about Novskoyy being convinced that it was the agents of the United States that had brought down the USSR. Maybe Novskoyy was right in opposing America's military forces, but not about the rest . . . Russia's problem wasn't McDonald's hamburgers in Red Square. Its economy had collapsed. Without oil exports it was a poor agrarian country.

Ever since he had agreed to Novskoyy's plan, under duress—hell, threat—its flaws nagged at him, and now seemed magnified with the admiral at sea. His rhetoric and powerful personality weren't there to melt away doubts. In the cold light of logic, the plan seemed extreme to the point of risking a nuclear war. Trust and arms control and reduction were the better way . . .

As the members filed in, Dretzski fought against his doubts. America was the *glavny protivnik*, the main adversary. That was ingrained in him, never mind what *seemed* to be the case. He was a military man. The military was at deathly risk. His country was *still* at risk . . . America's nuclear weapons were still the issue. Plus its still vast defense organization. Billion-dollar Stealth fighters, two-billion-dollar submarines, million-dollar cruise missiles, billions of dollars of space-based weapons systems. Novskoyy was a risk taker, but he could also be right . . .

The members took their seats at the slightly elevated panel in front of Dretzski's table, their panel forming a horseshoe-shape in front of him. All were present except the President, who would be a minute late.

Dretzski paused from his notes and his mixed feelings to look over the members. On the far left was General Anton Voskod, Chief of the Strategic Rocket Forces, the service that once owned the silo-based intercontinental ballistic missiles. With the arms treaties and the peace race, Voskod was out of a job. Voskod was one of the younger generals, in his early fifties, and had been a hawk during the time when his missiles were constantly pointed at U.S. cities.

On General Voskod's left sat General Dmitri Pallin, the KGB's Head of the First Chief Directorate, the KGB arm responsible for foreign intelligence. Pallin had come from the FCD's commando ranks. Pallin was also Dretzski's boss at FCD, which meant the presentation had better go well or it would reflect unfavorably on both of them.

On Pallin's left was the civilian KGB chief, Viktor Maksoy, a tired old man who tended to do whatever Pallin wanted, or whatever the highest ranking bureaucrat wanted. Maksoy had no backbone, which was the reason the President had chosen him—he had no taste for a KGB with teeth. Maksoy would go whatever way the wind blew.

In the center of the horseshoe was the empty chair for the President. The hearing could not go on without him.

Next to the empty chair was Tafel Fasimov, the Defense

Minister. A hard-liner like Voskod, he was never fond of capital-
ism or negotiations with the Americans. When, thought Dretzski, would the dinosaurs be gone?

To the left of Fasimov was the Foreign Minister Anatoly
Kirova. Kirova had spent much time at the U.N., Dretzski
thought, and had become, some said, Americanized, his conver-
sion measurable in the hot dogs and pizzas he consumed. Kirova
would be against the Novskoyy deployment, and would oppose
harassment of the Americans.

In the last seat on the right was Admiral Mikhail Barisov,
Supreme Commander of the Pacific Fleet, Novskoyy's opposite
number in Vladivostok. Barisov and Novskoyy were as different
as two men could be. Barisov was a thinker, a lover of ballet,
reader of history. Barisov too had become cozy with the *glavny
protivnik*, spending over a month at the U.S. Naval War College
in Newport.

President Misha Sergeiyvich Yulenski entered the room then.
Dretzski had not been able to read Yulenski, who could be
agreeable one moment and furious the next. He was one of the
new generation of democratic politicians.

After Yulenski called the hearing to order Dretzski addressed
the men at the table.

"President Yulenski, gentlemen, my name is Colonel Ivan
Dretzski and I have been asked to come here and brief you at
the request of General Pallin and Chief Maksoy. I am an intelligence specialist in First Chief Directorate, responsible for foreign intelligence estimates and nuclear-weapon intelligence. I
have a statement to read concerning the deployment of the
Northern Fleet, after which I will try to answer any questions
you have. Sir?"

"Yes, go ahead, Colonel Dretzski," Yulenski boomed, his
voice and manner jolly, as if trying to win votes.

"Gentlemen," Dretzski began, "on Tuesday, the Northern
Fleet's 120 nuclear-attack submarines deployed together from
their bases on the northern coast. They had been prepared for
this special exercise for several months, and at the order of Admiral Alexi Novskoyy, admiral in command of the fleet, the
boats began the exercise. The exercise involves several parts.
The first part is completed. The initial test was to see how
quickly and efficiently the fleet could be scrambled to sea—"

Dretzski could feel Admiral Barisov's eyes on him. It would not be easy to get anything by Barisov, which was probably why he had been flown in from Vladivostok.

"—with a minimum of notice. The second element of the exercise is to enter the North Atlantic and make a record-time-run to the east coast of the United States—"

The room filled with the buzz of voices.

"I need to stress that this is an exercise only. The ships are training for the possibility of a rapid-deployment. As Admiral Novskoyy has said, if a military unit is supposed to have a capability, and that capability is not regularly tested, the capability vanishes.

"After approximately one to two days on the coastline, the submarines will withdraw and return to their bases. That will be the third phase. We will evaluate the submarines on their ability to fulfill their missions. We have, of course, never gone into combat with our nuclear submarines—it is not like an army-artillery brigade, learning the science of warfare from centuries of firing cannons. Nuclear submarines are still a relatively new science, never taken into combat. We need to learn how to use this navy if it is to serve the defense of our newly constituted country. Admiral Novskoyy's exercise will rewrite the book on how we operate our ships."

"Colonel," the President began "why are you, a KGB First Chief Directorate operative, coming to brief us on this? Where is Admiral Novskoyy? Where is his staff?" Yulenski's meaning was clear: *Who are you, his boy?*

Dretzski knew he would face this, though had not been able to prepare a convincing answer.

"Sir, General Pallin and Chief Maksoy accepted Admiral Novskoyy's invitation to monitor his exercise and serve as referee. The admiral said that a deployment such as this would alert American intelligence agencies immediately. At FCD we were given the task to act as if the Northern Fleet was from a separate country—"

"It practically is," Admiral Barisov broke in. Apparently there was little cooperation between the fleets.

"—and determine if *we* could detect the deployment in advance when the fleet was provisioned and maintained."

"What were the results, Colonel?" Pallin asked, as if an encouraging attorney for the defense.

"We could not detect anything that looked like unusual activity. Not by satellites, radio surveillance, phone taps, warehouse activity, maintenance activity or even crew-member movements."

"Very convenient, Colonel," Admiral Barisov said. "Novskoyy hired you to see no evil, hear no evil—"

"I will give you a more impartial account than any Northern Fleet official or officer would. I would actually like to tell you that we detected Admiral Novskoyy's activity, but we did not. A failure for us, but a victory for our nation."

President Yulenski took the floor, his joviality gone.

"Colonel, why were the submarines sent to the coast of America without my knowledge or authorization? Why are we threatening the Americans? What do we expect them to do when they see all these submarines off their coast?"

"Sir, the intent is to avoid detection. If the boats get to their coast undetected, then we have proved the fleet can do it and Admiral Novskoyy's training and preparations are in order. If, however, every boat runs into defending submarines and ASW ships and aircraft, then we have learned something even more valuable, and we can fix it in case we should ever need the capability . . . It is an ingenious experiment—"

"So, Colonel Dretzski," Yulenski said, "shouldn't we give the Americans the courtesy of a phone call to tell them that our toys are wandering around practically in their territorial waters?"

Dretzski's armpits suddenly were wet. It was crucial that the Kremlin not call the White House—it would poison the controlled information and analysis being fed to the Americans through Agent Fishhook, whose role in the plan was its weakest and yet most vital element.

"I would advise against that, sir," Dretzski said, feeling very uneasy. "The whole point of this exercise, this experiment, is to see if an *unalerted* America knows we are coming. As suggested, if they do not, we have proved a capability. If they do, we have identified flaws to fix—"

"Very risky, Colonel. And Fasimov," Yulenski said to the defense minister, "this sort of thing will never happen again without my express orders. We can't conduct an open foreign policy if our generals and admirals are secretly playing with their toys. You people are tempting fate. I want to see Admiral Novskoyy this evening, Fasimov. Send him over, and you come also. We have some talking to do."

"Sir," Dretzski said, "Admiral Novskoyy is not in port."

"Where the hell is he?"

"Sir, he is on a new attack submarine that went on sea trials under the icecap. He should be returning shortly before his fleet."

"*Why* is he on a submarine under the ice? How can he monitor this exercise from there?"

Dretzski swallowed. If he said Novskoyy would surface and use *Kaliningrad*'s antennae, it would look too much like he had a command-and-control flagship, determining the destinies of his fleet. But if he lied and said Novskoyy couldn't receive radio messages, Admiral Barisov would know it. A morsel of truth was needed.

"Again, sir," Dretzski said, "Admiral Novskoyy felt that it would be best to get an unbiased opinion from an intelligence community that had no political obligations to him, someone completely impartial. That is why Naval Intelligence was not called in. The admiral wants the hard, cold truth, not a subordinate's possible sugar-coating. He is intent on finding out any operational flaws in the fleet. He deliberately left it to keep his own opinions and biases out of the exercise evaluation and execution. He is looking for the negatives, and the KGB will help him find them."

"Very well, Colonel," Yulenski said.

Dretzski suppressed a sigh of relief. Yulenski, it seemed, had bought the story, and with Yulenski went the others.

Yulenski stood, suddenly in a hurry, the meat of the briefing over. He left the room, aides coming in to collect his briefing papers from the presentation.

As the members filed out Dretzski felt confident—until Admiral Mikhail Barisov materialized in front of him.

Barisov, the Supreme Commander of the Pacific Fleet, was young for his job although he did not look it—thin to the point of gauntness, deep lines showing in his face, hair completely gray. Barisov had spent his youth in the submarine force, arriving for duty fresh out of the Marshal Grechko Higher Naval School of Underwater Navigation the same year that Yuri Gagarin had been launched into orbit. After twenty years in the submarine fleet, having commanded the VICTOR III submarine *Volgograd*, Barisov had cross-decked to the surface fleet and had commanded a destroyer, a cruiser and a helicopter/VTOL aircraft carrier. What followed were several dull years in the Moscow Defense Ministry, mostly spent fighting office politics, until Admiral Gorshkov had promoted him and given him command of the Pacific Fleet.

Barisov stared into the eyes of this weasely KGB officer, wondering why he was covering for Novskoyy.

"Dretzski, what's the real story on this deployment?"

Dretzski tried to look confused.

Barisov began asking questions, a prosecutor doing a cross-examination.

Dretzski tried to handle them calmly, all the while thinking that something might have to be done about Barisov. An aircraft accident on the way back to Vladivostok . . . ?

ARCTIC OCEAN
POLYNYA SURFACE
F.S. *KALININGRAD*

Admiral Novskoyy heard a knock at his door, looked up from his decryption of the last incoming message marked PERSONAL FOR FLEET COMMANDER.

Quickly he stowed the message and the attack-profile chart, then let Captain Vlasenko into the stateroom. Novskoyy turned his back on the captain and returned to the table. Vlasenko sat in front of it.

"Yes, Captain?"

"Admiral, we have been at the polynya now for two days. Isn't it time we went forward with the sea-trial agenda?"

Novskoyy stared at Vlasenko a moment. "The sea-trial agenda is postponed. Something urgent has come up. Fleet business. We may be here another week."

Vlasenko's insides turned over. "Then, sir, we should shut

down the turbine room. There is no sense in keeping the engines warm if we are going to sit here—"

"No, I want to be able to move quickly, I need flexibility. There is no predicting when the ice around the polynya may shift and threaten to crush us. We need to be able to run if we have to."

Vlasenko hesitated. He could not confront Novskoyy with what he had found out. That would land him in a locked storage compartment.

He reached for an alternative course. He could sabotage the radio-transmission gear at the base of the radio multifrequency antenna. Racking out perhaps five drawers and severing connections, perhaps pocketing some key components and destroying the spares. Of course, with Novskoyy on the control-compartment communications console, the tampering would be detected before he would be able to damage the gear beyond repair. There might be no way he could prevent the admiral from transmitting his message to the fleet. At least, Vlasenko was convinced, the operation was not on automatic. No one would actually launch unless Novskoyy transmitted his go-code. Otherwise, why would they be surfaced here? The ship was being used as a flagship. Which meant the only way to stop the time-on-target strike or threat of a strike . . . was to sequester Novskoyy. If necessary . . . kill him.

Vlasenko stood, turned and left.

Novskoyy returned to his message from Colonel Dretzski in Moscow:

1. KREMLIN IS SUSPICIOUS.

2. TODAY I BRIEFED THE KREMLIN AND DEFENSE MINISTRY PERSONNEL, INCLUDING PACIFIC FLEET COMMANDER ADMIRAL MIKHAIL BARISOV.

3. ALL EXCEPT BARISOV SATISFIED FOR THE MOMENT THAT YOU ARE CONDUCTING AN EXERCISE. TIME OF THE ESSENCE. ADVISE YOU COMPLETE OPERATION SOON OR THEY WILL WONDER WHY PIERS STILL EMPTY.

4. BARISOV VERY INTERESTED IN FLEET DEPLOYMENT. ASKED QUESTIONS, WANTED SPECIFICS. MENTIONED POSSIBILITY OF EMULATING OPERATION TO SEE HOW WELL HIS SUBMARINES COULD SCRAMBLE TO SEA. I TOLD HIM IT HAD TAKEN MONTHS OF PREPARATIONS, GREAT COST. THAT MAY HAVE

PUT HIM OFF OR MADE HIM MORE SUSPICIOUS OF YOUR MOTIVES. HE SAID NOTHING.

5. BARISOV REMAINS IN MOSCOW. MEANWHILE PACIFIC FLEET HEADQUARTERS IN VLADIVOSTOK BUSY. BARISOV MAY BE PLANNING SOMETHING. MORE REASON TO CONCLUDE OPERATION.

6. NEW INTELLIGENCE—U.S. ATLANTIC FLEET ATTACK SUBMARINES SCRAMBLED TO WEST ATLANTIC. OVER 60 VESSELS. SUGGEST RETHINK OPERATION IF THEY ARE ABLE TO TRAIL OUR SUBMARINES. THEY MUST BE PRESUMED TO CARRY JAVELIN CRUISE MISSILES. PROVOCATION COULD BRING DANGEROUS CONSEQUENCES.

7. MORE INTELLIGENCE—A U.S. ATTACK SUBMARINE, PIRANHA CLASS, IS EN-ROUTE NORTH ATLANTIC, POSSIBLY TO ICECAP.

8. U.N. CREW WITNESSED DESTRUCTION OF 120 "WARSHOT" SSN-X-27 CRUISE MISSILES TODAY. WORLD BELIEVES WE NOW HAVE NONE.

9. FISHHOOK, AS ORDERED, TRYING TO CONVINCE U.S. LEADERSHIP THAT NORTHERN FLEET DEPLOYMENT IS EXERCISE.

10. RAPID REPEAT RAPID CONCLUSION OF THIS OPERATION VITAL. GOOD LUCK.

Novskoyy read the message again, then shredded it in Vlasenko's shredding machine. He consulted his calendar. With a decent speed-of-advance, his fleet should be off the coast of the U.S. in two days—by the 18th of December.

What remained was for Agent Fishhook, General Tyler, to hold off the U.S. submarine force long enough for his ships to get in position.

CHAPTER
14

SATURDAY, 18 DECEMBER

The periscope video-repeater showed the dark water, the ridge of ice ahead and the low arctic sun shining coldly in the local morning. This far north, in the marginal ice zone, where the sun lingered low on the horizon most of the days, the MIZ was a dangerous area of icebergs and drift-ice, the transition between open water and the cover of the polar icecap.

Submarines usually avoided going to periscope depth in the MIZ. The risk of collision was great, and the hull could easily be torn open by an iceberg. But Pacino had insisted on one last look and for twenty minutes had trained the scope around in slow circles.

What Pacino saw looked like snow-covered, mountainous terrain on the horizon. Cold, deserted, desolate, dead. Still, at least it was the surface, complete with the sun and the sea and the ice. And fresh clean air not filtered by charcoal, not scrubbed of carbon dioxide by an amine bed, not fed through carbon-monoxide burners, not electrified by the precipitators. Not the dry coppery artificial air generated by the "Bomb," the oxygen generator that split water into hydrogen and oxygen, storing the oxygen and discarding the hydrogen, the mixture of gases dangerous enough to breach the hull in a violent explosion should it fail, and giving the machine its nickname.

Christman's voice, edged with uncertainty, interrupted Pacino's thoughts.

"Captain, range to the ice raft ahead is nineteen-hundred yards by SHARKTOOTH sonar."

Lieutenant Commander Christman, Officer of the Deck, stood at the under-ice sonar, the SHARKTOOTH, a console with a joystick and a vertical video readout. At the top panel was a stripchart used to record the depth of the ice overhead. The display on the center panel looked very much like a radar, was generated by a hydrophone on the forward edge of the sail that transmitted a faint high-pitched tone in a pattern like a police siren. If the sound pitch was plotted against time on a graph, the waveforms looked like shark teeth. With the changing transmission frequency, it could transmit and interpret the echo simultaneously, giving continuous ranges and bearings to ice-shapes ahead, which now formed a solid bank less than a mile away.

For a moment Pacino had a sense that this might be the last time he would see the surface and the sky and the sun . . . not an unheard of thought among submariners . . . and quickly censored the thought as he snapped the periscope grips up and rotated the hydraulic control ring. As the scope optic-module descended into the well the stainless steel pole felt extremely cold brushing Pacino's arm.

"Take her deep," he said without looking at Christman, then moved forward on the periscope stand to the pole of the number-one periscope, the World War II relic used only for surface navigation, and stared at the Conn sonar console on the port side. The TV screen was red to keep the OOD's eyes night-adjusted. The display was a waterfall cascading downward. The horizontal axis was bearing—north on the left, south in the center and north-northwest on the right. The vertical axis was time —the top now, the older data lower. All the data fell downward on the screen like a "waterfall."

Like the moon "following" a moving car, a distant contact would show up as a vertical trace on the display, its bearing constant, but a close contact would have a slanted slope, showing it moving from one true bearing to another.

At the moment the displays were only filled with static. Then a definite sloping trace appeared on the short-duration display. High-bearing rate, a close contact. Pacino reached for the microphone.

"Sonar, Captain, report the contact at zero four zero."

"CONN, SONAR, AYE, CONTACT NOW BEARING ZERO SIX TWO IS BIOLOGICS."

Pacino frowned. A whale or a school of fish.

"Sonar, Captain, select the narrowband beam on the trace's bearing and integrate on narrowband time-freq."

"CONN, SONAR, AYE."

Pacino pressed a selector-pad button below the display. The waterfalls disappeared, replaced by six graphs, each a plot of intensity on the vertical axis versus sound frequency on the horizontal axis. Fed by the towed array, the narrowband processors listened for specific frequencies known to be emitted by most Russian submarine classes, from such as their turbine-generator resonance, a 300-cycle-per-second sound. One of the graphs was centered on the anticipated 300-hertz tonal. If the contact was a Russian there was a high probability it would get a narrow vertical spike centered near 300 hertz.

The time-frequency data took about five minutes to come up with a meaningful display. Like the camera taking an evening-time exposure photograph, the sonar system "integrated" the sound data over a long-time period to make sure tonals weren't just background noises. For a full five minutes Pacino stared at the 300-hertz graph, not aware of Christman staring at him. The graph was flat. No spike anywhere near 300 hertz. Pacino shook his head, pushed a button on the selector pad and the broadband waterfall display returned.

"Sonar, Captain, return to your search."

The trace had definitely been biologics.

"CONN, SONAR, AYE."

The short-duration display began to fill with traces. Noise from rafts of ice shifting and grating against each other. Soon it would be audible to the naked ear.

Pacino moved through the gap between the port Conn console and the aft telephone-communications bulkhead, squeezing past the radar console, which was shut down and useless when submerged.

On the other side of the radar was the SHARKTOOTH under-ice sonar. Pacino looked down at the forward scan screen. The ridge of ice was now astern, and ahead were some more ridges, stalactites of ice hanging down from the ice canopy overhead. Just gentle ridges now, but soon they would stab down deeply enough to smash into them if the OOD made a mistake. Dimly Pacino heard Christman giving slight rudder adjustments to avoid the ridges. For the rest of their time under ice the OOD or his assistant, the Junior Officer of the Deck, would stand here at the under-ice sonar steering the ship. The JOOD would also help with under-ice navigation or man the fire-control computer, ensuring a weapon was programmed and ready. In case.

"Off'sa'deck, clear baffles," Pacino ordered. "And don't go more than two hours without a baffle clear. I don't want to be surprised out here."

"Clear baffles, Off'sa'deck, aye. Helm, right five degrees rudder, steady course one three zero." Christman picked up a microphone at the under-ice sonar console. "Sonar, Conn, clearing baffles to the right."

"CONN, SONAR, AYE."

Pacino climbed back up to the periscope stand and stared at the short-duration waterfall display, thinking of the Russian that came out of the *Stingray*'s baffles decades before.

NORFOLK, VIRGINIA
COMSUBLANT HEADQUARTERS

In Flag Plot Admiral Donchez stared up at 120 flashing red X's. The sons of bitches had arrived, he thought. The subs were lining up from off the coast of Maine down to the Carolinas. The southernmost portions of the coast were still clear, the last Russians still on the way to these more distant stations.

His attack submarines were in force off the coast, but 67 boats against 120 . . . not good odds for a face-off, if it came to that. His message to his submarines had been carefully worded to be as vague as possible yet still give their commanders some leeway to engage . . . if necessary.

1. RUSSIAN SUBMARINE ATTACK UNITS EXPECTED TO TAKE STATION OFF U.S.
   EAST COAST IN WESTLANT BY 182000ZDEC.

2. ALL UNITS SHALL DO UTMOST REPEAT UTMOST TO GET IN TRAIL OF RUSSIAN
   UNITS. ESTABLISH TRAIL WITH MAXIMUM TRAIL RANGE FIVE THOUSAND
   (5000) YARDS. MINIMUM TRAIL RANGE AT DISCRETION OF INDIVIDUAL COM-
   MANDING OFFICER, WITH MISSION DIRECTIVE TO REMAIN UNDETECTED IF
   POSSIBLE.

3. RUSSIAN INTENT UNKNOWN.

4. COMMANDERS SHALL USE BEST JUDGMENT. SUBLANT RULES OF ENGAGEMENT
   APPLY, BUT SHALL BE INTERPRETED SO AS TO MAXIMIZE SAFETY OF U.S. AND
   U.S. INTERESTS.

5. ON DETECTION OF ANY HOSTILE FIRE, UNITS ARE AUTHORIZED TO ATTACK
   TARGETS.

6. ADM. R. DONCHEZ SENDS.

It was the best he could do. No one could shoot unless one of
the Russian attack boats shot first. But why would they be deploying? To test American nerves? Donchez walked to the elevator to go to his office and watch the construction on the
Stingray monument. For all the good he was doing in Flag Plot,
he might as well walk out to the site and help them pour concrete.

As he left Flag Plot he looked at the charts and promised
himself he would not come back to the room until the Russians
turned around and abandoned their game of chicken, or war of
nerves, or whatever the hell they thought it was.

ARCTIC OCEAN
POLYNYA SURFACE

Admiral Alexi Novskoyy sat at the communications console in
the control compartment and watched the laser printer reel off
page after page of papers from the computer's storage memory.
Only five minutes after the hour Novskoyy had appointed for
the boats to be on-station, he had 120 messages from his submarines. He picked up the ream of messages and took them to the
ladder to the upper level of the second compartment below,

nodded to the Deck Officer, Captain-Lieutenant Ivanov, the only other occupant of the space.

"Good night, Ivanov."

"Good night, sir."

Novskoyy continued down the ladder and through the passageway to his stateroom, where he turned on a small stereo and sat down at the desk. It took over an hour to decrypt the messages, but when he was done he stared down at the checklist with satisfaction.

Each of the 120 attack submarines was in position along the coast of the U.S., and none had encountered any harassment. The Americans seemed to be giving them a wide berth.

He leaned back in his chair and let his eyes unfocus. He had expected at least a dozen reports of bumps and collisions with the U.S. attack submarines in the Atlantic, perhaps lines of frigates and destroyers filling the water with sonar pings, aircraft doing low flyovers and dropping sonobuoys, squadrons of helicopters chopping over the waves dipping sonar receivers on long cables. But nothing. The Atlantic was deserted. Not even a sniff of the American attack submarines Dretzski had reported.

Something had to be wrong. It was too perfect.

Novskoyy took off his reading glasses and shut his eyes. It had to be Agent Fishhook coming through. That and the U.N. inspection. The plan had worked.

He sat back to listen to the sounds of the symphony music washing over him, but the nagging thought kept intruding . . . why had the fleet achieved positions without opposition?

WESTERN ATLANTIC OCEAN

The USS *Billfish* cruised slowly northeast at four knots, bare steerageway, at a depth of 658 feet. The ship was rigged for ultraquiet. All off-watch personnel were ordered to their bunks. Lights throughout the ship were off or switched to a dim red setting. The P.A. Circuit One speakers were disabled, an announcement on them might be detected outside the hull. In each space men stood with headphones and boom microphones, linked on a single shipwide phone circuit, ready to pass urgent orders by voice.

Every running pump or piece of equipment in the ship had redundancy; the equipment selected to be running was the one in a set that was the quietest. All maintenance activity was halted. Non-essential gear such as galley equipment was turned off—the crew would eat cold meals for the duration of ultra-quiet. Hard-soled shoes were prohibited, the crew had switched to sneakers and slippers. Stereos, radios, televisions were turned off. The spare gyro was shut down, as well as the Bomb, the oxygen generator. Reactor main coolant pumps were in slow speed.

The ship was dead quiet.

In the torpedo room all four tubes had signs on the inner doors reading WARSHOT LOADED. Tubes three and four were flooded, sea pressure equalized to the outside pressure, outer doors open and weapons powered up, their gyros spinning rapidly, their computers activated, ready for a fire-control solution.

In the control room only the whine of the gyro and the humming of the fire-control computer were audible. The watch-section fire-control team was ready to track and, on orders, shoot any contact.

Lieutenant Culverson, the Officer of the Deck, stood on the Conn and stared at the sonar-repeater console, a television screen covered with red filter glass. A heavily built Texan with a string tie around the collar of his blue poopy suit, Culverson wore a pair of blue Hushpuppy loafers. After all, the rig for ultraquiet had deprived him of his usual cowboy boots. Culverson, wearing red goggles to preserve his night vision in case the ship needed to come to periscope depth, stared at the sonar screen, straining to find a submarine in the mass of stringlike indications of random ocean noises and biologics.

Twenty feet aft the sonar space was rigged for black, with only the six sonar console screens showing light in the room. Sonarman Chief Dawson sat at the central console of the sonar panel, the space silent except for a faint high-pitched whine from the video screens. The center lower screen was tuned to the athwartships beam of the towed sonar array, a set of hydrophones towed astern on a mile-long cable. The beam examined a thin slice of ocean, looking for specific frequency tonals from an AKULA-class attack sub that COMSUBLANT Intelligence had predicted would come into the Billfish's patrol area.

The central console graphs were displaying the frequencies surrounding the anticipated 314-hertz tonal of the AKULA's turbine generators. As Dawson watched, the graph slowly grew a narrow hill in the center. The minutes clicked by, and the graph's peak, the hill, became a mountain, then a pillar, then a thin sharp spike.

314.0 hertz. Exactly.

Too clear and sustained to be a natural phenomenon. Dawson flipped through the other displays. One harmonic of 154 hertz was also spiking. With a 314 and a 154, it had to be an AKULA class.

Dawson selected the LOFAR display, the low frequency analyzer that examined a contact's screw pattern. The lines of frequency were showing the repetitious vibrations of an eight-bladed screw.

It all added up to a Russian AKULA-class attack sub where it had no business being—150 miles east of Norfolk, Virginia.

Dawson keyed his microphone.

"Conn, Sonar, narrowband contact Sierra One, bearing either three five zero or one seven zero, is a submerged contact, Russian nuclear type four, probable AKULA class, making three zero turns on one eight bladed screw. Recommend coming to course . . . zero three zero to resolve the bearing ambiguity."

"SONAR, CONN, AYE, WAIT."

Dawson switched the display to the broadband waterfall, the display of all frequencies in the ocean around them. He concentrated on the two possible bearings to the narrowband contact. There was the beginning of a trace at 350. He put his palm on the cursor ball set into the horizontal section of the console and rolled it, moving the computer cursor to the trace, thereby tuning his audio set to that direction and that direction only. He shut his eyes, listened. What he heard was static, white noise, like rain, or water flowing in a creek. Broadband noise.

He cut in a filter, removing the lower frequencies. He selected higher and higher frequencies and waited. Finally he heard it.

. . . poosh . . . poosh . . . poosh . . .

He dialed in a higher frequency and listened.

. . . roosh . . . roosh . . . roosh . . .

Still higher.

. . . floosh . . . floosh . . . floosh . . .

He turned up the volume. The new Russian reactor coolant pumps on the AKULA class made that sound.

. . . FLOOSH . . . FLOOSH . . . FLOOSH . . .

He keyed his mike.

"Conn, Sonar, trace on broadband bearing three four seven is definite AKULA class, bearing rate left and picking up. Contact is closing, approaching CPA. Recommend course one eight zero to get a second leg."

"Sonar, Conn, aye," Culverson replied in his headset. "Designate the new contact Target One. I'm coming around now to one eight zero to the left."

"Conn, Sonar," Dawson said to his microphone, "recommend coming around to the *right*. You'll be pointing at the contact. Otherwise you could hit him—"

"No, we're coming around to the left. Better to hit him than loose him in the baffles. Skipper's orders."

Dawson shook his head, this was how underwater collisions happened.

The word to man tracking stations spread throughout the ship by the watchstanders. The tracking teammembers hurried to their stations.

In the control room Culverson was programming the fire-control solution to Target One into the weapons in tubes three and four when Captain Harrison Toth IV arrived and looked over his shoulder. Culverson looked up at Toth, in his late forties, portly and bald. Not exactly a thing of beauty, but after coming up through the ranks as a former sonar chief he knew more about submarines than just about anyone in the fleet. He also never let his officers forget it. But for all Culverson's gripes about Toth, he felt relieved to see him on the Conn this day.

WESTERN ATLANTIC
FS *VLADIVOSTOK*

Captain Dmitri Krakov held onto the handrail of the periscope well as the AKULA-class fleet submarine *Vladivostok* tossed in the sea off the continental shelf of the United States. *Vladivostok* had been at her hold-coordinate off the city of Norfolk, Virginia, for some twenty hours, rolling and pitching at periscope depth, waiting for any further mission directive. During the last week the crew had become increasingly edgy, and no wonder. So far Krakov had been unable to tell them exactly what their mission was. He wasn't sure himself.

Now he tapped the deck officer on the shoulder to ask for the periscope. The junior lieutenant quickly moved away from the scope, and Krakov grasped the horizontal periscope grips somehow reassured by the feel of the antiskid etching on the cylindrical grips. He put his eye on the rubber of the eyepiece, still warm from the deck officer's face, and looked out at the waves splashing and spraying over the periscope-view. If it was sickening to stand in the control compartment in these tossing seas, it was worse looking out the periscope. A queasy stomach was a hell of a condition for a submariner, but there it was.

Krakov waved the deck officer to take the periscope back. He was as impatient as his crew. More so. Like Vlasenko, he had been aboard the *Leningrad* in 1973, but unlike Vlasenko he had not felt in conflict over the sinking of the American submarine. He was, after all, a military man, raised and trained to destroy the enemy, and the enemy had been . . . how soon some forgot . . . the Americans. The politicians had had their way and now the country was being disarmed, destroying its capacity to defend itself. He had long had such feelings, but under the tutelage of Admiral Novskoyy his feelings had not only been kept alive, they had been hardened. It was thanks to Novskoyy that he had risen through the ranks to gain his own command the previous year. The admiral was the man he most admired, most trusted to do what was best and right for him, and for the future of his troubled country. Indeed, he felt very much toward the admiral as a son might toward a father—his own having died when he was just entering his teen-age years. It was because of his admiration for Novskoyy that he had chosen the navy and submarine service. If Admiral Novskoyy wanted him here, he had his reasons, and that was good enough for Captain Krakov. Captain . . . he relished the sound of it, and the responsibility that went with it. He loved it, all of it . . . except, of course, the secret miseries his stomach still underwent. Well, nothing was perfect . . .

He thought now of the ultrasecret loading of the SSN-X-27, listed on the inventory as an "exercise unit," loaded in its canister in the number-four torpedo tube. He thought of the nursing of the ship's mechanical and electrical system in the months prior to this sudden deployment. He thought of the deployment itself, so obviously planned with their food loadout and equipment maintenance, but without immediate warning in the hours before the order to depart the pier.

Krakov felt sure that the long, tortuous hours at periscope depth would soon be rewarded. And in a special way that along with the legendary Admiral Alexi Novskoyy, he would be called on to play an historic role. The thought of it was strong enough to overcome even his rebellious stomach.

ARCTIC OCEAN
BENEATH THE POLAR ICECAP

Devilfish had arrived at coordinate A21.2-53.6 on top-secret Chart Z1, the position relayed by Donchez. Her position was drawn on the chart on the navigation table. The anticipated coordinate of the OMEGA was shown as an orange dot.

Pacino leaned over the chart in the navigation alcove, aware of the ghostly moan of the SHARKTOOTH sonar beams illuminating their way in the ice rafts and stalactites ahead, OOD Stokes giving slight rudder orders to the helm to steer the ship around the pressure ridges, and the creaking of the ice around them as the masses of ice rafts shifted and ground against each other.

The position report from Donchez had given the OMEGA's approximate position, but even drawing a 30-mile circle around the reported position had not led to a detection. The satellite coordinate must have been subject to some kind of error. There were no sonar detects on the OMEGA on broadband, and none on any of the guessed narrowband frequency gates they were searching in.

Was the OMEGA gone? Or was he going about this the wrong way? Instead of searching for the OMEGA, should he be searching for a polynya? Pacino walked to the SHARKTOOTH sonar console.

"Energize the topsounder," he told Stokes.

Stokes nodded and dialed in a rotary switch that activated the ultra-high-frequency hydrophones on top of the sail, which pinged upward, and "listened" for two pings—the first a reflection off the bottom of the ice, the second a reflection off the top. The comparison of the two showed distance to the ice overhead as well as its thickness.

"Looks like a pressure ridge above now, sir," Stokes drawled. "Thick ice. One-hundred-fifty feet."

Pacino called over the Junior Officer of the Deck, Lieutenant Brayton.

"JOOD, establish a zigzag search of this area for thin ice." Pacino drew a square around the OMEGA's reported position three miles on a side. "Do a search in this block, then search in blocks further outward from the position. Keep plotting ice thickness. And notify me the instant you've got thin ice."

Before Pacino left the control room, he glanced over at the SHARKTOOTH's topsounders. Still thick ice. 125 feet.

The possibility of not finding the OMEGA before she turned around and returned to port suddenly hit Pacino hard—the aching in his neck and shoulders feeling like knives going through him. Knives wielded by one Alexi Novskoyy . . .

All through the night *Devilfish* moved back and forth under the ice, the secure pulse topsounder clucking, finding only thick ice and pressure ridges.

At 0810 GMT *Devilfish* had to go down to 350 feet to avoid a deep pressure ridge. Back in the control room, Pacino watched in frustration as the ice got thicker. 90 feet. 120 feet. 130 feet. He glanced at the chart, seeing that this was the furthest block to the east they had yet tried. Obviously the east side of the OMEGA position would turn up nothing but thick ice. It was hopeless. Pacino marked on the chart in bold pencil the area to avoid on the east side and again summoned the JOOD.

"Just thick ice here. Get us back west, to this area. Maybe we'll get lucky and find the polynya there."

Brayton plotted a course to get the ship to the new search sector.

"One-hundred-fifty feet, thick ice," Stokes called out from the SHARKTOOTH console. Brayton moved up beside him and told him the new course. Stokes nodded, giving the overhead-ice-thickness readout a grimace before making the rudder order. He looked over to the helmsman. "Helm, left fifteen degrees rudder, steady course two seven zero."

After several minutes, for a split second, the ice-thickness readout on the SHARKTOOTH sloped from 145 feet down to five. But as the ship came around, the ice thickness grew back to 175 feet.

"Get back to zero nine zero," Pacino ordered.

Stokes understood. "Helm, shift your rudder!"

"Shift my rudder, helm aye, my rudder is right fifteen degrees, passing course zero one five to the right, no ordered course, sir."

"Aye, helm," from Stokes.

Pacino patted Stokes on the back as they watched the ice thickness, at the same time Pacino wondering if it had been only a phantom reflection from a void in the ice. But as they got under the thick part of the pressure ridge the ice thickness once again sloped down, from 155 to under five feet in less than thirty seconds. It was an inverted cliff overhead. *The polynya.*

"Helm, steady as she goes," Stokes said, trying to contain his excitement.

And *Devilfish* sailed out from under the pressure ridge to the underside of a wide flat lake of thin ice that stretched on for almost four thousand yards. Pacino allowed himself to believe. This had to be it.

"JOOD, map the polynya," Stokes called to Brayton, who turned on the plot table in the forward starboard corner of the control room. Actually the table was more a flat box with a glass top. Inside the box was a device that received inputs from the ship's gyro-and-speed indicator and moved inside the box in scale to the ship's motion in the sea. The device shined a small crosshair upward to the glass. Brayton taped down a large sheet of tracing paper to the glass top and began to plot blue dots on the paper at the crosshair-light's position every minute-mark of the chronometer. As the ship continued east, the ice remained thin, and Brayton continued with blue dots, connecting them with blue line segments.

Finally, two and a half miles east, the ice became thick again, coming down in craggy inverted mountains overhead until it was 190 feet thick. As the boat moved from thin ice to thick,

Brayton marked the crosshair and began to plot the dots in orange with orange dashes connecting them and indicating thick ice.

With Brayton's directions Stokes was able to drive the ship in a cloverleaf pattern to explore the boundaries of the polynya—a procedure that could be vital to the ship's survival . . . if there was a fire or flooding *Devilfish* would have to try to make it back to the polynya and surface through the ice. It was essential to know its shape so in an emergency with a loss of the top-sounder the captain could make an educated guess where the thin ice was by using the plot table.

It was low-tech, dating back to the 1950s, but it worked and would continue to work even if the computers died.

Finally Pacino ordered the ship to bare steerageway under the polynya, affixed his headphone and boom microphone and climbed the step up to the Conn.

"Sonar, Captain," he said into the microphone, "we're under thin ice at a two-and-a-half-by-three-mile polynya. The OMEGA may be surfaced here. Use maximum positive deflection/elevation and check for signs of him."

Pacino stared at the sonar panel on the Conn console as he flipped through the displays with the selector keypad.

The screen was blank. They were alone.

"Conn, Sonar," the headphone intoned, "even with max D/E selection we have no trace of a broadband detect on the OMEGA."

"What about narrowband?" Pacino pressed.

"Cap'n, Sonar, the towed array is dragging at this speed, but it's still negative."

The son-of-a-bitch either wasn't at this polynya or had moved on, Pacino decided. As the ship cruised at two knots, Stokes keeping it under the thin ice, Pacino returned to the navigation table to try to figure the next search-step. Maybe there was a new intelligence message in the satellite waiting to tell him the OMEGA had gone or been spotted elsewhere. No, an ELF transmission would have called him up from the deep if that were the case.

Which meant . . . the OMEGA still had to be on the surface.

Pacino reached into the overhead and grabbed the control ring for the number-two periscope.

"Lookaround number-two scope," he called out.

"Depth 300 feet, speed two knots," Stokes called back.

"Up scope," Pacino said, and rotated the ring a quarter-turn. The hydraulics thunked above him as the high-pressure oil fought the sea pressure outside the ship. It seemed to take an eternity for the pole to come out of the well. The smooth stainless steel climbed up and up from the well, until the control module peeked out from the well and climbed even with Pacino's midriff. Another clunk as the hydraulics stopped.

Pacino snapped down the periscope grips and trained the view upward with the left grip.

Nothing but darkness, until the view was almost directly overhead. And then there was a faint light, a glow from the thin ice above.

"Off'sa'deck, bring us up slowly to one five zero feet. Two knots."

Stokes made the orders.

Pacino rotated the periscope in slow circles, looking overhead, trying to see any sign of broken ice, any sign of the OMEGA. His earpiece crackled.

"Conn, Sonar, we have a transient, no, a whole lot of transients at bearing two seven five."

Pacino strained to see. Two seven five was on the aft-port quarter. Sonar could be hearing an ice raft collapsing the polynya. The polynya might not last if the two ice rafts on either side started to move together. The ice could crush a submarine hull if she was unlucky enough to wait too long on the surface. Maybe the OMEGA had heard the ice shifting and had submerged to avoid trouble . . .

Something dark was blocking out the top of Pacino's periscope view, now rotated up to the maximum, about seventy degrees from the horizontal. Not completely upward but almost.

"Conn, Sonar," Pacino's earpiece crackled, "we've got . . . broadband steam noises . . . definite near-field effect . . . transient broadband steam noises! Conn, there's a submerged contact directly overhead!"

"Sonar, Conn, aye," Pacino called, straining his eyes to see upward as the dark spot on the periscope view enlarged and became a line and then a blot that blocked out half the light from the surface. Pacino ordered *Devilfish* deeper so he could see the shape.

Fifty feet lower was not enough to see either end of the behemoth that was above him, but any deeper would cut off the light.

This had to be the OMEGA, he decided, and it was the biggest submarine he could have imagined. It dwarfed *Devilfish*. There must be room for at least ten Piranha-class submarines inside that huge hull. How could he hope to defeat something that big and invulnerable? And then he reminded himself that inside that . . . monster was the man who had killed his father. The same man that now threatened him, his crew and the ship that he loved.

When he looked away from the periscope he saw that the eyes of the men and officers were on him. He was, after all, the captain, and they were trained to trust him so that it had become a matter of instinct. They also had, short of mutiny, no alternative. There was the temptation to talk to them, to explain, but that was not his role.

Pacino put his eye back on the periscope and called to Stokes.

"Off'sa'deck, I have the Conn. Man silent battlestations. Rig ship for ultraquiet. Flood tubes one and two and open the outer doors. Spin the Mark 50's in tubes one, two, three and four. And prepare to hover."

As Stokes got busy, Pacino looked up at the OMEGA, which he could not hear until he was close enough to touch it. For a moment he wished Donchez had simply ordered him to sink the OMEGA outright, but then realized he couldn't do that. Don't shoot unless shot at, was the order. So if the OMEGA shot a torpedo at them . . .

"Attention fire-control team," Pacino announced, "the OMEGA is surfaced at the polynya above. Designate the OMEGA Target One. We will position ourselves directly under Target One. We will come up on the hovering system with the maximum rate and hit Target One's bottom. We'll get deep again and monitor Target One's actions. If Target One shoots at us, we will have verified hostile intentions, as COMSUBLANT has asked us to verify. And if that is the case, we will put Target One on the bottom . . ." Pacino looked around the room. "If Target One does nothing or attempts to communicate with us, we will need to make a decision, whether her actions are genuinely friendly or a deception. All right, carry on."

And what the hell do I do if the OMEGA refuses to be provoked, Pacino asked himself. Put a torpedo in the water? If the Russian could not be provoked, he would have no authorization to shoot it. The order to shoot would be unlawful. All right, you bastard, give me an excuse. Don't make me make one.

Pacino turned back to periscope and positioned the ship at 675 feet, her aft-hull directly underneath the OMEGA at a right angle to the Russian, the OMEGA pointed north and *Devilfish* pointed east. He was looking back aft at the OMEGA hull, which was above his own reactor compartment. That way any possible contact would spare the periscope and the sail, both of which he might need later to break through the ice of the polynya.

ARCTIC OCEAN
POLYNYA SURFACE
FS *KALININGRAD*

Captain Vlasenko opened his locker, hoping his service pistol was there. Or had he left it behind? Yes, he must have left it in his apartment, it was mostly ceremonial. Perhaps he had avoided wearing it since those days on the *Leningrad*, an unconscious attempt to distance himself from Novskoyy's affectations.

What he intended to do would be much harder without a handgun. Perhaps impossible. But this had to stop, and the only way to stop it was to remove the admiral from control of the ship. From overhead Vlasenko heard the sound of a mast rising up, reminding him of Novskoyy and the communications console. He had waited long enough. If the admiral actually intended to launch an attack, he could order it to commence any minute.

Vlasenko had tried hard to convince himself that this deployment was just an exercise. But seeing Novskoyy cover his papers with the chart, and the chart itself—how could he deny such evidence to the contrary? The operation profile in the red binder had chilled his blood.

The evening before, Vlasenko had gone to the control compartment to check out the weather through the periscope and found that Novskoyy had gone and had taken his stacks of messages with him. While Novskoyy was still gone, one message had come in. Vlasenko had pulled the message out of the discharge tray and the deck officer, Captain-Lieutenant Ivanov, had tapped his shoulder, telling him not to touch any of the admiral's messages. Vlasenko had ignored Ivanov.

The message was a lightning bolt through his guts. It was from the *Alexander Nevsky*, addressed to Novskoyy. *Nevsky* was a fairly new ship, an ALFA class. In his mind's eye he could still see the block letters on the crisp laser-printed page:

WILL NOT BE IN POSITION AT T-HOUR. ETA AT PORTSMOUTH, NEW HAMPSHIRE, HOLD COORDINATE IS 1230 GMT, T-HOUR PLUS 3.5. INTEND TO RENDEZVOUS LATE, ANTICIPATING FINITE POSSIBILITY THAT T-HOUR MAY BE DELAYED DUE TO WEATHER.

So it seemed that the chart was not just a theoretical plan— the *Nevsky* was on the way to a position off the U.S. coast.

And what was "T-hour?" The time of a time-on-target *assault?*

If *Nevsky* was three-and-a-half hours late at 1230 GMT, that put T-hour at 0900 GMT. But what day? Today? Tomorrow? Vlasenko had glanced at the chronometer, which read 0850 GMT. If it was today, it was in ten minutes!

Disabling the radio would stop any transmission of a go-code to launch cruise missiles. But then it would be repaired. Disable the radio after smashing all the spare parts? The *Kaliningrad* had too many back-up systems and redundant circuits, and in the computer cabinets functions were in some cases combined. You could think you were smashing the radio modules and end up disabling the ship-control system instead. Even in the best-case scenario the radio could be repaired and the go-code could be transmitted.

He could order the Operations Officer to open the small-arms locker for inspection and get an automatic pistol. Except Ivanov, the Operations Officer and Acting First Officer, was on watch in the control compartment as Deck Officer, and only he had the keys to the small-arms safe, which was to be opened only by him. Not even Captain Vlasenko could take the key without violating his own standing orders. It would surely make the admiral suspicious if he ordered Ivanov off the watch or ordered him to turn over the keys. And waiting for the normal rotation so that Ivanov was off-watch was too risky . . . the watch shifted at noon, *over three hours from now.*

Vlasenko had considered briefing his officers on what Novskoyy was apparently up to, but most were in awe—or fear—of Novskoyy. He was, after all, the Fleet Commander. An order to arrest the man would not exactly be popular in the officer's mess, and even if he did get the officers together, there was virtually no way he could do it without Novskoyy knowing about it. There was no time for persuasion, for a committee decision. It was too dangerous not to take some action now.

He hated the decision, but there was no escaping it. This was *his* problem. *His* responsibility. He took a deep breath, left the stateroom and walked aft to the third compartment and found the tool bench on the starboard side. He pulled open a cabinet and unlatched a heavy wrench from a restraining bracket.

He went back forward and climbed the long ladder to the control compartment, the heavy wrench in his right hand. He would have preferred a pistol.

He neared the upper rungs of the ladder, trying to keep the wrench from knocking against the rungs, still without a clear idea what he would do with the wrench. He could lean it in an inconspicuous place, and when the time came, when the chronometer neared 0900, he could knock Novskoyy unconscious and lock him up in the stores locker in the third compartment. With Novskoyy out of the picture, he felt reasonably confident there would be no one else to carry out his plan. With Novskoyy's need for total control of any mission, it was most likely he had issued instructions to his fleet not to fire the cruise missiles unless he sent his implementation message. Otherwise, why were they surfaced here at the polynya?

Vlasenko had two steps up to go. He heard the conversations of the control compartment clearly now, the officers at their posts. The wrench was heavy. Vlasenko's hands were wet with sweat. What if he was seen with the damned wrench? How could he explain it?

Vlasenko held the wrench behind his right leg with his right hand and proceeded to pull himself up to the landing with his left—

It was too awkward. The wrench slipped out of his hand just as Deck Officer Ivanov announced that the captain was in control. The heavy tool clattered down the ladder and landed at the base six meters below.

Novskoyy looked over at Vlasenko.

"So, Vlasenko," his hand reaching for his hip holster, "what brings you to control . . . with a wrench? Going to fix the fire-control computer? Ivanov, call security. Now!"

Ivanov looked first at Vlasenko, then Novskoyy, stunned, as his hand reached for the phone.

Novskoyy kept his service pistol trained on Vlasenko for the full two minutes it took the Security Warrant Officer to arrive in the control compartment.

Vlasenko looked to his officers, saw none was going to challenge the admiral. Who could blame them? He turned to Novskoyy.

"Sir, why are you provoking the Americans? Getting ready to attack them . . . ?" The watch officers stared, astonished, at the two men. "I saw your attack plan, Admiral—"

"It's an *exercise*, you fool. You are destroying yourself over an *exercise*. I'm afraid, Vlasenko, that you have gone quite mad. I am sorry for you, and all the years I wasted trying to make a man of you. You are not worthy of your commission."

"Admiral, your fleet doesn't move without orders from you. That's the reason for this surfacing. Your action begins in . . . five minutes? Is that when you send the message? Launch the missiles?" He was partly testing, but the look on Novskoyy's face, his lack of any rebuttal, the sound of Novskoyy's clicking off the safely on his pistol . . . it all added up to a horrible confirmation. It was the admiral, not Vlasenko, who seemed to have gone over the edge, to have gone from a threatening deployment to an actual attack mode . . .

The security officer had arrived at the landing from the ladder to the second compartment upper level. He looked at the two men, momentarily hesitating at the remarkable scene of the admiral threatening the ship's captain with a semi-automatic pistol.

"Warrant, place Captain Vlasenko under arrest." Novskoyy looked around, noting the clock. It read 0856. "Put him in the control-compartment escape pod and shut the hatch. Stand guard at the ladder, when we go deep we will transfer him to a holding cell."

"Sir, I can take the captain to the storage compartment now," Warrant Danalov said.

"No. For the moment I want him where I can be sure of his actions. Take him up, shut the hatch and stand guard. And make sure you disable the pod-disconnect circuit. We don't want the poor man blowing the bolts and rolling onto the ice. There is a better punishment for this man."

The ladder to the escape pod was three meters tall and led to a lower hatch. It was awkward for the warrant to push Vlasenko up the ladder and follow with his pistol drawn, and for a moment Vlasenko considered kicking Danalov and trying to disarm him. Except Novskoyy's gun was still levelled at him, the admiral's trigger finger in place.

Just before he opened the pod hatch and left the control room Vlasenko glanced at Deck Officer Ivanov, hoping for some sort of action. Any action. Ivanov seemed immobilized. It had all happened too fast, Vlasenko realized. Now, when it was too late, he decided he should have shown Ivanov and others the plans in Novskoyy's stateroom.

It was completely dark inside the pod. Groping for the light switch, Vlasenko felt only the clammy frozen wall of the titanium spherical-pod bulkhead. When he did manage to find the switch, he looked for some way to change the scenario being written below. He saw none.

The pod was round, about six meters in diameter, capable of holding two dozen men in an emergency. Wood benches were set against the bulkhead, but most of the occupants would stand or sit on the deck during an emergency ascent. The control station on the starboard side contained a depth gage, currently reading zero meters, and a release circuit tied into explosive bolts below. This was the circuit Novskoyy had ordered disconnected.

Vlasenko would try it anyway. He pulled the cover off a

switch marked ARM and put the switch in the ARM ENGAGE position. Below it was a lighted green button marked POD RE-LEASE. He pressed the button.

No light came on. No explosive bolts fired. As he had expected.

He returned the top switch to the NORMAL position and replaced the cover. Below the circuit was a manual release lever. He tried it, but it too was locked out from below.

One last possibility—the upper escape hatch.

The hatch was dogged shut with six heavy metal claws tied into a central ring. Vlasenko reached for the ring, startled by how cold it was, and tried to twist it.

It wouldn't budge.

Not surprising, considering that the hatch opened up to the outside, above the ice from the leading edge of the teardrop-shaped sail. When the *Kaliningrad*'s sail popped through the ice cover to the air outside, the water clinging to the metal surface had apparently frozen solid over the hatch fairing.

Not that it would have done him any good. His underway uniform would have offered slight protection from the cold. He would have died from exposure within minutes in the subzero temperature outside.

Finally Vlasenko sat on one of the pod benches. There was no ventilation in the pod, no fresh air, no heat. It was not long before he was shivering, the taste of terrible frustration acid in his mouth.

Novskoyy took his seat in the padded chair in front of the communication console. It was time to type in the message to be transmitted to his fleet.

Behind him, in the periscope well, Ivanov looked into the optics of the combat periscope, training it in slow circles, watching the storm above the *Kaliningrad*. An arctic blizzard had rolled in from the dark featureless thick overcast of the sky. The flakes were as big as bullets. Visibility was shrinking.

Below the *Kaliningrad*, a U.S. Piranha-class nuclear submarine named *Devilfish* floated to a halt, over 200 meters further below in the blackness of the frigid arctic water.

Eight thousand kilometers from the *Kaliningrad,* 120 nuclear attack submarines awaited Novskoyy's transmission.

The admiral finished typing and went over the message one last time.

---

* * * * * * * * * * MOLNIYA * * * * * * * * * *

FROM   NORTHERN FLEET COMMANDER/EMBARKED FS KALININGRAD

TO   ALL UNITS SUBMARINE TASK FORCE NF-ONE

DATE   19 DEC

TIME   0850 GMT

PURP   LAUNCH PREPARATION PER SEALED ATTACK INSTRUCTION NF-211-9

ACTION 1.   THIS MESSAGE AUTHORIZES AND ORDERS ADDRESSEES TO MAKE ALL PREPARATIONS FOR SSN-X-27 LAUNCH ON TARGETS OF PRIMARY CONTINGENCY AS LISTED IN NORTHERN FLEET SEALED ATTACK INSTRUCTION NF-211-9 OF 13 DEC.

2.   UNSEAL ATTACK PROFILE NF-211-9 AND PROGRAM SSN-X-27 MISSILE FOR PRIMARY TARGET LISTED THEREIN.

3.   ON 18 DECEMBER UNITED NATIONS INSPECTORS MONITORED DESTRUCTION OF SSN-X-27 NUCLEAR CRUISE MISSILES.

4.   CURRENT DEPLOYMENT INTENDED TO FORCE UNITED STATES TO DESTROY OWN SEA-LAUNCHED CRUISE MISSILES. WARSHOT SSN-X-27 MISSILES WITH EXERCISE-UNIT MARKINGS HAVE BEEN LOADED ABOARD NORTHERN FLEET SHIPS AS CONTINGENCY.

5.   DO NOT EXECUTE MISSILE LAUNCH UNTIL INSTRUCTED TO DO SO BY AUTHENTICATED MOLNIYA EXECUTION MESSAGE SCHEDULED FOR 0910 GMT.

6.   TRANSMITTED BY SUPREME COMMANDER, NORTHERN FLEET, ADMIRAL ALEXI NOVSKOYY.

CHAPTER
15

SUNDAY, 19 DECEMBER
O859 GREENWICH MEAN TIME

ARCTIC OCEAN
BENEATH THE POLAR ICECAP

"Captain," Stokes said, "ship is ready to hover. Depth is six seven five feet, speed zero, depth rate zero."

"Very well." Pacino stood at the periscope watching the distant glow of the ice overhead. "Attention in the fire-control team . . ."

The room quieted, the eerie silence filled only with the whine of the computers and the bass of the ventilation fans.

". . . Here we go. After we upset this guy, be ready to make the recovery and get deep. Off'sa'deck, to all spaces, rig ship for collision and prepare to report any damage. Diving Officer, engage the hovering system and give me max blow until Aux 2 is dry, report ascent rate."

This dangerous maneuver might go sour, Pacino realized. If the *Devilfish*'s hovering system failed they might rise up with a drift to the side and collide with the ice. Trying to induce your enemy to lead so you could counter-punch was a risky business. If he started the ascent from a shallower depth it might not be enough to affect the OMEGA. To a ship that massive, even a blow from *Devilfish* from a mere 200 feet would scarcely jar it.

There were just no guarantees, too many variables, too many ways his maneuver could turn against him. But to do nothing was to risk losing the OMEGA if she left the polynya and went deep. The thing was too damned quiet. He'd never catch up with it. The time was now.

Chief of the Watch Robertson at the wraparound ballast-control panel reached for the hovering joystick and pushed it to the BLOW position to put high-pressure air into the aux tank and blow out the ballast water to lighten the ship. A slight sound was perceptible above the roar of the fans, the sound of air blowing into a tank.

The digital depth gage clicked. The ascent had begun.

"Aux 2 empty, sir. Securing the blow," Robertson intoned.

Pacino snapped up the periscope grips and adjusted the control ring to lower the periscope so it would not be smashed by the ascent.

"Six hundred feet, sir," Diving Officer Lanscomb called from his seat between the planesmen. "Ascent rate five feet per second . . . seven . . . ten . . . fifteen . . ."

On the ship-control console in front of the Diving Officer the numbers on the depth gage began to spin rapidly. The deck now tilted to the port side. Pacino, behind Stokes at the forward end of the Conn, looked up at the bubble inclinometer, which showed a list of ten degrees. The sail must be dragging them into this tilted ascent. As the water flowed at great speed over the hull, the sail acted as a brake, heeling them over. Pacino grabbed a handrail set into the side of the Conn sonar console.

Now five hundred feet below the OMEGA submarine, *Devilfish* continued upward at terminal velocity, her hull level fore and aft but heeled over, her sail tilted to a fifteen-degree angle. She was a 4500-ton express elevator, roaring through the dark arctic depths toward the most advanced attack submarine in the world.

ARCTIC OCEAN
POLYNYA SURFACE

Admiral Novskoyy checked the bulkhead chronometer, set as usual to Greenwich Mean Time. As he waited for the seconds to click away till 0900, he again read his message.

Brief and official, Novskoyy thought. He typed in the next words in the sequence:

TRANSMIT SEQUENCE STATUS?

And the computer said:

READY . . .

It was time. Novoskoyy typed in:

TRANSMIT

And the computer replied:

TRANSMITTING . . .

There were now only ten minutes, until 0910, to decide whether to send the execution message for missile launch to his fleet. Novskoyy had told Dretzski at the Severomorsk shipyards that this deployment was to force U.S. compliance with his demands for total destruction of their nuclear weapons. And he had believed it, at least up to a point. He had also acknowledged to himself that if necessary he would take the next step, as he had done all those years ago against the USS *Stingray*. Well, his ships were deployed, the mole, General Tyler, had already gone to lengths to convince the U.S. authorities that this was merely another exercise. Would they seriously believe a sudden reversal, believe that the threat was real? Certainly not from Tyler. And certainly not from a Russian admiral. Never again would he and his forces have such an opportunity. Had he ever, in fact, really believed it would not come to more than a deployment?

As the *Kaliningrad*'s multifrequency antenna began transmitting the stand-by order to the COSMOS 21 communications satellite, Novskoyy doubted he would need the ten minutes to decide whether to follow up with the execution message for missile launch. The decision was made.

ARCTIC OCEAN
BENEATH THE POLAR ICECAP

The aux tank remained full of air, acting like a hot-air balloon, driving *Devilfish* screaming up to the surface toward the OMEGA.

"Four hundred feet, Cap'n." Chief Lanscomb said from the Diving Officer seat. "Ascent rate 20 feet per second and steady."

Less than 20 seconds, Pacino thought. Twenty seconds to . . . what?

"Two five zero feet, sir," Lanscomb called out. "Depth rate twenty-two feet per second ascent rate. Two hundred feet, twenty-three feet per second . . ."

"One five zero feet sir, twenty-three feet per second." Lanscomb said.

It was the last thing Pacino heard before the collision.

WESTERN ATLANTIC
F.S. *VLADIVOSTOK*

The Communications Officer at the radio console caught Captain Krakov's eye. Something was coming over the periscope antennae. The flashing red light on the console meant it was coming in on the emergency frequency.

A shot of adrenaline overcame the nausea Krakov had been feeling.

The Communications Officer pulled the printout from the discharge slot and handed the message to the captain.

"Deck Officer," Krakov said after reading it, "spin up the SSN-X-27 cruise missile. Keep the periscope up for communication reception, and alert me to any incoming *molniya*. The First

Officer and I will retrieve the attack plan and authenticator package from the war safe."

"Sir"—the Deck Officer could barely get out the words—"is this a drill or . . . ?"

Krakov looked at his First Officer Anatoly Tupov, holding up a hand before he could speak.

"No," Krakov said, "it is not a drill."

Krakov and Tupov hurried to the captain's stateroom, down the ladder and around a corner, in the door and behind a locker cabinet to the war safe. The outer combination was Krakov's. He spun the tumbler, his hands sweaty, and on the second try opened the safe.

As he stood back he heard the shipwide announcement:

"BATTLESTATIONS MISSILE! BATTLESTATIONS MISSILE! THIS IS NOT A DRILL, REPEAT, THIS IS NOT A DRILL!"

The inner-safe combination belonged to Tupov. Tupov had more trouble with the tumbler. The safes were configured this way so as to prohibit one man alone access to the war-authentication codes. With an authenticator packet from the inner safe, someone could send a fake message to launch a nuclear attack or send a fake cease-fire message after a valid attack order. Novskoyy's message to begin preparations could have been sent by anybody with a radio on their emergency frequency. But the execution message, when it came, would need the exact combination of numbers and letters inside the foil packet marked NF-008. All authenticators were at all times under two-man control or locked in a double-combination safe. If the execution message was complete with the authenticator, the message was valid.

Krakov handed First Officer Tupov the authenticators, bound together in a brick. While Tupov searched for NF-008, Krakov opened the sealed attack order. Inside the wax-sealed envelope was a single sheet of paper with an introductory paragraph at the top stating the general conditions for a release, including the requirement of a *molniya*. Krakov skimmed it and dropped down to the meat of the profile, the computer-printed instruction for their primary target:

VICTOR III HULL NUMBER 29

FS *VLADIVOSTOK*

PRIMARY TARGET:	NORFOLK, VIRGINIA, USA
	NORFOLK NAVAL STATION
	SUBMARINE BERTHING AREA
	PIER SEVEN
TIME DELAY AFTER	
TRANSMISSION:	60 SECONDS

The latitude and longitude of the primary target were given to the tenth of a second of arc.

By the time Krakov and Tupov returned to the control compartment with the red foil authenticator packet the expectant crewmembers were assembled at their stations.

"Missile status?" Krakov asked the Weapons Officer.

"Missile power engaged, gyro on, fuel cell nominal and pressurized, target program ready to accept coordinates."

Krakov handed over the latitude and longitude of the U.S. Navy base. "Program the 27 for primary target."

Nothing to do now but to wait for the communications console to show its red flashing light, which would signify transmission of the *molniya* execution message.

But the *molniya* did not come. At 0912 GMT the *molniya* was two minutes late.

"Status of the missile," Krakov called impatiently to the Weapons Officer.

"Nominal, sir. Still green board for launch. Missile remains on ship's power."

"Shift the missile to internal power."

"Aye, Captain," the Weapons Officer replied, and proceeded to manipulate his console. "Missile on internal power, sir."

"Very good," Krakov said, looking at his watch for the sixth time in two minutes.

ARCTIC OCEAN
POLYNYA SURFACE

Novskoyy had less time than he thought to prepare the second
message ordering the missile launch.

The next seconds occurred in slow motion.

Novskoyy, a hand on the radio console to help him stand, had
partially gotten up when the whole ship seemed to jump. It was
not as if he were thrown—it was more as though the railing
surrounding the periscope well flew up and hit him in the midsection. He felt helpless as his body, caught below its center of
gravity, flipped over the railing, over the deck of the periscope
stand, his body still rotating. As the aft periscope pole came
toward him, he was almost horizontal. When he hit the pole it
smacked him squarely in the buttocks and his lower back.

He had a brief impression of sliding down the periscope pole
to the deck, and of the deck seeming at odds with gravity. It had
become so tilted over that it was no longer a deck.

His head hit the deck with a crack, his vision dissolved in a
world of blue and orange sparks, he felt liquid in his mouth,
tasting coppery—and then all was black.

WESTERN ATLANTIC OCEAN
USS *BILLFISH*

Commander Harrison Toth IV stepped up to the periscope stand
of the USS *Billfish*, shouldering aside the heavy curtain surrounding the periscope stand that was used to screen out the
glow from the control-room instruments when the room was
rigged for black. The space outside the curtain was never
completely black, illuminated as it was by the light from
the fire-control consoles, the gages of the ship control panel
and the light from the meters on the ballast-control panel. Together, the light leaks were enough to interfere with the Officer
of the Deck's night vision.

The OOD was pressed up against the number-two periscope
peering into the black night. Although it was 0900 Zulu, Green-

wich Mean Time, the local time was 0400, and dawn in December came late even this far at sea. 0703 was the time the status board stated for sunrise.

Billfish rocked in the rough seas, trailing the AKULA Russian attack submarine *Vladivostok* at periscope depth 153 miles east of Norfolk, Virginia. The AKULA, designated Target One, was also at periscope depth.

"Very well, FT," the OOD was saying to the Fire-control Technician of the Watch, who had come up to the Conn. Toth tensed, knowing this could be a precursor to a problem with fire-control, something he didn't need now with the AKULA so close.

"Captain, sir," the OOD said, not removing his face from the periscope eyepiece, "weapon power has been applied to the Mark 49 torpedoes in tubes three and four for over an hour now, sir. The gyros are heating up. The FT wants to deenergize them."

"What's the status of tubes one and two?" Toth was reluctant to turn off the torpedoes with the Russian in weapons range.

"Dry loaded, Mark 49 Hullbuster Mod Alphas, both tubes, sir."

"Get a recommendation from the Weapons Officer. I want my six shooter loaded when I'm in the same corral with this guy."

"Should we flood one and two, sir? We could spin up their gyros—"

"No. Flooding the tubes will just make noise. Could alert our friend up ahead—"

"Conn, Sonar," the headset to sonar boomed in Toth's ear, "transients from Target One . . . water noises . . . flooding a tank . . . hull popping . . . Target One's probably going deep . . . Conn, Sonar, confirmed. RPM's going up on Target One's screw. He's speeding up and going deep."

"Sonar, Conn, aye," Lieutenant Culverson replied into his own headset's boom microphone, glancing at Captain Toth. "Sir?"

Toth stared at the line of dots on Pos Two.

"Take us down below the thermal layer and rig control for white."

"Diving Officer, make your depth five four six feet," Culverson called out. "Lowering number-two scope."

The OOD put on his red goggles and ordered the room lit. The curtain was pulled aside, and blinding white light flooded the room.

The ship's angle increased to ten degrees as Culverson ordered the Diving Officer to go down to 546 feet. As the ship passed 300 feet, the thick steel hull emitted a creaking groan, punctuated by a loud pop.

Target One was a mere 1500 yards ahead on the port bow.

FS *VLADIVOSTOK*

The deck of the *Vladivostok* took on a steep angle as she departed periscope depth for her 50-meter missile-firing depth.

Captain Krakov was furious that he still had not received the expected message from Admiral Novskoyy to execute missile launch.

"Captain," Tupov said, "we should come back up to periscope depth and await a transmission."

"Anatoly, this must be a transmitter problem. An American ship may have gotten to Novskoyy on the *Kaliningrad*. There won't *be* a transmission. We can't contact the other ships in the fleet without violating radio silence. I know the admiral's intent. We must proceed. Execute launch on primary target as per the 0850 GMT preparation order."

USS *BILLFISH*

As *Billfish* levelled out at 546 feet the broadband sonar trace on the video repeater winked out. Target One had just vanished. Commander Toth frowned as his headset earphone crackled.

"Conn, Sonar, deflection/elevation to Target One is very high, plus ten degrees. Signal-to-noise ratio is dropping fast. We've lost him . . ."

"Sonar, Captain, is it possible Target One is still above the thermal layer?"

"Conn, Sonar . . . yes."

Toth gestured to Culverson with his thumb. *Get back up.*

FS *VLADIVOSTOK*

"Depth fifty meters, sir," the Deck Officer reported.

Krakov turned to the weapons console. "Status of the 27?"

"Run check complete," Weapons Officer Vasily Geronmyy said into his console. "System checks are satisfactory. Chronometer input satisfactory. Navigation fix input satisfactory. Gyro spinup complete."

"Mark the target readback," Krakov ordered.

Geronmyy typed into his console and read the computer reply.

"Norfolk Naval Station, Submarine Piers, ground zero. Airburst at fifty meters."

Krakov nodded.

"Variable yield setting?"

"One point one megatons." Geronmyy turned to look at Krakov. "The targeting manual also gives us direct-hit credit for taking out the American Navy's submarine headquarters and the Atlantic Fleet headquarters. And most of the adjacent Naval Base and Naval Air Station runways and aircraft should be in ruins."

"Open the outer door," Krakov ordered.

USS *BILLFISH*

"Conn, Sonar, we've regained Target One, signal-to-noise ratio above threshold. Contact is definitely above the thermal layer."

"Sonar, Captain, aye," Toth responded. "Anything more from Target One? Anything unusual?"

"Conn, Sonar, yes. Transients from Target One now . . . scraping noise . . . Conn, Sonar, Target One is opening a hull . . . possible torpedo tube outer door."

Toth swore under his breath. When he was a sonarman he would know for sure, not have to guess. Was it a torpedo tube door or not? It didn't make a hell of a lot of difference. The contact could be dumping garbage, pumping his sanitary tanks, dumping some bilge oil . . . It wasn't exactly appropriate to consider dumping trash an offensive action. Toth could almost hear his own court martial.

"Sonar, Captain, did he open a fucking torpedo tube door or not?"

"Conn, Sonar . . . yes."

The sonar chief still sounded unsure.

What if this guy was about to shoot him? Did he really have to wait for the Russian to launch a weapon before shooting back? Of course he had to. Rules of Engagement said so, gut feel or not.

Toth looked over at Pos Two. The solution was set into the Mark 49 torpedoes in tubes three and four, overheating as they were. But it would take the 49s in tubes one and two a full five minutes to spin up.

Commander Harrison Toth opened his mouth to order the weapons in tubes one and two be powered up. Just in case.

FS VLADIVOSTOK

"Missile on internal power, sir."

"Stand by to fire on my mark," Krakov commanded.

"Standing by, sir."

"Five. Four. Three. Two. One. Mark!"

"Fire!" the Weapons Officer called, punching a fixed-function key.

The ship shuddered, Krakov's eardrums popped.

USS BILLFISH

"Conn, Sonar, launch transient from Target One!"

"What the hell was that?" Toth demanded. Was this a torpedo in the water or not?

"Sonar, Captain, did Target One launch or not?"

No answer for a moment, then: "Conn, Sonar, no torpedo in the water, but it was definitely a launch transient . . ."

A dry fire? Toth thought.

"Sonar, Captain, was that a water slug?"

"Conn, Sonar, no, but . . . we suspect a misfire of a weapon.

More transients from Target One. He may be lining up another tube."

"Any sign of a counter-detection? Does he know we're here?"

"No."

Then who the hell is he shooting? Toth thought. *Unless it's not a torpedo . . . in which case it might be . . .* Oh God *. . . a cruise missile!*

CHAPTER
16

19 DECEMBER, 0914 GREENWICH MEAN TIME

Western Atlantic Ocean
FS *Vladivostok*

"What happened?" Captain Krakov was furious.

"Relief valve lifted on the tube, Captain. The weapon is still in the tube. Warrant's working on it now," the Weapons Officer reported.

"Can we shift the weapon to one of the other tubes?"

"Only tube four is set up for the SSN-X-27, Captain."

"How long?"

"An hour to replace the valve, sir."

"No. Reset the relief valve and line up to fire again."

"Sir, it may work, but odds are it'll just lift the valve again."

"Today we shall test the odds," Krakov said. "Reset the damn valve. Shut the outer door, drain the tube, bring the weapon back onto ship power and do a recheck. Thirty seconds!"

Damned shipyard, Krakov thought. A ten-million-ruble cruise missile crippled by a forty-ruble relief valve. Now the power surge from reconnecting the missile might blow its circuit and leave him with a useless, inert bomb.

"Status," Krakov demanded impatiently.

"Tube drained. Missile power is external. System checkout is . . . complete . . . no errors. Weapon is nominal, sir!"

"Flood the tube, open the door and reinitialize the launch sequence." Goddamned relief valve, Krakov thought. This time it had better work.

USS BILLFISH

"Sonar, Captain, what's the status?" Toth shouted into the boom microphone.

"Conn, Sonar, several transients from Target One. Sounds like he shut the tube door and drained the tube."

He must be lining up for another try, Toth thought. Or it *could* still be an exercise. Did he have enough evidence to justify shooting the Russian? The Rules of Engagement still said no—

"Conn, Sonar, Target One has reflooded his tube . . . outer door coming open now . . ."

"Screw it. Snapshot, tube three, Target One!" Toth commanded.

FS VLADIVOSTOK

"Missile on internal power, sir."

"Stand by to fire on my mark," Krakov commanded.

"Standing by, sir." The Weapons Officer was on the phone to the torpedo warrant officer in *Vladivostok*'s first compartment in case the relief valve lifted again.

"Five. Four. Three. Two. One. *Mark!*"

"Fire!" the Weapons Officer called, punching the fixed-function key.

For the second time that morning the ship shuddered, and for the second time Captain Krakov's eardrums popped.

Before Krakov could ask if the weapon was away, the pressure pulse of seawater had started the ejection of the waterproof canister holding the SSN-X-27 nuclear-tipped cruise missile. As the missile travelled the length of *Vladivostok*'s number-four torpedo tube, the missile's accelerometers tied into the central processors reported the launch acceleration.

Two g's. Twenty meters per second squared.

The missile's onboard computer compared the two g's with the setting engraved in its read-only-memory software. The setting was 1.8 g's. The onboard computer recorded its satisfaction.

And armed the rocket-motor igniter.

Destination: Norfolk.

USS *BILLFISH*

Toth's "snapshot" order was an automatic-action command, a quick reaction torpedo shot usually used only when fired on by a hostile submarine. It had been worked out for times when battle stations were not manned and only the OOD and fire-control technician were on hand. Ironically, the snapshot tactic had been derived from several detailed studies of Russian submarine tactics.

Without further orders, Lieutenant Culverson switched Pos One to line-of-sight mode and twisted the solution knobs to match the bearing and rate to Target One, then moved two steps aft to Pos Three and keyed the weapon in tube one to accept the solution.

Set! Culverson said to himself.

The Chief of the Watch had picked up the P.A. Circuit One system mike and shouted into it, distorting the announcement.

"SNAPSHOT TUBE THREE!"

The P.A. Circuit One order was for the torpedomen so they would know why one of their tubes was being remotely fired. It notified sonar, so the sonar technicians could prepare to track the weapon. And it automatically manned battlestations.

Culverson reached for the trigger and rotated it to nine o'clock—the STANDBY position.

"Stand by!" he said, talking more to himself than to anyone in the control room.

He pulled the trigger on the firing panel, set flush between the Pos Two and Pos Three consoles, past twelve o'clock to three o'clock—the FIRE position.

"Fire!" he called out.

The deck jumped, the pressure-pulse of the torpedo room's air-ram piston slammed the crew's ears. With seeming detachment Toth checked the chronometer. Not bad. Culverson had pooped out the weapon in fourteen seconds. That had to be a COMSUBLANT record.

The control room was already starting to fill with the battle-stations watchstanders. Some looked haunted and grimly nervous, some simply drugged with sleep; the latter woke up quickly when they realized this was no drill.

"Conn, Sonar, own ship unit . . . normal launch," Toth's earpiece intoned.

With the same odd detachment, Toth gave the next order, wondering briefly about his peculiar feelings, or lack of them, as if he were watching the scene from far away.

"Snapshot, tube four, Target One."

The same sequence happened, looking so similar it could have been an instant replay. Culverson hunched over the Pos Three console, still standing up, ready to steer the weapons.

"Conn, Sonar, own ship's second fired unit, normal launch. First fired unit active, now homing. Second fired unit active."

"Detect on one! Acquisition, unit one, sir!" Culverson was flushed. "Detect on two . . . detect . . . detect . . . acquisition, unit two, sir! Loss of wire-guide continuity on both, Skipper!"

The first explosion rocked the ship, heeling the deck over to a 15-degree angle to starboard. The second explosion came as the ship was righting herself, preventing her from heeling over to port.

Toth allowed himself the beginning of a smile. Until sonar came over his headset.

"Conn, Sonar, explosions from Target One and hull breakup . . . wait . . . Conn, we have . . . oh God, a *rocket* motor ignition from bearing to Target One!"

Toth's half-smile drooped into slack-mouthed shock.

His snapshot had been too late to stop the AKULA's missile-launch.

USS DEVILFISH

The impact of *Devilfish*'s collision with the OMEGA had thrown all twenty-one control-room watchstanders into the overhead, Pacino included. A nasty cut showed on the Diving Officer's forehead from flying up into the inboard induction manifold. Supply Officer Alan Crane was barely conscious, lying in an uncoordinated heap under the Time Bearing Plot table.

Pacino was only bruised, he had grabbed a handhold on the Conn's sonar console. The ship had rolled into an odd port-list with a severe aft-trim, canting the deck 20 degrees to port and 15 degrees aft, leaving the forward starboard corner of the room at least ten feet higher than the after-port corner.

The room was eerily silent, except for a slight hiss from a leaking emergency air-manifold fitting.

Pacino recovered first.

"Helm, all ahead full and cavitate," he ordered. "Diving Officer, give me max down angle on the ship with fairwater and sternplanes."

"Maneuvering answers all ahead full, sir," the helmsman called, rubbing his waist where the seatbelt had taken his full weight moments before. "Screw is cavitating."

There was a groaning, scraping noise from aft and a crunching noise from above.

"Sail's scraping the ice, sir," the Diving Officer said.

"And we musta hit the OMEGA, Skipper," Stokes said, rubbing his bruised neck. "That must be the scraping sound aft."

"Stokes, check for damage, all spaces."

"Aye, sir," and Stokes pulled a phone off of the deck to his ear.

Rapier got himself to his feet, stunned after wrenching his shoulder falling onto the Pos Two console.

Pacino waited, hoping the ship could get deep again using her speed. It took a long, tense minute for the ship to respond, bumping and scraping on the ice and on the OMEGA's hull, but finally the noises and vibrations stopped and the boat picked up speed. The deck grew steep but the listing angle came off. The digital-depth gage, frozen at 125 feet since the accident, began clicking, at first slowly, then beating out a rapid staccato burst of clicks.

"Two hundred feet, sir," the Diving Officer called out. "Speed fifteen knots. No ordered course."

"Helm, all ahead flank," Pacino ordered. "Maneuvering cavitate, left-hard rudder, steady course two seven zero. Diving Officer, pull out at 1500 feet."

It was an emergency order given in a purposefully calm voice. Pacino's commands seemed to bring the crew to life, glad for orders to bring them out of their shock.

BOOM!

BOOM!

BOOM!

BOOM!

The main coolant check valves slamming the piping from the order to go to flank speed. Their descent from the ice had made a hellish cacophony. As the ship descended, the hull popping and cracking from the pressure, Pacino wondered if the OMEGA crew had started tracking them yet. Were they too in shock, wounded, not able to respond?

Okay, you bastard, Pacino thought, here I am. Come and get me.

FS *KALININGRAD*

Novskoyy's eyes were open but the pattern of the deck tiles swam in and out of focus. Slowly he moved his aching arms to get them underneath himself, pushed himself up, felt a shock of pain from his backside, where he had hit the periscope. His shoulders and head throbbed, but nothing seemed broken. He got to his feet, noticing that the list of the deck was not his senses deceiving him but evidence that something serious had happened to the *Kaliningrad*.

Something . . . what? What hit them? A problem with the polynya closing in would have been slow, an ice raft drifting toward them. Novskoyy looked at the compartment. Deck Officer Ivanov was lying face down in the periscope well, unconscious or worse. Men were climbing into the compartment from the ladder aft. The medic's assistant hurried to Ivanov, who was opening his eyes and trying to move his head.

"What happened?" Ivanov asked, grimacing.

Novskoyy didn't answer. He looked around the space at the computer screens, each one blank. The computers must have crashed from the impact. He went to the central breaker panel and switched off the master breaker switch for the combat computers, then reset it. The screens flashed for a moment, then went blank. He hoped the large frame machines were rebooting themselves.

Hurry up, Novskoyy thought, looking at the screen on the communications console. Finally it did blink back to life, the words on the screen reading:

SELF-CHECK IN PROGRESS. ONE MOMENT, PLEASE . . .

Novskoyy grimaced. A polite computer. The message vanished, replaced by a status readout. He went to the panel, where officers were again manning the consoles, Ivanov ordering the ship-control and deck officers. Novskoyy scanned the status readout, frustrated, staring at one line buried in the status display:

MULTIFREQUENCY ANTENNA: ALL CIRCUITS OPEN
NO READBACK

The impact of whatever . . . whoever . . . had hit them had either snapped off the multifrequency antenna or rendered it useless. Would he be able to transmit follow-up orders to his fleet? He hunted through the status panel, looking for the indication of the auxiliary antenna. What the computer screen read was:

UHF AUX ANTENNA: CIRCUITS NOMINAL
HYDRAULICS TO ANTENNA DISABLED

At least the UHF Aux unit was all right electrically though its hydraulics were inoperable. It would need to be raised manually with a hydraulic jack handpump. Novskoyy thought of his fleet waiting for instructions, like a pistol with the safety off and the trigger pulled almost to the firing point. The collision had forced his hand. There were no further thoughts of a diplomatic solution. His next transmission to the fleet would be the order to execute missile launch. He should never have delayed, should have given the go-code from the first. What had to happen had always laid there like an inevitability, predetermined . . .

He had finished connecting the manual hydraulic pump to the line to the UHF Aux mast hydraulic manifold when the ship abruptly shuddered.

Novskoyy looked to Ivanov, bending over the sonar console. Ivanov looked back at Novskoyy, dawning comprehension on his face. As the deck vibrated from a scraping noise below, Novskoyy hurried to the sonar console.

"What is it, Ivanov?" Novskoyy asked.

"Listen," Ivanov said.

Outside the hull, from below, came the whooshing sound of a propulsion screw, a big one, the noise growing louder even than the scraping noise. The whooshing rose to a crescendo and then passed, growing quieter. After one last shrieking scraping noise all that could be heard was the screw.

"A submarine," Novskoyy said . . . Either one of the Russian Pacific Fleet attack boats coming to stop his mission, *or*, and more likely, the American attack ship that Dretzski had alerted him to.

Four loud BOOMS reverberated from outside the hull—from the direction the intruding submarine had gone after it stopped scraping the underside of the *Kaliningrad*'s hull.

Ivanov stared at the sonar console, flipping rapidly from one graphic display in the software to another. Without looking up he gave his report to Novskoyy.

"It's an American attack submarine, Admiral. *Piranha* class. Probably up here to spy on us—"

"How could it have found us?"

"They are leaving the area at maximum RPM, sir. We must neutralize them . . ."

Novskoyy's own instructions to the Northern Fleet submarines allowed, even encouraged, the firing of a war-shot torpedo at any foreign submarine if there was a collision or clear evidence of foreign surveillance if both vessels were under the cover of the polar icecap. Ivanov knew this.

"No," Novskoyy said. The *molniya* go-code for attack still had to be transmitted to his deployed fleet.

"Sir," Ivanov said, "the intruder is getting away, we must prosecute them, your standing orders to the fleet, sir. We can return here after the American is on the bottom—"

"No. We will remain here. There is an urgent radio—"

"Sir," Ivanov persisted, "the American must be expecting an attack and will be planning to release his own weapons. Sir, isn't it a question of defending ourselves?"

Novskoyy waved an acknowledgment. By his lights, Ivanov was right. After the sinking of the American sub in 1973 the U.S. submarine fleet had no doubt been spoiling for revenge, but would the American shoot at them in what everybody considered peacetime?

He proceeded to answer his own thought . . . They would if they linked his transmissions to his attack fleet off the coast. What if they had broken the encryption codes and were reading his communications. Then they would try to sink the *Kaliningrad* before he could complete the attack *molniya* to the fleet . . .

There was no choice—the transmission would have to wait.

"Ivanov, submerge the ship, lock in the fire-control targeting instructions for the American submarine and launch a 100-centimeter Magnum to the target aim-point."

Ivanov paused. The watchstanders paused. The room's conversations died.

"Sir, a nuclear weapon could damage this ship. I'll have to overpower the reactors and use the polymer system. Would the admiral consider a 53-centimeter unit? Or several?" The conventional 53-centimeter torpedoes had conventional explosive warheads, not nuclear ones.

"Not fast enough. The *Piranha* will get away and the 53-centimeter unit would run out of fuel. Launch the Magnum and get us out of the area."

"Aye, Admiral."

USS *DEVILFISH*

"Captain, damage reports are in," Stokes said, replacing the phone handset in the cradle. "We're hurting. Evaporator and lithium bromide air conditioner are out. Just about every piping system we've got is leaking from the couplings and joints. Bilges are filling up with water—nothing the drain pump can't handle. Worst leaks look to be primary coolant, and the radiation level in the reactor compartment is climbing. But we've got full propulsion. Hovering system up forward is leaking both high pressure air and seawater. We're trying to isolate the leaks. But the hovering system is down hard. Sonar's got a real problem. The towed array is dead. We must have crushed the fiberglass fairing on top of the hull, maybe severed the cable. Total loss of narrowband sonar on Target One—"

"Status of the spherical array?"

"Still okay, sir."

"Well, we'll just have to keep tabs on Target One on broadband."

"Captain," Rapier said, turning from the Pos Two console he'd been studying, "Target One's in the baffles now. We can't hear him. Recommend you come around right or left twenty degrees and bring him out."

Pacino shook his head. Rapier frowned, not understanding.

"Mark range to the collision," Pacino ordered.

"Two thousand yards," Stokes replied, looking at the geographic plot.

Minimum weapon standoff range for the Russian's torpedoes, Pacino thought.

"Conn, Sonar," Pacino's headphone intoned, "Uh, transients now from bearing zero seven zero, edge of the starboard baffles . . . Conn, Sonar, we have a detect on an active sonar . . . it's a quick pulse-range check . . . OMEGA's transmitting Blocks-of-Wood active sonar in a beam at us, verifying our range . . ."

Good. The OMEGA had heard them and was responding. The range check was a classic Russian tactic immediately before a torpedo shot. The officers in the space, most of them wearing the same headphones Pacino wore, turned to look at him, waiting for him to get the ship out of trouble, or into it.

"Well, XO," Pacino said, "it seems the OMEGA may be hostile, after all. Are we ready to shoot?"

"Sir," Rapier said, thinking of the Russian submarines lurking in the seas off the coast of his hometown, "let's kick his ass."

FS *KALININGRAD*

The next few minutes seemed to go by in a blur, whether the result of the injury he had sustained in the collision or the stress of the moment, Novskoyy wasn't sure as he watched Ivanov and the team of officers submerge the ship and head east away from the American submarine, trying to get enough distance from it so that the safety interlocks on the Magnum torpedo would allow warhead aiming—too close and it could home in on the *launching* ship. The conversation in the space seemed to swim by Novskoyy's ears rather than register in them.

"REARGUARD sonar range to target, 1500 meters," Ivanov called out.

"Magnum torpedo loaded in tube six. Flooding tube six now," said Weapons Officer Chekechev.

"REARGUARD range to target, 2000 meters. Target range meets firing criteria. Target bearing 280, speed 65 clicks." Ivanov.

"Magnum in tube six weapon power on, gyro at nominal RPM, computer self-check complete. Target solution locked in," from Chekechev.

"Open outer door, tube six." Ivanov turned to Lieutenant Katmonov, the Ship Control Officer. "To Engine Control, overpower both reactors to 110 percent power."

Chekechev: "Tube six outer door open. Magnum fuel turbopump pressure increasing, increasing—"

"Engine Control reports both reactors at 110 percent power," reported Katmonov. "Ship's speed, 80 clicks."

"Magnum fuel pressure in limits. Computer ready indication," said Chekechev.

"Firing status?" Ivanov asked.

"Ready to fire."

"Fire tube six on my mark," Ivanov ordered. "Five. Four. Three. Two. One. *Mark!*"

"Firing six!"

The ship trembled, just slightly, as the heavy large-bore weapon left the tube.

"Engage the polymer system and report ship's speed," Ivanov ordered.

"Magnum turning to attack course."

"Polymer system engaged. Ship's speed increasing to eighty-five clicks," Katmonov intoned.

Chekechev: "Magnum steady on attack course."

Katmonov: "Ship's speed increasing to ninety clicks."

Chekechev: "Magnum speeding up to attack velocity."

Ivanov: "Status of the target?"

Chekechev: "Target no longer registers on REARGUARD. Must be on the other side of the Magnum now. Confirmed. Magnum is on the bearing to the target. Target noise masked by Magnum noise."

"Very good. Range to the aim point?"

"Aim-point range, fifteen kilometers. Ship's speed, ninety-one clicks. A record, sir."

Ivanov took it in. The most a Russian submarine had gone before was eighty clicks, at least in his memory.

Chekechev: "Aim-point range, sixteen kilometers. Four kilometers to go till outside blast-damage zone."

Katmonov: "Ship's speed, steady at ninety-one clicks."

"Target status?" Ivanov asked.

Chekechev: "Still masked by the Magnum."

"Aim point range?"

"Range to aim-point, sixteen point five kilometers."

They were going east at record speed, the polymer slipping down the metal of the hull, greasing their way through the cold water. With every passing minute they drove further from the aim-point of the Magnum torpedo, closer to safety. But at the same time they also drove further from the polynya, pushing transmission of Novskoyy's *molniya* order further into the future. He interrupted the smooth functioning of the three-man fire-control team:

"Deck Officer," he said to Ivanov, "turn the ship around and drive us back west to the polynya."

"But sir," Ivanov shot back, shocked, "that will put us in the blast zone—"

"*Turn the ship*, course, due west."

Ivanov stared at Novskoyy. Then: "Admiral, I can't do that. It means this ship will be destroyed."

USS *DEVILFISH*

"Conn, Sonar, more transients from zero seven zero . . . Conn, Sonar! Torpedo in the water! Large-bore weapon screw pattern! It's . . . Jesus, it's a Magnum!"

"Skipper," Rapier said, one hand on his earpiece, "the son of a bitch just launched a nuke at us!"

Pacino said nothing. The OMEGA had just responded as he'd hoped. This was the confrontation he'd been waiting for.

He took a deep breath and issued a string of orders.

"Helm, all stop." He watched as the speed indicator went from 34 knots to near zero, aware of the eyes on him. "Off'sa'deck, shift propulsion to the Emergency Propulsion Motor. And relay the word to maneuvering: group scram the reactor, secure all reactor main coolant pumps, engage emergency cooling, shut main steam valves one and two and secure steam to the engine room."

Rapier, standing down by the fire-control console, looked at Pacino, sweat breaking out on his forehead. Pacino had, after all, just ordered the ship to be completely shut down, the only lights remaining supplied from the battery.

Finally Stokes found his voice: "Sir, that torpedo'll be running up our ass in about three minutes. We've gotta run."

Rapier joined in, looking at the chronometer.

"Sir, we can't play possum here under the ice. With the reactor dead and no steam and without a hovering system we'll need to go two knots on the Emergency Propulsion Motor just to maintain depth control. That kind of current-draw will kill the battery in twenty minutes, maybe less. Under the ice we can't recover from that. We could try to restart the reactor right now and we'd never make it."

There was no time to argue. Pacino looked Rapier in the eyes.

"XO, when we shut down, that torpedo will never hear us. It'll go by like we're invisible. Besides, if we run we'll either hit a pressure ridge and sink from a ripped-open hull or get killed from the nuke—we can't outrun that SOB, it goes sixty god-damned knots."

Stokes' hand shook as he picked up the P.A. Circuit Seven microphone to maneuvering in the engine room and passed the orders.

As the reactor was shutdown the ventilation fans whined to a halt. The room grew immediately stuffy and lights winked out in the overhead.

The heart and lungs of the USS *Devilfish* had stopped.

She drifted south in the current, a 100-kiloton nuclear warhead crashing toward her at 60 knots.

CHAPTER
17

SUNDAY, 19 DECEMBER, 0917
GREENWICH MEAN TIME

WESTERN ATLANTIC OCEAN

The SSN-X-27 canister was buoyant, nose-light, tail-heavy. On leaving tube four of the *Vladivostok*, the canister was already going forty clicks and angling upward. Two fins had popped out from the stern of the canister as it left the torpedo tube, both fins horizontal, both slightly angled upward at their trailing edges. The nose-light canister, aided by the tail fins, rose to the surface of the Atlantic, leaving the *Vladivostok*, by then imploding and sinking to the bottom, far behind.

Launch depth had been fifty meters. It would take almost thirty seconds for the SSN-X-27 to broach the surface. Every second of those thirty was vital to the missile's success as it ran through internal checks and arming sequences. A failure on any of the dozens of logic circuits and interlocks would cause the weapon to inert itself and shut down.

But each interlock checked out.

Behind and astern of the missile, the twin detonations of *Bill-fish*'s Mark 49 torpedoes hit the *Vladivostok* amidships and forward, first blowing holes in the hulls, inner and outer, and filling a sphere thirty meters in diameter with hot expanding gases.

The gas expansion was much too slow to affect the missile. The disintegrating hull of the firing ship was also of no concern to the SSN-X-27. Long since separated from the *Vladivostok*'s fire-control system, the missile was completely independent. Autonomous.

It swam to the surface, encapsulated, waterproof. When the broach sensors indicated that the nose had broken through the waves and was touching air, the nosecone of the capsule would blow off from the action of thirty-two explosive bolts. The rest of the capsule, suspended momentarily half-submerged, half-broached, would serve as a launch pad, and the rocket motor first stage would ignite, lifting the missile out of the cylindrical capsule, which would then sink.

The SSN-X-27 would have proceeded in this fashion, oblivious to the death throes of its mother ship, if not for the shock wave that travelled at sonic velocity through the water, hitting the missile's capsule when it was just ten meters short of the surface.

But the only effect of the pressure pulse was to force the capsule to the surface a few seconds sooner.

The capsule broached.

Thirty-two explosive bolts fired the cruise missile's nosecone into the dark sky of the dawn, the fiberglass tumbling end over end, the faint moonlight, now peeking between the clouds, glinting off its orange surface with each revolution.

The computer software, knowing the next command in the sequence, lit a small grain can at the far aft-end of the solid rocket stage.

The grain can exploded into incandescence.

In a chain reaction, the solid-fuel rocket-motor ignited. Under the influence of almost 100,000 newtons of thrust, the missile lifted itself out of the elongated capsule. The capsule sank from the hot gas reaction forces.

The missile flew skyward with an acceleration of four g's that caused it to reach 600 kilometers per hour within five seconds. Three seconds later the rocket motor cut out. The missile arced over in a ballistic trajectory, feeling zero-g at the peak. On the way back down, the first-stage solid rocket-motor blew off from eight explosive bolts at an altitude of 500 meters; it was no longer needed.

The intake diffuser popped out of the underside of the missile's fuselage, ramming in the predawn Atlantic air into the suction box of the axial compressor. The high-speed air windmilled the compressor, spinning up the unit on its near frictionless journal bearings.

As the compressor speed came up to several thousand RPM, the computer processing unit amidships sensed that it was time for fuel injection. An air-driven fuel pump, also windmilled by the 400 click airspeed, pressurized the kerosene jet fuel in the fuel lines. The missile measured the pressure buildup in its fuel lines. When the compressor RPM was high enough a solenoid valve in the fuel line popped open, sending the pressurized fuel into the six-canned combustion chambers.

The air in the combustion chamber was very hot as a result of being raised to so high a pressure by the compressor vanes. With the injection of fuel, all that was needed was the lightoff of the chamber spark plugs, and black smoke came out the tail of the missile as the fuel partially burned in the cans.

The missile now activated the six-can spark plugs, the cans instantly coming up several hundred degrees in temperature, and the air fuel mixture burned at a rate just shy of explosion. The hot gases were passed into the turbine connected by a shaft to the compressor—the turbine designed to keep the compressor running during the journey.

The hot high-energy gases flew by the turbine and out the missile's aft nozzle, which sped the gases up to supersonic velocity, creating the reaction thrust. As the exhaust flowed out the nozzle, the missile felt the push of 50,000 newtons of thrust, and the jet engine was self-sustaining.

While the missile was injecting fuel into the combustion chamber cans it extended its amidships fins, horizontal square miniwings, then rotated the wings to pull out into level flight. Just in time. Altitude was a mere ten meters above the water.

At 790 kilometers per hour, the 1.1 megaton hydrogen bomb flew toward its target.

USS DEVILFISH

The engine room was the furthest aft compartment of the ship, going from the escape-trunk hatch all the way to the shaft seals near the screw and rudder. The compartment was conical and large, the biggest aboard. It was humid, miserably hot even in the arctic water, from the massive steam pipes threading their way through the space.

Maneuvering, the nuclear control room, was close to the forward bulkhead of engine room upper level on the starboard side. It was a closet-sized space filled to bursting with three control panels facing forward, a large panel on the aft wall and four watchstanders.

Nearest the door of maneuvering on the ship's centerline the throttleman stood at the steel wheel of the throttle. His panel was the steam plant control panel, his gages read steam pressures and temperatures—the heartbeat of the steam plant.

Touching the throttleman's right shoulder was the reactor operator, who sat in front of the reactor-plant control panel. It's slanting lower surface had a mock-up piping diagram of the main coolant system that showed the port-coolant loop on the left and its mirror image on the right.

In the center of the coolant system was a reactor core with a pistol-grip lever protruding from it that moved the control rods. With the plant critical, the rods only affected coolant temperature, but when the plant was shut down the rods were withdrawn to start the nuclear fission reactions that heated the main coolant water, boiling the water in the steam generators and thereby providing steam to the turbines.

The vertical section of the panel was mostly stuffed with electrical gages showing reactor-plant temperatures and pressures and the reactor-power meter, which went from zero to 150%. Above 100% the meter face was painted blood red. No naval reactor had ever been above 103% power. Much over 100%, the core would experience some fuel melting. At some level above that, say 130%, the fuel melting would get substantially worse, irradiating the crew.

Against the starboard bulkhead was the electric-plant control panel where the remote circuit breakers that channelled the electricity to ship's distribution were operated. Behind the electrical operator was the Engineering Officer of the Watch, the EOOW, a nuclear-qualified officer who supervised the watchstanders and was responsible for the engineering spaces.

The battlestations EOOW was Lieutenant Commander Matthew Delaney, a rotund red-faced man with a seemingly perpetual frown. Delaney, a deadly serious man, could be at odds with Captain Pacino over what he perceived as the sometimes not sufficient concern showed by Pacino toward the potentially dangerous reactor. After all, unlike civilian reactors with their low-power density-cores, a Navy reactor *could* blow skyhigh. Navy engineers called such a potential catastrophe a "rapid prompt critical disassembly." Delaney called it a nuclear explosion.

In the moments after the "torpedo in the water" announcement, the order to scram the plant took Delaney by surprise. An exchange of weapons with the Russian he could understand. Under the ice, it had been rumored to happen. But with an exchange of torpedoes came standard evasive tactics—all-ahead flank, cavitate the screw, run like hell at max speed until the ship was hit or the weapon exhausted its fuel.

Delaney, though assigned as the ship's engineer, was also qualified for command of a nuclear submarine. The U.S. Navy insisted on all officers being tactically qualified. So the goings-on in the control room were no mystery to Matt Delaney. However, the order to scram the reactor was.

Instead of continuing the run at flank, as the plant was just seconds before, the Conn had ordered all stop. That was wrong, Delaney thought. He realized that fear of an ice-raft collision and subsequent hull rupture was justified. But an under-ice collision was a roll of the dice. Maybe it would happen, maybe not. A Russian torpedo was not a game of chance. If the target failed to run it had less chance of surviving than a wide-eyed doe staring down a hungry wolf.

Pacino must be playing dead, Delaney realized. But under the ice there was no surface to go to when the battery died. Delaney would need power to restart the reactor, especially for the power-hungry reactor main coolant pumps. And without juice from the battery, the ship would die.

Worse, the loss of the hovering system after the collision meant the ship would need to keep bare steerageway over the fairwater and sternplanes to keep from sinking—which required propulsion—another reason to stay critical. But with a dead reactor they'd have to use the Emergency Propulsion Motor, another damned electricity hog. The battery would be exhausted in fifteen minutes, and when it died so would the *Devilfish*.

Delaney did not like the commands from the Conn, but he also believed in Navy Regulations, the Reactor Plant Manual and the Ten Commandments. In about that order. So, reluctantly, he gave the next orders:

"Reactor operator, shift reactor main coolant pumps one, two, three and four to slow speed. Manual group scram the reactor and secure pumps one, two and three."

The reactor operator, an aggressive first-class petty officer named Manderson, acknowledged and flipped each reactor main coolant pump T-switch on the lower reactor control panel to the slow speed position, then pulled each switch upward. The indicating lights at the pumps changed from FAST to SLOW. Manderson stood and lifted a square Plexiglas cover over a rotary switch at the top of the reactor control panel: the switch was marked MANUAL SCRAM.

Manderson looked over his shoulder at Delaney. Delaney nodded. Manderson rotated the switch. As the switch handle came to rest at the position marked GROUP SCRAM, a dozen things happened in the nuclear plant within fifty milliseconds. And as far as Delaney was concerned, all those things were bad.

The reactor siren sounded, a wailing police-car siren in the maneuvering room.

The control rod bottom lights lit for group one, the controlling rod group.

The rod position digital counter began dialing group one's indicated position down to zero.

The reactor power meter dropped from 15 percent, normal for all stop with slow pumps, to zero.

Within seconds, main coolant average temperature dropped from 496 degrees Fahrenheit to 465 and continued to fall.

The STARTUP RATE meter on the RPCP went from zero to minus 0.3 decades per minute as the power level crashed into the immediate range, enroute within minutes to the startup range.

These were only the indications at the reactor plant control panel.

Two compartments forward, inside the reactor compartment, the six control-rod drive mechanisms of group-one rods lost their magnetic latch voltage. As the electrical power was interrupted from the scram breakers tripping, the magnetic flux holding the rods engaged to the drive motors collapsed, and as the magnetic attraction disappeared, springs opened alligator assemblies, disconnecting the rods from the holding mechanisms. Massive vertical springs pushed the six control rods made of an obscure element named hafnium to the bottom of the reactor vessel.

The hafnium had the odd property of acting as a black hole for the subatomic neutron particles that made the *Devilfish's* screw turn. When the six rods hit the bottom of the core, most of the neutrons flying around in the center of the reactor were absorbed by the hafnium instead of by uranium atoms. As the uranium atoms stopped absorbing neutrons, the fission reactions came to a halt like popcorn removed from an oven, going from full frantic popping to sporadic pops at odd intervals.

The fissions stopped. The uranium atoms, stuffed deeply into the fuel elements, stopped splitting, and so no longer added 200 megaelectron volts each of energy to the fuel element material. The end of the energy input was sensed immediately by the water coolant flowing in the fuel elements that no longer were super-hot.

The coolant stopped being heated by the fuel and arrived at the steam generators relatively cool at 465 degrees. Such coolant in the steam generators was useless in boiling the water from the condensers to turn it into steam. Low steam pressure in the steam generators starved the propulsion turbines and turbine generators in the engine room.

For a moment, the blare of the alarms was accompanied by the sickening, shrieking howl of the two huge steam turbines aft as they wound down from 3600 RPM to a complete stop.

To Delaney it was the sound of the *Devilfish* starting to die.

The electrical operator opened the breakers to the turbine generators as the steam pressure went away. Now the ship was on battery power alone. The fans in the ventilation ducts spun down and stopped. The air stopped flowing. The room grew hot and stuffy as the air conditioning disappeared. For a few moments the residual heat of the plant was overcoming the arctic cold. Soon, however, the boat would be as cold as the arctic sea surrounding it.

"Cut out the reactor siren. Shut main steam one and two," Delaney ordered.

The alarm siren stopped, leaving maneuvering in an unreal quiet. Manderson rotated two more switches, and two eight-inch gate-valves shut in the main steam headers, eliminating hope of a fast restart of the reactor.

"Rig emergency cooling for natural convection and shift propulsion to the EPM, then secure the last reactor main coolant pump," Delaney ordered.

The electrical operator spoke slowly, almost a hiss: "Eng, twenty minutes on the battery at this rate."

Delaney nodded, reaching for a phone. "Conn, maneuvering, reactor scram, steam plant shutdown, twenty minutes left on the battery." Twenty minutes. The torpedo would be there any *second*, he thought.

The high-pitched sound of the Russian nuclear torpedo's sonar pinging was now audible through the hull of the *Devilfish*, echoing off the ice rafts around them.

WESTERN ATLANTIC OCEAN
USS *BILLFISH*

The eerie, detached feeling left Commander Toth abruptly. The adrenaline jolt of fear accelerated his sense of time, blowing up seconds into minutes. He had heard stories about time dilation but thought they were exaggerations. He looked over at Lieutenant Culverson, the Officer of the Deck, who stood frozen in his blue Hushpuppies.

The *Billfish* had blown the AKULA out of the water, but not before it had launched a cruise missile at the coast of the United States of America. Right at Norfolk, Virginia. *Home*.

"Helm, I have the Conn!" Toth shouted. "All ahead full!

Maneuvering cavitate! Dive, make your depth six six feet, *twenty* degree up bubble! Let's go, *now!*"

Despite the string of orders and the maneuver to periscope depth, the control-room crew was moving through a sea of molasses.

It was too late, anyway. There was nothing in *Billfish*'s torpedo room able to cope with a cruise missile on solid rocket fuel. Their only ally was time—the weapon was subsonic. Time to impact might be as long as fifteen minutes . . .

With an early-warning message to CINCLANTFLEET and the White House, an interceptor aircraft might have a chance at shooting down the weapon. Assuming there was a unit ready for takeoff, an aircraft with a lookdown-shootdown radar, a pilot ready to fly and no screwups in relaying the message to people who could act on it . . . they would have maybe two minutes grace time in which to shoot the thing down.

Which was all that stood between Toth and the annihilation of Norfolk, Virginia.

"Helm, mark speed eight knots."

At all-ahead full the ship would surge ahead at a knot a second. And nine knots would be enough speed to rip the periscope right the hell off.

The deck angled up steeply, forcing Toth to grab a handhold in the overhead. He felt the deck vibrate from the power of coming to fifty percent reactor power in mere seconds.

"Eight knots, Cap'n," the helmsman called out.

"All stop. Lookaround number-two scope," Toth replied while reaching for the P.A. Circuit One microphone. His own voice sounded fast and tight as it went throughout the ship.

"COMMUNICATIONS EMERGENCY. COMMUNICATIONS EMERGENCY. NAVIGATOR, COMMUNICATOR AND RADIO CHIEF REPORT TO RADIO IMMEDIATELY."

"Six five feet, sir," the Diving Officer called. The ship had levelled off.

It took what seemed like an hour for the periscope to come out of the well. Toth focused on the bearing to the AKULA's launch position, and his heart sank.

The bright white rocket exhaust traced a graceful arc up to several thousand feet, a beautiful fourth of July rocket, except that as Toth watched, the fire trail suddenly stopped. There were no fireworks. No more fire from the tail of the rocket. Only a smoky parabola etched in the night sky.

Which meant the first stage, the solid-rocket motor, had been exhausted and the jet-engine sustainer had kicked in, sending the rocket on its way. It was no longer visible, not just because of the jettisoning of the rocket motor but because it was cruising below the radar grass, maybe only forty feet above the water.

But the worst part was the direction of the liftoff. Toth had hoped the missile might have been knocked off course by the Mark 49 torpedo detonations' shockwave.

No such luck. The rocket motor exhaust pointed due west, in a perfect trajectory toward Norfolk.

Toth handed the scope over to Culverson. "You have the Conn. Secure battlestations. I'll be in radio."

The emergency nuclear-warning message was called an OPREP 3 PINNACLE for some forgotten reason. Just a code word for a flash transmission to the White House consisting mostly of numerals in preformatted fields. The mere fact that it was being sent would be drama enough at COMSUBLANT and CINCLANTFLEET Headquarters.

At 0917 Greenwich Mean Time the BIGMOUTH antenna of the USS*Billfish* came out of the sail and transmitted the remarkable, harrowing message. The communication went out first on the NESTOR UHF satellite secure voice circuit, then on a teletype burst communication coded to the satellite, also by UHF.

The messages sent, there was no sense lingering at periscope depth. Yet Toth wanted to stay at the surface to see if the transmissions on the HF frequency from COMSUBLANT HQ stopped suddenly, which would indicate their incineration. He especially wanted to see if the CINCLANTFLEET SIOP WARPLAN implementation message would come through at FLASH priority. The SIOP WARPLAN was the collection of detailed instructions on exactly how they were to proceed in the event of a battle.

Toth walked slowly forward to the control room. All eyes of the watchstanders were staring on him. He cleared his voice.

"Off'sa'deck, take her deep to 546 feet. Ten knots. Start searching for another Russian attack unit. Maintain the rig for ultraquiet. And stream the buoyant wire antenna. I want to be in synch on VLF in case anything is transmitted from ashore."

He stood at the red sonar monitor panel of the Conn, waiting to find another Russian submarine, waiting for radio instructions to reach him from his wire antenna skimming the surface 500 feet above—or much worse, for no instructions to come from an incinerated headquarters.

It was time to give one more order.

"Off'sa'deck, tell the Communications Officer to get into his top secret safe. Have him bring the CINCLANTFLEET SIOP WARPLAN to the Conn."

CHAPTER
18

19 DECEMBER, 0924, GREENWICH
MEAN TIME

Arctic Ocean
Beneath the Polar Icecap
USS *Devilfish*

"Captain, the fire-control system is overheating, we'll have to shut it down." Weapons Officer Lieutenant Commander Steve Bahnhoff looked very unhappy.

Pacino gestured for Bahnhoff to wait. He had a last chore in mind for the Mark I fire-control system.

"Two minutes since the Magnum launch, Captain," Rapier said, urging Pacino to return fire.

"Very well, XO."

What had his father thought over two decades before when an older Russian torpedo was on its way, just as a bright shiny Russian Magnum was now on the way to the *Devilfish*? Had Patch even had time to think? An image of his father coughing up blood and seawater, drowning in both, came to him, etched in his mind.

It was almost time. Time for payback.

Pacino literally felt the eyes of his crew on him, waiting for his lead. The quiet was palpable. No bass rumble of ventilation.

No whine of the SINS navigation system. Only half the lights, the sonar and fire-control systems were functional. Without air-conditioning the residual heat from the steam and reactor plants made the ship stuffy and hot.

Bahnhoff's voice broke the silence. "Captain, fire-control casualty . . . it's a disk crash. Fire-control is in tape mode." Which, of course, meant the system would be twenty times slower and all positions would show the same clunky tape-mode display, the line-of-sight view.

Pacino had no time to answer.

CHICK! CHICK! PWEEP! CHICK! CHICK! PWEEP! . . .

"Conn, Sonar, Magnum torpedo is doing a range check."

Pacino didn't answer.

Bahnhoff looked up at him. "Fire-control temperature is almost a hundred and fifty, sir. We're about to lose it . . ."

But Pacino had to wait. The Magnum was still on its way in. Would the fire-control system hold out till the torpedo passed? More to the point, would the *Devilfish* herself survive?

The Magnum torpedo, serial number 0011779, propelled itself through the cold arctic sea with an external combustion engine, combining fuel with liquid oxidizer in a combustion chamber and sending the expanding gases to twin B-end hydraulic motors, spinning the concentric propulsor shafts. The engine design was old but ingenious. The torpedo cruised through the water, its counter-rotating screws just on the verge of cavitation, its slippery surface enabling it to get up to its final intercept velocity of 110 kilometers per hour. One hundred ten clicks. Fastest torpedo on earth. At the moment, however, the weapon meandered beneath the ice at a leisurely 70 clicks, making sonar reception better. There would be time to speed up to intercept speed once the weapon identified where the enemy ship was.

At first the Magnum "listened" passively as it cruised out toward the target position that the *Kaliningrad*'s computers had described to it before launch. It had a great deal of memory devoted to the sounds of the American nuclear submarines. Tapes of every submarine class had first been analyzed and coded into the digital memory. Later, tapes of every hull of the

American fleet had been inserted. This target's hull-number, SSN-666, had been fed in only minutes before, but the data from its August sound surveillance, stolen by an industrial espionage agent from the DynaCorp International Sound Analysis Division, indicated that the 666 had a slight amidships rattle when it ran slow-speed reactor recirculation pumps. Its fast speed pumps were so noisy that no comparison data was needed.

After a few moments the weapon had "heard" nothing and switched to active sonar. The torpedo cruised on, "knowing" that the 666 was immediately ahead, and waiting for its noise to manifest itself in the listening-sonar gear.

USS DEVILFISH

"XO, set the Hullcrusher in tube one to passive-sonar mode with a circling pattern, orbit point 10,000 yards away down the bearing line to the OMEGA. Tubes two, three and four, the same. Tube-two unit at 15,000 yards, tube three at 20,000 and four at 25,000. All will need to transit at high speed to the orbit points." Pacino's voice was level but his thoughts of his father moments before had brought a sickening taste to his mouth.

"Sir," Rapier asked, "you sure you don't want active sonar mode with the snake pattern? The active mode will still screen out the ice noise. It's a doppler sonar. And the snake pattern will cover a hell of a lot more territory—"

"No." Pacino cut him off, wondering how Rapier could argue, with the pinging of the Magnum coming in louder every second.

Pacino looked down at the fire-control display. The snake search pattern was a superb open-ocean torpedo program that made the torpedo wiggle side-to-side and up-and-down as it searched, covering huge ocean sectors with the sonar gear either passive or active. But for an under-ice shot Pacino had decided on a passive circler, a Mark 50 torpedo shot out to a preset range, then instructed to swim in circles until a target came into its passive-search sector. Without some kind of solution, active or passive snake shots would just dud. They examined too thin a slice of the ocean. At least a circler would look around all 360 degrees. And active sonar was out—it would alert the OMEGA that something was there. There was even the possibility a torpedo would home in on another friendly torpedo. It might work, but the odds were still against the OMEGA blindly driving into one of the torpedo's search cones. Still, it was all Pacino had.

"With four active snake torpedoes out there," Pacino said to Rapier, "the whole icepack would be filled with pinging. Our solution is getting stale without maneuvers and own-ship speed. The OMEGA could be anywhere on this bearing line. Passive circlers are our only chance. All right, XO, program the weapons."

Rapier nodded. "Programming now."

The Magnum's sonar pinging still sliced through the hull, getting clearer and louder. How long would it continue inbound, Pacino wondered.

"We can't launch until this torpedo goes by, *if* it goes by, but if we fool it I intend to shoot everything in the torpedo room at Target One."

Rapier took it in.

"Conn, Sonar," Pacino's earpiece rattled, "loss of Target One. Signal-to-noise ratio went below threshold."

Pacino and Rapier looked at each other for a long moment. The Russian had disappeared. The torpedoes would be duds for sure now. Pacino pressed on, seeming to ignore the bad news. "And XO," he said, having to speak over the noise of the incoming Magnum torpedo's screw, "all units will have ASH disabled."

"Sir, with Anti-Self-Homing disabled, the units could swim back and acquire on *us*."

"I know, but you heard sonar. We don't even know a bearing to Target One now. He could be anywhere. Time for an educated guess."

Both men paused to listen to the whine of the incoming nuclear-tipped torpedo.

The plot and fire-control officers were staring at the two men. Then, as the torpedo's sonar sounded through the hull, all eyes looked sideways to port, as if they could see through the steel to the approaching torpedo outside.

The ping-pitch had dropped from a shrill squeak to medium tone, the screw noise had gotten deeper, the noise no longer coming from the port side but fading away to starboard.

Pacino looked at Rapier. "We fooled it."

"Kicked its ass," Rapier said, the stress leaving his face for a moment.

"Conn, Sonar," Pacino's earpiece announced, "we're getting *down* doppler on the torpedo. It's past CPA and opening."

"Sonar, Captain," Pacino said into his microphone, "any reacquisition on Target One?"

"Conn, Sonar, no . . ."

Pacino's relief quickly faded. "Attention in the fire-control team," he called out to the room. "We've gained a little time but the Magnum may come back around when it realizes it's been had. I'm going to try to get some weapons out before the Mark I system shuts down on high temperature. And since we no longer have sonar contact on Target One we will be firing on our best guess. Carry on."

Pacino paused, eyeballing his officers, adrenaline pumping, sweat pouring . . . an intense mix of feelings almost sexual.

"Firing-point procedures," he said, voice low and tight. "Tube one, Target One, passive circler, ten thousand yards . . ."

The *Kaliningrad* had had no accurate range at the time of launch so the Magnum swam out the bearing line toward the aim-point—the point that the target, hull number 666, was expected to be at expected detonation time, ten minutes after launch.

The Magnum was using its active sonar to ping and "listen," attempting to pick up the enemy. Its program codes had been modified by the under-ice subroutine. Normally the sonar would ping and pay attention to any solid return ping, but since this action was happening under the icecap, the ice rafts and pressure ridges and stalactites would return a ping as well as an enemy submarine.

The subroutine instructed the Magnum to use the doppler filter, the device that rejected stationary objects and only examined moving ones. When a ping went out from the torpedo, return pings at the same frequency were disregarded. Only pings with an upshift or downshift in frequency passed through the filter since a moving object physically changed sound waves. If it moved toward the listening ear, the object's speed compressed the sound waves—and the frequency went up. Motion away rarefacted the waves, shifting their frequency down. Like a moving train's whistle would be shrill and high-pitched when the train approached, low-pitched and fading when the train went away.

So the torpedo "listened" not for return sonar pings, which would be ice dumbly reflecting the sound, but for pings higher or lower pitched than emitted by the nosecone transceiver. But oddly, none of the return pings passed the doppler filter. None were upshifted or downshifted. Nothing but false returns from the ice.

The torpedo was stumped. It was now 17 kilometers from the *Kaliningrad*, and the range to the enemy, the 666, had probably been much less at time of launch. The next line of coded instructions told the Magnum to continue to a range of 20 kilometers from its launch point, and if there were no hints of the target, to execute the default-turn-back and run until it either found the target on the return vector or reached a point 10 kilometers from the launch point.

Twenty kilometers from the launch point the Magnum torpedo gave up. It had been unable to find the target and it was time to turn back and execute its nuisance-explosion. In response to its program, the Magnum ordered its rudder over five degrees, made the 180-degree turn in less than a minute and headed back and east toward the launch point.

After 14.5 kilometers of backtracking without a sniff of the target, the Magnum initiated the arming of the nuclear warhead. It was, so to speak, resigned if disappointed. It would have been much more fulfilling to have detonated mere meters away from the 666. But at least its detonation 10 kilometers from its launch point would do some harm to the target.

With the arming sequence begun, the Magnum had no thoughts about what would happen to it in the moments following the nuclear detonation. Like a human driving toward orgasm, the torpedo was a highly goal-oriented being. The only thing in its "mind" was getting to its detonation position and exploding. Never mind the aftermath.

USS *DEVILFISH*

The Mark 50 Hullcrusher torpedo in *Devilfish*'s tube had been waiting a long time. For over two hours its gyroscope had been spinning, its central processor had been awake and the fuel lines had been pressurized. It had been programmed with the solution to Target One ever since the target was acquired fifteen minutes earlier. Every few minutes the solution to Target One had been updated, making the Hullcrusher hypersensitive to Target One's every move.

The outer door of the tube was open. The small clearance between the tube and the torpedo was filled with water at outside pressure. The water had heated up, from the warmth of the torpedo and the heat from the submarine, but the nosecone, home to the flat sonar transducer, was cold, feeling the water temperature outside the ship.

When a slight electrical signal came down the guidance wire at the torpedo's stern section, the weapon "tensed." The signal was the final target solution update, now locked in, as the control room fire-control console's SET key was pressed. A locked-in solution meant that launch was less than a minute away. The torpedo was ready.

"Ship ready!" Stokes called out.

"Solution ready," from Scott Brayton.

"Weapon ready," from Bahnhoff.

Pacino paused. This was unprecedented, firing on a target without having sonar contact on it. Yes, this was a recipe for a miss, particularly under ice. But better to try and miss than sink with a full load of torpedoes. Pacino made up an order.

"Shoot on last sonar bearing."

"Set!" from Brayton on Pos Two.

"Stand by!" from Bahnhoff on the firing panel, taking the trigger to STANDBY.

"*Shoot.*" Pacino felt a shot of adrenaline.

"*Fire.*" Bahnhoff pulled the trigger to the FIRE position.

Without the usual underway noises of ventilation and SINS

navigation system, the torpedo-launch sounded more violent than usual. The pressure-pulse hurt twice as much. Pacino forced a yawn to clear his abused eardrums from the pressure. Something about a warshot that made the launch sound different—this time the noise meant business.

"Tube one fired electrically, Captain," Rapier reported.

"Conn, Sonar," the sonar chief reported on the headphone circuit, "own-ship unit, normal launch."

On the Hullcrusher's port flank a relay opened as tube external power turned off. The torpedo was now on internal power, no longer dependent on the tube or the mother ship. As the connector separated, the prongs of the "in-water" sensor shorted out, and the sensor completed the first of several arming safety interlocks.

The torpedo "heard" the sound of water flowing, just for a moment . . . it was the pressurized water from the torpedo-tube tank pouring into vents at the aft end of the tube to push it out of the ship. The torpedo underwent a powerful acceleration, like falling through a dark tunnel at supersonic velocity. The noise of the sudden flow was deafening. Would the torpedo "hear" its target? Behind the torpedo the guidance wire streamed out of one of the fixed vanes of its propulsor, and also out of the ship's torpedo tube. The wire would remain stationary . . . the ship had a length of wire that allowed it to maneuver . . . and the torpedo let out its own wire to allow it to move. The wire allowed the weapon to be steered if the mother ship had a better fire-control solution. It also carried transmissions from the weapon to the firing ship when the torpedo had a valid detect on the target. The firing ship could tell when the wire became disconnected from the torpedo—which was usually an indication that the weapon had hit the target and exploded.

As the torpedo tube and the *Devilfish* faded away astern of the weapon, a second safety-interlock contact shut the three-g accelerometer, confirming the launch. The three-g contacts completed a circuit to a grain-fuel canister next to the combustion chamber. The grain fuel then ignited, pressurized the chamber and brought it up to the fuel's ignition temperature. As the temperature rose, the self-oxidizing fuel was injected and ignited, the turbine of the engine began to spin, already wind-milling at 20 RPM—and the engine-rotor accelerated to transit velocity . . .

USS *DEVILFISH*

"Firing-point procedures," Pacino said, "tube two, Target One. Set for passive circler, range 15,000 yards. ASH disabled."

"Ship ready," from Stokes.

"Solution ready," from Brayton.

"Weapon ready," from Bahnhoff.

"Shoot on last sonar bearing!" Pacino ordered.

"Set!" Stokes said.

"Stand by"—Bahnhoff.

"*Shoot*"—Pacino.

"*Shit*"—Bahnhoff. The Weapons Officer looked up from the fire-control console. "Loss of fire-control, sir." Bahnhoff's voice sounded dead.

The three video screens of the Mark I fire-control system had winked out, their blind eyes staring back at Pacino.

Suddenly the crowded room and the residual heat from back aft seemed to overcome the arctic cold on the outside of the hull. The room seemed to be baking at 200 degrees. Pacino wiped sweat off his forehead.

Rapier pulled off his headset. No sense worrying about the plots and sonar now. "Well, that's it, Captain. Unless you want to restart the reactor."

"Check the battery," Pacino told him.

Rapier picked up a phone. "Eng, how long on the battery?" Rapier listened, hung up, face grim. "Ten minutes, Captain. Not enough if we started her up right now."

Pacino stared into the distance.

"Well?" Rapier asked.

"Well what?" Pacino said quietly.

"Are you going to order a reactor-restart or not?"

Pacino shook his head. "Not yet, XO. Sit tight."

Rapier started to say something, decided against it and shut his mouth.

ATLANTIC OCEAN
FORTY MILES EAST OF NORFOLK, VIRGINIA

The SSN-X-27 nuclear-tipped cruise missile flew on at a speed just under 800 clicks. The surface raced toward the missile, giving it the impression of even greater velocity due to the low altitude. The missile calculated. In a few minutes the sand of Virginia Beach would be slipping under the fuselage. Ahead, the horizon was lit with lights from the beach, hotels, restaurants, boardwalk illumination, even just after four in the morning, even on this off-season December Sunday.

The missile computed a navigation fix from the stars overhead and judged itself just a hair off course to the south. It rotated the engine nozzle to the right, then back amidships as the course was corrected. Now the flight path was perfect.

Seven kilometers from the beach now. Time to begin the arming sequence. After a self-check of the detonator, the missile rotated a thick metal plate so that two holes lined up. Which put the central detonator in line with the main explosion train for the six specially shaped trinitrotoluene charges. The arming sequence complete, the missile settled into its ride.

At ten meters altitude the missile screamed in over the sand of Virginia Beach, 35 kilometers from Norfolk Naval Station, 37 from COMSUBLANT and CINCLANTFLEET headquarters. The hotels and tee-shirt shops zipped by beneath the missile's fuselage. Minutes till detonation.

Now the missile flew over the outer boundary of the Navy's military complex, starting with the administrative buildings and supply depot area and flying on over the headquarters buildings of COMSUBLANT and CINCLANTFLEET.

At the same time electromagnetic pulses were washing over its fuselage from the Navy EA-6B electronic warfare jet, now fifteen miles astern of it.

NORFOLK, VIRGINIA
COMSUBLANT HEADQUARTERS

Admiral Richard Donchez rubbed his bald head as he tried to focus on the surface of the desk. He felt a hand on his shoulder.

"Admiral? Sir, it's an emergency, wake up, sir."

Donchez checked his watch. Just after four o'clock in the morning, Sunday. He had dozed off in Flag Plot after putting his head on the desk at two in the morning. Pain filled him, he hadn't felt this way since commanding the *Piranha* years before.

In spite of his own promise to himself he had not been able to stay away from Flag Plot. In fact, for the entire weekend he had decided to camp out in his headquarters, Christmas holiday notwithstanding. And as the sole flag officer in a duty station at this time on a Sunday morning he was also SOPA—Senior Officer Present Ashore. Which meant that, nominally, he spoke for COMAIRLANT, COMSURFLANT and CINCLANTFLEET. He was it. All of it.

He looked up and found himself surrounded. The watch officer, Lieutenant Commander Kodiak, the young Cherokee Indian, was in front. On his left, Lieutenant Vinny Bentson, an intelligence officer. On Kodiak's right, Senior Chief Ron Carter, a communications specialist and the leading technician on the watchsection.

"What is it?" he asked Kodiak.

"Sir, we've got a flash OPREP-3 PINNACLE from the *Billfish*, 155 nautical miles due east. She sank an AKULA-class sub, *after* it fired a cruise missile. The AKULA is on the bottom but the missile is still incoming. Probable target is Norfolk, targeted for us, sir. And it's an SSN-X-27. The warhead's a one-megaton hydrogen bomb."

Donchez struggled for control. The missile coming in was obviously a warshot, the Russians would never take risks like this to launch dummies. This was *his* fault. If he had been more persuasive, more forceful with Admiral McGee . . . His eyes refocused on Kodiak as thirty years of training began to take over. His actions became almost automatic.

"Kodiak," he said quickly, "how many missiles did you say were coming in?"

"One, sir. Aim point, Norfolk."

"Does the White House have the word? And the Pentagon?"

"Yes and yes, Admiral. We're confirming their receipt now."

Donchez's thoughts were racing. This was probably the leading edge of a time-on-target attack, or a miscoordinated attack. Or perhaps even a deliberately uncoordinated attack. Fire when ready.

Donchez glanced quickly up at the plot-room wall, at the Atlantic chart with the flashing red X's.

"Kodiak, get in touch with COMAIRLANT's shack and scramble an EA-6 electronic warfare jet and a Hawkeye radar aircraft if they've got one. I don't care if it's land based or in the near Atlantic, we need radar surveillance for any more cruise missiles. Scramble as many attack aircraft as they can fuel and load out. The immediate threat is the missile coming in now. Get that one shot down, then let's worry about any more. Go!"

Kodiak ran to the NESTOR secure voice phone.

"Bentson," Donchez barked, "open the SAS safe. Get the operational authenticator for today. I want the military put on alert. DEFCON *ONE*."

Bentson ran off, grabbing an officer with the combination to the inner safe.

"Senior Chief," Donchez said to Carter, "send a flash message to the submarine fleet offshore: Anyone in trail watch for any sign of launch transients. *Any* false moves, the trailing unit is to sink their contact. If a submarine is not in trail then by God get *in* trail. Get a flash message to the *Allentown* off Severomorsk. Tell them to stay at periscope depth and be in UHF satellite reception at all times. Second, prepare to fire a twelve-missile salvo of Javelin cruise missiles at targets on my order."

Carter read back his notes, got a nod from Donchez and disappeared.

Donchez reached for a secure phone, and ordered the operator to patch him into the White House Situation Room. He reeled off the OPREP-3 details, had them read it back to make sure the President got the straight story, hung up and dialed Admiral McGee.

Thirty seconds later Donchez had a helicopter on the way to McGee's house.

"How we doing on time, Kodiak?" Donchez asked.

"Four minutes since the launch, sir."

"We got planes up yet?"

Kodiak had a radiotelephone handset screwed into one ear.

"The *Enterprise* had an EA-6B on standby just in case. Admiral McGee's orders, sir. The EA-6 is airborne, about two-hundred miles northeast, and should be reporting in on possible radar contact on the missile."

"Well, that's all just fine but it's useless unless we can get an attack plane to shoot the bitch down."

"Yessir, we've got an F-14 that was doing night-landing quals at Oceana Naval Air Station just a few minutes ago."

"Good."

"But, sir, he needs a missile loadout. The F-14 is taxiing in now at the Oceana squadron hangar. The duty weapons crew is outfitting him with some Mongoose heat-seeking missiles. He should be ready any minute."

"Dammit, Kodiak, tell them to *move*. That missile is coming in at 650 miles an hour. We got nine, ten more minutes tops."

"Yessir, I'm in contact with Oceana's tower now."

Chief Carter called to Donchez from across the room. "Sir. Admiral. The President's on Secure One."

As Donchez reached for the secure phone he gave Kodiak another order.

"Lieutenant, get that F-14 airborne. It's the only game in town."

He put the phone to his ear. "Donchez here, Mister President . . ."

MOSCOW
THE KREMLIN
RUSSIAN PRESIDENT'S CONFERENCE ROOM

Colonel Dretzski had had a contingency plan in case Novskoyy's plan failed. Now that the Novskoyy plan had stumbled, with one missile in the sky and the rest of the deployed ships apparently having decided not to fire, Dretzski decided to reveal his hand to the President. Now the emphasis should be on keeping Russia from getting hit with a retaliatory strike.

Dretzski wondered what had happened, why Novskoyy had decided to launch instead of strong-arming both superpowers as he had promised. Further, once he *did* elect to shoot, why had the fleet refused to fire, why did only one boat decide to launch? Was it a problem with the radios? Ironic if Novskoyy's grand, ego-driven plan had ended up being undone by a faulty circuit chip.

Dretzski had been encamped at Yasenevo, headquarters of the photographic intelligence raw-data section, monitoring the photo-reconnaissance satellites. He had been there all weekend, napping a few hours between satellite passes, awake for the coverage of the U.S. east coast. He was exhausted.

The conference room he was in now bore little resemblance to the spartan qualities of the FCD. The room was fit for an old-fashioned American Robber Baron: the huge hearth big enough to roast a pig in, logs crackling and warming the room, a table stretching on and on in mahogany splendor with deep leather chairs set about it, the high ceiling inlaid with gold, the walls panelled with handcarved wood, the furniture seemingly from the days of Catherine the Great.

Dretzski sat near the end of the table near the President. On the other side were General Pallin, FCD chief, who looked ready to kill Dretzski, and Maksoy, head of the KGB, who looked abstracted. Admiral Barisov was, strangely, on Dretzski's side of the table, as well as Defense Minister Fasimov. Foreign Minister Kirova was absent. What a meeting to miss, Dretzski thought.

Dretzski began. "Excuse me, sir," he said, turning to the President, "this is an emergency. Just moments ago, in our monitoring Admiral Novskoyy's deployment exercise we detected on a satellite infrared scanner an actual cruise missile launch off the coast of Norfolk, Virginia, USA . . ."

Dretzski paused. He had the room's full attention.

"Dretzski," the President said, his face suddenly tense, "are you saying there was an accident? That someone accidentally launched a missile?"

"Yes, sir."

"Must be an exercise weapon," Maksoy said, coming awake. "We destroyed our warshots, the U.N. monitored it."

"That thought occurred to us also," Dretzski said, and considered that they would know soon enough what Novskoyy had been up to, that his plan was falling apart . . . better for Ivan Ivanovich Dretzski if they heard it from him, as if he himself had been the hero who uncovered the conspiracy. He would not be popular but at least he should escape being imprisoned. "Just after our last meeting," he continued, "I ordered an FCD team to check the disposal sites of the SSN-X-27 missiles that had supposedly been dismantled by the U.N.—"

"*And?*" the President demanded.

"We found, sir, that the warheads destroyed, the presumably plutonium nuclear warheads, were *not* plutonium. They were clay, doped with alpha and gamma and neutron radiation sources. The solid rocket fuel turned out to be clay also, with special granules and coloring so it looked to be the real thing. The team leader personally put a match to some of the rocket fuel. It should have exploded and killed him. Instead . . . The word from the inspection team, unfortunately, just reached us moments ago, as the missile was launched."

"So where did the warshots *go?*" Admiral Barisov put in.

"Aboard the Northern Fleet's attack submarines. And they are, as we speak, cruising at hold positions less than two-hundred kilometers off the American Atlantic coast."

"Does this mean what I think it does?" the President said, face not only tense but growing red.

"It means, sir, that Admiral Alexi Novskoyy's fleet is armed with warshot SSN-X-27 nuclear land-attack cruise missiles, armed for an attack on the eastern United States . . ."

The President's mouth opened and shut several times, and for a moment Dretzski wondered if he was having a heart attack. After a moment, he seemed to get hold of himself, at least to demand recommendations.

Dretzski was ready. "Sir, I suggest getting on the hotline to the American President. Tell him you were deceived, which is the truth. Tell him what Novskoyy has. Suggest his navy blow the Northern Fleet to the bottom of the sea for all our sakes. I recommend you do *not* send our aircraft or ships in that direction—it would just seem an added threat. I would also, sir, recommend a radio message to the fleet telling them that Novskoyy has made himself an international criminal and that they are to reject any plan for hostilities, surface and head home."

The President, without a word, motioned to Fasimov and Admiral Barisov to follow him and hurried out of the room, apparently headed for the Communication Center.

They don't always shoot the messenger, Dretzski thought.

BARENTS SEA
TEN NAUTICAL MILES OFF SEVEROMORSK NAVAL COMPLEX
USS *ALLENTOWN*

Commander Henry Duckett looked at the OPREP-3 message from COMSUBLANT ordering *Allentown* to prepare to fire, then handed it to the OOD, who read it and looked up in astonishment.

"Man silent battlestations," Duckett said, wondering if this were for real and trying to suppress the thought.

OOD Lieutenant William Mills stepped to the firing panel and called up the firing-and-targeting-mode menu for launchtube number one, paged down to tube two and on down the list to the last three tubes—ten, eleven and twelve.

Ten miles off a major Russian naval base was the firing position. After the first missile a radar was bound to find them, a destroyer or cruiser bound to come and depth charge them into scrap metal, Mills thought. It seemed *Allentown* had just become a new word for expendable.

CHAPTER
19

SUNDAY, 19 DECEMBER, 0931
GREENWICH MEAN TIME

Virginia Beach, Virginia
Oceana Naval Air Station

Lieutenant Commander Todd Nikels fastened both latches of his oxygen mask to his flight helmet. The weapon-loading team had just completed the Mongoose missile-loadout. There had been only time to load two of the air-to-air heatseekers—both missiles were aboard, one below each wing of the F-14 supersonic fighter. Nikels waved to the Weapons Officer and keyed up the throttles. His engines had been idling during the loadout in violation of navy ordinance-loading procedures but this was an emergency.

"Oceana Tower, this is Valley Forge," Nikels said into his radio set. "Taxiing to zero eight now. Request takeoff clearance and a vector to the northwest."

"Valley Forge, roger, cleared for takeoff runway zero eight, climbout on three two five."

Nikels was almost reckless with the big jet fighter as he turned the taxiway corner. He had never taxied the aircraft this fast before, but he understood he had only minutes, maybe seconds.

Nikels' backseater, the radar intercept officer, was Lieutenant Brad Tollson, a Virginia native. Tollson had just returned from a tour at Pax River's Test Pilot School, a rival to Nikels' own most recent school, Top Gun. The products of each school seemed to think they were God's gift to aviation. Normally the crew of an F-14 Tomcat was the best two-man team in the Navy, but so far Nikels hadn't been able to figure out the stony Tollson.

The lights of the runway were lined up in front of Nikels' canopy in the predawn darkness, the neat twin lines inviting him up to the heavens. He pushed the keys to the stops with full afterburners and the F-14 began its takeoff roll. As the jets came up to full thrust he felt the acceleration push him back into the seat, pull the flesh of his face back, every blood cell wanting to pool in his back and buttocks.

The takeoff roll seemed to take forever, but at last the airspeed needle pointed to 170 knots. Nikels pulled the stick gently back, giving the wings just enough lift to pull the jet away from the concrete, retracted the wheels and flaps with one motion of his left hand. Now streamlined, the jet surged ahead, airspeed coming up to 300 knots. He turned left in a three-g turn and headed toward his intercept point with the cruise missile. In the background he could hear Tollson talking with the EA-6B radar plane, calling a vector up to him to close the missile.

At an altitude of 100 feet Nikels swept back the wings of the F-14 and went supersonic, and within two minutes it seemed that half of Virginia Beach's glass windows were broken from the sonic booms. Nikels had no time to worry about a little glass.

ARCTIC OCEAN
BENEATH THE POLAR ICECAP
FS *KALININGRAD*

Captain 3rd Rank Dmitri Ivanov stared at Admiral Novskoyy, wishing Captain Vlasenko were in command instead of under arrest.

"Admiral," Ivanov said. "We must continue to the east, we must not drive this ship into the blast radius of the Magnum."

Novskoyy suddenly felt a heavy fatigue. Unless he could get back to the polynya and somehow transmit the *molniya*, his plan would fail. It might already be failing. If an American submarine had come for him here, what had they already done to the ships of his fleet? And here this Ivanov wanted to run away like a woman.

"Men are dying right now, our fellow submariners," Novskoyy told him. "The entire Northern Fleet is off the American east coast. I must warn them. I am certain they are being hunted down right now. Just as the American submarine was sent here to hunt us down. We must get back to the polynya, we must turn back to the west."

"Sir, the Magnum detonation will rip us apart, we have to continue east—"

"No," Novskoyy said, pointing to the fire-control panel. "Look, the Magnum is two minutes beyond the aim-point. Has it turned?"

Ivanov looked down at the graphic display. "No, it's still steady on course two eight zero."

"And it is two minutes beyond the aim-point."

"Yes, Admiral . . . Either it is in a tail chase in pursuit of the American or it has lost the target."

"It *is* a tail chase, Ivanov. The American boat is faster than we thought. He must also have a polymer system."

"But, sir, the Magnum could have just lost the target and continued down the bearing line."

"*No*, you heard the American as it fled the area after hitting us. He was loud as a train wreck. You heard his reactor recirculation pumps shifting to fast speed. And he was running at maximum speed when you launched the Magnum?"

"Yes, sir."

"So why would he *stop* or *slow down* with a nuclear torpedo on the way?"

"But, sir, what if he went silent? Shut down?"

"Those are not American tactics." Novskoyy was also a pedant. He had once been a naval instructor. "What would *you* do if you were the American commander?"

"I'd clear the area, sir. Run."

"Correct. The Magnum is in a tail chase and the American is running. Turn the ship. If the American is running, the Magnum is pursuing, and the blast radius is further to the west than the polynya. Get me to the polynya so I can radio the fleet."

"Yes, sir," Ivanov said, crisply obedient once again. "Deck Officer, Ship Control Officer, right full rudder, steady course west."

The officers acknowledged, and 60,000 metric tons of Russian attack submarine came slowly around to the west, enroute to the thin ice of the polynya, on the way to transmit the *molniya* of Admiral Novskoyy.

Even though Vlasenko had been in the titanium pod for only a half hour the temperature inside was subzero. Since the collision he had sat on a wooden bench watching his breath form vapor clouds in the cold, trying to decipher the meaning of the sounds of the ship without hard data. The collision must mean that an American submarine had been shadowing them. But did it stop Novskoyy's lethal transmission?

Vlasenko had felt the hull tremble with the power of speeding up. A few minutes later came the unmistakable sound of a torpedo launch, the deck had angled to the port side, then starboard—turning hard right. The hull had again trembled with speed, then become calm. The polymer injection system was smoothing the ride.

It seemed clear Novskoyy had launched a weapon at the intruder, then run like hell—it must be a Magnum! A conventional unit couldn't hurt the firing ship, but a Magnum could blast them to the bottom if they were closer to it than 20 kilometers. Strangely, though, several minutes later the ship had slowed again and the pod deck angled to and fro as the ship was turned. It made no sense, there had been no detonation shock from the Magnum! Maybe it hadn't been a Magnum after all. Vlasenko hated his position . . . from captain to passenger.

He had tried to distract himself with a mental calculation of the amount of air in the sphere, and his rate of oxygen-use. He had decided that the air was good enough for perhaps 12 to 24 hours, depending on the assumptions about his levels of metabolism.

He also realized he would probably not last half that long
. . . the cold was chipping away at both his body and his spirit.
It was extremely painful. He could feel the circulation slowing
in his arms and legs. His toes were numb, so were his fingertips.
His ears burned from frostbite and his nasal linings were on fire
from the frigid air. Pain. How long could he endure it . . . ?

The Mark 50 Hullcrusher torpedo "felt" the thrust of its spinning propulsor. It had never before cruised on its own power; it
had only been through simulated electronic checks.

As instructed, it counted out the range from the firing point
with a counter on the propulsor shaft so that it knew when to
start the circular orbits, swimming in circles until it found a
valid return.

Seven minutes after launch the weapon reached the orbit-
point, put the rudder over and turned left to the north as it
slowed to circling speed. Turning, it "listened" passively.

Nothing to the north.

Nothing to the west.

The weapon circled.

Nothing to the south.

Still orbiting, the weapon settled in for a long series of circles
to find the target.

Two minutes after Ivanov ordered the turn, the ship was steady
on course west, at first at her original polymer injection speed
but slower as the polymers ran out. When the ship neared maneuvering range of the polynya she slowed further. All the
while the officers continued monitoring the quickly retreating
Magnum torpedo, twenty kilometers away, still on its own way
west.

It was then that their Magnum turned back to the east, exe-
cuting its default turn-back, now approaching them. The officers did not hear or detect the Magnum as it turned around.

Because at that same moment, the *Kaliningrad* drove into the
search-cone of an American torpedo.

*   *   *

The Hullcrusher torpedo, circling five miles from the firing ship, the *Devilfish*, "heard" a sound, a loud one, bearing 130, a submerged submarine sound.

The unit searched the program codes for instructions. The first line instructed the torpedo to turn toward the sound and wiggle slightly; the unit obediently undulated its rudder and wiggled. The sound changed position from right to left, had a valid left-to-right tag reversal—signifying the target was dead ahead.

The second program line told the weapon to put a signal into its guidance wire, telling the mother ship that it had a detect on the enemy.

The third line told it to speed up to 50 knots. The propulsor wound up, and the weapon surged forward. *The target was just ahead.*

The unit executed its final arming sequence and strained to feel the magnetic hull-detection-proximity sensor shift from DISTANT to CLOSE. Not long now. Not much longer, and its mission would be fulfilled.

Just ahead, the target was coming closer, but then the target zoomed by so fast that it disappeared.

The torpedo put its rudder over hard and turned right, the g forces pushing the fuel in the fuel cell to the port side, almost starving the fuel pump. But then, up ahead, the torpedo received the rapidly retreating sound of the target's propulsor. It was fast, but it was slowing. Slowing, range decreasing.

Closer, catching up.

Closer.

Soon the target's propulsor passed by overhead, and the torpedo was under the midsection of the hull. The torpedo "watched" its magnetic-hull-proximity sensor, which sensed iron, followed by a cascade of electrical tickles. The feel of iron was like a reward. In a rush, a compelling sequence of events overcame the weapon, all reflex.

The detonators lit off in its belly, a tingling flash. The detonators caused the 1500 pounds of high explosives to go up in one final, colossal fireball. The torpedo exploded, vaporizing into fifty thousand fragments, and its awareness stopped, ending in a fulfilled blackness.

The explosion was focused in the exact direction of the maximum magnetic flux of the hull-sensor, putting 90 percent of the explosive force toward the enemy hull. Short of a nuclear weapon, it was the best, perhaps the only way to kill a double-hulled submarine.

The force of the torpedo's blast melted through the outer steel hull of the fifth compartment of the OMEGA, exactly amidships, vaporizing a hole fourteen feet in diameter. The annular tank space was the location of the external battery canisters, and the blast, though somewhat attenuated by the energy expended in breaking through the outer hull, blew the battery canisters into flat plates and scattered the remainder to the bottom of the sea.

The force of the blast was lessened by the canisters absorbing the energy of the expanding hot gases. The burst next sought out the titanium inner hull, initially finding the external heavy frames bent into hoops, with the sheet titanium stretching between each frame. Four frames were forced inward, breaking them apart. The titanium skin welded onto the hoop-shaped frames was blown inward, creating a gaping eight-foot-diameter oblong hole. The rest of the explosive force was, as designed, concentrated inward, ready to unleash its deadly force on the interior of the hull.

The blast shouldered aside the titanium and came rushing into the interior of the submarine, to find that it was inside a storage tank of fuel oil for the emergency diesel generator. Since the fifth compartment was aft of and adjacent to the reactor compartment, the fourth compartment, the oil served as a liquid-shield for the sixth compartment, the turbine room.

From the outside, the physical result of the Mark 50 torpedo's explosion, the pride of COMSUBLANT and DynaCorp International Underwater Systems Division, was little more than a dead battery and a small oil spill.

The story was inside.

FS KALININGRAD

The blast of the American torpedo they had stumbled into caused the deck of the control compartment to jump, though slightly.

"What was that?" Ivanov asked.

"I heard an explosion," Chekechev said.

"What's sonar indicate?" Novskoyy demanded.

Ivanov: "Sonar is out, so is fire-control. The communications and navigation consoles are still up. We must have had a computer casualty in the fifth compartment. All the computers located there are dead. Without sonar and fire-control we can't shoot any more weapons."

Novskoyy reset the computer power-breaker. No use. The sonar and fire-control computers were lifeless.

And without sonar and fire-control, as Ivanov had said, *Kaliningrad* was no longer an offensive-weapon system, was no longer able to track the American submarine or shoot at it again. But they could hope the American would be on the bottom within the hour, the Magnum torpedo inflicting their revenge. The Magnum had fuel for 60 to 90 minutes of pursuit, and it had only been 23 minutes since it was launched.

But without sonar and fire-control, Novskoyy thought, it would be difficult to return to Severomorsk. Well, at least the communications computer was still up and running, he only needed to reach the polynya to transmit the attack order, the *molniya* . . .

Without sonar, there was no way of him detecting that the Magnum had turned around and was heading back to the aimpoint a mere eight kilometers from the west side of the polynya.

Ivanov looked over at Novskoyy, a phone in his hand. "The communications circuits are intact, Admiral. Once we reach the polynya you will still be able to transmit your message."

Novskoyy nodded, the man echoed his own thoughts, which turned bitter as he muttered, "I wanted to put all the computers up forward in the first compartment but Vlasenko insisted that the systems be split out. If all four had remained up forward as I had envisioned the ship would be at full capacity—"

"Not full, sir," Ivanov said, looking at the damage-control display, "the oil-shield tank in compartment five is ruptured. The inner hull is compromised over more than half the circumference. Another explosion like that last one and we could be cut in half."

"There will be no more detonations. The Magnum will be taking care of the American and very soon."

"I wish we had some sonar, Admiral. Without it we'll have to guess at the boundaries of the polynya. And there is no way to see if the Magnum has turned toward us."

"We will find the polynya," Novskoyy pronounced. "And the Magnum will find the Americans."

Kaliningrad continued west, nearing the pressure ridge at the east end of the oval-shaped polynya.

NORFOLK, VIRGINIA
ALTITUDE: 100 FEET

Lieutenant Commander Todd Nikels pulled the F-14 into a final five-g turn and grunted against the g's as the plane whipped around on an approach vector to the SSN-X-27 cruise missile.

"Fifteen seconds to intercept," Tollson, the radar-intercept officer, called out. "Yeah, that's it. Okay, radar contact, I'm looking at five miles, come on, close the bastard, it's only doing maybe six-hundred knots."

Nikels pulled up his MASTER ARM switch and armed the Mongoose heat-seeking missiles, then held his breath, waiting for Tollson to call the firing point. At this hour of the morning he didn't expect to see the target missile at all.

"Range, one point five miles . . . come left five degrees . . . that's it . . . stand by, and . . . FIRE!"

Nikels pushed the launch button on the control stick and felt the plane jump as the rocket motor lit up the sky in front of him and the Mongoose left the rail on the port wing enroute to the target. Momentarily blinded, Nikels blinked rapidly while he spoke into the intercom.

"Firing one."

"Roger," Tollson said, "FIRE."

Nikels hit the stick button again, and again a Mongoose missile lit up the night sky as it flew away. This time Nikels had clenched his eyes shut so he would have the night vision to follow the missile to see if he got a kill.

"Fire two. Are you tracking?"

"Got 'em," Tollson said.

Nikels looked out ahead at the Mongoose tracks as the heat-seeking missiles flew on toward the cruise missile fired by the

Vladivostok as it neared the boundary between the air base and the naval base, passed over a fence and was now officially over Norfolk Naval Base . . .

ARCTIC OCEAN
BENEATH THE POLAR ICECAP
FS *KALININGRAD* CONTROL COMPARTMENT ESCAPE POD

The shock of the detonation had quickly penetrated Vlasenko's sluggish doze induced by exposure to the cold. The bare titanium of the escape pod was so cold that his cheek burned from the direct contact. With a major effort he lifted his head off the curved wall of the sphere, skin sticking to the metal, pulling off a patch of flesh. The wound was the least of his problems. The onset of hypothermia from the freezing pod was evident in his numb limbs, and if he had been able to check a mirror he would have seen that his lips were blue.

He tried to force himself to motion, struggling against the pain, struggling against the cold . . . The intruding submarine, he decided, must have managed to get a torpedo in close, and the fact that he was still alive at least meant that the enemy did not use nuclear warheads on their torpedoes—Severomorsk's intelligence estimates had been correct, after all. Conventional explosives were relatively ineffective against *Kaliningrad*'s hardened combination of titanium and steel, and Vlasenko allowed himself a moment of pride in the ship that had, after all, survived a direct hit.

He listened for the sounds of another torpedo-launch but heard none. Strange. If he had been in command he would have pumped out more weapons, even if he had already launched a salvo of Magnums. But the torpedo tubes were silent. Why?

USS *DEVILFISH*

A loud explosion reverberated from the port side of the stuffy control room.

The control-room watchstanders believed the OMEGA was sinking. Pacino, stone-faced, held up his palm for quiet.

A sound came from the other side of the control room, faint, high-pitched. A screw at high speed, coming from . . . the west . . . the direction the Magnum had driven off to.

Commander Jon Rapier's face lost its color. "Captain . . . it's coming back. The Magnum. We fooled it once . . ."

"I know, XO. It could be doing a default routine. Why else would it have turned around and come back? This thing may detonate with or without contact on us, a nuisance detonation—"

"A damned sight worse than a nuisance, skipper."

Pacino looked at Rapier, standing there at the base of the periscope stand, scanning his face, looking for answers.

Pacino was out of answers.

"Yes, XO. Much worse than a nuisance," was all he said.

FS *KALININGRAD*
CONTROL COMPARTMENT ESCAPE POD

Captain Vlasenko strained to hear sounds from the inside of the control compartment. What was going on below now? Was Novskoyy approaching the enemy to return fire? Was he headed back to the polynya to transmit his doomsday message? He heard nothing. Complete silence.

A new thought occurred—what if the attacking submarine was *Russian*? What if Northern Fleet Headquarters had pieced together Novskoyy's wild scheme and sent an attack submarine to stop him. It made sense—another Russian ship would try a collision before shooting them, to stop the transmission and try to save a crew held hostage by Novskoyy. The thought buoyed him as he began to hope for the success of the other submarine. Who would HQ have sent? The *Smolensk*? The *Novgorod*? The *Nevski*? The *Leningrad*? That would be an irony—Novskoyy sunk by his own former submarine *Leningrad*.

How could he himself help them? There was nothing to bang on the pod wall with, so he couldn't make noise. Wait—there was the lever for the manual-pod release. But then he realized the attacking submarine would not need noise. They had already found *Kaliningrad* with a close torpedo. Perhaps they would finish it off with their own Magnum.

Was it right to hope for the sinking of his own ship? After thinking on it a moment, he decided it *would* be better for the *Kaliningrad* to sink than for Novskoyy to let loose his incredibly destructive plan. Still, the thought of losing the *Kaliningrad* made him sick.

As Vlasenko sat in the cold of the pod, his breath still clouding the air, his mind on terrible events he had no power to change, a Magnum nuclear-tipped torpedo only seven kilometers away, launched by the *Kaliningrad*, began to explode.

CHAPTER
20

SUNDAY, 19 DECEMBER
0945, GREENWICH MEAN TIME

The main detonator of the Magnum's warhead was set in motion by a spark cap, making the thumb-sized high explosive burn into a white-hot miniature fireball. In turn the main detonator caused six larger igniters to explode within ten microseconds of each other. Each of the six igniters then caused its pie-shaped trinitrotoluene charge to detonate. The points of the pie-shaped charges faced the center of the forward section of the Magnum torpedo, and the charges went up in one coordinated explosion. More accurately it would be called an implosion, since the shaped charges were designed to cause a pressure pulse to move *inward*, toward the center of the torpedo. As the explosives at the skin of the warhead blew inward they forced a doughnut-shaped piece of plutonium to collapse into a dense sphere, the mass blown into the hole of the doughnut.

As the plutonium collapsed into a dense ball from the force of the explosion it achieved critical mass. There had long been a background of nuclear fissions, the splitting apart of the heavy plutonium atom's nuclei, ever since the plutonium had been assembled into the Magnum torpedo a year before, but each fission had sent its neutrons flying off into space. The leaking neutrons were lost forever, and continued to leak out of the doughnut, useless in causing any further fissions. And although each fission gave off a tremendous amount of energy, the fissions were sporadic, infrequent. But as the plutonium was blown into a dense ball, the critical mass, the neutrons stopped leaking. The sporadic fissions still happened but each neutron flew not out into space but directly into another plutonium atom's nucleus, splitting that nucleus into two smaller isotopes and sending out another three neutrons. And as those three flew away from the fissioning atom they didn't leak but collided with other plutonium nuclei in the densely packed mass. And each of the three neutrons of that fission generation created three more fissions, with three more neutrons. Those three caused nine new fissions, creating 27 neutrons that led to 81 fissions, then 243, then 729, then 2187, until after 47 generations of fissions nearly every molecule of plutonium present had experienced an energy-releasing fission. The whole process took less than fifty microseconds.

The result was a nuclear explosion, a fission bomb.

Even so, it was only the beginning. The original plutonium doughnut had been surrounded with a canister of deuterium, heavy water. The fission explosion was a trigger for the fusion reaction, giving the deuterium atoms' nuclei enough energy to come together and form a heavier element, helium, releasing even greater quantities of energy per reaction. The deuterium atoms experienced fusion on an incredible scale, forming the helium and bringing the area in the vicinity of what was once the Russian Magnum torpedo to the temperature of the sun's surface, several million degrees.

The icecap itself, 600 meters above, over 30 meters thick, jumped into the air. A series of cracks in the ice formed, some as far as 70 kilometers from the blast. The ice immediately above the blast zone was blown hundreds of meters skyward in a tower of steam. The sphere of million-degree gas expanded rapidly, growing hundreds of meters in diameter. But even the hydrogen bomb had met its match in the coldness and near-infinite stretches of frigid ocean water. As the gas cloud expanded at high pressure, the cold arctic water cooled it, calmed it and eventually collapsed it.

The gas bubble, defeated by the cold arctic sea, gave up and decomposed into several hundred trillion bubbles, all rising upward in the radioactive water that had rushed back in to fill in the hole left by the explosion.

Although the gas bubble was doomed, fracturing into tiny bubbles, the shock wave from the blast lived on. It traveled at sonic speed in the ocean depths, reinforced by the ice above and the ocean bottom below into a solid wall of a pressure pulse that propagated quickly from the blast zone, reaching out to the sea around it.

As the shock wave moved out it crushed hundreds of ice-pressure ridges, some stalactites of ice vaporizing from the energy of the shock. One slender ice stalactite, roughly the size and even the shape of the Empire State Building, except that it was upside down and submerged, disintegrated instantaneously into several thousand pieces, none larger than a few feet in diameter.

The shock wave travelled on in all directions, killing the few fish and animals that inhabited the area of the arctic north. It took three seconds to reach the USS *Devilfish*, then drifting in the current from the north some three kilometers from the polynya's west edge. The shock wave took slightly longer to reach the *Kaliningrad*, almost five seconds.

The shock wave was attenuated, eroded, weakened as it travelled further from its origin. With each meter it travelled it grew weaker, its destructive forces spread over more and more area as the wavefront expanded, growing weaker with the square of the radius from the detonation. The *Devilfish* was 5000 meters from the blast, the *Kaliningrad* almost 7000. It would seem both would sustain equal damage, but the extra 2000 meters meant that the shock wave force was twice as cruel to the *Devilfish* as it was to the *Kaliningrad*—though to both vessels it was more than cruel enough.

Hundreds of meters beneath the icecap, and several kilometers from the original polynya and the new one formed by the detonation, both submarines were in mortal danger.

NORFOLK, VIRGINIA
NORFOLK NAVAL BASE

The two officers in the F-14 looked toward the base as the cruise missile flew on, oblivious to the tail chase of the two Mongoose missiles.

The first Mongoose went wild and dived for the ground, exploding as it impacted on nearby Interstate 64. The hole in the interstate was three-lanes wide.

The second Mongoose flew toward the hot exhaust of the SSN-X-27 cruise missile, as it was designed to do, but 200 yards from the target the heat sensor in the Mongoose's nosecone failed and it lost its direction. It sailed off to the north, effectively blind and with no target, until its rocket motor ran out of fuel. It glided to earth and landed on the roof of one of Norfolk Naval Base's several administration buildings. Its fuselage was crushed and misshapen as it lay smoldering and inert.

The SSN-X-27 had escaped Nikels' and Tollson's attack and was now approaching the northwestern edge of the base—the surface ships and submarine piers.

ARCTIC OCEAN
BENEATH THE POLAR ICECAP
FS *KALININGRAD*

There was no warning when the shock wave of the nuclear explosion hit the *Kaliningrad*. With the sonar systems out, and the torpedo seven kilometers away, it was inaudible and unexpected.

Kaliningrad had slowed to approach the polynya and had turned to the north. In doing so she had exposed her fifth compartment's portside wound, the rip from the American torpedo that had ripped open the diesel oil shield tank. The rip came halfway up her port flank and had cut through four structural frames.

The shock wave smashed into the port side of the ship, a violent, instantaneous pressure-pulse, peaking at 8500 Newtons per square meter. Had the inner and outer hulls been undamaged, the ship would have rolled as the shock wave blasted over her, perhaps damaging only more of the delicate computers. But with that rip in the fifth compartment, there was no metal on the port side to hold the ship together.

The ship snapped in half.

The control compartment experienced an immediate seven g's in the starboard direction, then three to port. Anything not bolted down, including the men, was thrown into one side of the room, then the other. The room was not designed for such impact forces, no padding, no softened edges, practically all metal—metal cabinets, metal seats, metal deck, metal titanium ellipsoid hull, metal pipes and valves and periscopes and conduits. What was not metal was glass—the screens of the computer consoles, the navigation graphic chart table, display faces. The combination of high-g forces, the small metal-filled room, glass screens and vulnerable human flesh turned the room into a meat grinder. It took only seconds, and when those seconds were over not a single man was whole, not a single man was conscious.

The stern part of the vessel, the remains of the fifth compartment and the huge turbine compartment, sank backward into the sea, the port high-pressure turbine coming loose from its foundation as the hull fractured. It took only two minutes for the aft-hull to pass through its 2000-meter crush-depth, shallower than the ship's since the compartment bulkheads were weaker than the hull.

The only man conscious in the aft-hull as it sank at a precipitous tail-down angle was the engineer, Mikhail Geroshkov, who had been strapped into a control seat in nuclear control at the aft section of the sixth compartment, the turbine room. The lights had gone out and the battery had already been destroyed by the American torpedo. Complete darkness made the prospect of death that much more frightening.

Mikhail Geroshkov began a prayer, something his mother had taught him decades before. At one time it was a practice he had disapproved. Now he said it aloud, over and over. The deck had become almost vertical, leaving him lying in his seat on his back, strapped in like a cosmonaut in a rocket. "Our Father who art in Heaven, hallowed be Thy name—"

The forward bulkhead of the sixth compartment collapsed and ruptured at a depth of 1970 meters. With a thunderclap of pressure it compressed the contents of the sixth compartment like the air in an engine's cylinder, and like the air in a diesel engine, the compression shot up the air temperature thousands of degrees.

For just an instant the nuclear control room was lit by the bright flash of the approaching flame front, the leading edge of the compression wave. Geroshkov was allowed milliseconds to see the wall of flames coming toward him at sonic velocity, 5500 clicks, but he had no time to open his mouth to scream. By the time the pressure wave reached the aft bulkhead of nuclear control, the scattered tissues that a moment before comprised Mikhail Geroshkov had vaporized in the soaring pressures and temperatures of the fiery air.

The aft half of the *Kaliningrad* hit the Arctic Ocean bottom, a crushed lump of steel and titanium. The debris field it created was a kilometer wide, four kilometers long.

The once mighty submarine, the pride of the Northern Fleet, was now little more than a titanium coffin.

USS *Devilfish*

Anyone in the control room of the USS *Devilfish* at 0945 Greenwich Mean Time would object to being called lucky. Of course, none could know what had just happened to the men in the after-hull of the OMEGA submarine.

Pacino had not bothered to grab onto a handhold in the overhead when the Magnum had returned. Convinced that the Magnum detonation would mean his death, he had stood there, rooted to his spot on the Conn, his arms crossed across his chest.

The shock wave from the Magnum's nuclear explosion first hit the screw and passed through the ship longitudinally, its force accelerating the ship forward in an enormous four-g jerk. The ship control team sitting strapped into seats at the forward panel had no headrests, the backs of the seats coming only up to shoulder level. All three were jerked backward so abruptly and forcefully that their necks were broken. One, the Diving Officer, died not from a broken neck but from asphyxiation when vertebrae punctured his throat. The four men sitting at the fire-control console were hurled forward, resulting in broken bones, concussions, deep gashes, finger-amputations. The battlesta-tions watchstanders who had been standing were tossed, sands in a gale-force wind. After the shock wave passed the only sounds in the room were the groans and labored breathing of the wounded.

The acceleration first knocked Michael Pacino off his feet and onto the deck, then threw him aft. He fell all the way back down the operations-compartment upper-level passageway, back almost sixty feet to the hatch to the reactor-compartment tunnel, his headlong plunge broken only by the body of a yeo-man seaman just out of bootcamp, the upper-level phonetalker, who had hit the aft bulkhead first, fracturing his skull, breaking his back. Pacino's head had rammed into Miller's abdomen, soft enough to break the mad tumble but not soft enough to avoid a severe shoulder sprain and a hard knock on the head.

Dazed, he wiped his hand on his head, now drenched with blood and mucus, wondering briefly whether it was his or the dead seaman's. He stared for a moment at the boy's body, his blood now running over the deck. Dimly Pacino heard the sounds of men screaming and moaning in operations upper level, most of the sounds seeming to come from the direction of the control room. He dragged himself to his feet and skidded down the blood-covered deck forward to the control room.

As he moved forward, the sounds of agony were joined by a second, even more frightening sound—the flow-noise of water flooding the ship in the lower level.

FS *KALININGRAD*

Aft of the fourth compartment's after bulkhead, the steel and titanium skin and framework were mangled and shredded where the vessel had split in two.

The reactor-compartment forward-bulkhead at first remained intact in spite of the ship smashing in two. Then the liquid reactor coolant sprayed and flooded the compartment as the number-two reactor vessel flew off its foundation and careened to the aft bulkhead, where it punctured the titanium wall. The hole in the bulkhead invited in the cold arctic water, where the gushing wave mixed with the sodium reactor coolant. The highly reactive sodium and the water exploded with twice the power of the explosives in a 53-centimeter torpedo. The after bulkhead ripped fully open, dropping the number-two reactor vessel down the fifteen kilometers to the ocean floor. The so-dium-water reaction continued and melted the titanium walls of the compartment and began to melt through the forward bulkhead, at last breaching it and flooding the third compart-ment with seawater.

The loss of the aft part of the ship had left the forward portion unstable, no longer self-righting in roll or pitch. And the flood-ing in the first compartment, adding the additional weight of the water, made matters worse. The forward spaces took on a down angle with a list to port that increased as the loose weap-ons in the first compartment skidded into the port bulkhead, and the water in the lower deck washed over from the tilt.

On the first compartment's middle-level deck the grain can at the aft end of one of the 53-centimeter torpedoes sparked as the wrecked weapon crashed into the port bulkhead, and the spark lit the explosive self-oxidizing fuel. The resulting explosion first set off fuel fires in the other weapons in the compartment, and moments later the warheads of the weapons went off in a tre-mendous detonation, blowing holes in the side walls of the compartment and breaching the decks above and below. The Magnums in the lower level were crushed, setting off fuel fires and rupturing the warhead casings.

The forward bulkhead of the deserted second compartment dimpled from the explosions up forward but held, making it one of two compartments of the *Kaliningrad* to retain its structural integrity. The other to survive was the control compartment, the oval-shaped bubble of titanium anchored to the top of the second compartment and faired into the superstructure. But with the power loss the control compartment, the nerve center, in effect died—no hydraulics, no electricity, no lights, no fans, no displays or computers or live consoles.

Admiral Novskoyy lay unconscious at the lip of the periscope well, with a bloody head wound and concussion from one of the periscopes. He had sustained countless minor injuries, scrapes and bruises and sprains but was the one in the compartment who had been spared the wrath of the shock wave, having landed near the ship-control console.

Ivanov, Deck Officer and Acting Captain, had been at the ship-control console supervising Lieutenant Katmonov. He had been thrown into the ladder going to the escape pod, been spun around and collided with the bulkhead on the port side, a relatively smooth surface with nothing hanging from it, so built to allow entry up to the escape-pod ladder without snagging the climber's clothes or body. He collided with Warrant Officer Danalov, with only a moment to register the sound of bones crunching but did not yet feel any pain. On the trip to the starboard side Ivanov's leg was caught on the back of the ship-control seat while his body continued toward the starboard side. Finally he broke the hold of the seat, and when he landed he hit the starboard forward corner of the room, opening a gash in his arm. With a compound fracture of his leg and a gash in his arm, he regained consciousness in time to see arterial blood spurting from his arm and two bones protruding from his left thigh, one pointing forward and one sideways. He promptly fainted. When he came to the pain hit him like an electric shock.

Lieutenant Katmonov, the Control Officer, had been strapped into his seat and survived with cartilage damage to his spine and pulled muscles in his back. In shock, he stared straight ahead at his dead panel, illuminated only by the compartment's four weak battle lanterns, and waited, and waited . . .

Captain-Lieutenant Viktor Chekechev, Weapons Officer, had been at the fire-control console at the time of the Magnum detonation. He was thrown into the periscope well, smashing his back into the periscope. From there he was hurled back into his console, where broken glass in the computer display broke his fall, and cut his ear half off. Three ribs had been snapped jaggedly on the fall to the periscope well, one entering his left lung and piercing a pulmonary artery. Immediately his heart began pumping blood into his chest cavity, his abdomen swelling with the blood, his skin turning white as he silently bled to death.

The only other crewmember in the compartment was Warrant Officer Dmitri Danalov, head of the security crew. On hand only to guard Vlasenko in the escape pod, he had been standing at the base of the short tunnel to the escape pod lower hatch between the control console and the communications station. The shock of the Magnum blast had sent him into the smooth ladder bulkhead, only smashing his nose. But the acceleration to port brought a missile to bear—Ivanov's body travelling at some forty meters per second. Danalov's head was smashed against the bulkhead, fracturing his skull. The acceleration to starboard threw him into the opening mechanism to the escape-pod lower hatch. If he had hit the mechanism a few inches to the right he would have escaped with only the top of his skull fractured. No such luck. The opening mechanism of the escape-pod lower hatch was a steel wheel set horizontally onto a shaft that controlled the steel dogs of the hatch as above. At the outside of the wheel was a long handle that protruded horizontally and was used to crank the wheel by hand. Danalov's head hit the crank handle with sufficient force to send it through his forehead deep into his brain. The crank handle then rotated the wheel until the handle released him. Danalov was still breathing when the weight of his body pulled him off the handle and sent him to the deck, leaving a residue of brain tissue on the crank handle. As the deck developed a down angle, Danalov's breathing had slowed to a wheeze. By the time the self-oxidizing fuel of a Magnum had ignited below in the first compartment his body functions had shut down. And when the rest of the ship passed through a depth of 1000 meters, the deck at a 40-degree down-angle, Dmitri Danalov was dead.

USS DEVILFISH

Pacino pulled himself off the deck of the operations compartment and ran to the control room, his body a symphony of aches but intact. The sounds around him formed the cacophony of a nightmare . . . the rushing sound of flooding, the screams and moans from the control room not as loud but audible, a knife in Pacino's heart. The smell of the ship had changed. What before was oil residue, ozone, perspiration, sewage and cooking grease was now salty seawater, hydraulic fluid, burning insulation and the smell of burning hair.

The lights were still on in the narrow fore-and-aft passageway. As Pacino went toward the control room he nearly tripped over a body, half lying in the passageway at the door to Sonar, half in the sonar room. Chief Sonarman Jethro Helms was dead, eyes staring at the overhead, blood running out of his mouth. As Pacino forced himself forward past the door to Sonar, the overhead lights went out. The battery he thought. The battery has flooded with seawater and it's shorted out and the ship is dying with no power and the hull is filling with chlorine gas from the reaction of seawater with the huge wet cells.

He ran forward until he was in the control room, feeling his way by instinct from years of living with the geometry common to all Piranha-class submarines. He felt the deck under his feet give, he was sliding in the darkness, something wet on the deck. He reached into the overhead for the switch to a manual lantern, not sure if he was slipping on oil, water or blood.

The lights came back on as he struggled for the switch to the battle lantern, but he switched on the light anyway in case the overhead lights went out again. He realized the ship was running solely on the battery, and when it went he would be in an uncontrollable hulk, suspended in seawater with no depth control.

It took several seconds for him to take in the scene in the control room. Filled with smoke. No one moved. Watchstanders collapsed on the deck surrounded by the broken glass of the video fire-control and sonar screens and instrument faces. The plot table of the geographic plot had smashed itself into the narrow aisle behind the fire-control cabinets and the curving starboard bulkhead.

The ship-control team was still strapped into their seats, their heads lolling on their shoulders. The Chief of the Watch was nowhere in sight. The OOD, Nathanial Stokes, was collapsed on the periscope stand, a phone handset resting on his face, the smashed panel that was once the sonar-repeater screen half-lying on his chest. Jon Rapier sat on a fire-control bench, his head on the console, his arms dangling. Behind him the Pos Two console was in flames. Lieutenant Scott Brayton had fallen between the bench and the lower portion of the Pos Three console.

Ensign Brett Fasteen, the Pos One operator, was lying on the deck with his arms and legs in unnatural positions, his chest toward the deck, his head twisted clear around so that his face was upward. No sign of Steve Bahnhoff or Ian Christman, but there were still unexplored shadows and piles of rubble. Pacino heard a brief sound of an electrical arc. The sound of flooding had stopped, leaving the room deathly quiet.

Pacino grabbed the P.A. Circuit Seven microphone, clicked on its speak button:

"Engineer, Captain."

Pacino was talking to himself . . . the microphone was hanging from a severed cord. He threw it to the deck, grabbed the phone handset off of Brayton's chest:

"Maneuvering, Captain. Engineer, pick up the Circuit JA phone!"

Lieutenant Commander Matt Delaney's voice came over the JA phone circuit. Pacino got out his question before Delaney could finish saying, "Engineer."

"Eng, what's your status?"

Delaney was shouting, as if the line reception was poor. Or maybe he was just scared, Pacino thought. He had a right to be.

"Flooding in port main seawater isolated by the chicken switch. We took on maybe two feet of water in the bilges and I need the drain pump but it takes too much current for the battery. Battery's got maybe five minutes left. We had a fast leak in the primary coolant system. Not sure where it was from but I isolated both loops with the main coolant cutout valves and the leak stopped. We were watching loop pressures when you called —okay, it's starboard."

There was the sound of Delaney's voice getting distant as he shouted instructions to the maneuvering crew, probably the reactor operator.

"Skipper, you still there?" Delaney's hoarse voice.

"I'm here, Eng."

"I'm opening up the port loop cutout valves. Okay, pressurizer level's holding." For a moment Delaney's voice was muffled. "Charge to the port loop." Delaney's voice came back as he screamed into the phone. "Skipper, we gotta restart the reactor with an emergency heatup rate. If we wait any longer we won't have enough juice to run a main coolant pump to start up. We need an emergency fast-recovery reactor startup."

"Engineer, conduct a fast recovery reactor startup. Put the switch in battleshort and use an emergency heatup rate on the reactor. Do an emergency warmup of the turbines, SSTG's first. I want propulsion in four minutes."

"Cap'n, we'll be up in three."

The phone clicked. Pacino slowly put the phone handset back in its cradle and turned to look at the XO.

Rapier was breathing. When Pacino touched his cheek, his skin was warm. Pacino slapped his cheek gently, trying to bring him to. Rapier moaned, slowly moving his head from side to side.

"C'mon, damn it, wake up . . ."

Rapier's eyelids opened, then shut, then opened again. His eyes were out of focus, pupils dilated wide.

Pacino bit his lip, turned and hurried out of the control room and down the stairs to middle level, then up twenty feet forward nearly to the hatch to the bow compartment and down the stairs to operations lower level, to the torpedo room.

Once in the forward door Pacino froze.

It was worse than he had imagined.

FS *KALININGRAD*

Novskoyy looked through a dark tunnel with an odd pattern at the end. As the fuzzy edges of the tunnel faded and more of the pattern became clear, Novskoyy realized he was staring, close range, at the vinyl covering of the deck of the control compartment, his face on the cold deck. There was an electric, tingling sensation in his tongue, and when the tingling stopped, the taste of copper. Blood. He moved his tongue in his mouth, feeling the cut in his inner cheek where he had bit nearly through the flesh.

The tunnel was gone but his vision was still out of focus. He tried to pull his head off the deck, but the deck came spinning back up again. A wave of nausea and dizziness took over. When the feelings receded he again lifted his head off the deck, slowly, and realized his face was in the periscope well and his feet up on the main-deck level.

He felt his head, pulled back a hand covered in crusty warm ooze and realized he must have opened his scalp. He tried to drag himself upright but soon saw that he already was upright just by pushing his body slightly away from the deck of the periscope well.

Which meant the ship, what was left of it, was nearly vertical going downward into a dive.

His greatest disappointment was not at losing the ship or even dying, but that he would be unable to transmit the *molniya*, that his grand plan to neutralize the U.S. was dying with him aboard the *Kaliningrad*. He had lived to be a man of history . . . instead, it seemed, he would go down with the most advanced technological underseas craft on earth, a footnote, not an architect of events.

He turned to find the other officers in the compartment lying against what once was the forward bulkhead but with the dive was rapidly becoming the new deck. The eerily tipping room was illuminated only by the light of the battle lanterns, their beams uneven, leaving gaps of darkness.

On the forward bulkhead below, still strapped into the seat in front of the control panel, Senior Lieutenant Vasily Katmonov stared unblinkingly into his lifeless control screen, his body hanging limply from the straps. If not for his moaning, Novskoyy would have thought him dead.

To Katmonov's left, at the corner of the room below the compartment's escape-pod ladder, Warrant Officer Danalov was collapsed in a heap, eyes shut, face white, a hole in his forehead.

Under Katmonov's seat, lying in the corner of what was once the deck and the forward bulkhead, Captain 3rd Rank Dmitri Ivanov watched his blood drip from his arm onto the deck. His face was a grimace of pain as he held his fractured leg with two hands. Ivanov's pained breaths were the only sounds in the compartment other than the arcing of a stray electrical short circuit in the aft area now far overhead.

To Katmonov's right, on the forward bulkhead, now almost horizontal from the ship's dive, Captain-Lieutenant Viktor Chekechev lay half in the shadows, his lower body obscured. What was visible gave little hope . . . face deathly white, breathing uneven, blood trickling from his mouth. Novskoyy moved to go to Chekechev but dizziness enveloped him and he fell, landing on Katmonov's control seat. He ducked his head between his knees and hoped the blood would return, and finally the dizziness did ease and his senses returned.

The pod, he thought. Get to the pod. He limped across the tilted room and found the pod-control panel. He hit the toggle switch that would open the massive motor-driven hatch. Nothing happened.

Fighting dizziness, he looked for a pry bar, any piece of long metal. Nothing. The room was not designed to require pry bars or primitive valve-extension handles.

If the deck wasn't so tilted he might have gotten the wrench that Vlasenko had dropped, the wrench the captain had brought to kill him with.

He climbed back to the hatch and started to bang on the lower hatch with a flashlight, hoping Vlasenko would hear and open the pod from inside.

No response.

CHAPTER
21

SUNDAY, 19 DECEMBER,
0950 GREENWICH MEAN TIME

NORFOLK, VIRGINIA
NORFOLK NAVAL AIR STATION

Admiral Casper "Bobby" McGee, CINCLANT, exited the helicopter and hurried up the ladder rungs to the door of the DC-9
idling at the end of the runway. He had barely gotten to the top
of the ladder when his aide pulled in the ladder and shouted *go*
to the pilot. McGee had nearly been knocked off his feet as the
pilot throttled up, the concrete of runway zero five immediately
blurring outside the still open door as the aide struggled to shut
it.

McGee had never taken seriously the notion of an attack on
the U.S. . . . Nicaragua, Panama, Iraq, moves in the political
chess game far away. That is, until a half hour before when the
call came that a missile was on its way in. The helicopter had
landed in his front yard moments later, startling his sleeping
neighbors. Now McGee listened to his aide's briefing of the current threat—the positions of the enemy submarines, the status
of the U.S. units tracking them.

His conversation with Admiral Donchez replayed itself in his
mind. How could he have not thought that a nation . . . or

some renegade in it . . . with 27,000 nuclear weapons, a nation fractured apart, would never be tempted to use weapons one last time? How could General Tyler in particular so badly have misread the situation? A question for another day . . .

The NESTOR UHF satellite secure-voice circuit blooped, the crypto-gear making the strange noises that indicated its awakening. And as the DC-9 continued climbing to the east at full throttle, McGee took the call from the White House . . .

NORFOLK, VIRGINIA
COMSUBLANT HEADQUARTERS

The President's accent, clear even through the scrambled voice phone, grated on Admiral Donchez's nerves. Particularly when the voice was saying something he disagreed with.

"*Sir*, we've got one-hundred-twenty covert Russian attack subs off the coast. One of them just launched a nuclear cruise missile, headed for me and—"

"Admiral, my advisors tell me you're having it shot down, there's no danger. And there won't be any more missiles launched. I've just received assurances, and I believe them, from President Yulenski that this is a mistake . . . the deployment, the launch . . . He's ordering the fleet back home right now, said he'd order the subs to surface—"

"Can he bring back the dead? Sir, I've been warning about this sort of thing now for days, no one wanted to hear it. General Herman X. Tyler didn't want to hear any *doomsday* talk out of me. Shooting down this missile isn't exactly a done deal, sir."

"Dick," Admiral McGee's voice said on the three-way connection, "better listen to the President—"

"Donchez," the President ordered, "Tell your submarines not to fire on the Russian units. Have them call the Russians on underwater telephone-sonar and tell them to surface. If they won't, well, then you can bump or collide with them, but do not shoot them. Clear?"

"Sir," Donchez said, "We have a Los Angeles Javelin vertical-launch sub off the Russian northern coast right now. I have her on missile alert. One word from you and she'll have twelve Javelins on their way."

"Admiral, recall that submarine. *Now*, goddamnit."

"Admiral, McGee here. The situation is coming under control, don't make it worse—"

"What's your ETA to Pattern Charlie?" Donchez wanted to know when operational control of the fleet would pass to McGee, when he'd be 100 miles out of Norfolk.

"About ten minutes. I'll contact you on NESTOR."

"Roger, ten to Pattern Charlie, and will comply with your orders," Donchez said, trying to keep the anger from his voice. "I'll recall the Javelin sub. But I still recommend reconsidering retaliation—"

But the President had already hung up.

ARCTIC OCEAN
BENEATH THE POLAR ICECAP
FS *KALININGRAD* CONTROL COMPARTMENT ESCAPE POD

When the shock wave had hit the ship and the pod, Vlasenko had been bounced around hitting every surface in the pod. For a moment he wondered if he was blind, felt a warm drip and realized blood was flowing into his eyes.

The pod was turned on its side. The ship, he decided, must be in a terminal velocity dive for the ocean bottom. The rumbling sound of another weapon explosion in the first compartment indicated he had less than a few seconds to try to get into the control compartment and load anyone he could into the pod and detach. He wondered if they were close enough to thin ice for an attempt to escape. It was the only chance he had.

Vlasenko pulled the pod-release lever from the control panel and inserted it between spokes of the hatch-control wheel, then with a grunt pulled on the lever, using it as a pry bar until the wheel broke away. Now he pulled the steel rod out of the wheel and was shocked to see the wheel furiously rotate by itself. The rotating mechanism pulled the hatch-dogs—each a thick banana of steel holding the hatch shut—clear of the pod hatch jamb. He had to jump out of the way as the hatch flew sideways and into the pod.

And Vlasenko found himself staring into the eyes of Admiral Alexi Novskoyy, whose arms were occupied holding the ladder.

Vlasenko balled his fist and smashed it into Novskoyy's face, and the admiral collapsed, falling away into the darkness of the shattered control compartment.

BARENTS SEA
TEN NAUTICAL MILES OFF SEVEROMORSK NAVAL COMPLEX
USS *ALLENTOWN*

As the radioman handed Commander Henry Duckett the flash message, he felt the eyes of the crewmen on him, awaiting word to launch the Javelins.

When he read the message the breath went out of him, partly relief, partly disappointment.

He handed the message to Mills, the OOD.

"Goddamn, sir, first they want us to hightail it up here, then they want us to cock the gun, then they want us to forget it and come on home."

Duckett shook his head. "Secure battlestations, spin down the Javelins and bring us around to course three zero zero, all ahead two thirds. We're getting the hell out of here."

NORFOLK, VIRGINIA
COMSUBLANT HEADQUARTERS

The speaker monitoring the radio communications of the F-14 had just tolled its unhappy message.

"I'll be goddamned, the Mongooses missed, I don't *believe* it . . . they both missed. The cruise missile is still inbound . . ."

The F-14 crew lapsed into stunned silence, the commentary on the Mongoose missiles coming to a sudden halt.

In the COMSUBLANT Flag Plot room Admiral Richard Donchez was the center of attention. Donchez's eyes narrowed as he looked at Lieutenant Commander Kodiak.

"See if CINCLANT's DC-9 is at the Pattern Charlie point. If it is patch in Admiral McGee."

Kodiak nodded. Until McGee could get outside the 100 mile

radius of the city Donchez would remain in command, but once the DC-9 hit the Pattern Charlie point McGee was to take over.

"Sir, the DC-9 is at Pattern Charlie," Kodiak said.

Donchez took the red radio-telephone handset from Kodiak and clicked the speak button. "Nathan Hale, this is Underdog, over."

A longish silence, then: "Nathan Hale standing by," McGee's distorted voice replied. "Go ahead, Underdog. Over." The speaker rasped McGee's voice, ending with a beep as the NESTOR secure-voice signal made its way through the encryption equipment.

"Execute Pattern Charlie. Repeat, execute Pattern Charlie. Break. Acknowledge Pattern Charlie. Break. Over," Donchez said, transferring operational control of all CINCLANTFLEET to the airborne admiral. This operation was now officially Mc-Gee's problem, along with the President's and General Tyler's.

"Dick, McGee here. Copy your Pattern Charlie and acknowledge same. Break . . ." There was a pause, followed by Mc-Gee's "Good luck, Dick, see you soon."

When Donchez spoke, his voice was gravelly. "Kodiak, get on the horn to that F-14 driver. If he hasn't figured it out yet, you ask him if he remembers what a Kamikaze is."

BARENTS SEA
USS ALLENTOWN

Commander Henry Duckett heard the long, rumbling roar come through the hull followed by a vibration that started to shake the ship. The deck trembled, the rumbling got louder, then diminished to a dim growl, which after a moment faded, leaving Duckett's small cabin in silence.

Duckett went to the control room and stepped up on the Conn.

Senior Chief Sonarman Jameson emerged from Sonar. "The noise you heard was an explosion, Captain, a definite underwater explosion. Bearing was north-northeast, covered a broad sector. The bearing line points to an under-ice explosion."

"Was it a hull breaking up?"

"No," Jameson said, shaking his head. "There's a sonar blueout for ten degrees on either side of the bearing."

"A *blueout*? But blueouts can only be caused by bubbles and echoes from a . . . a nuclear detonation—"

Jameson gave him a look. "Exactly, skipper. We believe the explosion was nuclear . . . Was there any warhead test going on out here? Anything in the intel brief about Russian tests under the icecap?"

Duckett shook his head.

"Is there a chance there's a U.S. boat up here?"

"If there is I'm not supposed to know about it," Duckett said.

"British? French?"

"Don't think so."

But Duckett did know more than he was saying. The Squadron Twelve intelligence officer had told him about the weird Russian deployment. He'd also blabbed about a concurrent SNCP mission under the icecap, a secret OP involving covert surveillance. Who did the spook say was going north?

Devilfish.

"Oh, God," Duckett said slowly. Incredibly, the Russian must have gotten the *Devilfish*. With the Russian subs on the coastline, only *Devilfish* and *Allentown* were this far north, everyone else was tied down with the Russian attack boats. Which meant one thing. *Allentown* would have to go under ice and see for sure what had happened. Duckett had never liked that wiseass Michael Pacino and his screw-off boat, but they were American submariners.

"What's going on?" The voice belonged to the XO, Lieutenant Commander Pat Bishop, a short, slight man with a high-pitched, nasal voice. Duckett couldn't stand the voice, couldn't stand the man. The XO was competent, but he was a weasel. More than once Duckett had found him compromising his orders. He had tried to transfer him but the thing had gotten snarled in typical navy red tape.

"You didn't hear the explosion?" Duckett said. He turned to Jameson. "Any idea on range?"

"Negative."

Duckett went to the aft part of the Conn and peered down at the chart table.

"Quartermaster," he called, "plot a bearing line to this detonation."

The line pointed up under the icepack.

"Cap'n," Bishop put in, "you're not thinking of going north, are you?"

Duckett looked at the bearing line, calculating how long it would take to get to the pole.

"Because if you are, let me remind you this ship doesn't have the depth control for an under-ice transit. It also doesn't have a decent under-ice sonar—no SHARKTOOTH. We can't rotate the fair-water planes vertical for penetrating ice with the sail, and even if we could, the sail isn't two-inch-thick steel like on a Piranha, it's fiberglass over aluminum. If you tried to smash through ice we'd wreck it. Besides, we don't have the charts, damn little arctic gear, *and* we don't have a clearance from COMSUBLANT. We'd have to radio in a request for clearance and we can't transmit this close to Russia, they'd detect us . . ."

"You done?" Duckett asked quietly.

"Yes, I am."

"Good, because you're absolutely right. You got all the reasons not to go north."

"Well, sir, I'm glad you agree," and he moved off to his stateroom.

"God," Duckett muttered, "where does NAVPERS even get these bozos?"

The OOD, Lieutenant Mills, heard with pleasure the captain's thought, which he shared.

"Off'sa'deck," Duckett said to Mills, "bring us around to the north, course zero one five, fifteen knots, head under the ice. Keep following the bearing to the explosions. Break out the under-ice procedure. It's been a while since I've been under the icepack . . ."

ARCTIC OCEAN
BENEATH THE POLAR ICECAP
USS *DEVILFISH*

Chief Engineer Delaney wasted no time giving the order to restart the nuclear reactor. The procedures he was about to execute would have made a civilian nuclear operator faint dead away . . . the emergency reactor start-up procedure was so dangerous that it was not even practiced unless the ship was beyond fifty miles from land, and even then only with rigorous controls and supervision. This day Matt Delaney would see how sharp the pencils of naval reactors' design-engineers were. This startup would stress the reactor like it had never been stressed, *including* the shock from the Magnum hit.

Delaney started with a reactor plant in poor condition. With less than minutes left on the battery in this reduced-load status, the running of the reactor main coolant pumps to get flow through the core would exhaust the battery in three minutes or less. The coolant inventory in the core was dangerously low from the previous fast leak from the starboard loop. It would be like trying to start up the Three Mile Island plant in the middle of the accident.

Delaney scanned the instruments. The primary coolant, without the heat input from the nuclear fissions, had cooled to 350 degrees. To warm it to 500 Delaney would be using an emergency heat-up rate. Usually the core was warmed gently at a degree per minute to avoid stressing the thick steel reactor vessel already made brittle by radiation. The emergency heat-up rate had never been done before, on any reactor. It might put enough stress on the plant to blow the head off the reactor vessel, or fracture the six-inch-thick steel.

Even if the warm-up went well the plant was only partly operational. The leak had dumped one coolant loop of highly radioactive water to the reactor compartment bilges. The port steam system was useless with the condenser isolated from the seawater flooding, which left one coolant loop and one steam generator to power one electrical turbine and one main engine.

Assuming he could get the reactor critical fast enough.

Conventional wisdom held that nuclear reactors couldn't explode like nuclear weapons. Natural uranium, melted together with the zirconium fuel metal and control-rod hafnium, ordinarily would not sustain a critical mass to explode like a bomb. Of course, the key was the natural uranium fuel. The reactor of the *Devilfish* was not a natural uranium low-power density core like a civilian land-based unit. The *Devilfish*'s fuel modules were packed with uranium-238, highly enriched uranium. The core had the power of a reactor thirty times its size. If the fuel modules ever did melt down there was a slight chance that the core could form a critical mass and go critical. The result would be a "prompt critical rapid disassembly"—jargon for a detonation.

Well, if they melted down and went prompt critical, he wouldn't be around long enough to worry about it. He began his string of orders, each vital to waking the beast in the reactor compartment:

"Check battleshort switch. Secure emergency cooling—shut XC-9. Pass the word to the Engineering Watch Supervisor, shut all scram breakers and equalize around and open Main Steam Two. Manderson, take the operational-mode selector-switch to cutback override, low-pressure cutout switch to low-pressure cutout, source range channel selector switch to start-up rate scram cutout. Ready? Start number-two main coolant pump in slow speed."

Petty Officer Manderson, the reactor operator, stood and pulled up on pump two's T-handle. With a thump of check valves, the pump started. The battery amp-hour digital meter on the electrical panel immediately began clicking.

"Battery discharge rate is 800 amps, Eng," the electrical operator said.

Delaney frowned. They were sucking a tremendous current from an almost dead battery. This would be a helluva race against time.

"Apply latch voltage to inverter alpha."

Manderson grabbed the pistol grip in the center of the panel and rotated it to the RODS IN position as he pulled it out from the panel face.

The chronometer in the maneuvering room over the door clicked off the seconds. The digital amp-hour meter of the plant-control panel clicked three times a second, each click bringing the ship closer to total loss of power.

"Group one rods latched," Manderson said, releasing the pistol grip.

"RO, pull rod group one to criticality. Nine decades per minute start-up rate. Give me heatup of the reactor to 500 degrees."

Delaney then announced on Circuit Two, a general announcing system in the aft spaces of the ship:

"ENGINEERING WATCH SUPERVISOR, COMMENCE COOLANT DISCHARGE FROM THE PORT LOOP. PRESSURE BAND 1600 TO 1800."

Manderson began pulling the control rods out of the core and the group-one rod position indicator clicked up at tremendous speed. Manderson fought to keep the spring-loaded pistol-grip switch in the RODS OUT position. Usually during a fast recovery startup, control rods were quickly pulled to criticality at a rate of five decades per minute, ten times the rate of a civilian reactor startup. Today the engineer had ordered pulling at nine decades per minute, the needle at the top of the gage face. This reactor would fry them to a nuclear crisp if the startup didn't go perfectly.

"Start number four main coolant pump in slow," Delaney ordered, as reactor power entered the power range.

Manderson pulled on its T-handle. The amp-hour meter on the electric plant control panel ticked off the life of the battery.

"Eng," the electrical operator said, "we're losing the battery! I've gotta lower voltage!"

"No way," Delaney said. "C'mon, Manderson, heat this bitch up. Pull the rods."

Manderson pulled rods out of the core with the pistol-grip switch. As the rods passed 16 inches out the temperature-needle swam off 350 degrees and headed upward, a second later reading 390, 410, 420, 435, 450, 470.

As the core heated, the sound of a creaking, shrieking noise could be heard forward from the direction of the reactor compartment.

Manderson yelled over his shoulder, "Sir, it's gonna blow, thermal stress—"

Delaney yelled back, looking at the dangerously low battery voltage.

"Keep pulling, it's our only chance—"

"500 degrees, sir."

Delaney grabbed his P.A. microphone. "ENGINEERING WATCH SUPERVISOR, EMERGENCY WARMUP THE STARBOARD TURBINE GENERATOR."

"Sir, only seconds left on the battery!"

"Hold on!" Actually, Delaney knew, the electrical operator was just as helpless as he was to keep the battery from dying. If they lost power now there would be no main coolant pumps circulating hot water to the boilers, no steam and no turbine generators. The ship would never recover. It was now, or never.

The only acknowledgment from the Engineering Watch Supervisor was the howl of a turbine starting to come up to full revolutions in one massive burst of steam, sounding like a jet engine spinning up to full power.

Delaney had never heard so welcome a sound.

A shout came at the door from the EWS, a sweating chief. "Starboard TG at 3600 RPM! On the governor and ready for loading!"

Delaney was calling to the electrical operator before the EWS had finished. "Shift to a half power lineup on the port TG."

The electrical operator didn't need to be told. As he paralleled in the turbine generator's bus to the battery-powered vital bus, the battery breaker tripped open, the battery completely exhausted.

There had, literally, not been a half-second to spare.

The torpedo room was a wreck, a flooded hellhole. Pacino stood in three feet of water looking at the devastation. He had no idea how the flooding had been stopped. There was not a living person in the space, only men floating face-down in the water. Someone must have died stopping the flooding and had saved the ship.

Shattered weapons were scattered throughout the compartment, dumping explosive self-oxidizing fuel into the water, and self-oxidized fuel was reactive enough to burn underwater, Pacino realized. The water must be flowing into the battery well through the seams of the well's deck hatch . . . which meant that chlorine gas would be pouring out of it at any minute.

Pacino reached into the overhead, opened a cubbyhole, pulled out a gas mask and put it on, inhaling stale copper-flavored air.

The battery hatch blew open, sending up a pressurized geyser of green chlorine gas. Once the cloud escaped, the water in the space rushed into the battery well. There would be maybe ten or twenty seconds before the battery exploded, Pacino thought. He took a deep breath, unplugged his hose from the manifold of the air line and ran back up the ladders to the control room, thinking that he had not seen a living soul since slapping Rapier's cheek. As he rounded the bend at the top of the stairs at his stateroom door, it occurred to him that the lights were still on. In spite of the flooded battery. The engineer must have gotten the reactor critical! He hurried into Control, feeling the first glimmer of hope in a very long time.

When the battery exploded below, it was a searing thump. He finally made it into the control room two decks up from where he had unplugged his hose. Lungs near-bursting, he found the manifold above the smoking wreck of the Pos Three panel and plugged in. When he had sucked in a few breaths he was glad to see other air hoses snaking through the space. And he saw Rapier still sitting limp on the bench seat, but wearing a gas mask and looking at Pacino.

Suddenly a voice on the P.A. screamed from a speaker:

"CONN, MANEUVERING, HALF POWER LINEUP ON THE STARBOARD TG, PROPULSION SHIFTED TO THE STARBOARD MAIN ENGINE. PROPULSION LIMIT, AHEAD STANDARD."

Pacino reached for the microphone. "ENGINEER, CAPTAIN," Pacino's voice boomed throughout the ship, "AHEAD STANDARD! MAX TURNS!" Then as an afterthought: "TOXIC GAS EMERGENCY IN THE TORPEDO ROOM. ALL HANDS DON EMERGENCY MASKS."

Ahead standard, 16 knots, was all the speed the ship would make with one main engine. Pacino walked through the space, the men dazed except for the XO, and grabbed the helmsman's seatbelt.

With a click and a gentle nudge, the helmsman collapsed to the deck on top of the Diving Officer. Pacino kneeled on the seat, looked up at the gyrocompass, still functioning. He watched as the speed-indicator needle came off the peg and pointed up to 16 knots, then turned the helmsman's wheel to port, bringing the ship around to a course of zero three zero to get back to the polynya. Flying by the seat of his pants as he was, he could overshoot, undershoot or drive right or left of it.

But one thing was very clear. They were still under thick ice. If he couldn't get to the polynya, he and his crew would join his father at the bottom of the Arctic Ocean.

NORFOLK, VIRGINIA
NORFOLK NAVAL STATION

For the SSN-X-27 cruise missile, it was time. Time to detonate the device in the nosecone. A thick steel plate in the detonator train rotated, lining up two pieces of the main detonator. The electrical system sent a spark to the main detonator, and it exploded into a ball of flames. The flames propagated to the igniters, six pie-shaped explosive charges set in a circle around a doughnut of plutonium surrounded by a can of heavy water, the deuterium.

The flame front reached the six igniters. Two microseconds later the igniters imploded the plutonium doughnut inward, collapsing it into a massive ball.

Lieutenant Commander Todd Nikels didn't need to be reminded of what a Kamikaze was. He estimated the SSN-X-27 cruise missile to be about 500 feet ahead, beginning to fly over the deserted submarine piers below. The F-14's wings were already swept back, ready to let him go supersonic. Nikels slammed the keys on the port console forward to the stops and felt a burst of acceleration as the thrust threw the massive jet toward the missile ahead. The missile grew, and within seconds it was just slightly to starboard and above, putting out a visible hot gas exhaust in the dawning light.

Nikels pulled the control stick back, aiming the F-14's right-wing leading edge at the missile.

As the jet passed through Mach 2 the starboard wing sliced

through the cruise missile forward of its intake-duct. The missile, already exploding, blew itself apart in pieces that flew backward in the airstream outside the F-14.

The cruise missile was destroyed, making it almost harmless, only its cloud of poisonous and radioactive plutonium a concern. Compared to a nuclear explosion, the contamination was almost minor.

That was the good news for Nikels.

The bad news was that his starboard wing had been cut off at the fuselage reinforcement, ripping out the starboard engine compressor, turbine and intake duct with it. The debris from the ripped-off wing and engine removed both tail vertical stabilizers and the starboard horizontal stabilizer. The fuel, contained in the wings and the central fuselage, instantly caught fire, enveloping the already spinning aircraft in flames.

Nikels watched his aircraft disintegrate. As it began to tumble out of control, he felt the blast of air when the canopy flew off the cockpit. Only then did he realize his radar-intercept officer, Brad Tollson, had started the ejection sequence.

Nikels tried to pull his arms tight into his ribcage and grab the ejection seat curtain above his head, but apparently Tollson was too far ahead of him. The ejection-seat rockets fired while Nikels was still trying to pull his arms in toward his body. The cockpit flew away from him. As he cleared the canopy his flopping right arm was torn off by the force of the 1200-knot jetstream. Nikels stared at his shoulder, at blood flying off into the slipstream. Now the rest of the F-14 exploded, transforming it into a fireball.

As blood poured out of his shoulder wound, Nikels lost blood pressure, and with it consciousness . . . Mercifully.

Two seconds later his parachute opened, a mere ten feet from the concrete of Norfolk Naval Station's Pier Seven. Nikels hit the concrete at over 600 knots, his body scattering down the narrow strip some 200 feet. Almost immediately it became covered with radioactive contamination from the plutonium/deuterium fusion bomb he had just destroyed.

CHAPTER
22

SUNDAY, 19 DECEMBER, 0956, GREENWICH MEAN TIME

ARCTIC OCEAN
BENEATH THE POLAR ICECAP
USS *DEVILFISH*

Pacino visualized the geometry of the sea around him. He had always kept the ship's position in reference to a polynya committed to memory, just like they'd taught in Prospective Commanding Officer School. He estimated the ship to be only one nautical mile from the southwest edge of the polynya . . . one mile, only 2000 yards, and they could vertical surface as if nothing had happened. A quick radio call for help and this nightmare could be over.

Pacino's lifted spirits would have been crushed if he could have taken a single glance at Delaney's reactor plant control panel. The 2000 yards to the polynya might as well have been 2000 miles.

Matt Delaney looked over Manderson's shoulder at the reactor plant control panel. It was like the Three Mile Island nuclear accident all over again and there was nothing he could do about it.

The reactor leak from the starboard loop had not been completely isolated by the reactor main coolant cutout valves as he had hoped. The gate valves, designed to seal the coolant system off from a massive pipe rupture, had failed them. Probably from the shock. All the time the ship had been driving toward the polynya the starboard reactor-main-coolant cutout-valves had been leaking and dumping the radioactive coolant into the reactor-compartment bilges. The reactor's lifeblood was spilling into the bilges, setting off radiation alarms aft of frame 57, the entrance to the reactor-compartment tunnel.

Delaney had tried to compensate by charging to the coolant system with the charge pump and the valve-operating water-flasks, but he was soon out of pure water. The number one and two charging water-storage tanks, the charging-water day tank and the valve-operating water-flasks dry. The evaporator, which made pure water from seawater, had been out of commission since the collision.

So Delaney had been forced to charge seawater into the coolant system in spite of the fact that the plant had been specifically designed to prevent the introduction of seawater into the delicate nuclear systems. The chlorine could corrode the pressure vessel within hours, maybe minutes, in addition to the contaminants in the seawater becoming radioactive. The seawater hose had been hooked up and the seawater was charged in, but the high-pressure charging pump could only barely keep up with the loss rate, and finally the overworked pump had burned up in a cloud of black smoke. With no water makeup, the loss-of-coolant accident began.

While Delaney watched, helpless, the level in the pressurizer tank dropped from 65 inches to 10 in less than a minute. The pressurizer was what kept the 500-degree water liquid instead of steam; when the pressurizer emptied, the entire system would boil to steam.

The reactor siren broke the eerie silence of the room.

"Low-pressure port loop, sir," Manderson shouted. "Low-pressure cutback, group one rods!"

The reactor "realized" it was depressurizing and was trying to lower power by driving in control rods, as it was programmed to do.

"Override the cutback and silence the alarm," Delaney ordered. He would get every last ounce of propulsion out of the plant—it was a goner anyway, and who knew, maybe they were only a shiplength from thin ice . . .

As the level in the pressurizer dropped to zero, water still leaking out of the system, the little water remaining began to boil to steam in the core. The siren, just silenced a moment before, wailed again in the small room, which seemed suddenly even smaller.

"Low-level pressurizer, sir. Heater cutout."

As pressure dropped, Delaney ordered the plant to be shut down. "Manderson, insert a full scram."

"Rods aren't dropping, sir. The fuel elements must be melting!"

The nuclear reactor became uncovered, boiling away the last remaining coolant. The fuel elements in the core melted, fuel pooled in the lower head of the reactor vessel and began to melt through the thick steel. Up to this point Delaney hadn't notified Pacino in control—what the hell could the captain do about it?

An alarm bell sounded in the room, announcing the high radiation in the engine room. Delaney pulled the microphone down out of the overhead.

"CAPTAIN, ENGINEER. REACTOR SCRAM. CORE IS UNCOVERED AND FUEL IS MELTING. BATTERY'S DEAD AND STEAM POWER IS GONE. RECOMMEND YOU EMERGENCY BLOW TO THE . . . TO THE ICE."

Delaney put down the microphone. Suddenly it was very cold in the engine room.

FS *KALININGRAD*

Vlasenko lowered his aching body down the rungs of the ladder, now at a crazy 50-degree angle to the vertical. Actually he came more over than down—and stepped over a limp form . . . *Novskoyy*. Some previous head injury must have knocked out the admiral with more force than his punch. He hadn't really connected solidly.

A booming noise diverted him from his inspection of the escape-pod release-system, and he looked over to the port side to see the signal-analysis console explode. The deck was too steep to climb far enough aft to see exactly what had happened. But he didn't have to see the console at close range to know the cause of the console explosion—the titanium inner-hull framing was sticking out in a large bulge just on top of the console. The hull was beginning to fail, and as he thought this, the console under the bulge started to leak seawater onto the deck. Vlasenko stared at the leak, refusing to believe that this high-tech hull had actually been breached . . . Titanium failure could only mean that they had gone below 2000 meters, the maximum-safety depth, though there were no working pressure indicators in the space now that the computers were dead. The ominous flicker of the overhead battle lantern brought him back to grim reality.

The water stream was raining down at him now, the forward bulkhead was a deck as the submarine dived at a 90-degree angle. Vlasenko looked over at the ladder to the escape pod—it was completely horizontal. He realized he had only moments left to get the crew out before the hull of the compartment gave way. He decided on Ship Control Officer Katmonov, still strapped into his seat. He tried to release the five-point seat-harness, but with Katmonov's body weight on it the release lever wouldn't work. He left him and pulled Ivanov's body up by his armpits. Ivanov was still breathing, going in and out of consciousness. Vlasenko hauled him up and staggered over to the ladder to the pod. The straight-down angle of the ship actually helped at this point, giving him a level surface on which to carry Ivanov. But the treads of the escape-pod ladder would trip him. Vlasenko set Ivanov down on the ladder and slid him over to the hatch, then with one final push he got the man into the pod.

The compartment shuddered, the flooding got worse. Now there were ten centimeters of water covering the control console. Vlasenko pulled Chekechev over out of the water and checked to see if he was breathing. He was dead. Blood came out of his mouth. Vlasenko felt a rush of anger—at Novskoyy, at the attacking submarine.

The water was lapping now at the pod's hatch. If he took any more time the pod would be flooded, finishing them all. He waded back to Katmonov through the water that now submerged the long dead control console. Katmonov was still suspended by his safety harness to the control seat. The water had swallowed his arms and legs. His head hung into the black water but he was not conscious enough to raise up from it and sputtered while he tried to breathe, coughing the water out.

Vlasenko took a deep breath, dived below the oily water and grabbed Katmonov's seat harness, trying to release the kid's harness before the water drowned him. But the water was too high, now submerging the back of the chair. Vlasenko's fingers, numbed from the cold, fumbled at the harness release, jammed by the shock of the weapon or frozen by the cold.

Lungs bursting, Vlasenko forced himself back to the surface and gasped for air, spitting up the dirty water. He realized his feet were no longer touching bottom—

A rumbling explosion jarred the ship, then another.

The weapons in the first compartment were exploding.

Vlasenko dived into the water, pulled himself down by pulling on Katmonov's shirt. As he made his way into the blackness of the water he felt Katmonov's hand grab his arm.

The kid was still alive.

Vlasenko found the harness, pulled hard on it . . . the harness was still frozen. He gave the release lever one last jerk, and it finally yielded. He managed to pull Katmonov from the seat, then got to the surface. As he burst through, he saw Novskoyy, and felt a wave of fatigue that nearly destroyed his will to survive.

He looked up at the flooding from the upper bulkhead of the compartment, then hauled Katmonov to the pod hatch, now half underwater, and floated him in. It was easier now, with the water in the compartment. He was about to slide into the pod hatch himself when the face of Alexi Novskoyy came floating into view in the semi-darkness.

At first Vlasenko thought that the admiral must be dead, but as he turned to swim away Novskoyy's eyes fluttered open and the admiral looked directly at him, grabbed his sleeve and collar.

No time to gloat, no time even to push Novskoyy away, much as he was tempted. However mixed his feelings, he told himself it would take less time to pull Novskoyy into the pod than to fight him off. As he pulled the admiral to the ladder, the man lost consciousness and his head began to bump on the rungs of the ladder, now horizontal to the pod.

By the time Vlasenko reached the pod hatch it was half gone, the water flooding the pod. He pulled Novskoyy in, saw that the admiral had collapsed and was floating face down, pulled him up away from the water and struggled to shut the hatch. It took all his strength to push the hatch against the water and turn the wheel.

When he turned away from the hatch he saw that Novskoyy had fallen back into the murky water. He set him back up, out of reach of the icy water and draped his arm around a handhold. Ivanov and Katmonov had their eyes open now and were shivering. Ivanov, hands grasping his leg, rocked back and forth in pain.

Vlasenko began to make his way to the pod control-panel just as the lantern in the pod flickered and died, shorted by the water. He felt his way to the panel, maneuvering through the numbingly cold seawater, found the panel in the dark, reached to its upper right corner, shut his eyes and pulled up on the toggle switch, praying that the pod would release from the mortally wounded submarine. The switch clicked home into the RELEASE position.

Nothing happened.

USS *DEVILFISH*

Two thousand lousy yards from survival and the reactor melts down.

Pacino couldn't blame Delaney, he couldn't have done any better.

He let go of the yoke of the control panel and climbed to the ballast panel as the lights went out. The ventilation fans wound down again and the room plunged into silence, illuminated by the single bulb of the battle lantern Pacino had turned on just moments before after the blast.

He plugged his gas mask into the manifold of the ballast control panel, looking up into the overhead as if he could see through the dark water to the ice cover. The ice was probably 100 feet thick here, he thought, and ice that thick was equivalent to five feet of steel. Even if he could get the ship up to 20 knots on an emergency blow, wouldn't the ice crush them? Try, damn it.

Pacino got ready to blow all main ballast tanks under the thick ice cover. He reached up to the forward lever, pulled the plunger cap down and rotated the lever from straight-down to straight-up.

The six eight-inch ball valves in the high-pressure air lines were self-actuated by air pressure, the huge valves clunked open with a crash, then connected 4500 psi air in the air bottles with the seawater-filled forward ballast tanks. In an explosion of expanding air, the seawater was forced out of the tanks, making the *Devilfish* light forward.

The room filled up with a vapor cloud as the blast of air noise slammed into Pacino's eardrums. He pulled the aft emergency-blow lever up to the open position, the air noise got even louder. Now the aft ballast tanks, assaulted by the ultra-high-pressure air, gave up their seawater. Seconds later the air bottles of the emergency blow system were empty of air, and all main ballast tanks of the *Devilfish* were empty of seawater.

Pacino looked expectantly at the depth gage, waiting for it to click their depth up a foot.

It was silent.

Of course, it was dead . . . no electricity, the reactor down, the battery flooded and excreting chlorine gas. Pacino found a flashlight by the blow switches and turned it onto one of the back-up analog pressure gages, the primitive bourdon-tube type that didn't need electricity to sense pressure. It showed them deep—740 feet; it would take a while for the gage to sense the ship rising.

Pacino saw the first sign in the ship's liquid-filled inclinometer. It took on a degree-up angle—*they were on the way up*. The water in the forward and aft bilges must be rushing aft, he thought, the angle inclining upward much faster than during a normal emergency blow. He hoped the up-angle wouldn't spill the air out of the ballast tanks and, God forbid, send them back to the bottom.

He shined the flashlight around the room, taking in the stunned faces behind the gas masks. Even if they made it through the hundred-foot-thick icecap, how in hell would he get them out of the ship? And if he did, what then?

Concentrate on the control panel, he told himself. The depth gage read 690 feet. At last the ascent had started.

Pacino sucked the stale dry air of the emergency system, waiting, waiting for . . . ?

FS *KALININGRAD*

Vlasenko reached over for the release lever—gone, lost in the black water half-flooding the pod. He dived into the water, twice, and found it. He struggled back up to the control panel, took a long moment to find it again in the dark, pushed the lever into the retaining bolt and rotated the lever to release the pod.

Again, nothing happened.

Exhausted, frustrated, Vlasenko leaned back against the freezing bulkhead of the pod, then searched for the flashlight cradle. At least he could die with the lights on. It took a while but he found the flashlight bolted to a spot on the sphere skin, pulled it free and clicked on the switch. Its weak yellow light barely lit the pod.

The pod shuddered—the control compartment finally collapsing and imploding from the depth. Vlasenko aimed the lantern at the depth gage—2100 meters and still sinking. And the pod's interior-orientation still showed the ship pointed straight down, the wooden benches crazily vertical, a hatch on one side, another opposite it.

The air in the pod was not as cold as before, with the four of them breathing into it, but it was stuffier. The water was agonizingly cold. Vlasenko decided there was no longer any hope. He felt like grabbing Novskoyy's pistol and shooting himself. He glanced at the admiral. The pistol was gone, lost during the explosion.

The pod hull creaked, starting to dimple, to give from the pressure, the titanium flowing. Undergoing creep deformation, the pressure outside too much. It wouldn't be long now.

The depth gage read 2375 meters.

The ship, what was left of it, shuddered again and a long loud rumbling propagated through the water and steel, the last of it a ripping, tearing sound. The shock and vibration slammed Ivanov's head into the dimpling titanium bulkhead. Drifting in and out of consciousness, the last impact knocked him out.

The last remaining compartment of the *Kaliningrad*, the second, had imploded from the seawater pressure.

Vlasenko shined his light at Ivanov and saw blood on his collar. He shook his head, and then a crazy curiosity, irrelevant under the circumstances, came over him . . . he wanted to know the crush depth of the pod.

He directed the light at the depth gage again, expecting to see it read 2500 meters. Instead it read 1900. *1900.*

The pod was moving differently now, shaking and swaying—not the motion of the hull of the ship but of an escape pod on *ascent.* The last impact must have jarred the pod loose from the hull. He looked again at the gage. 1800 meters, then 1750 . . . they were rising quickly, even with the water they had shipped through the hatch. Vlasenko checked the gage. 1000 meters. They were rising like a bubble from the sea, soon they would be at the surface—

The surface is thick ice cover.

The gage needle unwound. 500 meters. 400. 300.

Vlasenko tried to steady the men against the shock to come when the buoyant pod, rushing up from the deep, slammed into the ice. He grabbed lifejackets and plastic-wrapped ration kits and tried to cushion the overhead of the pod. The pod was still rising sideways, with no stability. A final glance at the depth gage—50 meters and rising fast.

He could only hope that the ice had been broken up by the explosion . . .

The escape pod of the *Kaliningrad* hit the ice raft going five meters per second, causing a jarring impact in the pod. The depth gage read under 5 meters, by the look of the needle maybe only one meter. So they would float here, separated from the frigid world above, by a single meter of merciless, mocking, unforgiving ice.

Vlasenko could no longer feel any sensation in his arms or legs. He lay there in the trapped pod with the wounded, waiting for sleep and an end to the cold.

USS *DEVILFISH*

The USS *Devilfish* rose toward the surface at a 45-degree angle, speeding up to 19 knots from the buoyant force. Pacino held onto the control panel, watching the face of the analog depth gage, the needle unwinding as the paralyzed ship rose from the air in her ballast tanks. Still 1800 yards southwest of the polynya, they were about to challenge thick ice. Pacino had a final command decision: to shut his eyes or watch the gage as the ship shot upward. He decided to keep his eyes open. The needle unwound. 400 feet, 300, 150 . . .

Pacino changed his mind. He shut his eyes tight.

CHAPTER
23

SUNDAY, 19 DECEMBER, 0958
GREENWICH MEAN TIME

Arctic Ocean
Polar Icecap Surface

The pressure ridge at the southwest edge of the polynya was 80 feet thick. The molecules that formed the crystalline structure of the ice had been motionless, frozen for centuries, last existing as liquid water a thousand years before. For those centuries the structure of the ice had been solid as concrete, one piece of a massive structure forming the polar icecap.

At 0945 Greenwich Mean Time a nuclear explosion had detonated under the ice pack five kilometers to the northwest. Its chief effect was a multitude of hairline cracks formed throughout the structure of the ice, but being hairline cracks, the tremendous cold and pressure from the weight of the ice raft was already rewelding the ice together into one piece.

At 0958 a 4500-ton nuclear submarine smashed into the ice's underside. The submarine was travelling at 32 feet per second. The force of the impact was equivalent to that of a locomotive going 231 miles per hour, or twelve one-thousand-pound artillery shells fired at point-blank range. Or a small nuclear detonation.

The ice exploded upward as if slammed by the fist of God.

The *Devilfish*'s sonar sphere was crushed, flattened to a plate and slammed into the thick steel of the bow compartment, which was also crushed, rupturing and bursting. By the time the bow compartment had ruptured, the ice's protest was over and a hole 50 feet in diameter formed. The displaced ice flew upward and outward, splintering into fragments and shards.

The cylindrical hull of the *Devilfish* flew through the hole onto the ice, the first third of her smashed into a compressed lump, her sail sheared off at the hull. The rest continued up and forward through the hole, the entire length of her coming out of the ice like some giant whale, moving over the edge of a slight ridge and coming to rest two hundred feet from the hole on the downhill slope of the pressure ridge. At the bottom of the gentle slope, a thousand feet away, was the lake of thin ice that *Devilfish* had been aiming for.

The control room, already devastated by the shock of the Magnum, changed violently. Where before the room had retained its shape and symmetry, the collision with the ice fractured the steel hoop frames of the pressure hull. The energy of the sudden deceleration threw people and consoles and seats and chunks of steel forward, a rain of flesh and pieces of steel. Several of the men who had survived the first shock, including Lieutenant Rod Van Dyne, the sonar officer, were hurled forward and killed instantly.

Pacino was thrown face-first into the ballast control panel, the wraparound console in the control room's forward port corner, taking the force of the collision in the face. The emergency air-breathing mask Plexiglas faceplate caved in, the remainder of the impact-load transferred to Pacino's face. The mask came off as he slid down the panel, his face hitting the Chief of the Watch's seat, his arms limp. He hung there for a moment, then fell to the deck, his head facing the lower portion of the console, the deck slick with oil or blood or seawater—in the dim light of the lantern it was impossible to say.

And somewhere under the thin ice was a 90-ton titanium pod with four men inside, all losing consciousness from exposure to the extreme cold.

By 1001 GMT the eruption from the ice was over.

The black submarine, its snout smashed, lay on the ice like

some beached behemoth, tilted over into a 20-degree port-list and lying on the ice's downslope. The strange metal beast from the deep lay there, motionless, inert. Inside the vessel was like the outside.

Nothing moved.

For a long while Pacino had been staring at the underside of a seat and the face of a console. The light was very dim. His face was cold where it touched the tile of the deck. He tried to identify the console he was looking at but had never seen it from this angle before.

He heard a voice in the distance.

"Captain? You okay?" The voice was muffled, choked. Pacino tried to roll over toward the noise. It took a long time, and it hurt.

"Manderson, the skipper lost his mask. Get it on him; I'll try to open the bridge hatch."

It got hard to breathe. Pacino couldn't see. There was a cloud in front of him, he felt like his head was in a fish bowl. He tried to struggle against it, but as he brought in the dry coppery air to his lungs his mental fog seemed to dissipate.

And he knew where he was. Slowly, fighting the pain, he struggled to his feet and found himself at the darkened ballast-control panel.

Engineer Matt Delaney was trying to undog the hatch to the bridge trunk. It seemed stuck. Pacino found his flashlight and searched the overhead for the valve-extension handle, the one bolted into the overhead that was used to open and shut the drain and vent valves of the snorkel mast and induction piping. The valves were too far up in the overhead to reach by hand and were nestled behind layers of piping and cables. The valve-extension handle was a steel rod four feet long. Pacino found it, pulled it out of its retaining cradle and limped forward to the hatch.

Pacino could see well enough to make it to Delaney and jam the bar into the wheel of the hatch. The two men pushed on the bar, using it as a lever, and finally the wheel moved, undogging the hatch. While Pacino waited, he surveyed the control room in the dim light of Manderson's hand-held flashlight. It was listing to port and pitched slightly forward. Emergency-breathing air hoses snaked through the room, ending in faces that were mostly unconscious. The worst was looking at the bodies that had no masks.

"Skipper, look!"

Delaney had opened the bridge-trunk hatch. Except that there was no bridge trunk. Bright white glaring light poured into the room from the hatch. And with it, a blast of frigid arctic air.

Pacino went to the hatch and looked up. He grabbed the rungs of the ladder to the hatch and raised his head into the light.

He pulled off the gas mask and gasped the outside air, so cold it burned his lungs. It was a spectacular scene. The sky was overcast, but any sky was welcome after what the *Devilfish* had been through. Pacino could see that what had once been the sail was ripped completely off, making this hatch lead onto the scarred outer deck of the ship. The hull aft seemed intact but the sonar sphere and the bow compartment were gone, crushed. The diesel would be useless now.

The ship, amazingly, was lying on *top* of the ice, on some kind of hill, not afloat in a polynya. It took a moment for Pacino to comprehend this. They hadn't just smashed a hole in the ice, they had gone *through* it, and come to rest on the surface of it. By the time Pacino believed his eyes, the implications of reality hit him.

4500 tons of nuclear submarine on the ice surface. How long can the ice hold up that heavy a load, concentrated in one spot? Ice weak enough to let us through in the first place?

"Eng," Pacino said, "we got to abandon ship, *now*."

"Captain, it must be ten below out there. We can't get the crew out until we unstow the arctic gear—"

"Get a crew together and get the damned gear. Most of it's in the ship's office and ESM. The shelter's stowed in the fan room. Hurry up, God knows how long this ship will stay up here before it goes down through the ice. Get a couple men you can spare to go through the ship and help the survivors up here. We'll exit out this hatch. Did you bring all the guys from back aft?"

"They're here, still alive. For how long . . . with the reactor melted we probably got 800 or 900 rem. And you guys up here probably got almost half that much." Both knew that at 1000 rem of radiation there would be virtually no survivors.

Delaney rounded up half a dozen men and headed aft to get the arctic gear.

Petty Officer Manderson tried to slap awake the men in the space. Pacino walked to the passageway aft of the control room and stopped at the door to his stateroom.

One last look. It had its own battle lantern, which he flipped on, knowing what he would see. A complete wreck. Nothing salvageable. As he was about to leave he saw the framed Jolly Roger flag, still in its frame and bolted to the wall. He pulled the frame open, ripped the flag off of the backing, rolled it into a ball and put it into his pocket. He took a final look around and left, then with a second thought went back in and turned off the battle lantern. Sort of a gesture of respect, like shutting the staring eyes of a corpse.

Pacino went back to the control room, got a fur parka from Delaney and shrugged into it. The crew passed the arctic gear out the bridge-trunk hatch, and then the gear and crewmembers were out of the ship.

Pacino found himself alone in the control room with Delaney, who was at the foot of the ladder to the bridge-trunk hatch, ready to leave the ship.

"Come on," Delaney urged. "Every second in here is another couple million neutrons in your tissues. And like you said, the ice under the ship could collapse any second."

"I'll be out in a minute. Just make sure the ice camp is far enough away from the boat. When the ice goes I don't want it taking out the men we have left."

Delaney nodded, lingered a moment and climbed the ladder.

And now Michael Pacino was alone in the shattered, burning control room of his crippled submarine. He stood by the burned-out fire-control console and looked up at the periscope stand, at the Conn, and realized his command of the *Devilfish* was over. He looked back into the room lit only by the orange lights of the battle lanterns, and spotted the other Jolly Roger on the control-room aft bulkhead, the skull and crossbones white against the black field, the ship's motto sewn above and below the pirate emblem. YOU AIN'T CHEATIN', YOU AIN'T TRYIN'. Well, goddamn it, he'd tried.

He was only dimly aware of Lieutenant Commander Matt Delaney returning and pulling him up by his arms and dragging him to the bridge-trunk hatch.

Pacino sat on a sleeping bag near a wall of the shelter, sipping a mug of steaming coffee that Jon Rapier had handed him, staring at the leering ram's head of the *Devilfish* emblem on the coffee mug.

The arctic shelter was a semirigid polyethylene bubble with a rumbling emergency diesel generator for warmth and light. The shelter had food for several days for the number of men that had survived the emergency surfacing. Besides Pacino, Rapier and Delaney, thirty others from the ship had escaped alive.

Which meant that there were 33 potential survivors from a crew of 127. A lousy survival rate, Pacino thought, but just hours before the whole crew had seemed doomed by the Russian Magnum torpedo. Only a few men remained unconscious, some with head wounds, some with internal injuries.

It was snowing outside, ten degrees below zero, but there was no wind. The sun would be low on the horizon, daytime here. And arctic days could last for months at this latitude. Rapier had set up flares around the shelter in hopes of a satellite pass picking up the heat and vectoring in rescue aircraft.

Pacino drained his cup and set it on the liner deck. Deep-bone exhausted, he shut his eyes. He would sleep, just for a moment . . .

Pacino woke to the sound of a nearby explosion, a snapping violent cracking noise.

From the direction of the *Devilfish*.

The men in the shelter got to their feet and ran out the shelter door, some forgetting their parkas.

Pacino looked over the ridge of ice toward the ship—another nightmare vision to etch itself onto his brain. As Pacino watched, in a steady, slow motion, the huge vessel broke free from her position on the ridge and began to slide down the hill, picking up speed, a 4500-ton radioactive sled finally going slightly sideways the last 100 feet. The ice beneath Pacino's feet shook as the massive ship slid to the bottom of the slope and skidded out to the flats of the thin ice. The ice around her shattered into tiny slivers, and the ship settled into the black water that had appeared where there was once ice. The rudder and sternplanes vanished first. In a long loud agonizing slide, the vessel moved backward and resubmerged. As the ship sank, it took on an up-angle, then slid more quickly into the water with a rushing sound of a zillion exploding bubbles.

Pacino watched as the bridge-access trunk, through which he had stuck his head only hours before, sank into the arctic water, the foam and bubbles filling his control room. The nose of the sub, hopelessly mangled by the collision with the ice, was all that remained. For a long moment, only the twisted steel of the sonar sphere was visible, and then it too vanished in a geyser of white foam and bubbles. All that was left of the USS *Devilfish* was the wash of bubbles and the hole in the ice, the water in the hole already skinning over in the arctic cold.

Pacino's mouth was twisted downward. He wanted to scream, but knew he could not. All he could do was turn his face from the awful sight, and away from the eyes of his men.

CHAPTER
24

SUNDAY, 19 DECEMBER,
1230 GREENWICH MEAN TIME

Arctic Ocean
Polar Icecap Surface

The world in front of Pacino was a jumble of white and gray, but he did not see the snow and the ice and the sky. They were only the blank screen for his mind to replay the scene of the *Devilfish* sinking into the arctic water.

As he turned and trudged up the snowy slope to the ice shelter near the ridge the wind began, slowly at first, then gathering momentum, the snowflakes stinging his face. Behind him he heard the excited shouts of his men, their voices running together in a blur that seemed to blend with the wind and the snow. After what seemed hours he reached the large bubble of the shelter, the snow flying almost horizontally in the biting arctic wind.

He shouldered aside the heavy curtains at the shelter's entrance and walked to his sleeping bag. The shelter was deserted. Pacino sank down to his sleeping bag and leaned against the cold wall. The wind howled outside, blowing the snow against the shelter wall. The emergency diesel generator rumbled in the center of the shelter, its air coming from the inner pipe of the double-walled snorkel pipe to the roof of the bubble, the exhaust traveling in the outer pipe, preheating the diesel's intake air.

For a long while Pacino just sat leaning against the wall and stared into space. The shelter stayed empty, the only sounds the wind and the diesel. Strange . . . but he was too tired to ask himself where the others were.

Finally he slept.

Rapier watched the retreating figure of Pacino, called out but Pacino walked on, trudging up the ridge to the ice shelter. Let him go, he decided.

At the base of the ridge was the dark jagged hole in the ice where the *Devilfish* had consigned herself to the deep, the water nearly black and choppy in the wind. As the wind picked up, the far side of the hole in the ice was nearly invisible from the snow and the fog. The men, who had gathered on the side of the ridge toward the hole, began to turn to go back to the shelter when Rapier heard a shout from Stokes, standing down the slope of the ridge and pointing at the hole.

Rapier couldn't make out what Stokes was saying, and all he could see was the damned hole in the ice. As he walked down the slope, the fog receded and the far side of the hole in the ice was visible.

Floating in the water was something gray and round. Too round for a chunk of ice. Rapier started hurrying, catching up to Stokes.

"What the hell is it?" Stokes asked.

Rapier shook his head. "I'm not sure, let's go down and look."

The object became clearer as they approached the base of the ridge . . . it was a sphere, a metal sphere with a round hatch set into one side, floating in the water. Stencilled red letters were around the hatch, the printing unmistakably cyrillic.

Rapier stared hard at it. "Stokes, you remember the *Comsomolets* sinking a few years back? Some of them made it to the surface in an escape pod. They died later, I don't remember details . . ."

"You think that thing's from the OMEGA?" Stokes said. "An escape pod . . ."

"Their subs have pods, that writing by the hatch looks like Russian . . ."

"XO, you think someone's in there?"

Rapier looked at the ice around the pod, trying to gauge its thickness.

"Maybe, maybe not. It could just have ejected from the hull. If anyone's in there they're probably dead from the cold or lack of oxygen by now." On the other hand, he thought, if people were inside, if there were any survivors, they could be interrogated about the collision and why they fired the Magnum. There might be important documents onboard . . .

"You men stay here. Stokes, come with me."

The two slowly made their way out over the ice, over the hundred feet to the far side of the hole and to the pod that floated about a foot from the edge of the ice. Rapier grabbed onto a handhold set into the gray surface and rotated the heavy pod so that the hatch faced him. On each side were small ridges formed in the surface of the sphere for footholds. Rapier took a handhold and pulled himself up to the hatch with his feet in the footholds.

"Stay there, Stokes, keep a grip on the handhold so I don't float the hell away."

It took endless minutes of unscrewing the handwheel before the latches of the hatch retracted and Rapier could pull the hatch up. The air of the pod interior nearly made him sick. He held his breath, looked down into the blackness of the pod. After a moment he stood up and called to Stokes.

"Four men inside. Can't tell their condition. Call the others over here and get some rope from the shelter."

Rapier looked again into the sphere and shook his head. Poor bastards, he thought, wondering how he could feel this way about people who had sunk his ship, killed his mates, but up here, in this freezing hell-hole, well, they were all human.

WESTERN ATLANTIC OCEAN
150 NAUTICAL MILES EAST NORTHEAST OF NORFOLK, VIRGINIA
ALTITUDE: 6,000 FEET

The Navy DC-9 orbited at a point above the continental shelf of
the United States. Admiral Casper "Bobby" McGee peered out a
window, watching the scene as the U.S. Navy destroyer, the P-3
Orion ASW turboprop airplane and the destroyer's LAMPS helicopter danced around a point in the sea, a point that suddenly
erupted with white foam, admitting to the surface a nuclear
submarine. A Russian attack submarine, easily identified as a
VICTOR III by its trademark teardrop-shaped sail, bulbous bow
and ellipsoidal pod on top of its rudder aft. It immediately
turned northeast, heading home.

An aide appeared next to him, watching the scene from an
adjacent window.

"This is happening all up and down the coast," the commander said.

"What's the tally?" McGee asked.

"This one makes one hundred and five Russian nuclear subs
surfaced after President Yulenski gave the orders to come home.
That's out of a force of 120—wait, one was sunk by the *Billfish*,
which leaves fourteen boats to go. Once on the surface they're
covered by at least one U.S. escort unit, either an attack submarine, surface ship, Viking jet, P-3 turboprop, LAMPS chopper
and in some cases Coast Guard cutters and choppers."

"What about the fourteen left? What if they go sour and tell
Yulenski to stick it?"

The aide shook his head. "SOSUS is showing all 119 contacts,
including the fourteen not yet on the surface. We don't know
for sure if the fourteen are being trailed by our own attack subs.
As soon as one of ours turns over a surfacing unit to a P-3 he
goes deep to look for another one. The math is in our favor.
Sixty-six American attack boats, fourteen of theirs, with ASW
aircraft and helicopters and SOSUS sensors helping them
search. We've got a curtain of interceptor aircraft airborne along
the entire east coast to down any more cruise missiles launched

from the sea. We've got a line of surface ships pinging active sonar in a sweep from the shallow coastline toward the east."

McGee nodded and took the message from the communications technician at the forward communication console. He looked up at the commander.

"Four more units just surfaced. Ten to go."

McGee sat down and allowed himself the luxury of shutting his eyes for a moment.

It had been a very long morning.

WASHINGTON, D.C.
PENTAGON
SUITE OF THE CHAIRMAN OF THE JOINT CHIEFS OF STAFF

General Herman Xavier Tyler dismissed the staff members, civilian analysts and intelligence officers that had finished briefing him, shaking hands with them. After the last briefer had left he stared down at one of the summary sheets, the intent of the Russian submarines off the coast revealed by the one ship that had launched, apparently prematurely.

Tyler took the sheets to his inner office, stared for a moment at the view outside, the best in the whole Pentagon.

He walked away from the window and sat down in his leather chair at his desk, the desktop adorned with memorabilia of a long Air Force career: F-104 fighter, F-4 Phantom, a Minuteman missile, a B-52 bomber.

Tyler got out a pen and a calculator, scribbled, finished his calculation. With deceleration from the bone and tissue, with a subsonic muzzle velocity, the bullet would still pass from the bottom of his brain to the top in such a short time that no nerve would have time to register pain. He would feel nothing. He put down the pencil and unlocked the bottom right-hand drawer.

The Smith and Wesson .357 Magnum revolver felt heavy in his hand. He opened the box of heavy grain ammunition and loaded all six chambers. Five too many, but the pistol would feel more balanced with six rounds in it. He snapped the chambers into the body of the revolver and cocked the trigger.

The barrel, he noted, tasted metallic as he put it to his mouth.

He took one mad look out the window, at the panoramic scene of a Washington, D.C., still intact, and pulled the trigger.

In surprise, he realized his calculations had been incorrect. It seemed to hurt forever.

NORFOLK, VIRGINIA
COMSUBLANT HEADQUARTERS

Dawn. But no sunlight made its way to Flag Plot of COMSUB-LANT headquarters buried deep underground. Admiral Richard Donchez looked like he had been in a fifteen-round fight and lost. Deep dark bags surrounded his bloodshot eyes. His favorite Havana had gone out. He pulled a fresh one from his jacket and tried to light it but, of course, the Piranha lighter was out of fuel. So was he. Pooped, was the word. He stood in front of the Arctic Ocean plot that showed the ice cap in green. The graphics were being updated by the computer, and as he watched the red X and the black X were replaced by a black circle and a red circle about 400 miles south of the pole roughly north of Novaya Zemlya.

Circles meant sinkings. As he stared in disbelief, the watch officer hurried up to him.

"Sir," Lieutenant Commander Sam Lockover said, "SOSUS reported two explosions at the positions indicated a few hours ago. They, well, apparently they failed to report the explosions due to the priority of reporting the Russian boats offshore . . ."

"Go on."

"The first explosion was conventional. The second was . . . nuclear." Lockover paused, Donchez's looks could kill. "After the second explosion SOSUS heard the breakup of one hull—could have been our unit up north, the *Devilfish*, or the OMEGA class she was trailing. A few minutes later there was a sound like an emergency-blow or deballasting system. Within another few minutes there was a sound of a collision between one of the hulls and the ice. The collision sound was so extreme that we don't think there would be any way a hull could have survived."

"Lot of goddamned theories and hypotheses, you've got there," Donchez said, feeling a shot of hot bile in his stomach.

The *Devilfish* might be down, its crew and Michael Pacino could be dead. Or stranded, surfaced at a polynya with no radio. "Call COMAIRLANT and get a C-130 or a P-3 up there to look around, maybe one of the Keflavik units or one out of Norway or Alberta if they can vector one in quick. Call CIA PHOTOINT and on the next KH-17 satellite pass have the infrared and visuals trained to the SOSUS position of the sounds. Somebody could be up there on the ice . . ."

"Sir," Lockover said, feeling damn uneasy to be the messenger of this news, "there's a bad storm up there, I mean it's from Greenland to Siberia, gale-force winds, heavy snow. We're grounded. COMAIRLANT won't fly anything up there and neither will the Marine Arctic Resupply units flying C-130's. We could get a jet up for high altitude surveillance but doubtful we'd see through the storm clouds. And we just had a KH-17 pass. Kodiak's on the phone to CIA now."

Kodiak hung up and came over to them.

Donchez waited.

"The satellite didn't see a damned thing, sir. Not even a polar bear. There's a chance it's just not seeing through the blizzard . . . more likely there's nothing up there for it to see."

It was 1973 all over again, Donchez thought. Another U.S. submarine sunk at the pole by a Russian. Another Pacino, on the bottom. Unbelievable.

"Was there a SUBSUNK transmission from our boat to the satellite?"

Lockover shook his head.

"The Russians? Did one of theirs transmit a distress signal?"

"Sir, we're trying to find out now through their embassy but things are pretty confused up there. And, sir, even if there was a distress signal I don't think anybody is going to get up there for a while with this storm. It could last a week, maybe more."

Donchez glanced at the Arctic plot, looking for the *Allentown*. Her X flashed, but her position was a guess, SOSUS being unable to hear her in spite of her damaged sail. For a moment he considered sending *Allentown* under the ice cap, then rejected the notion. One lost submarine was enough. The Los Angeles–class *Allentown* under the ice cap would never survive . . . no SHARKTOOTH under-ice sonar, no strength in the flimsy fiberglass sail. She'd get lost and never emerge. Goddamned

L.A.–class, they were a giant step backward in submarine technology.

"Which Piranha is furthest north?" Donchez asked. "One that isn't in trail?"

Lockover turned to a computer console, typed into it, returned with a printout.

"*Barracuda* is off the coast of Maine, sir."

"Vector her to the SOSUS position of the explosions, max speed. Get her up there *fast*."

"Sir," Lockover said, "she's not loaded out for more than a few days. She was just about to head for overhaul at Portsmouth. She'll run out of food by the time she gets to the GI-UK gap. And she has no arctic gear onboard—"

"We may well have men dying up there. Tell her to flank it. I want a report soon as she can get to a polynya close to the SOSUS position. And watch the weather. The minute it breaks, I want aircraft scouring that ice pack."

Lockover left to get the messages out.

Donchez looked up at the plot. He'd done what he could for now. He got on the NESTOR circuit to Admiral McGee in the airborne DC-9. Maybe the admiral could get an answer out of the Russians.

ARCTIC OCEAN
POLAR ICECAP SURFACE

Pacino woke up with a start from the sound of the men entering the shelter, shouting and talking to each other in excitement. Rapier came first, followed by Stokes and the others, some of them huddled together carrying men into the shelter. The men being carried in had white frozen faces. Pacino found Rapier, who had started to boil snow for a pot of coffee.

"Jon, what's all this? Who the hell are they?"

Rapier's face was crusted white with snow and ice, now starting to melt and drip down his face. If he was surprised by Pacino's use of his first name instead of the usual 'XO' he didn't show it.

"We . . . we found"—Rapier shivered—"God, it's cold out there. We found an escape pod, I'm guessing from the OMEGA.

Had Russian writing on it. It was under the ice, freed up, for God's sake, by the *Devilfish* when she went down."

Pacino winced.

"We got four guys out of the pod," Rapier went on. "One was already dead. We left him on the ice by the pod. The others were damned near gone from the cold."

Stokes and Delaney were taking the Russian survivors' wet half-frozen clothing off and wrapping them in wool blankets. All three were unconscious. Pacino looked at their gray faces. Two were older, probably warrant officers or chiefs or whatever the Russian equivalent was for senior enlisted men. He was anxious to hear their stories, what had happened to *them*, how they had survived in the pod, how the pod had gotten out onto the ice.

Pacino ordered them to be clothed in spare arctic parkas and watched for signs of coming to. For a long time he stood over the two Russians, wondering what their story was, if they had families. And for the first time in a long time allowed himself to think of his family, the last time he'd seen Tony, the weekend before the *Allentown* OP when the two of them had gone to Mount Trashmore Park. And Hillary, who became even more desirable through the cushioning of memory . . .

"Sir?" It was Rapier. "Wind's picking up outside, starting to snow pretty hard. Visibility's down to less than a hundred feet."

Pacino stepped outside onto the ice and was shocked at how much the weather had changed. The horizon was gone, the ice and the fog melting together just a few feet ahead. A fierce wind blew quarter-size snowflakes horizontally, a wind that cut through Pacino's fur parka like it wasn't there. In seconds the wind was burning his cheeks and eyes. Pacino spit at the side of the shelter. As he expected, the spittle was frozen before it hit the wall of the shelter, shattering as it impacted. Which meant the temperature was somewhere around 30 below, with a 20-knot wind. He ducked back into the shelter, wondering how much wind the shelter could take. It was, after all, only a bubble-shaped, prefabricated structure, not a building, yet more than a tent. It was going to be a long night.

CHAPTER
25

MONDAY, 20 DECEMBER

POLAR ICECAP SURFACE

Occasionally during the night Pacino had gone to the curtain and cracked it open to bring air into the shelter, and each time there had been a drift of heavy wet snow that had to be burrowed through. The shelter was probably invisible from outside with the snowdrifts piling up on it, but the snow also served as an insulator, keeping the heat in the polyethylene bubble, as well as muffling the outside noise. The only sounds inside the shelter were the rumbling of the diesel and the distorted conversations of the men.

"If this storm doesn't break soon," Rapier was saying to Pacino, "we're going to be in trouble. Diesel's only got another day of fuel, maybe less. It was all we could get out of the ship."

"Maybe we should shut it down to conserve," Pacino said, his voice slow, monotonic. "It's warm enough in here to run it twenty minutes an hour."

"I don't know, the temperature'd drop too fast. The fuel would congeal. Plus, we'd waste fuel starting her up. Once we shut it down in this cold she's down for good."

"Keep it running, then," Pacino said, faintly annoyed at what seemed a dialogue to nowhere.

"Also," Rapier said, "the radio's batteries are dead. We've

been transmitting on it all night, no answer. It might not have been working in the first place . . . none of the radiomen made it. Even if it was working there's no way anyone could get to us in this blizzard."

"You been putting the flares out?" Pacino asked.

"Ran out yesterday, you know that."

"Oh, right. How about rations?"

"Two days left, tops."

"Great. No flares, no radio, food and fuel running out and a blizzard that won't quit."

Rapier looked down into his coffee. "We're alive."

"How are they doing?" Pacino nodded toward the Russians.

"Better," Rapier said. "One regained consciousness for a moment, the older guy, then fainted away again. Doc thinks they've gotten frostbite over a lot of skin, hypothermia."

Pacino drained his coffee and tried not to look at the ship's emblem on the mug. The coffee was cold.

Rapier had stopped with his recital. Pacino shut his eyes and tried to doze, let the buzz of the diesel carry him away, away from here, from the reality of an arctic prison . . .

Pacino awoke to a commotion at the diesel, where the Russians were. One, the middle-aged silver-gray-haired man, half sat up in Chief Corpsman Ingle's arms and sipped water from a cup. When he looked up at Pacino and Rapier he seemed confused.

Pacino spoke to him, starting slowly.

"Do you speak English?"

The Russian nodded.

"I'm Commander Michael Pacino, commanding officer of the USS *Devilfish*. Correction, I *was*. My ship is on the bottom now. Who the hell are you?"

"Yuri Vlasenko, Captain 1st Rank, Northern Fleet." The man's English was only slightly accented. "I *was* captain of the submarine *Kaliningrad*."

Pacino eyed him, assaulted with mixed feelings. He was, after all, talking to the captain of the Russian OMEGA submarine. They were hardly buddies after what had happened. On the other hand, they were fellow professionals, survivors. He wondered about the admiral that had sunk *Stingray*. Where was he? Dead?

Vlasenko's reaction was also guarded. With an appreciation of what the Americans had done. "My compliments on your skill in surviving the arctic climate."

Pacino nodded, decided to tell Vlasenko that one of his officers was dead on the ice.

"When we found your sphere or pod or whatever you call it, the other one inside was dead. Three of you survived!"

"What happened Captain?" Vlasenko asked. "I was under arrest, I don't know what happened, although I know what Admiral Novskoyy had in mind. When he found out he had me locked up."

Novskoyy. The real enemy. Pacino looked at the older Russian, now regaining consciousness. His face was gray and lined, his breath wheezing in and out of blackened, badly chapped lips, his skin afflicted with frostbite. Blood had matted into a mess above one eyebrow, and his face was swollen and bruised.

It was Vlasenko who finally broke the silence, his voice tight with anger.

"This is Admiral Alexi Novskoyy, Supreme Commander of the Northern Fleet—"

Pacino stopped hearing. Admiral Novskoyy, the man who had murdered his father, the man he had considered his nemesis. Instinctively, his right hand clenched into a fist, cocked itself at his shoulder. He had almost let it go, wanted to let it go, until he *looked* at the man's face. Novskoyy was half-conscious, beaten up. It would be like beating a dumb animal.

The fury that had been in him was gone, sunk to the bottom of the ocean with the hull of the *Devilfish*. Right now they were both seemingly condemned to this white bubble in the arctic, waiting for a rescue that grew less likely with every hour. Waiting for death.

Pacino dropped his fist to his side as Novskoyy fell back into unconsciousness.

NORFOLK, VIRGINIA
COMSUBLANT HEADQUARTERS

Admiral Donchez came into the blast door to Flag Plot, met by the grim face of Watch Officer Kodiak.

"No word from the polar icecap, sir. And no break in the storm."

"Anything from the Russians? Indication of a distress call?"

"Sorry, sir."

Donchez looked up at the Arctic Ocean plot. A blue X flashed in the Barents Sea, indicating the uncertain presence of a U.S. submarine. The legend next to it read USS ALLENTOWN SSN-764.

"Any word from *Allentown*?"

"No, sir. But we weren't expecting any, were we?"

"No, guess not."

Donchez looked over at the Atlantic plot, now nearly empty. A single blue X flashed, the legend below reading USS BARRA-CUDA SSN-663.

"We've got other bad news, sir. The *Barracuda*, the unit you're sending to the polar ice cap to investigate the explosions . . . she's reported a casualty in the airconditioning units. Total loss of the lithium bromide plant. And the R-114 unit is leaking refrigerant all through the engine room, contaminating the atmosphere. They've had to shut down all electronics up forward —sonar, fire-control and navigation. Temperatures aft are 120 degrees. The crew are in gas masks. We have to call her back, sir. Without sonar she really shouldn't even be submerged. Her captain wants an answer."

Don't we all, Donchez thought. "Tell the *Barracuda* to surface and come home. Anybody else still at sea? Any other Piranha's?"

"A few could be ready to go in a day, maybe even hours. But we'd want to load them out with food and arctic gear. And, sir, by the time they got to this explosion position two weeks will have gone by. Sir . . . there are no detects under the ice cap, no infrareds in the last half-dozen KH-17 passes, and this storm is severe enough that even if there were any survivors yesterday there's little possibility any of them are living through today . . . I think we need to face the likelihood that the crew of the *Devilfish* are dead—"

"Send up a replacement for the *Barracuda*," was Donchez's angry reply. "I want a Piranha submarine headed north by tonight. Make it happen, dammit. Any problems with that, you let me know."

Donchez left Flag Plot and headed back to his office, thinking that the Piranha class boats were getting too damn old. Maybe he was, too.

In his office he cleared his desk and went to the window overlooking the expanse of grass up to the fenceline, to the *Stingray* monument across the street. Two cranes were hoisting the marble slab up into position, getting ready to put it down on its foundation.

Donchez stood there, unmoving, watching. And wondering what he was going to tell Hillary Pacino and her son.

POLAR ICE CAP SURFACE

Novskoyy had not regained consciousness. Vlasenko, now sitting up, was telling the Americans around him about the *Kaliningrad* and her mission.

"What was the message he was transmitting? What did it mean?" Pacino said.

Vlasenko told him, hesitantly, feeling almost personally responsible even though he had been imprisoned in the pod by Novskoyy.

Pacino looked at Novskoyy, feeling not only outrage but frustration—here was his father's killer, the object of his revenge . . . and yet what would be the satisfaction in doing what he badly wanted to do when the man was half-dead, his ship on the bottom too?

Pacino looked over at Rapier, then back to Vlasenko.

"Did he transmit the go-message?"

Vlasenko looked grim as he felt. Outside the wind howled, shaking the walls of the shelter.

"I can't say. I told you, I was arrested and put into the escape pod. Was there any word from your headquarters?"

"Captain Vlasenko, we can't very well receive radio signals under ice. We can only get an extremely low frequency signal, transmitting at a snail's pace."

"Snails?"

Pacino shook his head. "Point is, there was no word from our headquarters. But then," Pacino added, not even wanting to consider the horror, "they might have been taken out by a cruise missile, maybe that's why so far there's been no rescue attempt."

"Perhaps you collided with us in time to stop the transmission . . ."

"Maybe, maybe not . . ."

On the other wall of the shelter Lieutenant Commander Matt Delaney started coughing. Rapier, Pacino and Vlaskeno rushed to Delaney's side of the shelter. Delaney lay in his own blood, which he had just retched to the plastic floor. The chief corpsman tried to clear his throat, and after a few minutes struggling, Delaney was quiet and able to lean back against the wall.

"He's lost consciousness," Chief Ingle said, wrapping Delaney in a blanket. Delaney's forehead was starting to break out in sweat. "He got quite a radiation dose, didn't he, Captain?"

"Afraid so."

"Well, these may be the first symptoms," Ingle said quietly. "I'd imagine Manderson and the other watchstanders aft will be showing them soon."

Behind Pacino the diesel engine coughed and missed, finally stopping. The shelter seemed to crash into silence. Pacino's ears rang from the engine's previous noise. The engine was surrounded by the men in the shelter.

Pacino pushed through to get to the diesel and found Rapier with the cap to the fuel tank in his hand.

"It's out of fuel," Rapier said. "The resupply cans are empty."

Now that the diesel was quiet, and the ringing in Pacino's ears was fading, he could hear the howling of the wind outside the shelter, blowing the snow up against the shelter with the force of a sandblaster.

"Skipper," Rapier said, "without the diesel there's no heat, no light. This place will be the same temperature as the outside in an hour."

Pacino looked at Vlasenko.

"Captain, you got anything in that pod that could help? A heater? Transmitter? Satellite locator? Flares?"

Vlasenko shook his head. "All that equipment was in the main escape pod. This one was just an auxiliary."

"All right, everyone, listen up," Pacino said. "Gather all the blankets and sleeping bags and clothing around the diesel in the center of the shelter. Get your parkas on. Drink some water before it freezes. Come here by the engine. Its residual heat will keep us warm for a while. After that, only crowding together will save body heat. We'll just have to wait out this storm."

By the time Pacino's orders were carried out, Matt Delaney and four of his engine-room watchstanders were dead. Their bodies were left by the wall of the shelter away from the group.

Pacino sat down next to Rapier, thinking he should have stayed in the *Devilfish*. At least the end would have been fast.

CHAPTER
26

TUESDAY, 21 DECEMBER

POLAR ICECAP SURFACE

Pacino breathed slowly through cracked and frozen lips, the air wheezing in and out of his lungs, feeling like it was freezing him from the inside out.

Inside, the air was a dense fog of condensation, temperature minus 40 degrees. The room was a glaring white, either that or he was snowblind. He tried to bring the room into focus, no use. He tried to move his right arm, his left. Couldn't. No feeling or motion. His legs had been gone for what he guessed was an hour. His old Rolex Submariner watch, a gift from his father, had not been designed to run in these conditions. Its hands were frozen at 1107. He couldn't remember whether it had been morning or night when it had quit, whether it had been set to GMT or Eastern Standard Time. The only muscles that seemed still under voluntary control were his eyelids, his chest muscles —he was still breathing—and his neck. While he still had control of his neck and eyes he decided to look around at the shelter, the last vestige of his command.

The fog in the room was too dense to see further than fifteen feet, but that was more than enough for him to see the men who had already died . . . Delaney and his nukes from back aft —Manderson, Patterson and Taglia. The living and the dead could only be distinguished by the plumes of vapor from the faces of the living.

He heard a hacking cough and turned to see Stokes slump over, the vapor-breathing clouds no longer coming from the Kentuckian's nose.

Pacino waited for sleep.

The wind outside howled at a fierce 40 knots, gusts blowing up to 50. With the crazed wind came tons of snow falling horizontally. The snow piled up on the windward side of the bubble-shaped shelter, nearly obscuring it, climbing easily up its sides, threatening to collapse it at any moment.

Three hundred yards east of the shelter, near the two-foot-thick ice that two days before had admitted the doomed submarine back to the sea and had yielded the pod of the *Kaliningrad*, came a vibrating, trembling, crashing sound. At first it would not be heard even by someone standing directly on top of the thin ice, so strong was the blasting noise of the wind. But soon the roaring from the ice drowned out even the violence of the storm, and in a massive upheaval the ice that was once the *Devilfish*'s hole exploded upward. As ice blocks flew from the center of the hole, a huge, black finlike structure emerged, its surface cracked.

It was the sail of a United States Navy attack submarine.

The USS *Allentown*.

"Blow the hatch! C'mon, right *now*!"

Commander Henry Duckett was furious. After tracking the noise of the ice camp's diesel generator it had taken forever to find a polynya. The diesel sounds had died before they could get a decent fix on the noise. In arctic conditions it would do no good just to get close. Duckett had wanted to surface directly under the diesel. A rescue attempt was useless if near-frozen survivors had to walk a mile in the violent blizzard.

Finally he had decided this polynya was close enough and smashed the unhardened sail through it, shattering the unprotected BIGMOUTH radio antenna. The plot had shown the estimated position of the diesel over 400 yards into thick ice, which made no sense. But then, it hardly mattered. With the diesel silent for a day there was little chance he'd pull anyone out alive. Still, he had to try.

Duckett and Corpsman Denny Halloway stood at the base of the bridge access tunnel hatch with four enlisted men. Duckett was sweating beneath the layers of heavy arctic clothing. Halloway opened the lower hatch and turned a radial switch, energizing the light in the long tunnel through the leading edge of the sail and up to the bridge twenty-five feet above. From the bridge they would lower themselves down, using the handholds in the side of the sail.

Halloway started up. Duckett waited while Halloway opened the upper hatch and crawled into the cramped bridge. Before they could go outside Halloway had to open the clamshells that faired in the bridge cockpit. Already the cold from outside was making Duckett shiver, the sweat from the wait below adding to the cold.

A white glare from the world above lit up the upper-access trunk as Halloway latched the clamshells open, and with it came the thunderous sound of the gale blowing the heavy snow. Halloway shouted down for the landing team to follow him, his shout mostly drowned out by the wind.

Duckett now climbed the final rungs of the ladder leading to the bridge, the frigid wind slipping past his fur parka and pants as if he were naked. As he climbed out of the access trunk into the weather, the storm was a total physical shock . . . the wind blew by at what must have been 50 knots, flew the gray snow as if shot from a machine gun.

Duckett climbed over the coaming of the bridge cockpit, the subfreezing metal of the conning tower sticking to the crotch of his fur trousers as he felt for the foothold with his boot. It was a long trip to the ice below, and with visibility down, the sail seemed disembodied, floating in a gray mass of flying snow.

When he finally got to the hull, which was even with the two-foot-thick ice of the polynya, he looked over at Halloway, who was standing on the ice lake and shouting something at him. Duckett signalled he could not hear him over the storm, and Halloway pointed to his own eyes, at the same time yelling, "Captain! Your goggles, put on your goggles!"

Duckett nodded, pulled the yellow goggles over his eyes,

climbed out onto the ice next to Halloway. The four seamen followed out of the sail and joined them. Duckett scanned the horizon with infrared binoculars.

"Sir, look!" one of the men shouted over the roar of the wind, pointing in the direction of the rudder, which had penetrated the ice far aft of the conning tower. On the other side of the rudder was a hump of ice and snow, a bubble, too perfect to be a chunk of ice.

They hurried to the igloo-shaped snowmass and began to scrape the object with their knives. The bubble was made of metal, covered with a layer of ice and snow. Duckett tried to climb on its side, pulling himself up on the handhold.

"It's some kind of escape pod," he shouted.

Its hatch was open. Duckett cleared the snow away, took a flashlight from one of the seamen and shined the light into the pod.

"No one here," he said. He stood and again scanned the horizon with the goggles.

"Anything?" Halloway shouted to Duckett.

Duckett shook his head.

"Captain, there's a ridge up on the west side. If we climb it maybe we can see further."

Duckett waved the team on up the ridge, and the six proceeded to climb for what seemed an eternity.

At the top of the ridge, the team stopped and looked around. Duckett used the goggles, scanning the horizon for thermal detects. At one bearing he stopped, then continued. But then he scanned again at a bearing northwest of where they stood, looking toward the other side of the ridge.

"You got something?" Halloway asked.

"Not sure, doc. But something looks different over there," and he pointed in the direction he'd been looking.

They walked behind Duckett, who paused every few steps to look through the goggles. Eventually he stopped at the base of a small rise and shook his head, about to turn around.

"Go a little further, Captain," Halloway said, thinking he saw a clearing in the blizzard to the northwest.

They turned around, and Duckett found himself walking into

a deep drift rather than the rise of a high point. He was about to turn when his boot, by then deep under the snow of the drift, hit something hard, something that gave slightly with his weight. It felt strange. Not ice, not snow but something . . . *flexible.*

When the snow was cleared Duckett found himself looking at a section of plastic. Something man-made.

"It's for sure a shelter of some kind," Halloway said.

"Find the damned entrance," Duckett told him, excited now.

It took a while to find the entrance, a double-curtain device.

Duckett led them into the entrance, pulled off his goggles and mask and shook his head out of his hood. The shelter was cold and smelled like a meathouse. He looked around and saw bodies scattered throughout, not one of them moving.

They had been too late.

Halloway had dumped his pack and gotten out his stethoscope. He bent over each body, checked for any signs of life. He looked up at Duckett and shook his head.

Duckett and the others crouched down and began unbundling the faces of the men collapsed at the now quiet diesel. The first five were dead, in a frozen rigor mortis. He unbundled the sixth.

It was Michael Pacino, swollen eyes black and blue, lips nearly black, lower face white but skin not yet frozen.

"Doc! Over here!"

The corpsman put his stethoscope to Pacino's chest.

"His heart's stopped," the corpsman said.

A moment of silence in the shelter. Duckett stood up and looked around again.

"Jesus."

SANDBRIDGE BEACH, VIRGINIA

Admiral Richard Donchez's staff car pulled up to the house, a redwood three-story structure on wood pile–stilts driven into the sand of the wide beach just north of the North Carolina border. The name on the carved wood sign read "PACINO."

Donchez got out of the car and went up the steps to the entrance deck, located twenty feet above the elevation of the sand.

Hillary Pacino came to the door, and despite his mission

Donchez could not help noting how attractive this woman was, even in a shapeless Annapolis sweatsuit, her pretty face without makeup.

"Dick," she said, "come in."

When she saw the staff car waiting for him below she looked back at him, taking in his dress blue uniform.

"Mommy, who is it?" Tony's voice behind her.

She didn't answer him.

"Hillary," Donchez said, "it's Michael. There's been an accident. We think the *Devilfish* went down."

"Oh, God," was all Hillary could get out, collapsing in a chair. Finally she looked up at him. "What happened?"

"Hillary, we're not positive, but it looks like *Devilfish* was returning early from the mission, trying to get back before Christmas. There was a flooding accident. Crew couldn't stop it. The reactor shutdown and we think her battery exploded. We're starting a search for the hull now . . . I'm sorry, Hillary. God, I'm so sorry."

He hated the lie, but it was what the White House and Pentagon had ordered him to say.

Hillary put her face in her hands, Tony began to cry. Donchez crouched down and took the boy in his arms.

After a long while Donchez left, hating the Russians, himself, the whole damn world.

CHAPTER
27

WEDNESDAY, 22 DECEMBER

ARCTIC OCEAN
BENEATH THE POLAR ICECAP
USS *ALLENTOWN*

Corpsman Denny Halloway sat at his small desk in the space he used as an "office" and locker for his medicines. Duckett tapped twice on the door frame.

"Doc?"

"C'mon in, Cap'n."

"Well," Duckett said, "they still alive?"

"Yessir, Rapier and the Russians are sleeping. I think the Russians'll pull through. Rapier . . . he could go either way. Captain Pacino, well, I'm not sure we did him a favor, resuscitating him. He's in a deep coma. It wasn't just the hypothermia. I checked his and Rapier's dosimeters, you know, the little widget on your belt, measures radiation."

"Yeah?"

"Well, Pacino and Rapier both got big doses of radiation. Pacino's seems worse, though. They must have taken a nuke torpedo or melted down their reactor core. Maybe both."

Duckett thought about the bad blood between him and Pacino, going back to his first-class year at Annapolis, Pacino's plebe year. He remembered his resentment that Pacino seemed

297

to have it made . . . athletic ability, academic success, street smarts, self-assurance . . . all things he had to struggle for. All that plus his stunts, his one-upmanship. He'd damn near hazed him out of the Academy. Until Pacino's father died and he laid off the plebe's case. But something of the old feeling had persisted, like after that exercise when Pacino again got the better of him and his boat.

But now . . . "Will Pacino live? Can you save him?"

"Cap'n, he's got radiation sickness. Complicated by hypothermia. The cold restricted circulation to his arms and legs. He may need an amputation, a blood transfusion and a bone-marrow transplant—which is damned hard to do because finding a match for bone marrow ain't like a blood-type match. And the loss of oxygen to his brain, probably from partial cardiopulmonary failure in the cold, has put him in this coma. We don't have the gear to test him here, but he doesn't respond to light or touch or sound. You put all that together . . ."

He didn't need to spell it out further. Duckett grabbed the phone and dialed the Conn.

"Off'sa'deck, increase speed to full . . . I know, I know, I'll take the risk on collision with the ice. Keep me posted on our ETA to the MIZ. Soon as we're in the marginal ice zone I want to pop up and radio for a chopper, then get down and flank it till the chopper meets us."

"Doc, once we're in open water, if we can fly these guys out, where will they go?"

"Navy Hospital in Faslane, Scotland. They've got a good hypothermia unit. Maybe we could ask for that miracle-worker doctor who did all those bone-marrow transplants after Chernobyl blew up. And we'll request a brain specialist, someone who knows his way around a coma."

Duckett nodded and walked slowly to SES, the Sonar Equipment Space up forward. The makeshift sickbay consisted of a few cots set up in between the sonar electronic cabinets in SES.

Michael Pacino lay on one of the cots, shrouded in blankets, an IV bottle snaking into his arm, twin-oxygen tubes penetrating both nostrils, a catheter tube coming out from under the blanket terminating in a urine-collection bottle. His frostbitten face was completely wrapped in a moist bandage. Only his eyelids and lips showed.

For a long time Duckett stood and looked at Pacino.

"You son of a bitch," he said quietly. "I ain't done hazin' your ass yet. Now goddammit, you get better and get back to your wife and kid and you and me'll take up where we left off."

Pacino, for once, had no answer.

EPILOGUE

TWO MONTHS LATER

"Admiral, Captain Pacino is here to see you, sir," the intercom buzzed.

"Send him in." Donchez stood and walked around his desk to the door to greet Pacino. Pacino had been released from Portsmouth Naval Hospital only the day before.

Pacino slouched over his crutches and braced himself so as to hold out his hand to Donchez. He was dressed in blues, his fourth gold-braid stripe added onto the end of his sleeve since his promotion from commander to captain. His extended hand shook slightly. He was thin, twenty pounds underweight. His eyes were shrouded by dark circles and his cheeks hollow. His once nearly black hair showed distinct traces of gray.

Donchez took Pacino's hand, noticing it was clammy. "Mikey, come on over here and have a seat. You look a helluva lot better since last time." He had visited Pacino the week before when Pacino had looked white enough to be embalmed. "Hey, you've made an incredible recovery, thanks in part at least to sheer guts. Even the medical people didn't give you much of a chance."

"Thanks," Pacino said, his voice still hoarse. He sat on the couch facing the wide glass window that looked out on the *Stingray* monument. "It looks good from here," he said, and Donchez knew what he meant.

300

"I think your old man would have liked it. Well, I'm sure Commodore Adams is happy to get you back."

"Not exactly. He doesn't know what to do with me. And without a ship I'm not much good to him."

"You want me to talk to him?"

Pacino said nothing. An embarrassed silence followed. Pacino was right in a way, Donchez thought, he'd been labelled a captain who had lost his ship, a captain who'd come back without his crew. Never mind what really happened . . . once again international politics prescribed a cover-up for a nuclear confrontation and exchange. At least in the days of the *Stingray* the U.S. and Russia were still cold-war adversaries. Today they were *officially* friends. Pacino had been promoted to full captain and his Navy Cross was sailing through the Chief of Naval Operations' office, signed personally by Admiral McGee. But a Navy Cross was not much to a man who had commanded a ship and who now had none.

"Admiral," Pacino said, "I came to give you this."

He reached into his jacket and pulled out a folded piece of paper on Squadron Seven letterhead. Donchez put on his reading glasses. The letter was Pacino's resignation of his officer's commission.

Donchez said slowly, "Have you seriously thought about this?"

"Yes and no, sir. But it's where I am now. Later, maybe . . ."

"What would you do if you leave the Navy?" Donchez pressed.

Pacino shrugged. "The first thing I'm going to do when I get sprung from the hospital . . . they're still doing tests to see if I need that damn bone-marrow thing on account of the radiation . . . is go home and get reacquainted with my wife and son."

"Mikey, after things shake down at home, you've got to do something. Any ideas at all?"

"Well, maybe, if they want me, I'll go back to Annapolis. There's an opening in Rickover Hall, I hear, teaching fluid mechanics. I could work some more on boundary-layer polymer injection. At least now I know it works." He didn't smile when he said it.

"Sounds interesting . . . just don't be a stranger, Mikey."

"Absolutely not, Admiral. And, sir . . . thank you for

sending me on the OP. I got to go one-on-one with Novskoyy. It didn't work out the way anybody could predict, but at least our collision with the *Kaliningrad* kept Novskoyy from getting a chance to send his go-order. Jesus, when I think of that . . ."

"Right. We were lucky to neutralize that SSN-X-27 cruise missile seconds from detonation. If it wasn't for you, 119 more of those things might well have been flown at us."

"I'll try to remember that, sir," Pacino said as he saluted and left the office. Neither man needed to mention the pilot who had lost his life defeating that single cruise missile. There'd be no monuments to him. By orders from on high . . .

OUTSIDE WASHINGTON, D.C.
ANDREWS AIR FORCE BASE

The black sedan screeched to a halt. Inside were four men in suits and overcoats with mirrored sunglasses and shoulder holsters. Around the car United States Marines gathered, in utilities and carrying M-16s. To the east the Tupolev jet transport landed, jets roaring as the pilot applied reverse thrust, then taxied to the concrete apron, where the black sedan was parked.

A door opened behind the cockpit windows while a stairway ramp was wheeled to the plane, and out of the door stepped four men in heavy overcoats and fedora hats. They walked down the steps two by two. Behind them eight infantrymen followed, each hoisting a Kalishnikov. They walked across the stretch of concrete to the black sedan, their faces blank and unsmiling.

Now the four men in the black sedan got out, and one of them opened the right rear door and pulled out a man in handcuffs. The M-16s of the Marines were at the ready, as were the Kalishnikovs. The man looked to be in his late fifties or early sixties, his hair unkempt, his most striking feature his penetrating eyes, which squinted angrily at the men around him. He was escorted to the Russian delegation, one of whom took charge.

Papers were signed, radios in the sedan spoken into, a camera appeared in the hands of one of the men from the sedan and clicked away. The ritual moved on. The Marines and the men from the dark sedan watched as the handcuffed man was guided to the Tupolev transport, hurried up the steps to the jet. Once he was inside, the stairs were pulled away and the door was slammed shut. The transport throttled up, its massive turbines howling, taxied back to the runway on which it had landed. At first the Tupolev barely moved, finally started to pick up speed until, at the far end of the field, it tilted toward the sky, the sound of its engines slowly fading as it climbed into the overcast sky, shrank to a cinder-sized dot and vanished.

Onboard the aircraft Alexi Novskoyy was strapped into a net-type military-transport seat on the centerline of the jet facing the starboard wing. A man in a greatcoat and fur cap walked down the length of the transport toward him, then sat down next to him.

Novskoyy looked at him. "Colonel Dretzski, Ivan Ivanovich, you came . . ."

Dretzski unlocked Novskoyy's handcuffs.

"When they said I was being turned over to the KGB, I wondered who in the KGB it would be. How did you . . . how did you stay out of trouble? What exactly happened?"

"One of your boats launched before receiving an order. The *Vladivostok*. It alerted the Americans. I had to tell Yulenski that the KGB had discovered a conspiracy in the Northern Fleet. Yulenski recalled the submarines, apologized to the Americans and arranged for your return for trial."

"How convenient for you, Dretzski. And how typical of our President."

"I'm sorry, Admiral, but—"

Novskoyy waved him away, then: "What became of Vlasenko?"

"He is now a ranking member of Yulenski's staff."

Novskoyy's face tightened, fists clenched.

"What happened under the ice cap?" Dretzski asked. "Did your transmitter fail?"

"We were trailed by an American submarine," Novskoyy said bitterly. "Smashed us up, disabled the antennae. I went after him but he put me on the bottom . . . All those years building the *Kaliningrad*, all that planning . . . the plan . . . all for nothing."

Dretzski shook his head. "Look at this, Admiral," he said, and handed Novskoyy a copy of that morning's Washington *Post*. The banner headline read:

PRESIDENT CABINO TO U.N.: "NO NUKES"
ALL JAVELIN CRUISE MISSILES
TO BE DESTROYED IMMEDIATELY
SUPERPOWERS TO BE NUKE-FREE

"Do you believe this?"

"We do, sir. You did it, Admiral. Your plan was to get rid of the Javelins, and now they are gone."

Novskoyy nodded slightly, then read the article below the headline. At the bottom of the page was a small two-column headline: JCS CHIEF'S DEATH AT PENTAGON RULED SUICIDE—REASON STILL A MYSTERY. Novskoyy looked up.

"Fishhook? You had him sanctioned at the *Pentagon*? You are better even than I imagined."

Dretzski smiled. "No, Admiral, he did it. He had told the U.S. officials your deployment was an exercise. After the *Vladivostok*'s launch he was in danger of being exposed. He took the better way out . . ." Dretzski looked closely at Novskoyy, wondering if he had gotten his message.

The two were silent, Novskoyy's eyes were closed and Dretzski began to wonder if he was asleep.

"You know, Ivan Ivanovich," Novskoyy said, eyes suddenly open and looking straight ahead, "it is a long trip back to Russia for a dead man."

"A very long trip, sir," Dretzski said, knowing that the admiral had, indeed, gotten his message.

NORFOLK, VIRGINIA
COMSUBLANT HEADQUARTERS

As Donchez watched from his office window, a black staff car pulled up to the parking section behind the stone walk to the *Stingray* monument. A man in Navy blues got out of the car and limped on crutches to the wall of the monument.

The monument was a large black marble slab twelve feet tall

and eight feet wide. At the top of the slab was a submarine carved from the solid marble, the hull shape of the *Skipjack* class. In letters on the marble hull were the words USS STING-RAY SSN-589. The wall went north-south. Almost. The length of the wall pointed to bearing zero one four, the exact bearing to the location of *Stingray*'s wreck under the polar ice cap. On the wall were inscribed the names of the men lost in the *Stingray*, Commander Anthony "Patch" Pacino's name at the top. Surrounding the monument, at the four points of the compass, were Mark-37 torpedoes mounted on marble bases, the torpedoes painted a gleaming black to match the marble.

Donchez watched as Michael Pacino slowly made his way to the marble wall, stopping at the base and looking up at his father's name. After a while he pulled a small black bundle from his pocket and slowly bent and placed the bundle at the base of the marble slab. He straightened, as much as possible with crutches, and saluted the monument, his arm and fingers straight as a ruler. Finally Pacino dropped the salute and limped slowly back to the staff car, which sped off.

Donchez grabbed up his cap and left his office, then walked out into the cold February sunshine, around the corner and across the street to the monument. He went by one of the black torpedoes to the face of the wall and stared up at it, looking for a moment at the sleek marble hull in the shape of the *Stingray*, then down at the base of the monument at the bundle Michael Pacino had left there.

He picked up the bundle. It was a black fabric triangle, a folded flag. He unfolded the flag and saw the white form of a grinning skull above the crossbones. A Jolly Roger pirate flag.

Pacino's tribute to his father, and a long-ago conversation with Patch Pacino replayed itself in his mind, about flying the Jolly Roger after a big OP. That was why Mikey had always flown the pirate banner from the *Devilfish*.

Donchez felt an intense desire to do something to honor *both* Pacinos. It seemed wrong that *Devilfish* did not have her own monument. He searched for an idea, and as he made his way back to COMSUBLANT headquarters in the February gloom, the obvious came to him.

He walked up to the flagpole and grabbed the halyard of the COMSUBLANT flag, a boring emblem on a dingy blue field. He

hauled it down, unlatched the hook and dropped the COMSUB-
LANT flag to the pavement. He attached the Jolly Roger to the
halyard, and slowly hauled the pirate flag to the top of the pole.
He stepped back to look at it flying in the sky, then snapped to a
smart attention and saluted it.

That day, and every day thereafter while Admiral Richard
Donchez was Commander Submarines U.S. Atlantic Fleet, the
Jolly Roger flag flew from the flagpole high overhead at the entrance to the COMSUBLANT building, the skull and crossbones flapping in the wind beside the Stars and Stripes.

GLOSSARY

ACCELEROMETER An instrument that measures acceleration in g's.

ACQUISITION A torpedo being convinced that the signals from its sonar gear, active or passive, indicated a confirmed target.

ACR (ANTI-CIRCULAR RUN) A torpedo interlock that prevents the weapon from acquiring on the firing ship. When the torpedo turns more than a 160 degrees from the approach course to the target, the onboard gyro sends a signal to the central processor to shut down the unit. It then sinks.

ACTIVE SONAR The determination of a contact's bearing and range by pinging a sound pulse into the ocean and listening for the reflection of the ping from the target. The time interval between transmission and reception gives target range using the speed of sound in water. The direction of the return pulse indicates the target bearing. Generally not used by submarines since it gives away the ship's position. Used by some Russian units for a confirming range check immediately prior to shooting a torpedo.

AFT GROUP The main ballast tanks aft—four are aft of the engineroom, and four surround AMR 2. During an emergency blow, all six of these ballast tanks are blown dry simultaneously.

AKULA One of the newest classes of Russian attack submarines. Similar in appearance to a VICTOR III with the bulbous bow and stern pod on the rudder. Believed to be as quiet as an American *Piranha* class.

ALFA One of the recent Russian submarine classes. Very small and, until the appearance of the OMEGA class, the fastest nuclear submarine in the world. Also one of the loudest. Manned by a tiny crew of officers, the ship is totally automated. ALFA Unit One apparently suffered a massive reactor accident in the late 70s.

ALPHA RADIATION A positively charged particle emitted by heavy elements undergoing radioactive decay. Essentially a helium nucleus.

AMINES Chemicals used in CO_2 scrubber, a bed of amines over which

307

air is blown. Eliminates carbon dioxide, a by-product of human respiration.

AMP-HOUR A unit of electrical energy that measures the capacity of a battery.

AMP-HOUR METER Digital indicator on the Electric Plant Control Panel that measures the discharge of the ship's battery in amp-hours.

AMR 1 (AUXILIARY MACHINERY ROOM 1) (*Piranha* class) A mechanical equipment room in operations compartment lower level aft of the torpedo room. Contains the bomb (oxygen generator), forward auxiliary seawater pumps, air compressors, and other ship systems.

AMR 2 (AUXILIARY MACHINERY ROOM 2) (*Piranha* class) A two deck high compartment aft of the reactor compartment. Only two decks since it is surrounded by ballast tanks. The upper deck contains electrical switchgear and the reactor control cabinets. The lower deck is home to the main feed pumps, reactor auxiliary systems, and the second bomb.

ANALOG As opposed to digital—an analog instrument has a gage face and a pointer. An analog signal is smooth and continuous, while a digital signal is either on or off.

ANECHOIC COATING A thick foam coating attached to the outside of the hulls of Russian submarines. It absorbs incoming active sonar pulses without reflecting them back while damping out internal noises before they can get outside the ship. Analogous to stealth radar absorptive material on a stealth aircraft. Not used on American submarines since it is bulky and easily torn, and American ships are internally quieter.

ANGLE ON THE BOW The angle between an observer's line-of-sight to a target ship and the target's heading. A ship coming dead on has an angle on the bow of zero degrees. If the contact is going on a course at a right angle to his bearing from the observer, the angle on the bow is port (or starboard) 90 degrees.

ARRAY A collection of sonar hydrophones or transducers that work together to track a contact.

ASH (ANTI-SELF HOMING) A torpedo interlock that measures the distance from the firing ship. If the torpedo comes back toward the firing ship, at 80% of the return trip, the ASH interlock will shut down the unit, and it floods and sinks.

ASROC Antisubmarine rocket. A depth charge in the nosecone of a solid rocket fueled missile carried by ASW surface ships. The missile puts the depth charge in the water miles away from the firing ship, allowing the depth charge to be a nuclear warhead.

ASW (1) Antisubmarine warfare. (2) Auxiliary seawater system.

AUTHENTICATOR A packet containing a computer written group of letters and numbers. Packets are under two-man control at all times from production to destruction, and are locked in double safes. No one man has both safe combinations. Used by Russian and American forces to validate or authenticate orders to use nuclear weapons so that a single madman would be unable to launch nuclear weaponry. Destruction is done by first shredding, then burning under two-man control.

AUX 2 (*Piranha* class) A depth control tank (variable ballast tank) beneath the torpedo room.

B END HYDRAULIC MOTOR (ROTARY PISTON MOTOR) An external engine used in some designs of torpedoes. Hot gases enter from a combustion chamber under high pressure. The gases are expanded in a rotary mechanism of pistons connected to a canted swash plate, converting the thermal energy to mechanical work.

BAFFLES A "cone of silence" astern of most submarines where sonar reception is hindered by engines, turbines, screws, and other mechanical equipment located in the aft end of a submarine.

BALL VALVE A total shutoff valve using a ball inserted in a pipe. The ball has a hole in it to allow flow when aligned with the pipe. When rotated 90 degrees, the flow is stopped by the ball.

BALLAST Weight added to a ship to allow it to submerge, to counter buoyancy. Done by flooding tanks, main ballast tanks or variable ballast tanks.

BALLAST CONTROL PANEL Control panel in the port forward corner of an American submarine's control room. The console controls the ballast tank vent and blowing system, the hovering system, and the trim system. Also home to the chicken switches, the levers controlling the emergency blow system. Panel is manned by the COW, the Chief of the Watch.

BALLAST TANK Tank that is used solely to hold seawater ballast, weight that allows a ship to sink, or when blown allows a ship to be light enough to surface.

BALLISTIC MISSILE SUBMARINE Nuclear submarine that carries intercontinental ballistic nuclear missiles (SLBM's—submarine launched ballistic missiles). Mission consists entirely of hiding from all other ships and staying in passive radio communication with Washington in the event the President orders a nuclear assault on a foreign country. As opposed to fast attack submarines that do not carry SLBM's.

BALLISTIC TRAJECTORY Path of an unguided flying object, in a free-fall path determined by gravity, initial velocity, magnetic, Coreolis, and aerodynamic forces.

BARE STEERAGEWAY Minimum speed to allow the rudder and planes to work. About two knots.

BATTLESHORT A condition in which the nuclear reactor's safety inter-locks are removed. Used only in a severe emergency or in battle, when an accidental reactor shutdown is more dangerous to the ship due to loss of propulsion than the potential risk of a reactor meltdown. Only the captain can order Battleshort.

BATTLESHORT SWITCH Rotary switch on a cabinet in AMR 2 upper level that removes reactor safety interlocks.

BAT-EARS SONAR Slang name for the AN/BQQ-7 sonar suite, including the spherical broadband array, the hull broadband array, and the towed narrowband array. Also known as the "Q7."

BEAM (1) To the side of the ship.   (2) An active sonar cone stretching out into the ocean like the beam of a flashlight.   (3) A passive sonar reception cone—noise outside the cone will not be received.

BEARING Direction to a contact, expressed in degrees. A contact to the north is at a bearing of 000. A contact to the east is at 090, etc.

BEARING AMBIGUITY When a target is detected on the towed array, its noise could be coming from one of two directions. The ambiguity must be resolved by turning the ship and seeing which new two direc-tions the tonal seems to be coming from, or correlating a narrowband towed array bearing to a broadband bearing. Broadband bearings are never ambiguous.

BEARING DOT STACK A method of finding a firecontrol solution on the Mark I firecontrol system. The operator "stacks dots" using a knob. The display is a graph of the difference between actual target bearing and solution generated target bearing versus time. When the dot stack is in a vertical line, the difference between where a target is and where he should be is zero, indicating a firing solution. If a target zigs, the dots diverge off either left or right, indicating the target is no longer where the computer's solution says he should be.

BEARING DRIFT The direction of change of a contact's bearing, i.e., bearing drift is right when the contact moves from 090 to 095.

BEARING RATE The speed (or rate of change) of a contact's bearing. A contact that has a bearing change from 090 to 095 in one minute has a bearing rate of 5 degrees per minute right.

BIGMOUTH ANTENNA Slang name for the AN/BRA-34 multifre-quency antenna. A radio antenna suitable for transmission or recep-tion of several frequencies including HF, VHF, and UHF. Shaped like a telephone pole, it protrudes from the sail about 25 feet.

BILGES The space at the very bottom of the cylindrical hull of a subma-rine below the lower level deck. In the engineering spaces, the bilges capture leakage from piping systems for pumpout by the drain system. The bilges also capture any water from flooding so that it can be pumped out before it rises above the lower level deck to damage equipment.

BIOLOGICS Ocean noises generated by marine life forms: shrimp, whales, and other fish and mammals fill the sea with clicks, groans, grunts, and even tonals. The sounds can sometimes be mistaken for submarine sounds. A current theory holds that submarines transiting at low speeds can attract marine animals, thus shrouding the submarine in a cloak of biologics. For this reason, biologics are usually investigated with narrowband sonar to prove they do not hide an enemy submarine.

BLOCKS-OF-WOOD SONAR Code name for a Russian active sonar that sounds like two wood blocks clicking together. Used almost exclusively by Russian submarines to verify a target's range immediately prior to weapon launch. Immediate action for an American submarine hearing Blocks of Wood sonar is to call a Snapshot.

BLOWDOWN Opening a valve in a pipe from a steam generator (boiler) to the sea to blow out sediment and boiler chemicals. High pressure of the boiler forces the water out to lower pressure of the sea when at fairly shallow depths. Usually done only at periscope depth. Extremely noisy operation that destroys sonar reception completely.

BLOWING SANITARY Application of high pressure air to a sanitary (sewage) tank to force the sewage out of the tank into the sea. The air trapped in the tank must be vented to the inside of the ship to avoid telltale bubbles that could allow the ship to be detected. The venting makes the ship stink.

BLUEOUT Reverberations and noise from the bubbles caused by an underwater nuclear explosion. Masks sonar reception for hours, sometimes days.

BOMB GRADE URANIUM U-235, capable of fissioning and causing nuclear energy release. High concentrations of U-235 are used only in nuclear bombs and in high power-density naval reactors.

BOMB (OXYGEN GENERATOR) An electrical device that puts an ultrahigh voltage on distilled water, causing electrolysis, the breakdown of water into hydrogen and oxygen. The oxygen is put into the oxygen banks and bled into the ship for breathing. The hydrogen is discarded overboard through the auxiliary seawater system. The device, making the explosive combination of oxygen and hydrogen, has the potential to explode violently enough to breach the hull and sink the ship. Affectionately nicknamed the Bomb.

BOOMER Nickname for an FBM, fleet ballistic missile submarine. When used by SSN (fast attack submarine) sailors, it can be a derogatory term. A badge of honor to boomer sailors who see themselves as the lone defenders of America.

BOTTOM CONTOUR NAVIGATION Navigation by using a bottom bounce sonar pulse to map the contour of the ocean bottom and comparing the contour to computer memories. When the actual contour matches the computer's memory, the ship's position is known and the ship has a "fix." Advantageous since it allows obtaining a fix when deeply submerged without need to slow down and approach the surface. Disadvantages are that it emits an active sonar beam, allowing detection, and is useless when over a sandy flat bottom.

BOTTOM CONTOUR (BC) SONAR Sonar set allowing bottom contour navigation with a secure pulse (narrow frequency, short pulse duration) sonar.

BOTTOM SOUNDING Distance from the keel to the ocean bottom, measured in fathoms using the fathometer or BC sonar.

BOUNDARY LAYER Region of fluid flow around a solid object where the flow is slowed by friction with the surface of the object. Causes drag, slowing the object.

BOURDON TUBE A bent tube of metal that straightens when increasing internal pressure is applied. Used in primitive depth gages.

BOW COMPARTMENT Furthest forward compartment in a *Piranha* class submarine, containing crew berthing in the upper level and the emergency diesel generator in the lower level.

BOX A rectangular area of ocean, about ten miles wide and thirty miles long. A transiting submarine is required to stay inside the box. The box moves through the ocean at the same speed as its center, called a PIM (point of intended motion). Used so that an ASW surface ship does not mistake a transiting U.S. sub for an enemy. Any submarine contact inside the box is assumed to be a friendly. Not used in wartime, when submarine safety lanes are used, entire lanes devoted to transiting U.S. subs.

BRIDGE Small space at the top of a submarine's sail used for the Officer of the Deck to control the movement of the ship when on the surface. The height allows a better view of the surroundings of the ship.

BRIDGE ACCESS TRUNK Tunnel from the interior of the submarine to the bridge.

BROADBAND Noise containing all frequencies; white noise, such as heard in radio static, rainfall, or a waterfall. Broadband detection range is high for surface ships, which are noisy. Broadband detection range is low for submarines, usually less than five miles, due to quiet submarine designs.

BUBBLE (1) The ship's angle in degrees, as in the order "five degree down bubble." A relic of the days when bubble inclinometers were used to measure the ship's angle. Modern angle indicators take input from the gyro. The old style bubble is retained as insurance against electrical failures. (2) Control. Loss of control is known in slang as "losing the bubble."

BULKHEAD Seagoing name for a wall. Compartment bulkheads are the reinforced steel walls between compartments, hardened against seapressure so that one flooded compartment will not flood the neighboring compartment.

BURST COMMUNICATION Satellite-to-submarine and submarine-to-satellite radio transmissions using computers to compress messages. Allows high data rates, so that a ream of messages may be transmitted or received in mere seconds.

BUS Electrical term for a collection of loads. Vital bus loads include reactor main coolant pumps and control rod control. Nonvital bus loads are also "vital" and include sonar, firecontrol, etc., but are called nonvital since their loss will not immediately cause the loss of the ship.

CAVITATION Noise generated by a ship's screw. Always generated on surface ships, but only on submarine screws when a ship accelerates. A screw blade moving in the water, like an airplane wing, causes a low pressure region on one side and a high pressure region on the other. The low pressure (suction) side pulls the ship forward while the high pressure side pushes the ship forward. When the low pressure side's pressure gets too low, the water actually flashes to steam (boils) since the pressure can no longer keep the water molecules together in liquid form. A steam bubble is formed that is moved out into the water. When the steam bubble sees the higher pressure in the water away from the screw, it collapses again into liquid and emits a loud high frequency screech. A dead giveaway that a submarine is accelerating. To minimize noise, a submarine accelerating does so deliberately slowly. When running from a torpedo, in an emergency, the Conn will order maneuvering to cavitate since speed is more important than stealth.

CHAIN REACTION When a nuclear fission reaction causes at least one more fission reaction from the release of neutrons. The fission neutrons leak when subcritical, but when a reactor is critical, the number of fissions is constant since one reaction leads to another.

CHARGE PUMP A high pressure pump that forces water into the high pressure nuclear reactor cooling system to make up for any water lost from a rupture or leak.

CHECK VALVES Valves that allow flow only in one direction.

CHICKEN SWITCH One of two levers in the control room that emergency blow the main ballast tanks. So named since they are used when the captain is chicken and can no longer remain submerged. A term sometimes used for the hydraulic levers aft that shut ball valves on seawater systems for isolation of flooding.

CHIEF OF THE BOAT (COB) The most senior non-nuclear chief petty officer aboard, who is administratively responsible for the enlisted men on the submarine.

CINCLANTFLEET Commander-in-Chief, U.S. Atlantic Fleet. Admiral in command of the fleet, who has COMAIRLANT, COMSUBLANT, and COMSURFLANT reporting to him. Little known fact: as a CINC, the admiral has nuclear weapon release authority separate from that of the President. He will out of courtesy not release nuclear weapons without Presidential orders, but is authorized to use his own judgment during an emergency. CINCLANTFLEET also is the name for the organization supporting the admiral's command.

CIRCLE PATTERN Mark 49 and Mark 50 torpedo search pattern in which the torpedo swims in a circle until it finds the target.

CLAMSHELLS The steel or fiberglass hinged plates that cover the top of the bridge cockpit when rigged for dive and are opened when rigged for surface. When shut, the top of the sail is completely smooth.

CLEAR BAFFLES A maneuver to turn the ship around so that the sonar system can examine the conical slice of ocean previously astern of the ship, the blind spot called the baffles.

CLEAR DATUM Tactical euphemism meaning run away.

CLEARANCE Permission from COMSUBLANT for a submarine to submerge and go to a certain place for a certain mission. Also called a SUBNOTE, the clearance specifies the travel of the box and the PIM through the ocean.

CLICK A kilometer per hour.

CLUTCH A device aft of the reduction gear that allows uncoupling the ship's drive train (main engines and reduction gear) from the shaft, allowing the EPM (emergency propulsion motor) to turn the shaft, and hence the screw, without having to turn the massive main engines. Very similar to the clutch on an automobile.

CO BURNER/CARBON MONOXIDE BURNER A device that combusts carbon monoxide to produce carbon dioxide. CO is able to knock a crew unconscious with low concentrations, so the burners are vital pieces of the atmosphere control equipment.

CO2 SCRUBBER Atmospheric control equipment that rids the ship of carbon dioxide (from breathing, the diesel, and the CO burner) by blowing it over an amine bed.

COCKPIT The small space at the top of the sail. The bridge.

COMAIRLANT Admiral in command of Naval Aviation in the Atlantic Fleet.

COMMINT Intelligence gained from intercepted enemy communications.

COMMODORE Commander of a squadron of submarines. Usually a Navy captain. For a few years, the old rank of commodore was recommissioned, and commodore was essentially a one star admiral. The admirals complained, wanting to be called admirals. In recent years the rank of commodore has been replaced with the rank rear admiral (lower half).

COMPARTMENT A section of a submarine with hardened bulkheads and the pressure hull as its envelope. Able to withstand almost full crush depth pressure. Separating a submarine into several compartments makes the ship more survivable.

COMSUBLANT Commander Submarines U.S. Atlantic Fleet, the admiral in command of the Atlantic's submarine force. Also the name of the organization that supports the admiral, including intelligence, liaison, supply, communications, and procurement.

COMSUBRON 7 Commander of Submarine Squadron Seven. Also the name of the organization that supports the commodore. SUBRON 7's physical command includes pier 7 at Norfolk Naval Base and the submarine tender ship *Hercules*. The Squadron staff and the commodore occupy several O-level decks of the *Hercules*.

COMSURFLANT Commander Surface Force U.S. Atlantic Fleet, the admiral in command of the Atlantic's surface fleet. Also the name of the organization that supports the admiral.

CONDENSER A piece of equipment that converts low pressure steam to water by passing the steam over tubes with cold seawater flowing inside them. The main seawater system exists to pump the seawater through the truck sized main condensers. The condensate water is pumped back into the steam generators (boilers) to be boiled to steam for use in the turbines for power production and propulsion.

CONN (1) The act of directing the motion and mission of a submarine. Done by the Officer of the Deck, the Junior Officer of the Deck, or the captain. Whoever has the Conn is the conning officer. (2) The elevated periscope stand in the control room where the Officer of the Deck usually conns the submarine.

CONN OPEN MICROPHONE RECORDER (COMR) A black box in the overhead of the control room that records conversations during sensitive operations for use of reconstruction. Submitted with patrol reports after an OP. Monitored in the radio room and sometimes in sonar.

CONNING TOWER The fin on top of a submarine's hull allowing the ship to be conned safely on the surface. Called the sail in the U.S. Navy.

CONTACT Another ship, detected by visual means, sonar, or radar. A contact can be hostile or friendly.

CONTINGENCY 12 A section in the CINCLANTFLEET SIOP WAR-PLAN outlining options for a submarine captain when he suspects the United States has been the victim of a decapitation nuclear assault. Boomers and Javelin cruise missile submarines are given the option of launching nuclear weapons at the enemy without orders from Washington, NMCC, or CINCLANTFLEET. Fast attack submarines without land attack weapons are given the option of attacking enemy surface ships and submarines without further orders.

CONTROL COMPARTMENT Bubble shaped compartment above the main pressure hull of some Russian submarines, where all control activities are centered.

CONTROL ROOM Nerve center of a submarine, where the depth, speed, and combat actions of a submarine are directed.

CONTROLLING ROD GROUP The group of nuclear control rods that are raised and lowered to control reactor temperature or dropped to the bottom of the core during a partial (group) scram.

COOLANT DISCHARGE Discarding reactor coolant (water) overboard. Done during the heatup of a fast recovery startup, when the raising of water temperature from 300 degrees to 500 degrees makes it expand dramatically.

COOLANT LOOP One of two piping loops going from the reactor vessel to the loop's steam generator (boiler) and then to the loop's reactor main coolant pumps and back to the reactor vessel. The piping is called the primary coolant system and is highly radioactive.

CORE The inside of the reactor's pressure vessel. The core contains fuel elements including enriched (bomb grade) uranium sheathed in zirconium metal; a moderator to slow down the fission neutrons so they can be absorbed by uranium nuclei to cause more fissions (water is the moderator in a Navy core); and control rods that absorb neutrons so that the reactions and power level can be controlled.

COSMOS Russian communications satellite.

COUNTER ROTATING SCREWS Propulsion method using a screw that turns clockwise with another coaxial screw that turns counterclockwise. Efficiency increased since the first screw's exit vortex energy is used by the second screw to create more thrust. Disadvantages include complexity of design.

COUNTERDETECTION When submarine A sneaks up on submarine B, the detection by submarine B of submarine A is a counterdetection.

COUNTERFIRE When submarine A fires on submarine B, a counterfire is the launching of a weapon by submarine B at submarine A.

COUNTERMEASURES A small object launched by a signal ejector or a torpedo tube designed to decoy an incoming torpedo. Some low-tech countermeasures are bubble generators designed to fool active sonars. More sophisticated countermeasures for use against passive sonar torpedoes are torpedo-sized noisemakers programmed with the firing ship's own sound signature, broadcast louder than the firing ship.

COW (CHIEF OF THE WATCH) Member of the ship control team manning the Ballast Control Panel.

CPA (CLOSEST POINT OF APPROACH) The closest range a tracked contact will come to own ship. Prior to CPA the contact is closing. After CPA the contact is opening.

CPO (CHIEF PETTY OFFICER) Enlisted rank somewhat equivalent to sergeant in the Army. Possesses infinite knowledge and wisdom regarding submarines.

CRAZY IVAN A Russian submarine's maneuver to clear baffles. Due to the Russian submarines' frequently being trailed by U.S. subs, the Russians clear baffles suddenly and come back on the reciprocal course. An intimidation tactic designed to deter American boats from trailing too close. The cause of several undersea collisions.

CREEP Property of some metals at elevated temperatures to stretch when failing instead of rupturing or fracturing. Titanium has the property of exhibiting creep at low temperatures.

CREEP DEPTH A titanium submarine's depth at which the hull begins to fail in creep.

CRITICAL The point that a nuclear reactor's fission rate is constant without an external source of neutrons. The chain reaction keeps fissions going on using neutrons from fissions.

CRUSH DEPTH The depth that a pressure hull ruptures from seawater pressure.

CSLINST COMSUBLANT Instruction. An administrative document with administrative orders from COMSUBLANT.

CURVE A curve is obtained when a firecontrol solution is reached. Derives from the days of manual plots when bearing to a target was plotted against time. After two or three legs, the Z shaped curve defined a solution to the target.

CUTBACK An automatic reactor protection circuitry action to lower reactor power by driving the controlling control rod group into the core.

The cutback allows propulsion to continue while saving the reactor from an overpower meltdown accident. A Navy engineering compromise action between a scram (which eliminates propulsion) and continued criticality, which could lead to a nuclear accident.

CUTBACK OVERRIDE Action to stop a cutback by taking the mode selector switch to the cutback override position, stopping control rod motion inward. Used when a cutback is caused by an instrument failure rather than an actual hazard.

C.O. (COMMANDING OFFICER) Official title of the captain of a ship.

DANCING WITH THE FAT LADY Periscope watch. When rotating the number two periscope (type 18 scope), the observer's pelvis is pressed up against the hot optical control module of the unit. Physically exhausting when done for hours at a time.

DEBALLASTING SYSTEM Russian alternative to an emergency blow system. Explosive charges are placed in the ballast tanks to blow water out and replace the water with hot gases. Cheaper system than an emergency blow system, but rumored to have worsened Russian emergencies by rupturing the hull instead of blowing out ballast tank water.

DECADES PER MINUTE Measure of speed of increase of reactor power during a startup. A decade increase means that there are ten times as many fission neutrons in the core as before. There may be several dozen decades between the startup range and the power range. Normal startup rate is one decade per minute (about two to ten times faster than a civilian reactor startup rate). Fast recovery startup rate is 5 decades per minute. Absolute emergency rate is 9 dpm, since the maximum visible on the meter is 10 dpm.

DECK OFFICER Russian equivalent to the American Officer of the Deck.

DELOUSING When a submarine temporarily trails another friendly submarine; done to ensure the first sub is not being trailed by an enemy sub.

DEPLOYMENT Extended submarine OP to a distant OPAREA.

DEPTH CONTROL Ability to control a ship's depth within a narrow control band. Done either manually, with a computer, or with the hovering system (when stopped). Particularly vital at periscope depth because failure to maintain depth control can cause the sail to become exposed (broach), giving away the ship's position.

DEPTH RATE Speed of change of depth in feet per second. Vertical speed.

DEPTH SOUNDER Fathometer. Measures distance from the bottom of the ship (keel) to the ocean bottom.

DETECT (Noun) When a torpedo is in search mode, a detect is a positive confirmation that a target is where the solution theoretically shows him to be. When a submarine is discovering a target, a detect is the initial sonar bearing to the broadband noise or the initial sonar frequency of the tonal.

DEUTERIUM Heavy water. Used in nuclear fusion reactors or fusion (hydrogen) bombs.

DIALEX Phone system used on submarines for administrative and unofficial communication.

DISK CRASH The failure of the disk module of the firecontrol computer. Memory access and operating system actions are done using the tape module, which is infinitely slower than the disk system. Severe failure, but still allows limited firecontrol and weapon launch functions.

DISTRIBUTED CONTROL SYSTEM (DCS) Computer system that controls a complicated process such as a nuclear propulsion plant.

DIVE POINT The point a submarine plans to submerge. Traditionally where keel depth is greater than 600 fathoms.

DIVING OFFICER Officer or Chief who sits aft of the sternplanesman and helmsman. Responsible for depth control.

DOGS Banana shaped pieces of metal that act as clasps to keep a hatch shut.

DOPPLER EFFECT Effect responsible for train whistles sounding shrill when the train approaches and low pitched when the train is past. When a moving platform emits sound waves, the waves are compressed ahead and rarefacted (spread apart) behind the source. The compression of the waves raises their frequency, making a higher note.

DOPPLER FILTER A sonar receiver that blanks out reception of the frequency of transmission of a sonar pulse. The receiver listens only for higher or lower frequency returns, thus screening out stationary contacts and only detecting moving contacts. Used in police radars and torpedo under-ice active sonars.

DOT STACK Same as a bearing dot stack.

DOUBLE HULL Construction of the pressure hull inside an outer hull. The space between the outer and inner hull is used for equipment and ballast water. Creates a very survivable platform at the cost of weight and expense.

DRAIN PUMP Main component of the drain system. Pumps out bilges of flooding spaces and discharges the water overboard.

DUTY OFFICER Essentially the Officer of the Deck when the ship is tied up at the pier or in drydock.

D/E (DEFLECTION/ELEVATION) The spherical array of the BAT-EARS sonar suite has hydrophone sonar receivers placed over most of its surface. A sound received on the upper surface (high D/E angle) means the contact is above the submarine or its noise is bouncing off the ocean above. A sound received at low D/E is either reflected from the ocean bottom or directly transmitted from beneath the submarine.

ELECTRIC PLANT CONTROL PANEL (EPCP) A console in the maneuvering room that controls the electrical distribution of the ship including the turbine generators and the battery.

ELF (EXTREMELY LOW FREQUENCY) Long wave radio waves capable of penetrating deeply into the ground and underwater. Requires large high power land based antennae and has very low data rates (taking several minutes to transmit one letter or number). Usually used to call a submarine up to periscope depth to receive a burst of communication from the satellite.

EMBRITTLEMENT A reactor's pressure vessel is impacted by trillions of neutrons, altering the physical structure of the metal. The steel vessel becomes brittle and fractures easily when subjected to sudden temperature changes, like a frozen coffee mug shatters when hot coffee is poured in.

EMBT BLOW Emergency main ballast tank blow.

EMERGENCY BLOW Blowing the water out of the main ballast tanks using ultrahigh-pressure air. Empties ballast tanks in seconds, lightening the ship, allowing the ship to get to the surface in an emergency such as flooding.

EMERGENCY COOLING (XC) A system that uses a seawater heat exchanger to cool the nuclear reactor when flow through the core is lost. Uses natural convection flow, which is flow motivated by the tendency of hot water to rise and cold to sink.

EMERGENCY DEEP An emergency procedure used at periscope depth to avoid collision with a surface ship. Involves cavitating, flooding a depth control tank, and putting a diving angle on the ship to get deep in mere seconds. Designed to avoid hull rupture from collision with a surface ship that cannot see the sub at PD. Era of supertankers makes this a vital procedure because supertankers have so much oil volume forward of their engines that they are quiet as a sailboat and are often undetected by sonar.

EMERGENCY HEATUP RATE Emergency procedure used on startup when heating a nuclear reactor after a scram. Instead of a nice slow warmup at a half degree per minute or one degree per minute, the plant is heated up at up to several hundred degrees per minute to save the ship, ignoring the risk of a possible vessel rupture from thermal stress.

EMERGENCY PROPULSION MOTOR (EPM) A large DC motor aft in the engineroom, capable of turning the shaft to achieve 3 knots using battery power alone. An electricity hog.

EMERGENCY SSTG WARMUP Emergency procedure to get a turbine generator to make power within seconds from its cold condition after a reactor scram. Done to achieve power quickly, ignoring the risk of turbine destruction, case rupture, and major steam leak.

ENGINEROOM Largest and furthest aft compartment on a U.S. submarine. Holds the maneuvering room, propulsion and electrical turbines, main condensers, numerous pumps, evaporator, air conditioners, reduction gear, clutch, EPM, and shaft seals.

ENSIGN Lowest officer rank. Also a flag flown aft when the ship is tied up.

EO (ELECTRICAL OPERATOR) Enlisted nuclear qualified watchstander who mans the Electric Plant Control Panel and reports to the EOOW.

EOOW (ENGINEERING OFFICER OF THE WATCH) Nuclear qualified officer who runs the nuclear power plant. Responsible to the OOD for propulsion and propulsion plant damage control.

ESCAPE POD Device used on Russian submarines to escape a sinking ship.

ESCAPE TRUNK A spherical airlock used on American nuclear submarines. The device can be used to make emergency exits from a sub sunk in shallow water. Principally used for divers to lock in or lock out.

ESM MAST An antenna that is raised to allow detailed analysis of enemy radar or radio signals. Supplements the equipment installed on the periscope.

ESM (ELECTRONICS SURVEILLANCE MEASURES) The gathering of intelligence through the analysis of enemy signals, including radars and radio transmitters.

EVAPORATOR Device that evaporates seawater using steam heat. The vapors are condensed and used as potable (drinking) water or steam plant/reactor plant makeup water. The plant comes first.

EWS (ENGINEERING WATCH SUPERVISOR) A Chief who is a roving supervisory watchstander in the engineering spaces. Reports to EOOW.

EXPLOSIVE BOLTS A hollow fastener with an explosive charge inside for quick disconnection. Used in rocket motor stages and escape pod latches.

EXTERNAL-COMBUSTION ENGINE Engine in which the fuel and oxygen burn in a chamber remote from where the work is done.

Examples include jet engines and oil burning steam plants. As opposed to internal combustion engines where the fuel is burned where the mechanical work takes place, as in an automobile engine.

FAIRWATER PLANES Winglike surfaces protruding from the sail of a submarine, used for depth control. Can be rotated to a vertical position for breaking through polar ice.

FAMILY-GRAM Short three line personal radio message from a crewmember's family, transmitted by COMSUBLANT when a ship is on a deployment. Family typically gets one message every six weeks.

FAST ATTACK SUBMARINE An SSN, a submarine designed to be small, light, quiet, fast, and lethal. Carries torpedoes to sink surface ships and other submarines. Carries cruise missiles for anti-ship warfare and for land attack. Used also as a covert intelligence gathering platform. Can put covert troops ashore using the escape trunks. Capable of months of submerged, undetected operations.

FAST LEAK A rather nasty leak from the primary coolant system of a nuclear reactor. If not isolated, will empty the water from the core and lead to a meltdown, and possibly to a prompt critical rapid disassembly.

FAST NEUTRONS Neutrons emitted by uranium nuclei undergoing fission. Mostly useless for causing another fission reaction since they want to leak from the core. Water (moderator) slows the fast neutrons down through collisions with water molecules. The slow (thermal) neutrons can then be accepted by a uranium nucleus to cause another fission. Under some conditions, uranium can be critical on fast neutrons. One example is a bomb undergoing a nuclear explosion. A second is a core in a reactivity accident such as a control rod jump, where the core becomes prompt critical, critical on the fast neutrons that are emitted "promptly" by the fission reaction.

FAST RECOVERY STARTUP Emergency procedure to recover from a reactor scram at sea, using a 5 decade per minute startup rate and abbreviated turbine warmups. One of the compromises between ship safety (requiring the reactor be up for propulsion) and reactor safety (requiring a scram if there is the slightest reactor fault).

FATHOM Unit of depth equal to six feet.

FATHOMETER Bottom sounding sonar that directs an active sonar pulse down to the ocean bottom and measures the time for the pulse to reflect back and hence the distance to the bottom. New units transmit a secure pulse, using a short duration random high frequency pulse.

FBM Fleet ballistic missile submarine. Official name of a boomer.

FINAL BEARING AND SHOOT Order of the captain to shoot a torpedo after he takes one last periscope observation of a surface target.

FIRECONTROL SOLUTION A contact's range, course, and speed. A great mystery when using passive sonar. Determining the solution requires maneuvering own ship and doing calculations on the target's bearing rate. Can be obtained manually or with the firecontrol computer.

FIRECONTROL SYSTEM A computer system that accepts input from the periscope, sonar, and radar (when on the surface) to determine the firecontrol solution. The system also programs, fires, steers, and monitors torpedoes. If a ship is cruise missile equipped, the system will program and fire the missile.

FIRECONTROL TEAM A collection of people whose task is to put a weapon on a target. Includes the sonar operators, OOD, JOOD, Captain, XO, firecontrol operators on Pos One, Pos Two, Pos Three, the firing panel, and the manual plotters (geographic, time-bearing, time-range, and time-frequency).

FIRING PANEL A console section between Pos Two and Pos Three. The vertical section is a tube/weapon status panel. The horizontal section has the trigger, a lever used to fire a torpedo or cruise missile.

FIRING POINT PROCEDURES An order by the captain to the firecontrol team to tell them to prepare to fire the weapon, done during a deliberate approach when the solution is refined, as opposed to a Snapshot. The solution is locked into the weapon and the ship is put into a firing attitude.

FIRSTIE A first class midshipman at Annapolis. A senior.

FISSION A nuclear reaction during which a uranium or plutonium nucleus is split apart after the absorption of a neutron. Releases two to three neutrons, two nuclear fragments, and 200 megaelectron volts of energy.

FIX A ship's position. Determined by visual triangulation or radar when close to land on the surface, or by NAVSAT or BC sonar when at sea.

FIX ERROR CIRCLE The circle that the ship could be in as a result of time since the last fix, steering errors, speed errors, etc.

FLAG PLOT A chart room used by flag officers (admirals) to plot strategy or determine the distribution of forces.

FLANK SPEED Maximum speed of a U.S. submarine. Requires fast speed reactor main coolant pumps and running at 100% reactor power.

FLASH The highest priority of a radio message. Receipt required within minutes or seconds.

FLOATING WIRE ANTENNA A bouyant wire trailed from a submarine's sail used to stay in passive radio communication when the ship is deep. Tends to snag fishing boats. Seagulls love to ride on them. Not generally used by SSN's.

FLOODABLE VOLUME The amount of a compartment that can flood before it causes the ship to sink.

FORWARD GROUP The main ballast tanks forward of the operations compartment. During an emergency blow, all six of these ballast tanks are blown dry simultaneously.

FRAME Hoops of steel or titanium that serve as the skeleton for the pressure hull.

FRAME 57 The frame between the operations compartment and the reactor compartment on a *Piranha* class submarine. The start of the engineering spaces. Anything beyond Frame 57 is called "back aft."

FREQUENCY GATE A narrow range of frequency that the sonar is tuned to listen to.

FUEL ELEMENT An assembly of uranium with zirconium cladding in a nuclear core. The uranium heats the water, making steam in the steam generators, allowing power production in the turbines.

FULL POWER LINEUP Electric plant lineup when the reactor is critical and self-sustaining. Both turbine generators are at 3600 RPM and are supplying power to the ship's loads. The battery is not discharging.

FULL RUDDER When the rudder is turned 30 degrees.

FULL SCRAM When *all* control rods (not just the controlling group) are pushed to the bottom of the core. It takes much longer to recover from a full scram than a group scram.

FULL SPEED Maximum speed of a U.S. submarine with slow speed reactor main coolant pumps running the reactor at 50% power. A *Piranha* class does about 25 knots at full.

FUSION A nuclear reaction in which several light nuclei come together and release tremendous quantities of energy. Usually requires initial temperatures of several thousand degrees.

G   A measure of acceleration. The acceleration due to gravity is one g. Two g's is twice, etc.

GAMMA RADIATION Electromagnetic radiation released in a nuclear reaction. Generally similar to X-rays.

GEOGRAPHIC PLOT (1) A manual plot saved from World War II submarine days using the plot table to deduce a firecontrol solution. Works well on unsuspecting targets. Target zigs cause confusion on this plot. Useless in a melee situation. (2) A mode of display of the Mark I firecontrol system showing a God's eye view of the sea with own ship at the center and the other contacts and their solutions surrounding it.

GEOSYNCHRONOUS SATELLITE A satellite orbiting at an altitude of about 33,000 miles. The orbital velocity matches the earth's rotational speed, making the satellite stationary with respect to the earth's surface. Ideal for communication satellites.

GI-UK GAP (GREENLAND-ICELAND-UNITED KINGDOM GAP) The northern entrance to the Atlantic, choked by Greenland and Iceland to the northwest and Great Britain to the east. Any sortie of Russian Northern Fleet units would need to pass north of Norway, then south through the GI-UK gap.

GMT (GREENWICH MEAN TIME) A worldwide time standard using the time at longitude zero at Greenwich, England. Also called Zulu time.

GO CODE Slang for a nuclear release message to units ordered to fire nuclear weapons.

GPS (GLOBAL POSITIONING SYSTEM) A series of satellites and shipborne receivers enabling extremely precise navigation fixes. Also called the NAVSAT.

GRASS/RADAR GRASS A region within about 50 to 100 feet of the ground that surface search and air search radars are unable to penetrate due to ground clutter. An aircraft or missile flying in the grass can sneak up to its target without radar detection.

GREEN BAND Normal limits for T-AVE during critical reactor operation. Between 480 and 500 degrees F.

GROUP ONE One of three control rod groups in a Naval S5W/S3G Core 3 core. During about half of core life these control rods control reactor temperature and power level.

GROUP SCRAM A reactor scram using only the few control rods in the controlling rod group. Enough negative reactivity to shut down the reactor for several hours, but not so much that recovery is difficult.

GUIDANCE WIRE A neutrally buoyant wire streamed from the rear of a Mark 49 or 50 torpedo allowing communication between the weapon and the firecontrol system. Used to pass steer commands from ship to torpedo and information about the target from torpedo to ship.

GYRO/GYROSCOPE Electrical compass using a rapidly spinning gyroscope.

HAFNIUM Element used in Navy control rods. Acts as a black hole for neutrons. Without neutrons, fission reactions stop, and a core is shutdown.

HALF POWER LINEUP Electric plant lineup when the reactor is critical and self-sustaining. One turbine generator is at 3600 RPM and supplying power to the ship's loads. The battery is not discharging.

HARD RUDDER A rudder angle of about 37 degrees. An emergency order because it risks being unable to return the rudder to an amidships position.

HARDENED SAIL A sail constructed of 3 inch thick HY-80 steel designed to break through polar ice.

HEAVY WATER Deuterium. Used in nuclear fusion reactors or fusion (hydrogen) bombs.

HELM The wheel that turns the ship's rudder. Also short for helmsman.

HF (HIGH FREQUENCY) Radio waves capable of reception continents away. Reception is often unreliable, susceptible to various atmospheric conditions.

HOMING A torpedo in the final stages of arming and pursuit of a target.

HOT RUN A serious emergency resulting from a torpedo that starts its engine while still in the tube or in the torpedo room. Hazards include the toxic gas exhaust and probability of warhead detonation.

HOT STANDBY A condition of a shutdown reactor and steam plant such that the systems are kept as warm as possible to allow a more rapid startup.

HOVERING SYSTEM A depth control system managed by a computer that keeps the ship in one point underwater. Used by boomers when launching missiles. Used by fast attack submarines to establish a desired vertical speed (depth rate) to vertical surface through polar ice.

HULL ARRAY One of the sonar hydrophone element assemblies (arrays) of the BAT-EARS sonar suite, consisting of multiple hydrophones placed against the skin of the hull over about 1/3 of the ship's length. Used mostly as a backup to the spherical array because the hull array's sensitivity is reduced by own ship noise inside the hull.

HYDRAULICS Use of oil under pressure to cause motion in large equipment. Used to move the planes and rudder and to raise masts and antennae. In the nuclear plant, primary coolant (water) is used to move valves.

HYDRODYNAMIC FORCES Lift, downforce, or drag caused by the flow of water over the surface of a moving object.

HYDROPHONE A device that converts mechanical motion of soundwaves into electrical signals to be amplified and analyzed by the sonar system. Somewhat like a large microphone. A set of hydrophones forms an array. Hydrophones are passive devices designed for reception only. A transducer can either receive or transmit sonar pulses.

HY-80 STEEL A special alloy of steel made for the Navy. HY stands for high yield. 80 stands for yield stress of 80,000 psi. One of the strongest and toughest steels made. Used for the pressure hull plates and frames of the *Piranha* and *Los Angeles* classes.

IMMEDIATE The priority of a radio message just below FLASH. Receipt required within an hour.

IMPLOSION An inward explosion, such as a pressure hull crushed by seawater pressure.

INCLINOMETER A liquid filled tube in the shape of an upside down U with a small bubble at the top. A low-tech method to measure the angle or roll of the ship.

INDUCTION PIPING Piping from the snorkel mast to the ship for use by the diesel generator when the ship is snorkeling.

INTAKE DIFFUSER The air intake of a jet engine. A diffuser is the opposite of a nozzle. It slows down the incoming airstream and raises its pressure.

INTEGRATE The accumulation of data of the BAT-EARS narrowband sonar processors. Tonal frequencies are examined and plotted against time. The longer a tonal is heard, the more certain the computer is that the tonal is not random but is a contact.

INTERLOCK An electrical circuit or mechanical device that prevents unsafe actions. A mechanical example is the shaft that prevents opening a torpedo tube inner door when the outer door is already open, thus preventing opening a hole to the ocean. An electrical example is the reactor protection circuits scramming the reactor if the plant exceeds 103% power to prevent a meltdown.

INTERMEDIATE RANGE A region of reactor power that is passed through on the approach to the power range. When increasing power, the reactor is just slightly supercritical. When decreasing power after a scram, the core is subcritical. The region of neutron level between the startup range and the power range.

INVERTER An electrical device that converts DC power into a step AC current. Used to drive control rod motors.

INVERTER ALPHA The inverter normally used for the controlling rod group.

JAM DIVE An emergency that results from either the sternplanes or fairwater planes failing in the dive position, forcing the submarine toward crush depth. A high speed sternplane jam dive is the classic accident taught at Submarine School in the diving simulators. Immediate actions include reversing the screw to All Back Full and emergency blowing to the surface. Only one in five simulations results in recovery of depth control—most students are blasted down to crush depth no matter what they do.

JOOD (JUNIOR OFFICER OF THE DECK) Assistant to the OOD. When in transit, the JOOD is usually an unqualified officer in a training position, given the Conn and supervised by the OOD. When in a tactical situation, the JOOD is a senior qualified officer who shares the firecontrol duties with the OOD and is generally responsible for the firecontrol solution and release of weapons.

KEEL In the old days of sail, the keel was the plank that the ribs of the ship were attached to, forming the backbone of the hull. Cylindrical submarine hulls do not have a physical keel. The keel is by definition the lowest point of the hull.

KH-17 Newest generation of Bigbird spy satellites. The KH stands for Keyhole—appropriate for a spy platform.

LAMINAR FLOW Smooth, layerlike, near frictionless flow over an object.

LATCH RODS The order to increase the voltage of the electromagnets on the control rod drive mechanisms to engage the motors to the rods after a scram or shutdown.

LATCH VOLTAGE The increased voltage applied to the control rod drive mechanisms in order to latch rods.

LD-50 The radiation dose that will statistically kill 50% of a population exposed. About 500 rem.

LEFT-TO-RIGHT TAG REVERSAL The result of a torpedo in passive search mode doing rudder wiggle. If the target moves left and right, the target is confirmed as valid. Much like a dog cocks its head when it hears prey.

LEG The straight line travel of a submarine doing passive sonar Target Motion Analysis (TMA) between maneuvers. During a leg the crew attempts to establish a steady bearing rate to the target and establish speed across the line-of-sight to the target. Two legs determine a firecontrol solution. Three legs confirm the solution.

LINE-OF-SIGHT (1) The line from own ship to the target ship. (2) A mode of the firecontrol system used in Tape Mode and during a Snapshot. The display shows own ship as a rowboat, the target ship as another rowboat at the end of the line-of-sight. The operator matches the target bearing and the bearing rate to get a crude firing solution. (3) A description of the travel of UHF radio waves, which travel in straight lines.

LIQUID METAL COOLANT Use of liquid metal as reactor coolant instead of pressurized water. Sodium and barium are two popular coolants. Abandoned by the U.S. Navy due to the dangers of a sodium-water reaction.

LIST Tilt of a ship to the side.

LITHIUM BROMIDE AIR CONDITIONER One of the air conditioners onboard that uses the absorptive method of heat transfer.

LOCKING IN/LOCKING OUT Entering or leaving a submerged submarine through the escape trunk (airlock).

LOFAR Low frequency analyzer used to determine number of screw blades on a contact's screw.

LOOKAROUND (1) A periscope observation. (2) A warning by the OOD or captain to the ship control team that the periscope is about to be raised. The Diving Officer and helmsman report ship's speed and depth as a reminder, since high speeds can rip the periscope off and flood the ship through the periscope hole.

LOOKDOWN-SHOOTDOWN RADAR A radar capable of seeing down into the radar grass for the purpose of destroying low flying objects.

LOOP (1) A set of piping in the primary coolant system. (2) The VLF antenna.

LOS ANGELES CLASS The class of submarines built after the last *Piranha* class. Faster but limited in depth. Hold more weapons and run quieter. Disadvantaged by inability to go under the polar icecap. Also less survivable than the venerated *Piranha*s due to the reduction of compartments from 5 to 2.

LOSS-OF-COOLANT ACCIDENT Nuclear accident caused by pipe rupture or system failure such that coolant is lost, leading to extreme temperature excursions and probable reactor meltdown. Three Mile Island was a loss-of-coolant accident.

LOW PRESSURE CUTBACK A cutback due to low pressure in the core. A protection against oncoming loss-of-coolant accident or loss-of-pressure accident.

LOW PRESSURE CUTOUT SWITCH A switch that alters reactor scram trip setpoints based on the current operation of the system.

LOW PRESSURE TURBINE A turbine that accepts low pressure steam from the high pressure turbine and extracts energy from the steam for mechanical work.

MAD (MAGNETIC ANOMALY DETECTOR) A detector flown on an aircraft that measures changes in the earth's magnetic field that could be caused by the iron hull of a submarine.

MAD (MUTUAL ASSURED DESTRUCTION) The theory that a nuclear enemy will be deterred from launch of his nuclear weapons by the knowledge that if he launches, he will be destroyed by America's nuclear arsenal.

MAIN BALLAST TANK Tank that is used solely to hold seawater ballast, weight that allows a ship to sink, or when blown allows a ship to be light enough to surface.

MAIN COOLANT AVERAGE TEMPERATURE (T-AVE) A rough

estimate of in-core temperature found by averaging water inlet temperature and outlet temperature.

MAIN COOLANT CUTOUT VALVE (MCCOV) A large gate valve designed to isolate a coolant loop from the core in case of a fast leak.

MAIN ENGINES (PROPULSION TURBINES) The large turbines that extract energy from steam and convert it to power to turn the screw.

MAIN SEAWATER SYSTEM The seawater piping and pumps that force seawater through the main condensers to condense steam into water for boiler feed.

MAIN STEAM VALVES ONE AND TWO (MS-1, MS-2) Large gate valves on the port and starboard main steam headers at the forward bulkhead of AMR 2 that can isolate the main steam system in the event of a major steam leak.

MANEUVERING The nuclear control room, located in engineroom upper level. Smaller than most closets.

MANEUVERING WATCH The watch stations manned when a ship gets under way in restricted waters.

MARK 37 TORPEDO Torpedoes used in the early nuclear submarine classes. Driven by electrical motors.

MARK 49 TORPEDO (HULLBUSTER) Current version of the torpedo in use by the submarine fleet. Has a range of about 20 to 25 miles, carries a 1500 pound load of shaped charge explosives, and has a top attack speed of 50 knots. Depth limited to 3500 feet.

MARK 50 TORPEDO (HULLCRUSHER) Experimental prototype of the weapon designed to replace the Mark 49, for use against large double hulled deep diving submarines. Maximum depth is 10,000 feet. Shaped charge warhead 100 times more effective at hull rupture than the Mark 49. Maximum speed is 55 knots.

MARK I FIRECONTROL SYSTEM Full name is the CCS (Combat Control System) Mark I. The system has three positions, each capable of some two dozen displays for finding target solutions and programming weapons.

MATCH BEARINGS AND SHOOT Captain's order to shoot a torpedo after resetting the firecontrol solution to match the actual bearing and bearing rate of the target. Used with older firecontrol systems. (See Shoot on Generated Bearing.)

MELEE A condition in which two submarines in combat are aware of each other's presence. Firecontrol situations using passive sonar become impossible to ascertain due to constant maneuvers of the target. Both combatants tend to switch to active sonar and get weapons in the water. If the ships are too close, weapon targeting becomes nearly impossible and collisions become highly likely. In some situations, commanding officers may elect to clear datum until the battle can be controlled.

MEGATON Nuclear warhead yield equivalent to a million tons of TNT.

MELTDOWN Gross fuel element failure and melting in nuclear core due to overheating, usually from overheating. Overheating can be caused by lack of cooling in a loss of coolant accident or by excess reactivity addition as in a control rod jump. Hazardous because highly radioactive products of fission are released to the environment (a typical Navy reactor midway through core life has enough radioactivity to rival the release from Chernobyl). Also dangerous because the melted fuel can collect at the bottom of the reactor vessel and melt through the metal, breaching the hull. Finally, there is a slight chance of the melted fuel mass becoming critical at the bottom of the core, leading to a prompt critical disassembly.

MOTOR GENERATOR One of two large machines located in AMR 2 upper level. It is a motor connected to a generator on the same shaft. The unit can convert DC electrical power to AC power, when the battery is supplying ship's AC loads, or from AC power to DC power, when the turbine generators are charging the battery.

MIZ (MARGINAL ICE ZONE) An area of drift ice and icebergs in the region between open water and the polar icecap.

NESTOR SECURE VOICE A UHF radiotelephone communication system that encrypts a voice signal prior to transmission and decrypts it after reception. Can be transmitted to the satellite and beamed worldwide. Fast, secure means of communication.

NEUTRON FLUX The amount of free neutrons in a specific volume during a specific time interval. Roughly proportional to reactor power level, i.e., to the fission rate in a core.

NEUTRON LEVEL Number of neutrons per second received at a probe outside the reactor vessel. Directly proportional to reactor power level (fission rate).

NEUTRON RADIATION As a result of uranium fission, each fission yields two to three neutrons. Many of these leak from the core, irradiating neighboring compartments and people. Elaborate shields are constructed, but nothing stops all the neutrons. Also a result of spontaneous fissions in nuclear warheads.

NEWTON A unit of force named after Sir Isaac Newton. Roughly one fifth of a pound.

NLACM (NUCLEAR LAND ATTACK CRUISE MISSILE) A cruise missile capable of attacking a land target using stellar or radar contour navigation. Examples include the Javelin (American weapon, built by

DynaCorp International) and the SSN-X-27 (Russian, built by the Severomorsk Weapons Industrial Company Number 427).

NMCC (NATIONAL MILITARY COMMAND CENTER) A nerve center in the Pentagon where, in theory, orders would originate for fighting a nuclear war. Seasoned officers scoff at the idea that NMCC would survive the first ten minutes of a surprise decapitation assault.

NOFORN A level of classification of information that indicates no transmission allowed to foreign nations.

NONVITAL BUS A misnomer for a group of electrical loads supplied off the same turbine generator breaker. While the loads are indeed vital, their loss will not immediately lead to loss of the ship. Examples include sonar and firecontrol, fast speed reactor main coolant pumps, and the wardroom video machine.

NOZZLE The opposite of a diffuser. Converts pressure energy of a fluid stream to velocity (kinetic energy).

OIL SHIELD TANK A tank surrounding a reactor compartment used to shield against neutron radiation since oil is an excellent shielding material and needs to be carried aboard for the emergency diesel generator anyway.

ONE THIRD SPEED First speed up from All Stop. Usually gives about 5 knots. Equivalent to the British Dead Slow Ahead.

OOD (OFFICER OF THE DECK) Officer in tactical command of the ship, a sort of acting captain. Directs the motion of the ship, giving rudder, speed, and depth orders. Responsible for ship's navigation, operation of the ship's equipment, and employment of the ship's weapons. Usually has the Deck and the Conn. Needs captain's permission to do certain operations, such as go to periscope depth, startup the reactor, transmit active sonar or transmit radio, or launch a weapon.

OP Operation or mission.

OPAREA A specific ocean area devoted to a particular exercise or operation. Some OPAREA's are permanent, some are established only for one exercise.

OPERATING ENVELOPE A region of speed and depth defined for submarine operations. Outside the envelope, the ship could suffer a casualty and sink (the warranty is off). Example: going flank speed at test depth is outside the envelope, because a sternplane jam dive would send the ship below crush depth before she could check the speed and emergency blow to the surface. Operating outside the envelope is done only with captain's permission.

OPERATIONAL MODE SELECTOR SWITCH A rotary switch on the Reactor Plant Control Panel that determines reactor operational mode, such as shutdown, normal, and cutback override.

OPERATIONS COMPARTMENT Forward compartment containing the control room, torpedo room, crew's mess, and crew berthing.

OPREP 3 PINNACLE Name of a message that is sent with FLASH priority to the White House and NMCC telling of a dire emergency requiring immediate action, such as an incoming nuclear assault.

OUTBOARD (1) Away from the centerline of the ship; toward the outside of the ship. (2) A small motor with a screw lowered from AMR 2 lower level; the outboard can be trained in any direction to give the ship thrust out from the pier when getting under way.

OUTCHOP Formally leaving one commander's authority and entering another's. Also has the meaning of leaving one ocean and entering another.

OVERHEAD Nautical term for ceiling.

OWN SHIP Firecontrol term for the firing ship.

OXYGEN GENERATOR See Bomb.

PARALLEL Electrical term, meaning connecting two bus AC load centers with a circuit breaker. The loads have to have the same frequency and be at the same point in the sine wave or else equipment can be damaged and fires can start.

PASSIVE SONAR Most common mode of employment of most submarine sonar systems. Sonar system is used only to *listen*, not to ping out active sonar beams, since pinging gives away a covert submarine's presence. Use of passive sonar makes it difficult to determine a contact's range, course, and speed (solution). TMA is the means of obtaining a solution when using passive sonar.

PATROL QUIET Ship systems lineup to ensure maximum quiet while allowing normal creature comforts such as cooking and movie watching. Maintenance on equipment is allowed, if it does not involve banging on the hull. Noisy operations are only permitted with the captain's permission, such as reactor coolant discharge, steam generator blowdowns, etc.

PATTERN CHARLIE The point in space and time when a CINC's airborne command post is a safe distance from its base, so that it is no longer vulnerable to nuclear destruction. The CINC can then take over from an operational commander in a bunker.

PCO WALTZ A melee situation where two submarines are aware of each other in a combat situation. Firecontrol situations using passive sonar become impossible to ascertain due to constant maneuvers of the target. Both combatants tend to switch to active sonar and get weapons in the water. If the ships are too close, weapon targeting becomes nearly impossible and collisions become highly likely. In some situations, commanding officers may elect to clear datum until the battle can be controlled. Term originates from Prospective Commanding Officer School at Groton, Conn., where many sub-vs-sub exercises are done.

PD (PERISCOPE DEPTH) An operation when the ship comes shallow enough to see with the periscope. Certain operations can only be done at periscope depth by decree of the Submarine Standard Operating Procedures manual. Such items include steam generator blowdown, shooting trash from the TDU, and blowing sanitary. Some things can only be done at PD, including radio reception of satellite broadcasts, reception of a NAVSAT pass, and ESM activities. Slows the ship down since high speeds can rip off the periscope. Dangerous operation since quiet surface ships can get close without being detected by sonar. See Emergency Deep.

PHOTOINT Photographic intelligence, such as the interpretation of satellite photos.

PILOT A person who has detailed knowledge and experience of a port and approach waterways. Taken on prior to entering or exiting port to serve as an advisor to the captain.

PIM (POINT OF INTENDED MOTION) The center of the box. The moving point in the ocean that a transiting submarine stays within a predefined range of at all times. See Box.

PING An active sonar pulse.

PIRANHA CLASS The SSN-637 class of submarines, headed by the lead ship of the class, the USS *Piranha*. Press release from the program at the launch of the USS *Piranha* reads: "*Piranha* is a streamlined, highly advanced, and maneuverable antisubmarine warfare platform which uses the most advanced technology to accomplish her mission. . . . Super quiet, deep diving, and swift, *Piranha* is one of the most capable warships of the United States Fleet."

PLEBE A first year man at the U.S. Naval Academy at Annapolis.

PLOT TABLE A glass topped boxlike table that has a mechanism that moves in scale to the ship's motion in the sea. Table accepts input from the ship's gyro and speed indicator to do this. When tracing paper or charts are taped to the table top, the ship's motion can be plotted and recorded against time. Used for the geographic manual plot to determine contact solution. Also used to map polynyas. Ancient low-tech method of doing all these things, it has the advantage of not relying on computers, and is thus "bulletproof."

POLYMER A chemical formed of long chainlike molecules.

POLYMER INJECTION The injection of a polymer into the boundary layer of a submarine at the nosecone. The slippery liquid reduces the skin friction of the ship, reducing the drag. The result is the ability to dramatically increase ship's top speed for short periods of time. Ideal for torpedo evasion.

POLYNYA Thin spot in the polar icecap where a submarine can surface by breaking through the ice.

POOPY SUIT Underway uniform worn by American submariners. Usually cotton coveralls. Origin unknown.

PORK CHOP Nickname of the Supply Officer.

POSITION ONE (POS ONE) Furthest forward console of the Mark I firecontrol system. Usually set up with the captain's and XO's guess solution to the contact or displays the geographic display for a God's-eye view of the sea.

POSITION THREE (POS THREE) Furthest aft console of the Mark I firecontrol system. Usually set up to program torpedo tubes and weapons.

POSITION TWO (POS TWO) Mark I firecontrol console between Pos One and the Firing Panel. Usually set up on the Line-of-Sight mode so that the Pos Two officer can come up with his own independent firecontrol solution under the XO's supervision.

POSITIVE DISPLACEMENT PUMP A pump that uses pistons, diaphragms, or moving rotors to force liquid from a low pressure area to a high pressure area.

POWER RANGE Nuclear power level above the intermediate range. In the power range, steam can be produced by the reactor for propulsion.

PRECIPITATOR A device that removes particles and oil droplets from the air by passing the air over a highly charged set of plates or wires.

PRESSURE HULL Hardened steel section of a submarine able to take sea pressure at depth. The "people tank."

PRESSURIZED WATER REACTOR A PWR produces power using water at high temperature and pressure as both a moderator and coolant. Also uses a primary water coolant loop that keeps the radioactivity confined. A secondary system, the steam system, takes energy from the primary coolant and uses it for propulsion—the secondary system is not radioactive. As opposed to a BWR, boiling water reactor, that acts as a reactor and boiler, in which the reactor's coolant is used in the turbines, making the drive train's internals radioactive.

PRESSURIZER Tank in the primary coolant system that keeps the water in liquid form even up to 500 degrees by using heaters and raising the water in the pressurizer to even higher temperatures and pressures.

PRESSURIZER LEVEL The level of the pressurizer tank is the main indication of the amount of primary coolant in the primary coolant system. Large changes in core temperature can raise or lower the level due to thermal expansion or contraction of the water. A loss-of-coolant accident is detected by a falling pressurizer level.

PREUNDERWAY CHECKLIST Set of checklists used to get a submarine under way, including valve lineups and switch position checks. Considered of equal complexity and scope to a Space Shuttle countdown checklist.

PRIMARY COOLANT SYSTEM The piping system that circulates primary coolant from the reactor core to the steam generators (boilers) using reactor main coolant pumps. As opposed to the "secondary" coolant, the steam going from the boilers to the turbines for propulsion.

PRIORITY A level of urgency of a radio message below IMMEDIATE and above ROUTINE. Reception guaranteed on the same day.

PROMPT CRITICAL Under some conditions, uranium can be critical on fast neutrons instead of thermal neutrons. One example is a bomb undergoing a nuclear explosion. A second is a core in a reactivity accident such as a control rod jump, where the core becomes prompt critical, critical on the fast neutrons that are emitted "promptly" by the fission reaction. A core that is prompt critical is milliseconds from either a steam explosion or a prompt critical rapid disassembly.

PROMPT CRITICAL RAPID DISASSEMBLY Polite term for the unlikely event of a core undergoing a nuclear explosion.

PROPULSOR Sophisticated screw that uses ducting and multistage water turbine blades for propulsion instead of a conventional screw. Similar to a water jet. Extremely quiet and nearly impossible to cavitate. Disadvantage includes slow response and acceleration due to relatively low thrust compared to conventional screws.

P.A. CIRCUIT ONE Shipwide Public Address announcing system.

P.A. CIRCUIT SEVEN Speaker announcing system used between the Conn, Maneuvering, the bridge, and the torpedo room.

P.A. CIRCUIT TWO Similar to P.A. Circuit One, except that it only announces in the engineering spaces (aft of frame 57).

RANGE Distance to a contact.

RANGE GATING The action of an emitter of active sonar pulses. The ship being tracked can tell how close the pinging platform is by the time between pulses, assuming the transmitter does not ping the second pulse until it receives a return ping from the first pulse. The closer the pinging object gets to own ship, the shorter the interval between pings.

REACTOR Nuclear core. An assembly of fuel elements containing U-235, control rods, shielding, and inlet and discharge of primary coolant. Heat source that allows steam to be generated in the steam generators to produce propulsion and electricity.

REACTOR COMPARTMENT Compartment housing the reactor, pressurizer, steam generators, and reactor main coolant pumps. Access fore and aft is through a shielded tunnel, since anyone inside the compartment when the reactor is critical would be dead within a minute from the intense radiation.

REACTOR MAIN COOLANT PUMPS Massive pumps, each consuming between 100 and 400 horsepower, that force main coolant water through the reactor and then to the steam generators. Three are in each main coolant loop. Special design allows zero leakage.

REACTOR PLANT CONTROL PANEL (RPCP) Control panel in the maneuvering room where the Reactor Operator controls the reactor.

REACTOR PROTECTION Circuitry containing safety interlocks and control functions preventing reactor damage in an accident.

REACTOR VESSEL Heavy steel shell housing the reactor core.

REARGUARD SONAR New Russian passive and active sonar that looks astern into the baffles. Mounted in the aft section of the pod atop the rudder of the Project 985 (*Kaliningrad* or OMEGA) class Russian submarines. Eliminates need to do baffle clearing maneuvers.

RECONSTRUCTION Six hour period following a watch when an enemy submarine is trailed. The off-watch firecontrol team meets in the officer's wardroom and compares data from charts, geo plots, computer readbacks, and logs, in an effort to "get the story straight" for the patrol report. Conflicting information is resolved during reconstruction.

REDUCTION GEAR The mechanism that converts the high RPMs of the two main engines (propulsion turbines) to the slow RPM of the screw. Solves the problem of how to get two turbines to drive a single screw. Also solves the problem of how to let the main engines rotate at high RPM where they are efficient while letting the screw rotate at the low RPM where it is efficient. Unfortunately, the reduction gear is one of the noisiest pieces of equipment aboard.

RELAY Electrical device that acts as a smart switch.

RELIEF VALVE A spring loaded valve that will open and relieve the pressure on a tank or vessel instead of allowing the tank to rupture or fail.

REM Roentgen Equivalent Man. A unit of radiation dosage that takes into account tissue damage due to neutron radiation. Convenient since it allows gamma, alpha, and neutron radiation to be measured with the same units. 1000 rem will kill. 500 rem may kill. Yearly dose for submarine personnel is restricted to less than 25 to 100 millirem.

RIG FOR BLACK Submarine term meaning "turn off the lights in the control room."

RIG FOR COLLISION A shipwide lineup consisting of shutting hatches in bulkheads and shutting hardened ventilation dampers in bulkheads to minimize possible risk to the ship during a collision. Generally same as rig for flooding.

RIG FOR DIVE A detailed valve and switch lineup done in preparation to dive. Initially done by a dolphin-wearing enlisted man and checked by a dolphin-wearing officer.

RIG FOR FLOODING Similar to rig for collision. Bulkhead hatches and ventilation dampers are shut to isolate each compartment from the neighboring compartment. Ship is buttoned up to ensure maximum survivability.

RIG FOR PATROL QUIET Ship systems lineup to ensure maximum quiet while allowing normal creature comforts such as cooking and movie watching. Maintenance on equipment is allowed, if it does not involve banging on the hull. Noisy operations are only permitted with the captain's permission, such as reactor coolant discharge, steam generator blowdowns, etc.

RIG FOR WHITE Submarine term meaning "turn on the lights in the control room."

RO (REACTOR OPERATOR) Nuclear trained enlisted man who mans the Reactor Plant Control Panel and reports to the EOOW.

ROUTINE A message priority below PRIORITY. Delivery assurance in weeks or months.

RULES OF ENGAGEMENT A formal manual detailing what actions a U.S. vessel may take in response to enemy actions, such as an intentional collision by an enemy vessel in peacetime. In general, the rules require that no weapon may be shot unless the enemy ship has already launched a weapon.

RUN-TO-ENABLE Initial torpedo run taking it away from own ship. During the run-to-enable, the warhead is not armed and the sonar is not operational. When the run-to-enable is complete, the weapon activates the active or passive sonar and swims the search pattern. The warhead is not armed until it has a detect on the target.

R-114 AIR CONDITIONER Two air conditioning units that control the high temperatures and humidity caused by the steam plants. Ship is air conditioned to allow electronic equipment to function, not for creature comfort.

SAFETY LANES Special routes for submarine transit in time of war. Submarines detected by U.S. forces inside these lanes are assumed to be friendly.

SAIL Conning tower. Named because, unlike the conning towers of World War II diesel boats, which were misshapen and asymmetrical, modern nuclear submarine conning towers are smooth fins with square profiles when viewed from the side. Someone called it a sail in the distant past and the term became official.

SCI (SPECIAL COMPARTMENTED INFORMATION) A classification of information separate from the Confidential/Secret/Top Secret system. SCI information is compartmented or sectioned, so that no one person has the full story. Capture or compromise of one compartment of the information will be damaging but not catastrophic. SCI information is usually so sensitive that it is generally considered a higher classification than Top Secret. SCI is also information that compromises intelligence methods and sources.

SCRAM An emergency shutdown of a nuclear reactor, done by driving control rods to the bottom of the core using springs. A term left over from the 1940s when primitive lab reactors had a single control rod suspended by a rope. An emergency shutdown would be done by cutting the rope and letting the rod drop by gravity. The safety man was called the Safety Control Rod Ax Man—hence SCRAM.

SCRAM BREAKER A circuit breaker that interrupts power to the latching electromagnets of the control rod drive mechanisms. When the breaker opens, electrical power to the electromagnets is shut off, the magnets lose their magnetism, and the latches of the rods open, allowing springs to drop the rods to the bottom of the core.

SCRAM SETPOINTS The power level that will result in the protective circuits scramming the reactor. There are also setpoints for amount of flow through the core and core pressure.

SCRAMBLED EGGS The gold branches of leaves sewn onto the brim of a senior officer's cap.

SCRUBBER CO_2 scrubber. Atmospheric control equipment that rids the ship of carbon dioxide (from breathing, the diesel, and the CO burner) by blowing it over an amine bed.

SEA TRIALS Post construction shakedown cruise of a ship. Done to ensure the equipment lives up to the specifications and that the ship is ready to perform its mission.

SEARCH CONE A cone of ocean extending forward from the nosecone transducer of a torpedo. Anything inside the cone can be detected and homed on.

SEAWOLF CLASS Newest class of American fast attack submarines, the successor to the *Los Angeles* class.

SECTION TRACKING TEAM A firecontrol team stationed to man the plots and firecontrol system when tracking a hostile contact for extended periods of time. Modified battlestations. So named because each watchsection (similar to a shift) has its own tracking team.

SECURE PULSE FATHOMETER A fathometer (bottom sounder or bottom contour sonar) that bounces a downward focused secure pulse off the ocean bottom to determine depth below the keel. Pulse is secure because it is short duration and high frequency. High frequencies are quickly attenuated by the ocean.

SELF-OXYDIZING FUEL Fuel such as hydrogen peroxide that contains its own oxygen. Needs only a spark to react and explode violently. Capable of burning underwater. This fuel is frequently used in torpedoes. Its use makes a fire in the torpedo room that much more hazardous.

SELF-SUSTAINING (1) When a jet engine's turbine has enough power produced to turn the compressor shaft and sustain engine operation. (2) When a nuclear reactor's steam plant is producing enough electrical power to power its own reactor coolant pumps and electrical circuitry (taking about 10% power). The ship can then divorce from shorepower.

SES (SONAR EQUIPMENT SPACE) A room in the operations compartment taken up by large electrical cabinets containing power and signal circuits used by the BAT-EARS sonar suite.

SEWER PIPER Another derogatory term for submariner, used by aviators and surface sailors.

SHAFT SEALS The mechanism used to allow the screw's shaft to penetrate the aft bulkhead of the engineroom without seawater leaking in. Furthest aft point inside the ship.

SHAPED CHARGE An explosive charge that is designed to focus the energy of explosion in a particular direction. Used to break through tank armor and double submarine hulls.

SHARKTOOTH SONAR Slang name for the AN/BQS-8 under-ice sonar. The transducers are in the forward edge of the sail. Sonar is active, transmitting a high frequency police siren sound, able to transmit and receive simultaneously to chart ice obstacles ahead of a submarine under ice. Also includes a network of topsounders on the sail and hull to look up to find distance to overhead ice and ice thickness. Named SHARKTOOTH because the emitted frequency, when plotted against time, resembles a series of ramps, like shark teeth.

SHIP CONTROL OFFICER Russian equivalent to a helmsman, except the watchstander is an officer directing a highly automated distributed control system that controls the motion of the ship. Reports to the Deck Officer.

SHIP CONTROL PANEL (SCP) The console from which the ship's depth, course, and speed are controlled. On American submarines, this console resembles a 747 cockpit, with the Sternplanesman on one side, the Helmsman on the other, and the Diving Officer behind and between them. On Russian submarines, the console is the control station for the automated distributed control system that directs the motion of the ship.

SHIP CONTROL TEAM The watchstanders manning the Ship Control Panel, including the Sternplanesman, the Helmsman, and the Diving Officer. Sometimes includes the Chief of the Watch, off to the port side at the Ballast Control Panel.

SHIPS INERTIAL NAVIGATION SYSTEM (SINS) A multimillion dollar complex navigation system using a sophisticated gyroscope and support electronics to estimate the ship's position accurately at any time.

SHOCK WAVE An instantaneous change in fluid properties (a disturbance) that travels outward at the speed of sound in the fluid (sonic velocity). Examples include a sonic boom and the shock wave from a nuclear blast.

SHOOT ON GENERATED BEARING Captain's order to shoot a torpedo based on the firecontrol solution's estimate of where a target should be, not on the last actual bearing from sonar (See Match Bearings and Shoot). Generally considered best way to shoot with the Mark I firecontrol system. When ordered, the firecontrol team locks in the firecontrol solution to the target, and when the torpedo reports back, the captain is given one last chance to say either "Shoot" or "Check fire."

SIDESCAN SONAR Sonar used to examine objects on the ocean bottom. Used to find the *Titanic* and wreck of the USS *Stingray*.

SIGINT Signal intelligence. After intercepting an enemy radar, the emitting platform can be identified.

SIGNAL EJECTOR A small torpedo tube used to eject flares (for signalling surface ships), communication buoys (which can transmit hours after the ship has cleared datum; also used for SUBSUNK buoys), and countermeasures (torpedo decoys).

SIGNAL-TO-NOISE RATIO (SNL) How loud a contact is relative to the surrounding ocean noise. Measured in decibels.

SIOP WARPLAN The Top Secret plan for waging a major sea war, including the use of nuclear weapons. SIOP stands for Single Integrated OP-Plan.

SKIMMER Derogatory term for a surface ship or sailor of a surface ship. Surface ships only skim the surface.

SKIPJACK CLASS Early fast attack submarine class that was the first to feature a streamlined cylindrical hull.

SLBM Submarine launched ballistic missile.

SNAKE PATTERN A torpedo search pattern in which the torpedo wiggles, tracing a snake shaped pattern. Enables narrow search beam to cover more ocean by forcing the torpedo to look on either side of its heading.

SNAPSHOT A quick reaction torpedo shot, usually only done when fired on first.

SNCP (SPECIAL NAVY CONTROL PROGRAM) Top Secret series of covert submarine operations.

SNORKEL A mast designed to bring air into the submarine so that the air-breathing diesel generator can use it for combustion when the reactor is scrammed.

SOLENOID An electrical device that causes motion by the action of an electromagnet. Used in remotely actuated valves.

SOLUTION A contact's range, course, and speed. A great mystery when using passive sonar. Determining the solution requires maneuvering own ship and doing calculations on the target's bearing rate. Can be obtained manually or with the firecontrol computer.

SONAR SYSTEM A system of hydrophone/transducer arrays, computers, and displays enabling a submarine to determine what is in the water surrounding it, including other ships.

SONIC VELOCITY The speed of sound waves.

SONOBUOYS Small objects dropped from ASW aircraft that float on the surface and listen to the ocean below, then transmit that information up to the aircraft. A method of giving an aircraft sonar capability.

SOPA Senior Officer Present Afloat or Senior Officer Present Ashore.

SORTIE An exodus of a group of ships from a port or anchorage.

SOSUS Sound Surveillance System. A network of underwater passive hydrophones and data relay cables buried in secret locations in the Atlantic to track enemy submarines. Triangulation gives enemy submarine positions accurate enough to know their approximate location but not accurate enough to fire on them, even with nuclear weapons.

SOUND SIGNATURE The collection of characteristic sounds, both broadband and narrowband tonals, that uniquely identify a class of ship, and sometimes, the exact ship itself.

SOUNDING The depth beneath the keel as measured by the fathometer.

SOURCE RANGE CHANNEL SELECTOR SWITCH A rotary switch on the Reactor Plant Control Panel that energizes or deenergizes certain nuclear instruments and turns on or off some reactor protection circuits.

SPEED OF ADVANCE (SOA) The speed the ship plans to go during transit. Also the speed of the PIM or box.

SPHERICAL ARRAY A sphere in the nosecone of a submarine fitted with transducers over most of its surface to be able to hear in all directions (except the baffles). Useful since it not only tells the bearing to an incoming noise, but also its D/E (deflection/elevation). The D/E can give clues that the sound is relayed via bottom bounce or surface bounce, or even that a close contact is deeper or shallower than own ship.

SPIN UP Start the gyro and computer system of a weapon in preparation for launch.

SPL (SOUND PRESSURE LEVEL) A detailed recording of an enemy submarine's sound signature obtained by covertly driving an attack submarine in circles around it with a special tape recorder energized. Very dangerous operation requiring approaches to within 10 feet of the enemy hull. Risk of collision is great, but intelligence gained is considered worth the risk.

SQUADRON An organization of about a dozen submarines of the same class under the command of the Commodore. The Squadron usually owns the piers, the tender ship, and a torpedo recovery salvage ship. Squadron commander (Commodore) has only administrative control over the submarines—operational control at sea is done by COMSUB-LANT.

SQUIGGLE (SGWLC) Steam generator water level control system.

SSBN A boomer. Literally stands for Submersible Ship, Ballistic missile, Nuclear.

SSN A fast attack submarine. Literally stands for Submersible Ship Nuclear.

SSTG'S (SHIP SERVICE TURBINE GENERATORS) The two turbines aft that turn the ship's electrical generators and provide electrical power.

STANDARD SPEED Speed between All Ahead Two Thirds and All Ahead Full. Gives about 18 knots.

STAND-DOWN Rest and relaxation period for an attack boat crew after an extended 4, 5, or 6 month deployment.

STARTUP RANGE Lowest reactor power level, in which neutrons are generated by radioactive decay and occasional spontaneous fissions.

STARTUP RATE The speed, in decades per minute, that reactor power level is changing. Positive startup rate means power level is increasing. Negative means the power level is decreasing. See Decades Per Minute.

STARTUP RATE SCRAM A scram caused by a high startup rate. Setpoint is about 9 decades per minute.

STATION NUMBER ONE Position off the Russian northern coast used by either a submarine waiting in ambush in wartime or a covert intelligence gathering ship in peacetime. Location coordinates are in the SIOP WARPLAN.

STATUS BOARD A white board in the control room used to indicate the status of miscellaneous things of interest to the OOD such as torpedo tubes (empty, flooded, door open, or warshot loaded), time of sunrise, etc.

STEADY A report from the helmsman that the ship is on the ordered course and is not turning.

STEAM EXPLOSION One possible result of a reactor overpower accident, in which too much heat is added to the coolant in a short time. The water expands into steam, and the pressure rises dramatically, finally breaching the reactor vessel, causing it to physically explode.

STEAM GENERATOR A large heat exchanger with superhot primary coolant flowing inside tubes, with cold water from the condensers pumped in the bottom. Primary coolant boils the water to steam for use in the turbines. Also called a boiler.

STEAM LEAK, MAJOR When one of the large steam pipes ruptures in the engineroom or AMR 2. Result is rapid cooking of engineering crew unless the leak is isolated using MS-1 or -2 valves. Steam leaks are also dangerous because they will overpower the reactor.

STEAM PLANT CONTROL PANEL (SPCP) Console in the maneuvering room that monitors the steam plant. Has the large throttle wheel in front that controls the speed of the main engines. Manned by the throttleman.

STERNPLANES Horizontal control surfaces at the tail of a submarine. Similar to the elevator tail surfaces of an aircraft, the sternplanes cause the ship to rise or dive.

STERNPLANESMAN Enlisted watchstander in the Ship Control Party who controls the sternplanes at the Ship Control Panel.

STRAIGHT BOARD Indications on the Ballast Control Panel showing green bars, indicating that all hatches and vents are shut—final announcement indicating ship is ready for dive.

SUBEX Submarine exercise.

SUBMERSIBLE Small deep-diving submarine designed for short trips to the ocean bottom to gather data. May be manned or a robot.

SUBROC Submarine launched rocket with a nuclear depth charge. Obsolete and eliminated since analysis indicated it would severely damage the firing ship due to the nuclear blast.

SUBSUNK An emergency transmitter that releases from a submarine hull automatically at a certain depth that calls a distress signal to the satellite that a submarine is sinking. System taken out of service for fear of it going off mistakenly, giving away the ship's position.

SUCKER An emergency air breathing mask for use during toxic gas emergencies or radioactive contamination release to the submarine's atmosphere.

SUPERCRITICAL A condition of a nuclear reactor when power level is increasing and each fission neutron generation's population is exceeded by the next generation's.

SURFACED-AT-ICE Ship rigged to stay for a long period of time surfaced at a polynya. Ballast tanks are partially filled with air and monitored.

SUSTAINER ENGINE The jet engine of a cruise missile. It sustains continued flight.

SYNCH A radioman's term meaning the ship's radio equipment is tuned and receiving radio signals from the transmitter.

TAPE MODE A firecontrol casualty condition in which the tape module is used as the operating system instead of the disk module. Reduces speed and capability of the Mark I firecontrol system.

TARGET ONE The designation of a sonar, radar, ESM, or visual contact as a target to be fired upon or tracked.

TARGET ZIG A term used to describe a target's maneuver, either a turn, speed change, or both. Requires the ship to do more TMA to get a new solution.

TDU (TRASH DISPOSAL UNIT) A vertical torpedo tube used to jettison garbage overboard. Garbage is first bagged and weighed down with lead bricks to ensure it does not float to the surface and give away the ship's position.

TERMINAL VELOCITY A falling or accelerating object in a fluid (air or water) eventually stops speeding up when fluid drag balances accelerating force. The velocity that is reached is called terminal velocity.

TEST DEPTH A depth about 2/3 of crush depth. Maximum allowed depth a submarine is allowed to go in peacetime.

TG'S (TURBINE GENERATORS) The two turbines aft that turn the ship's electrical generators and provide electrical power.

THERMAL LAYER A layer of warm water near the surface of the ocean. The water is warm because of agitation by waves and sunlight. Further down, the wave motion is nil and there is no sunlight, leaving the seawater near freezing at all times. Sound waves originating below the layer bounce off it and come back down, making it difficult for surface ships to detect deep submarines, and the reason surface ships use dipping sonars or deep towed arrays. Sound waves originating above the layer will bounce off the layer and come back up, making surface ships difficult for submarines to hear when approaching the surface to come to periscope depth. Sometimes the layer confines surface noise into sound channels, enabling a submarine to hear a contact above the layer hundreds of miles away. Layer depth is typically 150 to 200 feet deep.

THERMAL NEUTRONS Neutrons slowed by water moderator in a reactor core, enabling them to be absorbed by another uranium nucleus to cause fission.

THERMAL STRESS Stress in metal caused by one side being hot and the other being cold. The hot part wants to expand, the cold part wants to contract, and the result is the metal trying to tear itself apart. An example is a rapid heatup of the massive metal of a reactor pressure vessel when raising plant water temperature after a scram. The inside surface of the vessel can be 500 degrees, while the outside and the "meat" of the thick metal is still at 300 degrees. The vessel can rupture, causing a loss-of-coolant accident. Neutron embrittlement of the vessel makes thermal stress effects even worse.

THERMOLUMINESCENT DOSIMETER (TLD) A small piece of plastic worn on a crewmember's belt to measure that person's radiation dose.

THREE-WAY VALVE A valve, usually a ball valve, that can direct inlet flow one of two ways.

THROTTLE The valves at the inlet of a steam turbine that determine how much steam flow the turbine will receive, and thus, the amount of power the turbine will produce (and its speed). Done at the Steam Plant Control Panel.

THROTTLEMAN Nuclear trained enlisted watchstander who monitors the steam plant at the Steam Plant Control Panel and positions the throttle based on the speed orders of the control room (which are transmitted by the engine order telegraph).

TIME-BEARING PLOT A large graphical plot of target bearing versus time. Plot can be used to calculate contact range based on knowledge of own ship's speed across the line-of-sight. Also used to call or verify a target zig when target bearing rate diverges from expected bearing rate.

TIME-FREQUENCY PLOT A large graphical plot of target tonal frequency versus time. Useful in zig detection, when a down shifted frequency shows the target moving away and an upshift shows the target turning toward own ship.

TITANIUM A special metal with high strength that is useful in submarine hulls due to its creep properties. Very expensive and almost impossible to weld.

TMA (TARGET MOTION ANALYSIS) Means of establishing a target solution using passive sonar. Own ship does maneuvers to generate speed first on one side of the line-of-sight, then on the other. Several maneuvers or legs can quickly find the target solution. Stealthy method of determining what the target is doing. The system is weak when the target is himself doing TMA. Result is a melee or PCO Waltz, where both submarines are maneuvering and neither knows what the other is doing. In worst case, submarines may need to shift to active sonar to determine range or clear datum until the target can be ambushed stealthily.

TONAL A steady sound frequency emitted by a target submarine. Usually very narrow bandwidth. Very much like the pure tone put out by a tuning fork. Caused by rotating machinery such as turbine generators.

TONAL SEARCH GATE A filter set up on a narrowband passive sonar that only listens to a small range of sound frequencies in anticipation of finding a particular tonal.

TOP SECRET Classification of information, the disclosure of which could "cause grave damage to the national security of the United States." Detailed information regarding U.S. warplans and some U.S. OPs. Old submarine saying: confidential on the table, secret on the bed, top secret under the pillow.

TOP SECRET—THUNDERBOLT When the classification of top secret is followed by a codeword, it indicates the SCI classification, making the information classification essentially higher than top secret. Usually the very name of the classification is at least secret.

TOPSOUNDER A sonar transducer designed to transmit an active sonar beam upward to gage the thickness of the ice cover overhead.

TORPEDO IN THE WATER Announcement that a hostile submarine has launched a weapon at own ship, requiring immediate evasive action and a counterfire.

TOWED ARRAY A passive sonar hydrophone array towed astern of a submarine on a cable up to several miles long. The array itself may be a thousand feet long. The array is used to detect narrowband tonals at extreme ranges.

TRACK To keep tabs on a contact's solution over time. Merchant surface vessels are tracked to avoid collision. A casual maintenance of a firecontrol solution to a contact.

TRAIL The serious prosecution of a target intended to maintain weapons ready to fire at the target at all times while remaining undetected.

The constant maintenance of an accurate firecontrol solution to an enemy submarine. Trail ranges vary from 10,000 yards to 20 yards. The trick is to keep from being counterdetected, which can be embarrassing. U.S. attack submarines will keep Russian boomers in trail as much as possible to ensure they can be sunk if they get ready to fire ballistic missiles. Second priority for trailing is a Russian attack sub. Third priority is another U.S. unit, to see if they can be trailed without their knowledge. Trailing a U.S. unit is extremely difficult unless they are making transient noises or have broken equipment.

TRANSCEIVER Refers to radio equipment or sonar equipment that can both receive and transmit.

TRANSDUCER A sonar hydrophone that can ping active sonar pulses and listen and analyze the returning pulses.

TRANSIENT A noise that is made by an enemy sub due to a temporary condition. Examples include dropped wrenches, boots clomping on deckplates, slamming hatches, boiler blowdowns, rattling check valves, etc.

TRIM The balance of a submarine. The first step is to pump or flood variable ballast to achieve neutral buoyancy. The second is to pump from tank to tank to balance the ship fore and aft and port to starboard.

TRIM PUMP A large pump that can pump variable ballast from tank to tank or from a tank to the sea to achieve a good trim. Can be connected to the drain system for use as a backup for the drain pump.

TRIM SYSTEM The piping network, tanks, and trim pump used to establish a good trim. Can be cross-connected to the drain system as a backup for the drain pump.

TRIP The actuation of an interlock, such as a reactor scram.

TURBINE A mechanical rotating device with blades that converts the pressure energy, velocity energy, and internal (temperature) energy of a fluid stream (steam or combustion gases) into mechanical power.

TWO THIRDS SPEED An engine order between All Ahead One Third and All Ahead Standard. Gives approximately 10 knots.

TWO-MAN CONTROL Term referring to the handling of authenticators for nuclear release message validation. No one man is ever alone with an authenticator. The authenticators are locked in double safes, and no one man has the combination to both.

TYPE 18 PERISCOPE Modern periscope able to act as a means of seeing outside the ship at PD, but also is able to receive radio messages from the satellite and allow reception and analysis of incoming radar signals. Contains video camera and low-light capability as well as a still photograph camera.

T-AVE (AVERAGE REACTOR COOLANT TEMPERATURE) An estimate of in-core water temperature by electrically averaging the outlet high temperature water (T-Hot) and the inlet low temperature water (T-Cold).

T-HOT Hot leg temperature, the temperature of water leaving the reactor core. Usually about 520 to 560 degrees F.

T-HOT CUTBACK A cutback inserted when T-HOT gets above a trip setpoint.

T.O.T. (TIME-ON-TARGET) A land attack assault in which weapons are launched at carefully planned moments to cause all weapons to detonate on target at the same instant in time. More remote launching platforms must fire before closer units.

ULTRAQUIET Ship systems lineup done in a tactical situation such as a close trailing OP or in wartime. Only the quietest equipment is running. Offwatch personnel are required to be in bed. The galley, showers, laundry, movies, and maintenance of equipment are all prohibited to minimize noise. Hard soled shoes are prohibited. Lights are shifted to red to remind the crew of the need for silence.

UNDERHULL An operation in which a submarine sneaks up to a target when the target is in a surface transit or is running shallow. The submarine doing the underhull raises the periscope, starts the video recorder, and drives around the target taking video pictures of the ship's hull. Especially valuable when done on a new ship, since the pictures are better than if a cameraman were sent into the ship's drydock. Extremely dangerous operation.

UNIFORM WHISKEY MIKE Code for "your weapon missed me."

UNIT A torpedo launched by own ship. As opposed to a torpedo (after sonar calls "torpedo in the water"), which is launched by a hostile submarine.

UWT (UNDERWATER TELEPHONE) A sonar system using voice transmissions instead of tones or pulses, used for communication between two submarines that are fairly close.

VACAPES OPAREA Virginia Capes Operation Area. A region off the continental shelf east of Norfolk where submarines of the Norfolk base practice tactics.

VALVE-OP WATER FLASKS (VOWF) Tanks of pure water used for hydraulically operating nuclear system valves. Can also be used to charge to the primary coolant system by air loading with high pressure air.

VARIABLE BALLAST TANKS Tanks used to hold seawater for added weight, or conversely, seawater tanks that can be pumped out or blown out to lighten the ship.

VARIABLE YIELD Yield is a nuclear warhead's explosive power in kilotons or megatons. A warhead with variable yield can dial in the desired explosive power by changing the shape or size of the implosion charges or by altering the geometry or concentration of the fissionable (or fusion) material.

VECTOR Any quantity that has both magnitude and direction. Example: a velocity vector is speed (number of miles per hour) *and* direction (north).

VENT To release trapped air from a system.

VERTICAL SURFACE When a hovering submarine blows water from a variable ballast tank to establish a vertical velocity and then rises vertically from the water. Generally only used to surface through the ice.

VICTOR A class of Russian attack submarines built to counter the threat from the *Piranha* class submarines.

VICTOR III A class of Russian attack submarines that are much more refined, quieter, and faster than the VICTOR class (only a few VICTOR II's were built, and may be considered experimental models of the VICTOR III's). Built to counter the *Los Angeles* class submarines. Precursors to the AKULA class attack submarines.

VITAL BUS A group of electrical loads supplied off the same motor generator breaker, able to be fed either from a turbine generator or the battery. These few loads are vital to the survival of the ship. Examples include primary ship control circuits, slow speed reactor main coolant pumps, reactor protection circuitry, and the wardroom coffee maker.

VLF LOOP An antenna capable of receiving VLF transmissions at depths down to several hundred feet.

VLF (VERY LOW FREQUENCY) Radio transmissions on a longer wavelength than LF but not as long as ELF.

VLS (VERTICAL LAUNCH SYSTEM) New missile launch system on later *Los Angeles* class attack submarines, in which space in the forward group of ballast tanks has vertical torpedo tubes for launching Javelin cruise missiles. Allows torpedo room space to hold more torpedoes.

WARDROOM (1) Officer's messroom. Used also as a conference room, briefing room, reconstruction room, junior officer's office, movie screening room, and place to converse. (2) The group of officers assigned to a ship.

WARSHOT A weapon that is used to sink an enemy ship or inflict damage on a target. As opposed to an exercise shot.

WATCH/WATCHSTATION A watch is an 8 hour shift during which a group of men at specific stations run the submarine. A watchstation is a person's station or assignment during the watch.

WATCHSECTION A collection of watchstanders who run the submarine for an 8 hour shift called a watch.

WATER SLUG Shooting a torpedo tube when it is only full of water. A "slug" of water is ejected from the tube.

WATERFALL A display of broadband sonar with bearing on the horizontal and time on the vertical. Broadband noise traces fall down the screen, looking like a waterfall.

WIGGLE RANGE TMA range obtained by the wiggling of an advanced sonar system's towed array hydrophones due to the tow cable moving in the water flowstream. Each hydrophone has accelerometers and instrumentation to determine its position and motion with respect to the contact and own ship.

WIRE GUIDE CONTINUITY A low electrical resistance in the wire guide to a torpedo, indicating the wire is still intact. Loss of wire guide continuity means the weapon got fouled in the wire and cut it, or that the weapon has exploded.

XO (EXECUTIVE OFFICER) Officer who is second in command of a nuclear submarine, responsible to the captain for the administrative functioning of the ship. At battlestations, the XO coordinates the firecontrol team and makes recommendations to the captain.

ZIG A term used to describe a target's maneuver, either a turn, speed change, or both.

ZIRCONIUM A metal used as cladding on uranium fuel elements because of its corrosion resistance and low neutron absorption characteristics.

ZULU Same as Greenwich Mean Time.